EX LIBRIS

VINTAGE **CLASSICS**

THE MATCHMAKER

Stella Gibbons was born in London in 1902. She went to the North London Collegiate School and studied journalism at University College London. She then spent ten years working for various newspapers, including the *Evening Standard*. Stella Gibbons is the author of twenty-five novels, three volumes of short stories and four volumes of poetry. Her first publication was a book of poems, *The Mountain Beast* (1930), and her first novel *Cold Comfort Farm* (1932) won the Femina Vic Heureuse Prize in 1933. Amongst her works are *Christmas at Cold Comfort Farm* (1940), *Westwood* (1946), *Conference at Cold Comfort Farm* (1959) and *Starlight* (1967). She was elected a Fellow of the Royal Society of Literature in 1950. In 1933 she married the actor and singer Allan Webb. They had one daughter. Stella Gibbons died in 1989.

STELLA GIBBONS

The Matchmaker

VINTAGE BOOKS
London

Published by Vintage 2012

11

First published in Great Britain by Longmans, Green & Co. Ltd in 1949

Vintage
Random House, 20 Vauxhall Bridge Road,
London SW1V 2SA

www.vintage-classics.info

Addresses for companies within The Random House Group
Limited can be found at: www.randomhouse.co.uk/offices.htm

The Random House Group Limited Reg. No. 954009

A CIP catalogue record for this book
is available from the British Library

ISBN 9780099529330

Penguin Random House is committed to a sustainable future for
our business, our readers and our planet. This book is made from
Forest Stewardship Council® certified paper.

Typeset in Bembo by Palimpsest Book Production Limited,
Falkirk, Stirlingshire

Printed and bound in Great Britain by Clays Ltd, Elcograf S.p.A.

To
Enid Gibbons and The Blue Idol—affectionately, peacefully

1

On the journey from London down into Sussex, Major Ronald Lucie-Browne was entrapped into conversation by an elderly gentleman, who lost no time in revealing that he had once been a Captain, and went on to relate that he was an expert in the science of firing a revolver. This (as you would of course be aware) was no easy performance; none of your shutting one eye and taking aim at the target; no, it was a highly complicated operation; it was a science; but neither in the war that was just over, nor in the one before that, had he found it properly accepted as such. There will just be time, before we reach your station, to explain it.

Ronald Lucie-Browne listened in silence, not once letting his eye stray towards the satchel upon his knee containing reports from the Liberal Party's office in the constituency which he hoped to contest during the next General Election. Born and educated as a gentleman, he had earned his living during the fourteen years since coming down from Oxford as Reader in French Language and Literature at one of the older provincial universities, but his nature was not completely suited to the calm of modern academic life in England (which lacks the excitement of intellectual speculation characterising such life in the great American universities) and also—like so many of his generation—he was cursed with a sense of social responsibility. It had seemed to him, after much uneasy and earnest thought, that it was his duty to try to enter politics. His voluntary enlistment during the first months of the war and his subsequent military service had interrupted this plan, but now that the date for his demobilisation was in sight, he hoped to enter seriously upon it.

He had intended to study the reports during the journey into Sussex because he knew that he would have neither the time nor the inclination to read them after he got there, but he had not the ruthlessness necessary in dealing with elderly gentlemen who explain to us about revolvers, being a kind, grave, affectionate young man who proposed, thus handicapped, to enter the political sewers for the good of his fellow beings.

It appeared that *you fired at the chap's stomach when you intended to hit him in the heart.* There! It was out! The elderly gentleman relaxed; he leaned back; he repeated the secret several times in a lulling diminuendo which seemed to marvel at the simplicity and infallibility of the method just revealed; and then, having accepted one of Ronald's cigarettes, he became silent, as if exhausted by his efforts, and gazed rather glassily out of the window.

As it was now too late to begin upon the reports, Ronald also looked out of the window. The scanty copper and bronze leaves of late November burned along the hedges and far down in the brown and purple woods under a breaking grey sky, and the autumn landscape, that for six years had seemed to be watchfully, patiently submitting itself to darkness and danger and cold, was now settling into its natural winter sleep. There was relief in the very air, but his thoughts always became sad when he found himself alone, and presently, as he watched the woods gliding past, the familiar despair with the state of the world began to invade his mind—until it was suddenly banished by the realisation that in a few moments he would be with his family.

'Nearly there; yours is the next station,' observed the elderly gentleman, coming out of a reverie-doze. 'Ah yes, this is where *we* began to get *our* luggage down when *we* lived at Sillingham.'

He went on to inquire if Ronald himself lived there? (having asked no personal questions during the journey because he had been busy explaining about the revolvers).

2

'My wife has just taken a furnished cottage down here,' was the answer.

'Oh, really? She was lucky to get it. I wonder if I know it?' with a gleam of reviving, but this time purely civilian, interest.

'It's called Pine Cottage. It's about two miles out of Sillingham on the Froggatt road, near a small farm called Naylor's.'

'In-deed! Pine Cottage! Yes, I do know it; I know it *well*, and so does my wife.'

His tone was far from encouraging; indeed, it combined dismay with commiseration in a manner that would have alarmed Ronald, had not his anticipations about Pine Cottage already been coloured by knowledge of the tastes and habits of his wife, to whom he had been married for twelve years. He forbore to comment, merely remarking that Pine Cottage stood in the fields, about a quarter of a mile from the Froggatt road. That (added Ronald, deliberately inviting comment) would be a disadvantage in winter weather, he feared.

But the elderly gentleman suddenly went into his shell; he said no more; he only nodded and gazed out of the window with his lips portentously compressed, rather as Bottom's may have been when hinting marvels to honest Snout. Ronald had his luggage ready and was waiting by the door for the train to stop.

They were now passing low-lying meadows, mounting into hills crowned with the leafless woods of winter through which evening light was shining, and both travellers simultaneously became aware of a row of faces confronting them along a white gate in the hedge below. There was a woman in a gay plaid coat, with bright hair blowing about, and three little girls, one a mere baby, all cheering and waving as the train went by. It looked quite a party of pleasure in the midst of the silent fields under the fading light, and even above the noise of the train they could hear the children's shrill voices; blankets were scattered about on the grass, and there was an old pram in the background, and bunches of autumn leaves were being waved above the laughing faces.

'Evacuees,' announced the elderly revolver expert, settling his tie with a well-kept hand. 'We have suffered greatly from them down here, poor things. Both sides have done their best, but there *is* a fundamental difference in outlook, so why not be a realist and admit it? Is your wife meeting you by car?'

Ronald, smiling for the first time that afternoon, shook his head.

'We hope to have ours in use again next week and damned glad I shall be, too. Well, here you are. Good-day; give my love to the Ruhr. It's twenty-five years since I was there in the last Army of Occupation.'

'I will, sir. Good afternoon.'

A moment later he was hurrying down the platform, looking nowhere but towards the ticket-barrier, and some ten minutes later (the train having been most irritatingly delayed over some matter of eggs) the elderly gentleman had the shock of seeing him walking along the road arm in arm with the bright-haired woman in the plaid coat.

'Married beneath him, poor fellow,' he thought, as the train moved away.

Alda Lucie-Browne pushed the pram with one hand and clung to her husband with the other, while the two little girls skirmished on the outskirts and the baby twisted herself round to join in the conversation. They all talked at once except Ronald.

'——and we shall just have time to see the cottage before it gets dark, darling,' said Alda.

'We always have high tea at Pagets, Father, and it's sausages to-night. Every night we have something different. Tomorrow it's macaroni cheese,' said Jenny, the girl of eleven. 'They're going to save you some sausages, too.'

'Will there be remartoes for Meg's tea?' demanded the baby, who was aged three and a half, in a clear, precise voice.

4

'*To*-matoes,' muttered Jenny.

'Don't pick on her, Jenny, you know mother likes to hear her,' whispered Louise, who was ten, as Alda turned the pram aside through a gate which Ronald swung open.

'Thank you, dear. We go across this meadow and the next one, and there we are,' she said.

'It's getting very dark.' He glanced doubtfully across the still, damp fields where mist was already rising. 'Is Meg well wrapped up?'

'Oh yes, she's got her winter vest on to-day.'

'And me cardigan,' added Meg, pulling half of that garment out from her overcoat. 'Look, Farder.'

'*And* her rubber boots,' said Louise. 'And on Tuesday we have bacon and egg pie, Father, and on Wednesday boiled shell eggs . . .'

'Look!' Jenny stopped short in a patch of long moist grass and pointed upwards. She was smiling, as if offering her family a present. They all gazed at the heavens, following the dark line of her finger in its woollen glove and there, hidden until now among the clouds but at last revealed as they thinned and rolled away at sunset, was a pink November moon.

'A moon!' said Jenny. 'Now it doesn't matter how late we are, because we can see,' and she ran off into the meadows, followed by Louise.

'Meg will get out,' announced Meg, struggling with the strap that confined her.

'Oh no Meg won't. It's too wet. Father will push the pram now, because the ground is bumpy, and Meg will have a nice ride,' said Ronald, taking over the pram from Alda, who placidly dropped her hands into her pockets and strolled along smiling absently at the ground, while he steered the pram round molehills and the tussocks of last spring's grass, and patiently extracted details from her about the lease and rent for Pine Cottage and the terms of the agreement.

'But there *is* inside sanitation, Ronald. Didn't I tell you? I thought I did. *And* a bathroom. But no electric light. Oh look, children, there's a rabbit! Quick, Louise, there by the hedge! You can see his white scut.'

'Oh Mother, *where?*' Louise's voice was anguished. 'Quick!'

'There,' said Jenny scornfully, and her finger came steadily over her sister's twisting shoulder, and pointed, 'In a direct line with my finger.'

But it was no use; Louise could not see, and the rabbit, startled by their voices, suddenly whisked and was gone. Louise came silently over to her father and slipped her cold hand into the one that left the handle of the pram to meet it.

'And four bedrooms, Alda?' Ronald went on. 'That sounds all right. Is it properly furnished?'

'Indeed it is, rather too much so. You wait till you see the pictures. You'll hate them.'

'I shan't have much opportunity to hate them, sweetheart.'

'Oh Ronald, why?' Startled, she looked up at him.

'I'm being sent to Germany.'

'Oh *darling*! Oh Ronald, how unutterably sickening. When did you hear?'

'Only this morning. I didn't want to spring it on you the minute we met.'

'How long for, in heaven's name?'

'Indefinitely, but I shall get leave of course.'

'Won't you even be here for *Christmas*, Father?' demanded Jenny, outraged. 'I do think, now the war is over, they might let you. They are beasts.'

'I'm afraid not, old lady.'

Alda was silent for a moment; then she said: 'Well, we must just look forward to leave, that's all. It's too bad, losing you again after we'd just got you after four years, but it's no use grumbling, I suppose, and we'll have a lovely time while you *are* here. You'll be out altogether soon. When do you go?'

'Next week, I'm afraid, lovey.'

She said no more, but slipped her arm through his and pressed it. Her gay, rebellious spirit would never learn patience but she no longer wasted energy in defying the inevitable, and they had long ago decided that, should he be sent to Germany, they would not risk her accompanying him with the children.

'Over here,' she said presently, withdrawing her arm and beginning to climb a slip-gate marking the entrance to the next field. Beyond its bars of silvery oak, Ronald could see another dim green meadow placidly extending away into the gathering twilight, while overhead the pink moon had changed to gold amidst fragile grey clouds. The evening bus to Horsham with all its lights blazing cheerfully was passing along the main road three fields away.

'How would you have managed with the pram if I hadn't been here?' he demanded, when he had lifted the pram over the slip-gate. 'Seriously, Alda, is it much further? How on earth you're going to manage in the winter——'

'Oh, this is the *long* way round,' she laughed, turning back from hurrying up the rising slope of the meadow with her daughters. 'The cottage is only two or three hundred yards from the Froggatt road. We came this way to-day to meet your train. There!' She stopped, pointing. 'There it is.'

He had not realised, so gradual was the incline which they had been ascending, that they now stood on the highest point for miles around, and could command a wide prospect over dusky woods and darkening meadows ending at last in the long, rolling line of the downs fifteen miles away, sable and mysterious against the fading yellow sky. Immediately below lay a group of barns and other buildings with black wooden walls and mild grey thatched roofs, and beyond these, standing upon another low incline and surrounded by dark pines amongst whose pointed tops flashed a star, was a small, square house.

But stronger than his admiration of the scene was his relief that a cart track, unmistakable even in the dusk, ran across the meadows from the farm buildings to the cottage, and even as he looked, the headlights of a car, reassuringly close, glided past on the Froggatt road.

'Isn't it a marvellous position?' demanded Alda.

'Those pines will make it damp,' he pronounced, beginning to push the pram forward again. 'How far did you say you are from the village?'

'Not more than a mile and a half—well, say a mile and three-quarters——'

'Or two miles,' he muttered.

'And there's a good road, downhill all the way. And there,' pointing away towards the woods, 'is the convent where Jenny and Louise are going.' (Here Louise made a remarkable face expressing repugnance and despair, but Jenny looked attentively at her mother.)

'I went to see Sister Alban yesterday. It *is* so lovely and clean there, Ronald, with that marvellous feeling convents always have—you know?'

Ronald said, 'H'm.'

'You can h'm, but they do.'

'How do you feel about it, Jen?' turning to his eldest daughter.

'I will deal with the situation as it arises,' answered Jenny sedately, quoting one of his own expressions. 'All schools are beastly except Miss Mottram's, so what does it matter?'

Louise looked at her sister respectfully, as one who hears of an ancient and honourable grief. She herself could barely remember the school in Ironborough which the sisters had attended before their home had been destroyed and their present nomadic existence had begun, but Jenny remembered it all; every schoolfellow, every detail of the day's routine, every article of furniture in the large old-fashioned mansion converted into a school, and longed to return there.

Alda thought it wisest to ignore this, and said cheerfully:

8

'Here we are.'

They had now arrived at the house, and its square little face, with windows reflecting the yellow remnants of day, stared aloofly above them. Sussex tiles, pointed and decorated, covered the upper walls; there was a tiny porch over the front door, and the pines stood about it in a close half-circle. The front garden was primly enclosed by a wooden fence, and every foot of it was filled with thick, strong, bushy laurels whose branches pressed against the small front windows. Even on a bright day Pine Cottage never seemed full of light—the pine trees saw to that—and this evening in the eerie owl-light it actively breathed out darkness; the porch was a cave; the room beyond the laurel-shadowed windows might have been filled with squid-juice, so black was it, and every shadow from the surrounding woods seemed drawn into the circle of those sighing pines.

'Meg doesn't like that little black house, Mudder,' remarked Meg, who had been silently looking up at Pine Cottage.

'We'll soon make it light,' answered Alda cheerfully, pushing open the gate. It had a rustic catch, and it stuck.

When they tried to unlock the front door with the key produced by Alda, that stuck, too.

'Here . . .' said Ronald, putting his shoulder to it. 'Let me try . . .'

'Meg, you may come out now,' said Louise in a low authoritative tone, beginning to unbuckle the strap round her sister's middle. 'You must be a very good girl, because mother and father will be busy looking at the house and they won't want to be interrupted. *Come* along,' and she set Meg's tiny boots of patched rubber down on the path (which was of gravel; there was nothing so pleasant as a firm path of large stones, that could steam after a light spring rain or hold the heat of a long summer day, at Pine Cottage).

'Merciful heavens,' exclaimed Alda, as the door gave way with a wounded screech and Ronald fell into the black passage, 'Are you all right, darling?'

He answered rather shortly that everything was comparative and then, as Alda lit the lamp on a table, they all burst out laughing; Meg was especially pleased to do so and held her face up to the light, making loud ha-has with her eyes shut. A passage was now revealed which apparently ran slap through the house and out the other side through a back door. It was covered in worn oilcloth. The yellow walls glistened with damp and the air struck deathly cold.

'B-o-r-l-e-y——' spelled Ronald, with a significant glance at his wife.

'Borley Rectory, the Most Haunted House in England,' took up Jenny promptly. 'It was always cold there because of the ghosts. Do you think this is haunted, Father? How *super*!'

'Of course not, don't be absurd.' Ronald put his hand on the shoulder of Louise, whose eyes suddenly looked very large. 'Come along, let's explore.'

'What a howwid smell,' said Meg heartily, as Alda with some difficulty opened a door on the right.'

'Look, darling, the living-room *is* rather small; I expect we shall live in the kitchen,' said Alda, withdrawing her head.

'I should think so too; beastly little morgue. What's this?' as they approached another door at the end of the long passage.

'The kitchen. It isn't too bad.'

'Everything seems fairly clean,' he said, glancing suspiciously about him when they had succeeded in getting the door open.

'And there's a little boiler that heats the water, and the coal lives in a shed out here——'

She hurried with the lamp from room to room, only pausing when held up by a door which stuck; demonstrating, explaining, throwing open cupboards and generally casting her own glow so successfully over Pine Cottage that her husband found himself in the familiar position of thinking that the place was not so bad after all. The children followed her, with their three heads of flaxen hair palely reflecting the warm gold of her own; all three had a water-fairy look, with pale grey or green eyes and lily skins, but Jenny's hair had the darkest tint and her eyes the deepest colour.

'Now let's go upstairs,' said Alda, when they had inspected coal shed and larder and even ventured out into a small back garden overlooking the fields. 'Now, the bedrooms really are the best part of the house.'

It occurred to Ronald that this was as well, since, when damp and lack of sun and endless mud had done their work, his family would probably spend much of their time in bed. But he did not say so; the house was taken; the contract signed and stamped, and Alda and the children, in their own minds, already settled at Pine Cottage. If he put his foot down and insisted upon an upheaval, he would have to go to Germany in the following week leaving his family still unsettled for the winter, and he felt that he simply could not endure any fresh anxiety about them. They and he were so newly re-united, their shared happiness was still so sweet, that he could not cast a shadow over it by trying, perhaps unsuccessfully, to improve upon Alda's plans. After all, they were sure of a roof for their heads when much of England and most of Europe was living in a damaged house, or homeless. Here his flock of excitable, talkative feminine creatures must stay, in this depressing little place that was neither villa nor cottage standing so unexpectedly in the lonely fields; and here at least, while he was quartered in some dying town in broken Germany, he would be able to think of them on the long winter nights; safe, and in a home . . . of a sort.

'This reminds me of the seaside lodgings we used to stay in when I was a boy,' he remarked, as they wandered in and out of the bedrooms, which were furnished with large brass bedsteads and solid Edwardian wardrobes and chests of drawers.

'*We* always stayed in hotels,' said Alda, whose father was a wealthy general practitioner in the provincial city where she had been born.

'Yes, you poor little beasts.' He was standing in front of a picture and shaking his head over it.

'We adored it; Jean and I used to get crushes on the waiters.'

'Jean? What was she doing there with you?'

'She used to come away with us whenever her wretched mother wanted to get rid of her.'

'The beds do bounce, Mother!' shouted Jenny from the next room.

'Don't let Meg lie on them; they may be damp,' Alda called back. 'It's good that they bounce; they'll be comfortable.'

'Didn't you tell me that Mrs Hardcastle died recently?' Ronald went on.

'Yes, about three months ago. I was so glad for Jean.'

'Oh *Mother*!' Louise was standing at the door with a face expressing double distress; that someone should be dead and her mother so unlike her usual self as to be glad because of it.

'Mrs Hardcastle was very beastly, Weez,' said Jenny judicially. 'You know what revolting teas she always gave us.'

'Perhaps she meant them to be nice.'

'Hur-hur! Perhaps not! Mother, I'm absolutely starving. How much longer are we going to stay here?'

'I shouldn't let Louise and Jenny have this room, Alda; it gets no sun at all,' said Ronald, turning away from his picture. 'All right, Jen, we're going in a minute.'

'Have you seen enough to set your mind *at ease*, darling?' Alda asked, putting an arm about her husband's neck and pulling his dark thin cheek down to her own. The gold in her hair, and her pale face and widely-curving smile, suggested a sunlit Amanda or Anthea, whereas 'Alda' has an echo of the witch-like flowers and black berries of the elder tree, with some grey Norse sorceress weaving beneath its shade, but it means 'rich,' and Ronald thought that it suited her.

'Nothing could do that,' he answered, sighing, and held her

close for a moment. 'How far are you here from Pagets?' (the house where they had been staying with the Friends).

'Only a mile across the fields in fine weather, but it's a good three miles round by the road and the fields are impossible in the winter, unfortunately.'

'I wish you could have stayed on there.'

'So do I, but it just wasn't possible. They'll have no help in the house at all after next week, and the old lady is really ill. They've been so good to us; I can't worry them any more.'

Ronald walked across to the window (which was a modern one, set flatly in a metal frame and interposing none of the comfort of wood and deep-sunk panes between the room and the chilly night) and stared out across the faintly moonlit fields. A low wind was sighing round the house and swaying the tops of the pines.

'And who are the people at the farm? Have you seen them?'

'The Hoadleys, man and wife. They have the keys of this place and I had to call there for them. They weren't particularly forth-coming but they seemed harmless.'

'Could you go to them if you got in a hole? Have they a telephone?'

'Oh yes; I telephoned to the agent from there. It's a little farm that used to belong to gentry, so I hear, but they got tired of it and the Hoadleys bought it. But I shan't get in a hole; do I ever?'

He smiled, and pulled her ear. No, she did not get into holes; nevertheless, he mistrusted her feminine rashness and enthusiasm, her passion for the open air and flowers and picnic meals and her impatient overlooking of such details as damp rooms and inconvenient sinks.

'You won't be completely isolated . . .' he muttered, turning away from the window and looking slowly round the walls, distempered an icy blue and stained with damp. 'This really is a most depressing room, darling. Everything looks as if—as if——'

'It's been underground for weeks,' she said cheerfully. 'But the beds are really good and in the spring these woods will be brimming with primroses; you just wait! And Mrs Prewitt is going to let us have Use of Linen and Cutlery.'

'Is that the owner? Who is she?'

'She went to Ireland in 1939 and just hasn't come back. She owns several houses round here.'

'Are they all like this one?'

'Pretty much,' Alda said carelessly, smoothing her hair in front of the misty mirror. She had been too charmed by the situation of the cottage and the promise of those woods to pay much attention to a certain expression upon the faces of the Sillingham tradespeople, and a note in the voices of the Friends at Pagets, when she announced that she had taken Pine Cottage.

'Well,' Ronald said heavily, 'I suppose we'd better be going. What are the children up to?'

Alda went out on to the landing, where there was the sound of giggling, and he slowly followed.

It added considerably to his depression that his family should have been victimised by a *rentier*. Naturally he did not share the Left view of *rentiers* as a class, but this specimen seemed to him to justify it. Pine Cottage had walls of single thickness and its doors and windows and fittings were cheap and mean. He thought of Pagets; built three hundred years ago, with an oak staircase solid as the decks of the ships upon which the original Friends had sailed for the New World; the house sunk deeply in its old, wide, sweet garden, and house and garden set secretly amidst the mild turnings of an ancient lane. He wondered (for his picture of the proletariat was Ruskinian rather than Marxian) that Mrs Prewitt had been able to find Sussex workmen willing to throw her matchboarding and her bad bricks together, and he remembered how, when he looked out of a certain window at Pagets, his gaze travelled slowly up a massive, slabbed, sloping precipice, warmly grey as April clouds and fledged with emerald moss at the meeting of each slab and carrying little white flowers in spring; it was the roof of Horsham stone.

'What is all this?' he demanded, beginning to laugh as he came out on to the landing and found his wife kneeling with her head close to those of her three daughters, and all in fits of laughter.

'Meg says——' began Jenny, lifting a pink face.

'Oh no, it's rude!' from Louise.

'——that when you sit on the seat in *there*,' jerking her head towards an open door, 'it——' she went off again and could not get a word out.

'Come on, Jenny, we don't want to be here all night,' commanded Alda, putting an arm round the two eldest. 'You then, Meg. What does it do?'

'FLIES up and smacks your botty!' shouted Meg, and off they all went again, the four fair heads close together and their laughter ringing through the house.

Ronald laughed too, but he told Alda that she had 'better have that seen to,' and the laurels in the front garden thinned, as well; it would make the living-room lighter and Mrs Prewitt should be grateful. (Not that he wanted her gratitude, he added.)

Meg was asleep on his shoulder as they walked home through the winter moonlight. The way from Pine Cottage to Pagets was even rougher than the way from Sillingham to Pine Cottage and it became increasingly clear to Ronald that during the winter months at least his family (unless Alda made determined efforts towards a social life) would be almost completely cut off from what society the neighbourhood afforded.

2

On a still morning some days later, Fabrio Caetano—of ITALY, as the flash on the shoulder of his uniform proclaimed—lay on his back amidst the stumps of oaks and birches in the middle of a sunny slope.

The slope was enclosed on all sides by woods; eighteen months ago a camp had been hidden there, and deserted huts stood in the thickest parts, and dumps of rusty petrol tins and other rubbish were being gradually revealed as the leaves fell from the blackberry bushes. A track ran straight through the middle of the north wood down to the main road a mile away, with its iron-hard mud monstrously rutted by the sprockets of tanks and blackened at intervals by fire, but that was all over now; the men with their casual blasphemy and jokes, and the alien spirit which came with them like another language although they talked in English, had gone away. Sussex people no longer drew in to the roadside to let the trucks race by, each delicately and instantly blazoning its nationality by a leaf or star painted upon its side; and the urgent sense that these men must take, or be given, everything that they wanted (space, the peace of the woods, food and drink and love) because at any moment they might have to go away to be killed, had gone too; and a robin was singing on its short flights from bough to bough.

An Italian lying in the sun! So many times that might have meant a dark face showing mere animal enjoyment of warmth or (since this was a prisoner's face) a sullen relief in temporary freedom, but this time, for once, the face whose eyes beneath their lowered lids were watching an insect moving along a leaf was sensitive: not with the nervous responsiveness that belongs

16

to the faces of educated people, but in an older and simpler way difficult to paint in words. People would glance at Fabrio, as he passed them cycling back from his work to the camp, and think: 'That one minds; he's taken it to heart.'

He came from a tiny fishing village on the Ligurian coast, lonely in its loveliness and uncorrupted by the money of tourists; his father was very poor and ignorant but lived a satisfying human life because, at eighty, he was still a healthy, handsome old man and undisputed head of a large obedient family and because he owned a piece of land and also a boat; that boat came next in importance, in the Caetano household, to the land and to Gianni Caetano himself and far, far ahead of the family tradition that they were descended from a wicked and beautiful *principessa* of the old days who had been the mother of famous tyrants.

Fabrio's childhood had been passed in a poor, dirty, noisy home where there was plenty of excitement and affection and plenty of food—*pasta*, and garlic and tomatoes cooked in oil, and small sweet peaches. The boat and the piece of land were responsible for all this abundance; the former was small, but it was seaworthy and sound, and Fabrio's father could go fishing in it at night and bring home a netful of luscious tiny fish, enough to feed all nine of the Caetani for a day; or occasionally take out a party of tourists from the nearest port, into which he sailed twice a week (tourists were not so numerous, alas, since the coming of Il Duce, who did not want the foreigners to come and see how poor Italy was, and then this accursed second war).

The Caetani's boat was the opposite number of the English odd-job man's bag of tools or small van, making it possible for them to rely on their own efforts for their sustenance rather than upon weekly salary packets and the caprices of an employer. Capitalist in a tiny way, Gianni lived outside the modern economic system; and some of the Caetano girls made lace and some made love, some of the boys fished and some of them hung about Pietro's garage and Giorgio's bench in the nearest port and learned a little about cars and a little about carpentry, and so they managed, not to exist, but to live.

For although there are slums in Italy and as bitter winds there as anywhere in the world, the Ligurian coast is sheltered and warm, and poverty and beauty, the ancient lovers, still go hand-in-hand there, lingering on in an ancient corner of the world. It is easier to be poor in the sunlight. Zola said so even of Rome, which endures more bitter winters than Fabrio's village ever knew; and if those who are most earnest for the education and comfortable housing of their fellow-men could have seen Fabrio and his brothers lying half-naked in the shadow of the brown sail of their father's boat, laughing and quarrelling over a few cigarettes or a handful of fruit, even they would have admitted that poverty does not always mean misery, and that in Europe, at least, those who have the gold of the sun find it easier to do without paper money.

But what, the Gentle Reader will ask, of politics? What of the Fascist Movement and Benito Mussolini, who came to power in the year that Fabrio, child of his father's old age, was born of a young second wife? Was it possible for any Italian, however poor and obscure, to avoid the pernicious scourge (or cleansing flame, as you please) that swept his country from 1922 to 1944? Yes, Gentle Reader, it was possible. Of course the Caetani sons joined the *Balilla* when they were seven and the *Avanguardia giovanile* when they were fifteen, and last of all the army got them and three of them were killed, but in the Caetani—in Fabrio especially—Fascism (an old idea) met something much older than itself. It met a deep indifference to ideas of any kind. The Caetani did not have ideas; they felt; and what they felt about most strongly was life, not politics; food, not Fascism; their boat, not Mussolini's *Balilla*. They heartily agreed with every word that Mussolini was reported by rumour to have said, and forgot it the next minute. This very healthy attitude of mind, or rather body, prevented the Caetani from becoming what is called politically aware, and it also prevented them from attracting unwelcome attention from the local tyrantissimo at the port (who afterwards, we are pleased to relate, fell in the sea while drunk and was drowned). They also had a deep, cheerful sense of their own importance as individuals which made them more interested in themselves than in anyone else. That helped them to keep out of trouble, too.

So if the Gentle Reader was afraid of being told—at some length—how Fabrio at the age of eight felt a mistrust of the *Balilla*; which increased to a hatred of Fascismo and all its works when he joined the *Avanguardia giovanile* at fifteen; finally swelling into a dedicated purpose when he was taken into the army, and leaving him firmly established as an active one-man-Underground-Democratic-Movement at the age of twenty-three, the Gentle Reader need have no fears. Fabrio shouted when he was told to shout, like the rest of them, and went on living his secret life undisturbed.

He had been taken prisoner in Libya in 1943, and had now been at the camp in Sussex for two years. Since the end of the war in Europe he had been permitted, together with other Italians who professed themselves collaborators, much more liberty; and at the moment he and his fellow prisoner, Emilio Rossi, were supposed to be working, unsupervised, at clearing a ditch for Mr Hoadley of Naylor's, but the morning was so warm, the still air so caressing, that Fabrio had stopped work some time ago and was lying among the bracken, doing nothing, while Emilio was busy on his own affairs down at the far end of the slope.

There had been no rain for some weeks and the rusty fern, the few large curled leaves lingering on the chestnut trees, the withered grass underfoot, and the twisted copper leaves of the oaks were dry; there were even primrose clusters with green shoots in their hearts along the bank where Emilio lay in the cavern made by roots of an ancient holly bush, his body curved round the dark hole of a rabbit burrow and his hand waiting, relaxed yet ready, above the burrow's mouth. He kept so still that he did not seem to breathe or to be alive; his very eyes were half-closed, and all he could see between his eyelids as he looked steadily downwards was the break in the bank where the burrow began. His brown uniform was the same colour as the autumn leaves.

Fabrio knew what his friend was after, and every now and then he turned on his side and gave a glance in his direction, but it was too much trouble to go rabbit-hunting; though he liked eating rabbits when they were cooked.

Presently there was a flicker, so quick that it might have been a shimmer of air, at the burrow's mouth. Emilio relaxed his hands and body and waited. Suddenly a young rabbit was sitting upright in the burrow's mouth against the sunlight. Its ears looked as if they were made of transparent pink satin edged by a tiny silver fringe. Emilio did nothing; he hardly breathed. The rabbit suddenly flicked back into the burrow. In less than a minute it came back again and took a few steps forward. It was not uneasy; this was the way it always came out from the darkness into the fresh scented air. It was so young that its bones and fur seemed liquid; mere fragility and silverness blent into warm, moving life.

For an instant it sat there sniffing, with delicate paws pressing the freshly turned soil, and then Emilio flung himself on it and gripped it between his small hands. It made one convulsive plunge and then a few weaker ones and at last lay limp. He had not pressed very hard.

Then he got up, brushed the leaves from himself, and walked slowly up the slope towards Fabrio, putting the rabbit in his pocket as he went.

'I got one,' he said in Italian.

'I know; I saw you.' Fabrio rolled over on his side and sat up, linking arms round his knees and looking up into his friend's face. 'I wasn't asleep.'

'Shall we stew it? I've got the can down there,' jerking his head towards the ditch.

'What's the time?' Fabrio glanced at the sun. 'Not quite noon. All right, only we must be quick. *He* was telling *her* this morning that he was coming up here some time to look at our work. What about water?'

Emilio showed his yellow teeth in a laugh. 'I've got that, too. I took a bottle from their cellar and filled it at the rainwater butt.'

'Your lighter wasn't working last night.'

'It is now; *he* gave me a drop of juice.'

He held up a little metal object no bigger than a matchbox, carved with a dragon's head in a vigorous primitive style and hinged and polished. He pressed it open and a tiny flame burned thinly in the sunlight.

'All right!' exclaimed Fabrio, jumping up, all his melancholy vanishing. 'We'll put it on to stew and do a bit of work while it's cooking.'

'Ah-h-h! No, wait a minute,' said Emilio softly, in a changed tone. He glanced under his eyelids, towards the north face of the wood and Fabrio, following the direction of his stealthy movement, saw a woman, a little girl and a pram straying along by the edge of the trees. They were talking to one another and their clear voices in the unfamiliar language came down to the two men through the sunny stillness.

'She's come to live at the villa near our farm. She wouldn't say anything if she did see us,' said Fabrio, putting his hands in his pockets and beginning to stroll away towards the ditch where their spades and mattocks had been left.

'How do you know? Do you like her looks?' jeered Emilio, following him, and added something frank.

Fabrio laughed but did not answer, and they would have

reached the ditch without seeming to notice the two intruders, had not the child run as fast as she could towards them, ignoring a command from her mother, and planted herself in their path.

'Hul-lo!' she exclaimed with such smiling and delighted surprise that both men paused, smiling too.

''Ul-lo,' they said, looking down at her.

'Bambina,' added Emilio, turning to Alda, who now drew near. His eyes moved boldly yet wistfully over her shape, which had the roundness natural to a woman in the early thirties who has borne several children, but Fabrio, after a glance at her face, turned away his head. Alda noticed his chestnut hair and blue eyes with interest, for she had supposed all Italians to be dark.

'Nice day—good,' she said, with her friendly smile, pointing at the sun.

'Yes. Good-a. You-a bambina?' said Emilio, and began to feel in his pocket.

'Yes. Meg,' said Alda, pointing this time at her daughter.

'Ah-ha. Meg-g.' Emilio nodded. 'I show-a Meg a little—a pret-ty——' and before Alda's gradually widening eyes he was beginning to withdraw a bundle of limp fur from his pocket when Fabrio, saying something quickly in Italian, pushed it back into its hiding-place.

'Oh—thank you so much, I'm afraid we must be going now,' said Alda hastily, taking Meg's hand and beginning to retreat, 'Good-bye,' and she directed a special smile at the other Italian, the 'nice' one, as she now thought of him, who did not return it; she just caught a glimpse of a sullen face as he walked away.

'You live-a at villa?' said Emilio, moving a few steps after her.

'We, him and me, Fabrio Caetano, Emilio Rossi, at Naylor Farm.'

'I expect we shall see you again, then,' said Alda.

'You give-a cigarette,' said Emilio coaxingly, still following her. 'We have no cig-arette; we only——' he rapidly opened and shut his ten fingers three times in front of her face, leaving

22

five fingers extended in the air. 'For a week. No good. You give-a cigarette?'

Here Fabrio, who was half-way towards the ditch where the spades were, turned back, as though waiting, and called out something. Emilio laughed and shrugged his shoulders, then, exclaiming 'Buon'giorno, signora,' he followed his friend.

'Was it a dead bunny in that man's possick?' demanded Meg, the instant she and her mother were alone.

'I'm afraid so, darling.'

'Oh, poor little thing. Why wouldn't you let it see me, Mudder?'

'You didn't *want* to see it, did you, Meg?'

'Yes, Meg did want.'

'You shall next time, dear,' soothed Alda, reflecting with complacence upon the advantages of having three children; the variety of response was in itself an endless entertainment. Louise would have shuddered for the rest of the morning over that glimpse of fur, while Jenny would only have inquired whether the Italians were going to cook it for their dinner.

Then they turned their steps homeward, for there was still much packing and arranging to do on this, their last day at Pagets. Jenny and Louise were there now, fitting their especial treasures into the large old suitcases in which they had travelled for the past three years, but Alda was always conscious of a desire, sometimes subdued and sometimes imperative, to wander out into the open air and to-day, which promised to be one of the last fine days of the month, she had not even attempted to resist it.

As they were lost to sight along the rutted track through the woods, Fabrio said angrily to Emilio:

'Why must you beg from her?'

Emilio sat down and pulled the rabbit out of his pocket and began to skin it deftly with a razor blade set in a wooden holder.

'She has a pretty face, and she's as good for a cigarette as any other bit of skirt. Why shouldn't I?'

'I won't beg from anyone.'

'Oh yes! You won't beg! Who let me pay for his beer yesterday?'

'I had no money, as you well know.' Fabrio's voice rose and there was colour on his high cheekbones.

'All right, all right.' Emilio pushed some billets of wood across with his foot. 'Get the fire going, will you. Here's the water,' and he pulled out an orangeade bottle from the rolled bundle of his coat.

Presently, when the smoke was going straight up into the still air, while the flames darted below it and the water in the petrol can was beginning to steam, Emilio broke the long silence by saying:

'Anyway, I did it to get cigarettes for you too,' and dropping his arm for an instant over his friend's shoulders.

'All right, all right!' mocked Fabrio, shaking the arm off, but after a moment he began to sing.

'What's that?' asked Emilio lazily, lying back amidst the skeleton leaves and the bronze fern with arms behind his head.

'The fishermen sing it at San Angelo.' Fabrio broke off to say this, then resumed, sitting by the fire with arms linked round his knees and head thrown back. His voice was a tenor; no phenomenon, but behind it, lightly and easily floating the words out through his throat and into the air, was the desire to sing that makes a bird sing and—in spite of his captivity and the consequent martyrdom of all his young instincts—the bird's joy in living.

'Ah, that old stuff! That's dead. You want to sing——' and he burst into *Giovinezza*, but after a few bars stopped again and shook his head, muttering, 'I never did like that much, I like this better,' and he swung into a tuneful little song consisting of an American scaffolding and an Italian façade recently broadcast from Rome and exactly like all the other tuneful little songs with American scaffoldings and German, French or English façades recently broadcast from Berlin, Paris and London.

'That's good, too,' and Fabrio joined in joyfully and the rabbit in the petrol can began to bubble. It was now nearly two hours since Fabrio Caetano and Emilio Rossi, of ITALY, had done any work.

Mr Hoadley, a giant of a man, coming down through the fern in the direction of the singing with a hound-puppy, which he was 'walking,' at his heels, did not know exactly how long this had been going on but he did know when a fire had been burning for some time and the fire was the first thing he looked at. A cavern of red heat and frail oak-ashes had gathered beneath the penthouse of charred logs.

He walked so swiftly down the slope that he was on them before they knew it, and they had only time to scramble up before, with a vigorous thrust of his stout stick, he had sent the petrol tin sideways into the fire. There was a hissing, and a cloud of rabbit-steam and wood smoke rolled out as the broth poured over the logs and dripped down to sink into the ground. The hound-puppy, who had been eagerly advancing towards the smell, yelped and leapt back from the boiling steam with tail between his legs.

'You pair of lazy bastards,' said Mr Hoadley, scattering the fire with his boot. 'Get on, I don't want to hear anything about it, I'm sick of the two of you,' and whistling to the dog he turned and marched away, with his cap pulled over his eyes and his usually good-natured lower lip thrust out. He had, when he thought about such matters at all, a low opinion of every race except the English, and since his employment of Italian prisoners his opinion had sunk lower still.

Emilio had made a hasty movement towards his abandoned spade and mattock as the farmer loomed over them, but Fabrio had stood his ground, and now thrust his trembling hands into his pockets and stared down at what was to have been their feast; the blackened, steaming wood, the joints of rabbit, cooked to a turn and looking very pink amongst ashes and brown leaves, and the moisture, the delicious broth, dripping from the over-turned can. He swore, and his blue eyes glittered.

'Ah, come on—it's still good to eat!' cried Emilio impudently, down on his knees in the moist ground and rubbing a rabbit-leg clean against his sleeve. There was a scurry at his side and the beautiful head of the hound-puppy suddenly appeared under his arm, with such mingled pleading and aristocratic confidence in his eyes that Emilio unhesitatingly gave him a piece of the meat. An angry shout from the distance, however, sent him bounding off, and the watching Italians saw his treasure snatched from him and tossed into the bushes.

It was now after two o'clock and the light was brightening and the shadows lengthening. Fabrio pulled a packet of food from his pocket and ate, sullenly ignoring Emilio's offer of rabbit, and presently both were at work again, clearing and reshaping the ancient ditch overgrown with brambles and broken down by rabbits and foxes, and did not cease until it was time to stop for the day. Emilio straightened the last breadth of ditchwall with a downward stroke of his spade; Fabrio was already cleaning his, with his heel and a piece of wood. The air was very cold and the primrose sunset looked down on them from behind the oaks; sharp scents of bracken and holly leaves, beaded with moisture that would later freeze, assailed their nostrils. They were hungry, and they longed with passion, as at this hour exiled Sussex men in Italy were longing, for home. The sea below San Angelo would be growing dark, the evening wind blowing the boats home, lights shining out from the windows of the *Leone d'Oro*. The keels make a soft crunch-ch-ch as they come up through the sand. A girl's dress glows richly through the dusk as she loiters on the shore. Yellow light and the smell of frying food come out through an open window. The stone-pine that is a landmark on the *Capo* stands out black against the violet sky, and inland rolls the wooded country, ancient and beautiful, with wheat and hill-perched villages. Mother of God, thought

Fabrio, it is like that *now*, as I stand here in these cursed wet leaves and must take such care to clean my spade. It is like that *now* at home, at San Angelo, and I am here.

'Ready?' asked Emilio, hunching himself into his coat. 'Hullo, what do you want?' It was the hound-puppy, his tan and white coat looking very distinct in the soft, clear light preceding dusk, who came up to greet them.

'He got his rabbit-leg after all,' said Fabrio, pinching the supple dewlap while the dog stood still to be caressed, looking from one to another with wise eyes. 'Didn't you see him just now?'

'He can come back to the farm with us,' said Emilio as they began to climb the slope towards the woods.

'Be careful; the old——will think we're trying to steal his dog,' said Fabrio roughly. 'Better not get too friendly with him. There! go home, can't you? We don't want you,' and he motioned with his boot, but the puppy made a polite movement of avoidance and in a moment was back at his side. Fabrio's sore, homesick heart was comforted by his friendliness.

3

'How long will it take us to get to Pine Cottage?' asked Jenny, who inherited her mother's forward-looking temperament.

'I don't know. Perhaps Mr Bolliver does,' and Alda leant forward to attract the attention of Mr Bolliver, whose car she had hired to transport herself, her daughters, and no less than fourteen pieces of luggage, to their new home.

'About twenty minutes,' smiled Mr Bolliver, slightly turning his head. The winding lane that led down into Pagets was now far behind them, and the car was travelling along the main road to Sillingham, with the chicken farm and orchards on the right, and on the left the meadows and woods rolling southward to Christ's Hospital, whose tower soared forth from the purple forest ten miles away. The sky was lowering and throughout the morning everybody had been hoping that it would not rain.

'Jenny! Your spear!' Louise sat upright and gazed distressfully at her sister. 'Oh, we've left it *behind*!'

'No, we haven't. Mr Bolliver kindly put it in the back with my big case,' soothed Alda.

'And the eggs and my jar with the beetles in and my Alison Uttley books?'

'All safely in, darling. Do not *flap*.'

'Now we're going to Pingcottage,' announced Meg, who was sitting on her mother's lap and gazing first at Jenny, then at Louise and then at Mr Bolliver's back; she wore the shabby siren-suit in which Louise had gone through the first air attacks on Ironborough, and a Norwegian bonnet of white wool printed with huge crimson roses. Alda always contrived to find some brilliant jersey or pair of red boots or fur mittens to relieve the shabbiness of her children's clothes, which were even more worn than those belonging to most families of garment-sharing sisters because of the roving life led by the Lucie-Brownes for the past few years. Their outfits thus possessed originality and distinction, and the three were often taken for 'artists' children'—to the shame of Jenny, whose conventional nature vaguely felt the expression as derogatory. Alda herself dressed the year round in old tweeds or faded cotton, and expended most of the coupons and money on her daughters; she had never found that her looks and her charm needed setting off by clothes.

'Oh Mother! *Did* you put in my Christmas cards?'

'*Yes*, lovey. Do not *flap*.'

Alda's spirits began to sink as they left behind the extended, straggling village street that was Sillingham and passed the railway bridge and the ugly new cottages on the road leading to Froggatt. She thought of Pagets, encircled by a barrier of bushy bronze oaks whose green trunks enclosed mysterious shadows. There was a feeling of protection there, yet a sense of light, of freedom and movement, too, of air blowing through widely spaced branches; but here, all was low and damp. She was extremely susceptible to dreary surroundings and bad weather, but she seldom realised what was depressing her spirits, and her only method of raising them was to seize upon whatever could be delighted in and delight in it slightly more than was natural. 'All Alda's geese are swans,' her sisters said indulgently, and her husband sometimes called her The Golden Goose. She was now preparing to delight in the view from Pine Cottage.

Their arrival was made more cheerful than she had anticipated by Mr Bolliver's good nature in carrying all the luggage, including Jenny's Masai spear, across to the cottage for them, the children joyfully expanding the small jokes which arose every other minute and assisting him to deposit the heavier cases upstairs. While he was thus employed Alda hurried out to the cellar and saw with relief that the coal had arrived. There was also a pile of freshly-chopped wood. How kind of someone, she thought, and hastily filled a scuttle with coal and her skirt with billets and went into the parlour.

'Mother, the groceries have come. All our rations and a lot of lovely soap. The tradespeople seem very *reliable* round here,' called Jenny from the back door.

'Digestive biscuits. Goody!' from Louise.

'Meg doesn't want a biksit.'

'Charmed, I'm sure. All the more for us.'

'That's the lot,' smiled Mr Bolliver at the parlour door, thinking that this was the nicest lot he had so far delivered at Pine Cottage. How many he had set down at that gate full of hope and strength! and how many he had called for three months later! broken in mind and body and cursing their landlady as he drove them away.

When he had been paid and had driven off, Alda knelt before the fire, now burning strongly but heatlessly in the cold air, and gazed with unwonted pensiveness into the flames. Overhead, the children could be heard dragging their possessions out of the suitcases and putting them away in carefully chosen places from which she would afterwards have to remove and rearrange them.

She glanced round the room. Dim grey light came in between the scanty curtains and showed a grubby pink cushion, a row of tattered paper novels and other books in such dirty covers that she decided then and there to lock them out of the children's reach, a steel engraving of a mythological figure weeping in a grove. The air smelled of staleness and old carpets. Save for the distant sound made by the children and the fluttering of the fire, all was silent.

Alda had been homeless for so long that she had almost ceased to grieve (or so she told herself) for the elegant yet homely double-fronted house in the old quarter of Ironborough which she and Ronald had been carefully, lovingly filling with furniture and books. Home, for her, was now wherever Ronald and the children and she herself could gather together in front of a fire or about a table, and sometimes she congratulated herself that she was not tied to a house, a routine and a neighbourhood as her married sisters were, but whenever circumstance compelled the family to pull up its shallow roots and move on, she felt their homelessness keenly for a week or so, until those roots had re-established themselves. At Pagets they had struck into deeper and richer soil than any they had so far discovered, and this afternoon Alda was not cheerful.

She jumped up and ran to the children, leaving the fire beginning to warm the room. I'll soon have *you* down and packed away in a cupboard, she vowed, grimacing in passing at a print, executed in strong reds and browns, of four bald old men smoking churchwarden pipes amidst some hounds in an inn parlour. Ruskin himself, in the chapter on Late Venetian Grotesque, never in his worst nightmares imagined art sinking to such bathos. Yet beside it hung a Victorian water-colour of an Italian lake surrounded by mountains, painted in harmless clear blues and framed in broad gold, that she liked and resolved should stay there. Her fancy leaned towards whatever was pretty and immediately enjoyable, and some years previously Ronald had quietly, with amusement, abandoned his attempts to alter his Golden Goose's taste.

'It's raining,' announced Jenny, glancing up from the confusion of possessions spread about the floor in the biggest bedroom, and Alda looked out of the window and saw some distant wooden structures already half-hidden in weeping mist.

'Those are chickens' houses,' said Louise, who had followed her to the window and stood looking out with an arm about her mother's waist. 'Look, you can see the chickens walking about.'

'A man in a sack did come and gib them their tea,' put in Meg, who was busy untidying a box of hair ribbons. 'Meg did see him.'

'When can we have our tea, Mother?' sighed Louise. 'I *could* peck a bit.'

'Could you peck a bit, my lovey? Well, you shall. Let's just put some of these things away and then we'll have tea. Toasted buns and butter!'

They worked until the light failed, filling drawers with shabby little clothes and rolling mattresses down the stairs, with shouts of laughter, to air by the parlour fire. Jenny was really helpful, for she inherited her mother's impatient energy tempered by an organising capacity handed down from her paternal grandmother; Louise dropped things and went off into daydreams, and Meg bustled off on explorations, returning at intervals with reports, usually of an alarming nature, about the house and its contents.

'*May* we have it in front of the fire, Mums darling?' asked Jenny, lifting a crimson face from toasting the buns.

'Of course. Oh dear, if only Father were here . . . never mind. The time will soon pass. Come along, Meg; Louise, come and warm those frog-hands. There! now let's be cosy.'

Firelight, and curtains drawn against the rain and deepening twilight, and four laughing faces, framed in hair as palely golden as the flames. The mean, tastelessly furnished room is hidden in kind shadows; they play over the ceiling and bow and waver as if dancing an accompaniment to the story Alda reads aloud. Five hundred miles away, the father driving through a dark, sighing forest of pines in Oldenburg imagines that group gathered about the fire, as he has so often seen it, and amidst the black night and the dreary confusion of the journey, he smiles.

(. . . The mighty George Eliot once commented with acerbity upon those readers who 'demand adultery, murder and ermine tippets on every page,' and we ourselves, confronted whenever we open a volume of contemporary fiction by explosions, lust, perversion and despair in every line, join our feeble voice to hers. Though often tempted to show that we, too, know all about That—yes, *and* That, to say nothing of the Anglo-Saxon Words (all nine of them) we refuse to be bounced into writing what we do not enjoy writing. Our themes are gentle, it is true, but

> We do but sing because we must
> And pipe but as the linnets do,

and our final decision is that enough is going on everywhere without our starting in.)

After a game of Rush Hour, and baths which were necessarily scanty because of the short commons in fuel, Alda put her family to bed in the chilly, unfamiliar rooms and left them to fall asleep as quickly as excitement would permit, while she herself went round the house looking for tramps, burglars and lunatics (of escaped prisoners from the German camp six miles away, or deserters from the American Army still lurking in the woods, she did not think until later that evening).

She opened cupboards, glanced into the large cold pantry, and shone her torch into a closet filled with chipped crockery and yellow newspapers by the kitchen door: then, satisfied that nobody lurked there and smiling to herself, she went into the now comfortably warm parlour and sat down beside the fire prepared to enjoy a peaceful hour or so before going to bed.

It was almost eight. She had wound the ugly little clock on the mantelpiece and its loud hasty tick—a vulgar sound if ever there were one—now filled the silence. She could hear the rain falling steadily outside, and occasionally a car going past on the Froggatt road. As she picked up the knitting which she preferred to reading, she glanced round the room for the second time that day and decided that when she had packed away quite half of the pictures and ornaments, those dull pink walls and that thread-bare carpet would look less offensive; but oh! if only the room had had clean white matting and apricot distemper!

The fire settled itself lower into the tiny basket grate, the clock ticked sharply, quickly. Alda's needles flew skilfully in the intricacies of a jumper for Louise and her thoughts flew to Germany. She had been working and dreaming for perhaps half an hour, when there sounded a loud, single knock at the front door.

She stopped knitting, and turned her head in the direction of the summons, and her eyes opened a little wider. She was not a nervous woman, but at that moment she did realise that she was alone with three children in a cottage a quarter of a mile across the fields from the nearest house, and that if she opened the front door to that knock, there was no reason why— whoever was there—should not come in.

She waited, her knitting resting in her lap. Rain drove against the window, the fire gave forth its faint sounds. The knock was not repeated.

But she did not find this reassuring. Was the intruder waiting at the door? or, worse still, prowling noiselessly about the house— perhaps even now peering into the room through that gap in the curtains? She forced herself to glance at the window and of course nothing was there; no white face half-revealed, no hand pressed menacingly against the pane.

Suddenly she got up, dropped her work on the chair, and hurried down the passage. She did listen, it must be admitted, just for a moment before she actually turned the catch of the front door, but when she did so it was without hesitation.

The rainy moonlit sky, vast and vacant, looked down at her; cold and sweet, the wet air blew against her face. No one was there, and across the fields, sheeted with fresh pools, shone reassuringly the lights of the farm.

She took a lengthy look all about her. A sixty-foot ash tree stood up in the wind, sighing steadily, and she could hear the pines at the back of the house sighing too; their sound was like the sea's sound, the sea fifteen miles away across the black, turfy downs. Suddenly, something made her glance down at her feet, and there, neatly arranged upon the doorstep, was a pile of books.

'Oh, how kind!' Alda exclaimed, and stooped to examine them, not realising that the unknown might have put them there as a lure to engross her while creeping up to bash her on the head.

She had just read the title of the first one, *In Touch with the Transcendent*, and had time to experience dismay, before a gust of rain blew in over herself and the books and she shut the door.

Back in the parlour she put them on the table and finished her inspection. The titles were:

With Rod and Gun in Jugoslavia; *Foch, Man of Orléans*; *In Touch with the Transcendent*; *Peter Jackson, Cigar Merchant*; *To Haiti in a Ketch*.

In Touch with the Transcendent, a volume of vaguely religious essays, was the most worn of the five, and was clearly a favourite with its owner, but *Peter Jackson, Cigar Merchant* also bore traces of frequent use. It was not easy to conjure up a personality who should delight in both works, and when Alda went up to bed an hour later she had got no further than the conviction that he was good-natured, eccentric, and a man.

4

At breakfast the next morning Jenny and Louise instantly assumed that the unknown was a spy, and worked out an elaborate plan by which he could be identified and trapped, while Meg methodically worked her way through a large bowl of cereal and milk, glancing continually from one animated face to another.

The subject kept them absorbed until breakfast was over and before them—long, rainy and dull—stretched the day. The irregular nature of their lives during the war had never permitted Jenny and Louise to acquire the sense of order and routine which is alleged to play such an important and valuable part in a child's upbringing, and Alda herself was no routine-lover; the impromptu picnic, the unheralded treat, were what she enjoyed, and her housekeeping was slapdash and cheerful. She was well fitted to bring up children (who do not miss routine and order if they have security and love) and her daughters, with imaginations kept in play by the many home-diversions provided by an ingenious mother, were happy children.

They each had a paint-box; there was the hoard of old *Bestway* and *Weldon's Fashion Books* that travelled round with the family for colouring and cutting out; there was Louise's box of dolls' clothes and the unfailing interest to be obtained from swapping them with those in Jenny's box; there were books (two of Louise's favourites were *Bessie in the Mountains*, a pious mid-nineteenth-century American story, and *By Order of Queen Maud*, a Late Victorian tale in which the highly exhibitionist heroine ended up as a cripple for life, just to learn her); and finally, *all three owned raincoats and sound rubber boots*. This meant that they were made free of the pleasures of an English winter; if all else failed to amuse, they could go for a walk.

Alda knew that bread, vegetables and groceries would be brought to her door, and she reckoned that it would not be necessary to shop in the village more than twice a week. There was, therefore, no sound excuse, after she and Jenny had whisked through the washing-up and sketchily made the beds, for going out.

But the fire burned cheerfully in the kitchen and three heads were bent placidly (even Meg, who was too young for painting, was temporarily entertained in watching) over the painting books. Alda went across to the window and looked out; green, wet, fresh and empty the fields stretched away to the brown woods. She felt the raindrops on her face and the suck of wet mud at her boots and the cold crystal scatter of water over her hand as she pulled at a late blackberry; she could taste its soft rotten sweetness on her tongue. I'll go over to the farm, she decided, and see what happens about letters and milk. She had received an impression that the Hoadleys did not want to be friendly but there was no harm in asking.

When she came down in her oilskins, Meg was sitting on the floor.

'Just getting on me boots,' she explained. 'Meg will go with Mudder.'

'Oh now, Meg darling, you can't come this time, it's pouring with rain,' exclaimed Alda impatiently, wild to be off. 'You stay here goodly with Jenny and Weez.'

'Meg doesn't want to.'

'*We* don't particularly want *you*, goodness knows,' said Jenny, without looking up from her work.

'I should think not, indeed,' from Louise.

'Dwell, if vey don't want me and you don't want me, what shall I do?' roared Meg, bursting into tears and standing up with one boot off and one on. 'Oh, oh, oh, what shall I do?'

'Put your silly ass boot on and come with me,' said Alda crossly and gaily, snatching her up and pulling on the boot. 'Oh, for goodness' sake don't make that noise!'

A few minutes later she was splashing across the meadow with the rain driving in her face and the laughing Meg on her back. A raised track strengthened by flints led from the cottage to the farm, but in parts it had been broken away and deeply worn down by the passage of hay wains and herds of cows, and in these places the pools were inches deep, while on either side extended quagmires. Alda would have preferred to enjoy this wet day by herself, but Meg's weight felt pleasant upon her shoulders and she liked the clasp of the little hands round her throat.

Keats said that poetry should *steal upon the senses*. Even so, Naylor's Farm stole upon Alda's eyes. At one moment she was plodding along the track, moving her wet eyelashes to free them from the raindrops, while ahead of her lay a group of barns and sheds built of tarred weatherboarding and thatched with ancient straw that had changed in the course of years from gold to silver; the next moment, she had passed the buildings, and the farm (whose upper storey alone had been visible from the track) lay before her in a hollow. And what had been a pleasant country landscape was transformed.

It looks like the end of somewhere, she thought vaguely, lifting her hand again to wipe the rain from her eyes, and yet it is not shut in. How very beautiful.

There was nothing special or solemn in the scene: it was only that the guardian group of elms was perfectly shaped, and that a sheet of water brimmed between herself and the low, rose-red farmhouse so that the building seemed rising from a lake. Rosevines, on which masses of withered white blossoms and even a few living ones lingered, overgrew porch and windows; how sheltered the place must be! the gentlest possible slopes and folds in the surrounding meadows enclosed it and made it remote rather than lonely. A low wall of the same rosy brick surrounded the tangled garden, threaded by a narrow brick path; there was not much attempt at flower growing and the place seemed a little neglected, gradually settling into this hollow among the fields, where throughout the years the pond had gathered and white ducks sailed in the rain.

Having walked round the water, Alda pushed open the faded wooden gate and went up the path. After she had used the creaking knocker, she let Meg slip to the ground and stood gazing away at the endless gentle folds of meadow, the farm buildings and the disturbed grey sky. There were no signs of life until a man in a brown uniform came out of a shed with a sack over his head and a sullen face under it; she recognised the blue-eyed Italian of the woods, but though he glanced in her direction he made no reply to her pleasant 'good morning' and disappeared among the buildings towards the back of the farm-house. At that moment the door opened.

'Yes?' said the young woman who stood there, unsmiling under a coquettish turban, with a duster in one hand. 'Oh—good morning,' recognising her.

'Good morning, Mrs Hoadley. I hope I'm not disturbing you. Can you tell me what happens about letters here? Does the postman come or do we have to fetch them?'

'Sometimes she does (it's an old lady—or was, before she was taken ill a month ago) but most days we have to ride down to Burlham for them.'

She paused, obviously waiting for Alda to thank her, and go away; her manner was perfectly civil and equally perfectly designed to keep Alda at a distance.

'I see. That won't always be convenient for us,' said Alda, who sometimes did not notice when people intended to keep her at a distance. 'What a nuisance.'

'Yes, it is. Mr Hoadley or one of the men has to go down

39

there every day, never mind the weather or the work.' She did not add an offer to let one of them bring Alda's letters.

'You are going to let us have our milk, aren't you?' Alda went on, eager to get the details of their new life into working order.

'Yes.' Here Mrs Hoadley's eyes strayed to Meg.

She was sitting on the low brick wall supporting the wooden porch and kicking her boots and trousered legs against it, and such looks as she had were not improved by wet tails of hair hanging out of her pixie hood on either side of her fat pale cheeks. Her attitude and manner, which were detached to indifference, were not attractive unless the beholder happened to like children.

'Don't kick holes in the wall, please, it's bad enough now,' said Mrs Hoadley with a cross smile.

Meg stopped kicking and gazed up at her with interest. Then (for she was not accustomed to a tone lacking in affection) she turned inquiring eyes upon her mother.

'Perhaps you'd better take the milk now, it'll save one of us a journey later,' went on Mrs Hoadley. 'I won't ask you in, it's so wet and children make such a mess, don't they? I'll go and get it.'

She turned back into the house, leaving the door open, and with one impulse Alda and Meg peered into the hall to see what this cross lady's house was like.

All was in noticeably good taste; grey-papered walls, an etching of a cathedral, a grandfather clock with *J. F. Cole, Horsham* painted upon his face in a wreath of flowers, and on the floor a grey drugget. How boring, thought Alda, whose taste certainly did run to the Christmas Supplement in Colours. I would have white paper all over red grapes and green leaves, a brick floor, apple-green paint——

'Here you are,' said Mrs Hoadley, reappearing, and she handed her two open zinc cans filled with milk.

'Thank you, but I'm afraid I can't take them now; I've got

Meg to carry and I can't manage both,' said Alda decisively, putting them down on the brick coping. 'I'll come back for them later.'

Mrs Hoadley was plainly preparing to open her compressed lips with something hasty when a man came up the path, saying, 'Letters from Ironborough, Molly,' at the same time putting a packet into her eager hand; and when she did speak all that came out was:

'Here is Mr Hoadley; he may have some letters for you.'

'Yes, I have. We saw your lights last night and knew you must be in,' smiled Mr Hoadley and handed Alda a bundle which included two from Germany. Her face lit up.

'Oh, thank you. How kind,' she said.

'Somebody has to go down anyway (there's always a pile of forms for me to fill up by every post) so we may as well save you the journey. Is this your milk?'

Mrs Hoadley, apparently losing interest in the proceedings, had hurried with her letters into the house.

'Yes. I was coming back for it later. I've got *this* to carry,' giving a little shake to Meg, who was now on her back, 'and I can't manage both.'

'I'll take the milk for you, I'm going up that way,' and he picked up the cans. 'Gone up to see Mr Waite if anyone wants me, Molly; shan't be long,' he called to his wife, who was standing by the window reading her letters. She nodded impatiently without looking up.

'Now you can say I've been watering the milk,' he remarked with his friendly smile, when they were walking through the rain, which was now slightly less heavy, towards the cottage. A hound-puppy whom Mr Hoadley addressed as Ruffler had joined them and walked at his heels.

'It's delicious creamy milk; we had some for tea yesterday didn't we, Meg?'

'Meg hab milk?' said Meg questioningly; she had never taken

41

her eyes from the farmer since he joined them, and by the way he looked at her, though he said nothing, Alda knew that he liked children. She thought that he had none of his own, or Mrs Hoadley would not have made that remark about children making a mess. She's too right, thought Alda, they do; and if you don't like them that's your first thought about them; mess, and a noise.

'Was it you who kindly left some chopped wood for us?' she went on. 'I was so pleased when I found it yesterday.'

'Well, I thought you might be glad of some, it was such a nasty raw day, you'd want to get a fire going. I had one of the Italians chop it and take it up,' he answered, a little awkwardly.

'You have two of them, haven't you? Meg and I met them in the woods the other day and they told us they were working here.'

'"Working" isn't quite the word. They eat all they can get and do as little as they dare.'

Alda nodded sympathetically. At Pagets she had heard that many of the prisoners were hard-working and expert in hedging, ditching and other country crafts, but she was far too expert herself at getting on well with men to intrude a controversial statement into a pleasant conversation.

In a moment Mr Hoadley added grudgingly:

'As a matter of fact, Fabrio (that's the red-headed one) is a first-rate carpenter but he's bone lazy. They aren't much use to me; I've often thought about applying for a Land Girl.'

Alda made some suitable reply, and then inquired if she also had to thank him for the books left upon the doorstep?

'No, that wasn't me. I've no time for reading; never have cared for it much, either. That would be Mr Waite, I expect. He lives round the back of you. He's got some books.'

'Has he a farm, too?'

'A sort of a farm. It's a chicken farm.'

'Oh yes; we can see the little houses from our back windows.'

'Yes. Two hundred fowls he's got up there. Nasty, dirty,

42

heartbreaking work it is, too,' ended Mr Hoadley feelingly, and Alda now recalled seeing a distant form; a sexless, sack-draped, booted shape, moving slowly among the fowl houses and wire enclosures early that morning. Naturally, she had not connected it with *In Touch with the Transcendent*.

'This gate needs a drop of oil; I'll see to that for you,' said Mr Hoadley, marching up to the front door and setting down the cans in the porch, and Alda followed, thinking that life at Pine Cottage must certainly be pleasanter for the fact that this giant, whose burred Sussex 'r's were comforting as the scent of hay, was their neighbour.

The dog Ruffler, who had followed him, now came up to her and leant his fore-paws upon her skirt, gazing up into her face.

'You're a very handsome, fascinating boy,' she said to him softly, caressing his ears, while Meg, who had been set down in the porch beside the milk, now transferred her gaze from the farmer to the dog. 'Will he behave himself among all those chickens, Mr Hoadley?'

'He'd better,' said Mr Hoadley, giving Ruffler a severe look. 'That's why I take him up there with me, to teach him. I'm "walking" him, you see, for Mr Mead down at Rush House; he's come up to stay with me for a bit and learn how to follow and fetch and do what he's told. Training him, it is.'

He said 'Good morning,' smiled at Meg (who gratified Alda by smiling broadly in return), touched his hat and went off into the rain followed by the dog. Alda went into the house to read her letters.

Ronald's contained more about politics and economics than she really liked; having pursued the Liberal Cause through Greece, North Africa and Italy, on all types of Service stationery stamped with prohibitions in many different languages, Alda was still blithely indifferent to the Liberals (and the Conservatives and the Socialists and the Communists too) unless one of them happened to be ill or hard up under her nose. Then she helped generously, ignoring the sufferer's political views. Her husband, never ceasing to marvel at her lack of interest in theoretical politics, found her practical charities endearing.

However, there were loving sentences at the end of both letters, and some jokes about German cats for the children, and he was in a house which had a roof, and the work was 'tremendously interesting,' so his letters were, from all points of view, satisfactory.

The next one was not satisfactory from any point of view except that of the writer.

It was from the successful and efficient being known to Jenny and Louise as Father's-Only-Sister-Marion. She was thus distinguished from Mother's Sisters (who were five in number and naturally known as Auntie Marjorie, Auntie Peggy, Auntie Gwen, Auntie Brenda and Auntie Betty), and was called Marion at her own request. There was some reason, which Alda had never precisely fathomed, why she preferred her own sons and Alda's daughters to use her Christian name; it prevented complexes being set up or gave a sense of comradeship or something. Her letters were known among Alda's unmarried sisters as Getting on the Blower or Beefing Again; the married ones with young families viewed her activities more indulgently, for they did not extend to themselves.

She was busily getting through her second husband; from her first she had parted by amiable mutual consent, and he had left her the custody of two clever little boys. By the second one she had had two more clever little boys and all four (the youngest was six) were doing outstandingly well at school.

Her chief interest in life was politics, and she had ambitions to play an active part in the political life of Ironborough, but she would also have liked a daughter to mould and influence.

The spectacle of Alda's three girls—unconventionally dressed, scholastically backward, and wholly charming—moved her several times a year to sit down and dash off a letter full of suggestions to Ronald or Alda.

This time, she suggested (after listing the latest triumphs gained by her sons) that Jenny and Louise should be sent to a first-class boarding school with help from herself towards the fees, while Meg was farmed out at a progressive nursery school run by a friend of her own.

Alda could get a job to help provide the money for these schemes.

Alda folded up the letter with some irritation. She never attempted to argue with Marion, either verbally or on paper, and took refuge from her attacks in laughter, but it certainly was kind of her to offer to help with fees, and it gave her more right to be listened to.

For some time Alda herself had known that Ronald was becoming increasingly uneasy about the lack of regular schooling for Jenny and Louise, but circumstances and sheer lack of money had conspired to prevent the laying and carrying out of desirable plans. Alda's main object, strongly felt rather than thought out, had been to keep the three children with her, among a few cherished possessions that should mean to them Home, and this she had succeeded in doing. She told herself that it had not been possible, until now, to do more. Attendance at a village school for three months here, or a class for six children in some vicarage schoolroom there, was all the education that Louise and Jenny had received since leaving Ironborough.

She herself was no believer in highly-educated women and she took pleasure in her children's quaint, original ways. She feared that school might make little pattern-girls of them. Victorian women (her own family boasted a matriarch or so in every generation) had never been highly educated, and no one could accuse them of lacking character and energy!

As for Meg, she was quite progressive enough.

However, this time she had an answer for Marion. She could

write that in January Louise and Jenny would begin attending the school attached to the nearby Convent—*where the education is excellent, as it* always *is at convents.*

No doubt Marion, who was a robust T.C.P. (or Twentieth Century Pagan) would deplore the religious atmosphere in which her nieces were to be steeped, but she must just deplore.

Then Alda turned to the last letter, which was written in a backward-sloping hand.

Darling Alda,

I expect you are settled in the new house by now. I am down at *Worthing* for a few days (br-r-r! in this weather!) to see Aunt Alice who has been ill again, and it would be lovely if you could meet me for tea at Horsham on my way home. Do write *at once* and fix an Olde Tea Shoppe or somewhere where we can meet. I have got a doll's coatee for Jenny and a book for Louise and some sweets for Meggy. Kiss them all for me. *It's all off, I'm afraid.* All news when we meet.

Loads of love
from
Jean.

'Who's that from?' inquired Jenny, looking over her mother's shoulder.

'Jean.' (The young Lucie-Brownes had so many true aunts that the courtesy 'auntie' of an earlier generation was never applied to their mother's friends.)

'What's "all off"?' Jenny went on. 'Isn't she going to marry Mr Potter?'

'Who said she was going to?' said Alda, putting the letter away.

'You did. I heard you. When we were at Lyle Villas.'

'And before that you said she was going to marry Captain Roberts.' Louise was nibbling the end of a paint-brush and staring at Alda with huge pensive eyes.

'Dear me!' exclaimed her mother sarcastically. 'What was *Mr Parker* called in the bosom of his family?'

'Nosey!' they cried together.

'No-sey!' crowed Meg, and rushed round the room shaking her head and screwing up her eyes and muttering, 'Nosey—nosey—nosey—nosey—nosey!'

'No, but you did say she was going to. Truly, Mother.'

'Well, she isn't now. Clear those things off the table, please, and then you can set the lunch for me.'

'*Why* doesn't she marry someone, Mother?' asked Louise, obediently beginning to pack up her paint-box.

'She hasn't found anyone she likes, I expect. Hurry up, now.'

5

'And then not another word for three weeks! Not even a tinkle to ask if my cold was better! I didn't know quite what to do——'

'Oh Jean, you didn't telephone him?'

'Of course not, darling. I remembered your advice and was *firm* with myself. But I did just send him a book by Peter Cheyney.'

'Good heavens! Sent it to him as a *present*?'

'Of course not; only lent it to him. He'd been dying to read it and couldn't get it anywhere. I just put in a casual, friendly little note with it. And then, believe it or not, another long silence! And still I didn't ring him up. Wasn't I good?'

'You did all the right things—or nearly all,' admitted Alda.

'Oh yes, I did all the right things,' said Jean Hardcastle, without irony. 'At last, on October the seventeenth, the book came back with a letter. He apologised for not having given me a tinkle before, but his firm had put him on another back-room job (it all came out in the papers the other day, Operation Achilles it was called, I expect you saw it) and he'd been fearfully busy. He said we must meet again soon, and signed himself *Yours ever Oliver Potter.* Now, darling, what do you make of that?'

She paused and hastily ate some cake, keeping her eyes fixed pleadingly upon her friend's face.

A smart hat sat surprisingly upon her innocent brow but it made no difference: everything recommended by the experts in the women's magazines to make a woman noticeable and desirable had been done to her, but still it made no difference. The exotic perfume, the careful grooming, the paint, the hair gilded and dressed like that of a page boy in the fifteenth century—all these had been imposed upon a personality ordinary and gentle as a green leaf, and all without leading to that result for which she had longed since she was seventeen: marriage. She was now thirty-two years old, and she had never even been engaged.

'So what do you think I ought to do now?' she went on, not waiting for the answer to her first question but directing upon Alda a look of utter confidence and trust.

'You can't do a thing,' retorted Alda firmly. 'He's let you see very plainly that he doesn't mean business and you'll just have to write it off.'

'Oh, do you really think so, darling? He *was* so sweet in the summer. I don't see how anyone can be so sweet, and then a few months later be quite different.'

You ought to see it by now, if anyone ever did, thought Alda, looking at her with mingled affection and impatience.

'Well, people—men—can,' she said. 'But I think he behaved very badly, I must say. (More tea?) Did he kiss you?'

'(Yes, please.) Once or twice. Well—rather a lot, in fact, darling. But of course,' hastily, 'I didn't think *that* meant anything. I'm not quite a fool.'

'Jean, are you absolutely sure you didn't let him see you cared about him?'

'Oh, I think so, Alda. Yes, I'm fairly sure about that. I did try hard not to. And anyway——'

She paused, and took a cigarette from a handsome case and lit it from a gold lighter. Alda, who did not smoke, watched her slim hands, unroughened by housework, manipulating the small luxurious objects while four tinkling, surprisingly unfashionable silver bracelets slid about on her wrist. Alda's own hands were coarsened by housework and cooking in spite of her casual attempts to protect them, but during the war Jean had worked as secretary to her mother, an energetic and vital *charmeuse* who had run a hostel for Allied soldiers. The work had been exacting,

49

but not rough, and Jean's looks, such as they were, had not suffered.

'"*And anyway*" what?'

'Oh—I don't know.' Jean blew out smoke and stared down at the table while she played with a knife. She had suddenly realised how many of these sessions she had had with Alda, and the realisation had given her a little shock. They had sometimes joked about her eagerness to confide and Alda's readiness in advising, but never before to-day had she fully taken in the fact that this same conversation (with Captain Ottley or the Farebrother boy or Michael Powers in place of Mr Oliver Potter) had been going on for fifteen years. She had been momentarily silenced by wondering whether it would go on for another fifteen. That possibility was enough to silence any woman.

'Oh—mother dying,' she said vaguely, feeling for some reason unable to confide these thoughts to her friend, 'I couldn't give all my attention to him—though, of course, I was crazy about him,' she added hastily.

There were times when Alda found Jean both silly and irritating. This was one of them.

'It must have been just a relief when your mother died; do be honest, Jean,' she said sharply.

'I suppose it was—in a way. But it was a shock, all the same. And poor Dad has taken it so hard.'

'Yes—how is your father? No better?' Alda had always liked Mr Hardcastle, who was automatically at his best, like many a man before him, in the company of a pretty, lively woman whom he could not bully.

'He's really ill, you know. He just can't get over it.'

'It's queer, the way he came to adore her so as they both got older. I can remember them really disliking one another, when I was a little girl about eleven.'

'She was so beautiful, Alda.'

'But such a witch, Jean! You might have been married years ago if she hadn't taken all your young men.'

Jean looked slightly sulky. There was a pause before she answered:

'Oh, I don't know about that. Basil didn't like her at all.'

'Well, but you must admit she always made a dead set at them. It used to make Ronald and me feel slightly sick.'

'Well, it's over now, so what does it matter?' Jean sighed, and began to gather up her handbag and suitcase. 'I must go or I shall miss my bore-making train. It's been lovely seeing you, darling. You always make me feel so much better. And so you think I can't do anything about my Mr Potter?'

'Do use your common sense, ducky. What can you do?'

'I thought perhaps I might just give him a tinkle. He might be ill or something.'

'Not he. If he really wanted to see you he'd stagger up from his dying bed. No, it's just another of those things.'

'Mother wasn't always so bad,' said Jean irrelevantly, arranging the surprising hat. 'She gave me some advice once.'

'Now what sort of advice? Bad, I'll bet.'

'Oh, about—attracting men.'

'She should know, of course.'

Mrs Hardcastle had been the type of Eve-woman, at once imperious and intensely feminine, that all the virgin-huntress and the mother in Alda rose to detest. If anyone had told her that she had been afraid of Mrs Hardcastle's power over men, she would have contemptuously denied it; nevertheless, her dislike had been based on just that fear.

'Don't, Alda; she is dead, after all. Oh, I didn't take her advice. She could get away with things that other people couldn't, of course. I just remember what she said, that's all,' and, as if the memory were amusing, Jean smiled.

Alda asked no more questions, for she found the subject distasteful, and immediately afterwards Jean left to catch her train, having warmly kissed her friend and again assured her how delightful it had been to see her.

Alda watched her hurry past the tea-shop against a background of bright shop windows shining in the winter dusk; an ordinarily pretty young woman whose features were slightly too small, with an expensive fur coat wrapped about her nymphlike slenderness. Once she looked back to smile and wave, then she was lost to sight.

Poor old Jean, thought Alda, and poured out another cup of tea. She was to wait in The Myrtle Bough tea-shop until one of the Friends from Pagets, who had business in the town, called to take her back by car to the guest-house, where she would collect the children and catch the bus that would convey them the greater part of their way home. The dark branches and glittering decorations of a Christmas tree in the shop window were reflected in the mirror hanging above the table where she sat, and her own hatless head and irregular profile was seen there too; with chiselled upper lip and that type of nose which is perhaps the most attractive known to mankind, the Extra Short Greek with slightly wide nostrils. The curves of her mouth were full yet delicate and her eyebrows were shadowy as a child's. Her face and lips were unpainted, and this permitted every tint and curve to attain its full natural value. It was the face of a slightly insensitive wood-nymph, with sparkling hazel eyes.

Her thoughts played complacently about her own flirtations in the days when she herself had been—as her sisters put it—'in circulation'; and she recalled the laughing but efficient kindness with which she had handled her team of admirers. Never had she felt compelled to do the telephoning or make the advances, and always it had been a problem to choose an escort from the eager group; of course, she had had to refuse a proposal now and then, but there had never been hurt feelings or broken hearts afterwards. She had been used to the society and admiration of men since her middle teens, for her father's large house in a prosperous suburb of Ironborough had been the scene of delightful dances and parties, providing the perfect setting in which young love with honourable intentions could see its beloved in the home setting, and afterwards declare itself on the tennis court or in the vegetable garden, and her married life, on its personal side, had been cloudless and happy as her happy youth.

She thought with pity of Jean, whose upbringing and environment had been so different from her own.

Jean's parents had married one another to spite two other people, and her own birth had been dreaded as an additional complication in lives already over-full with social activities and money. Her childhood had been conscientiously organised, and luridly brightened by too many visits to cinemas and theatres and the company of smart, corrupt servants, while her holidays had either been passed at whatever expensive school she happened to be attending (because her parents 'can't cope with Jean at home') or with Alda's casually kind family. Her hygienic nursery was filled with elaborate and extravagant toys, and in it her mother's maid used gigglingly to read extracts from *Lady Chatterley's Lover* to Jean while smoking her father's Turkish cigarettes. Lady Chatterley and her lover rolled off Jean without effect, and her budding nature was saved from becoming precocious, bitter and shallow partly by its own qualities and partly by that lonely help of the lonely child: reading.

She was not clever, but she was affectionate, and her instincts were sound, and upon this surface, as she entered her teens, the hierarchy of the English novelists imposed their pictures— romantic or picaresque, subtle or passionate—of the world. Through Dickens and Scott to Rider Haggard and Baroness Orczy she passed by way of Conan Doyle to Kipling; she lingered hand in hand with Stanley Weyman to discover Hugh Walpole and Arnold Bennett, and thus, through Thomas Hardy and Marion Crawford, she walked out into the contemporary world of Charles Morgan and Ethel Mannin, Aldous Huxley and Graham Greene, and—so led and comforted—her poor little nature was saved alive.

It will be remarked that her taste was catholic, and none the worse, we believe, for that. It is doubtful if your picker and chooser and sniffer gets as much pleasure (not that pleasure is what he reads for, of course; he reads because, like Guinness, it is Good For Him) from his careful choice as does your plunger and wallower and gasper, who enjoys *Ben-Hur* equally with *Tess of the D'Urbervilles* and is usually devouring three books at once.

By the help of the novelists, and her own nature, Jean had slowly learned to tolerate her unsatisfactory life and to find amusement and entertainment, even some contentment, in watching the scene about her. But she was affectionate; novels could not satisfy her need to love, rather than to be loved, and she began with crushes upon Gary Cooper and Clark Gable and ended by fixing all her longings and hopes upon marriage— and upon any personable man who showed any signs of interest in her.

The reader will have gathered what had been happening at intervals to Jean and her personable men during the past fifteen years, and all that she gained from each successive disappointment had been an increase in her own responsiveness to life, and the slow development of a half-amused, half-rueful philosophy. And Alda and her sisters, who did not notice such developments in their friends' characters unless they were verbally announced, continued to tease old Jean about her passion for reading novels.

Alda, having worked out her train of complacent reflections, began through force of habit to wonder if there was any man in the neighbourhood who would 'do for Jean,' and decided that the only hope was Mr-Waite-who-has-some-books. True, she herself did not know him, but he had provided her with an excellent excuse for getting to know him when she returned his loan, and she resolved to rush through *To Haiti in a Ketch* and the rest and make his acquaintance as soon as was possible. If he were at all presentable, she would cultivate him.

However, the few remaining weeks before Christmas passed so busily and quickly that she almost forgot Mr Waite and his books; she put the latter into a cupboard to get them out of the way and never even opened one of them, for she spent every evening after the children were in bed making toys and paper decorations. Her family had a tradition of splendid old-fashioned Christmases, which she had determined to carry on with her own children, and she was also anxious that Jenny, Louise and Meg should harvest a few rich memories, at least, from these restless, homeless years. Therefore she fashioned silver stars from the tops of milk bottles and dolls' clothes from scraps of old silk and miniature furniture from cotton reels, and saved sugar and points to expend upon the Christmas dinner—at which there was now a faint hope, though only a faint one, that Ronald might be present.

Sometimes from her window she saw that hooded figure which was vaguely reminiscent of the Ku-Klux-Klan, moving among the coops on rainy mornings, and wearing an equally concealing hat drawn down over his eyes on finer ones. There was something dreary about the sight, and she felt disinclined, when she did remember him, to make Mr Waite's acquaintance. She disliked the company of depressed, complaining people so much that she would put up with more than most women if only the offender were cheerful, and she sometimes showed strong impatience with the doleful whining fits that overtook Louise.

Jenny was growing to be a companion to her mother, for she was in some ways older than her age, and could reply to Alda's remarks with something more than childish chatter. She was intelligent, and had a robust humour of her own, but whether she was also clever, or sociable, or ambitious, or possessed a bump of veneration, her mother was not in a position to know. These are qualities which require the presence of other children to draw them forth, and Jenny saw no children but her sisters. In education she was backward even for a child whose schooling had been interrupted, reading with difficulty those childish books which she preferred, but Louise quickly discovered the tattered, grubby hoard concealed in the cupboard and had read every book at Pine Cottage within the first week. Alda, whose own judgment of books had been formed by twelve years of marriage to a clever man, dismissed *Pat Takes a Hand* and *Mystery at Red House* as 'not *books* at all,' but Louise, with the aid of that Philosopher's Stone, a child's imagination, extracted golden pleasure from the shoddiest story. As for Meg, she had only just been introduced to the Flopsy Bunnies (to whom we recently saw a reference in *The Condemned Playground* which convinced us that Mr Connolly would see eye to eye with Mr McGregor).

Every morning the children went down to the farm to fetch the letters. Sometimes they came back rejoicing, when Mr Hoadley had already bicycled into Burlham for them; sometimes the comely, cross girl who brought them in on her breadvan every other day was late, and they returned empty-handed. The letters were then brought up in the middle of the morning by one of the Italians.

There was some confusion in the family over the Italians, for to Jenny, Louise and Meg, Emilio, with his teasing and his gifts of tiny baskets deftly woven from straw, was 'the nice one,' while Fabrio, who seldom spoke, and handed in the letters with a brief smile or none at all, was 'the nasty one.' Alda, however, while pitying both young men, preferred Fabrio's reserve to his friend's over-bold stares.

At the children's request, she asked Mr Hoadley if they might give the prisoners some cigarettes and, permission having been somewhat unwillingly given, a shopping expedition was made into Sillingham.

At Bettany's, the biggest grocery shop in the High Street, two of the four young ladies employed were married to Canadian soldiers and hoping to sail for their new homes within the next few months, and one had tender memories of an American private. Louise could hardly have chosen a less appreciative audience to hear her announcement that they were 'going to buy some cigarettes for the poor Italians,' and only the fact that the four young ladies of Bettany's knew the children as old acquaintances from Pagets prevented their comments from being sharp indeed.

'*May* we go and have tea at the Linga-Longa?' implored Louise, casting a wistful glance at the bedraggled curtains of the only café in Sillingham, as Alda hurried the pram past it on their way home. The winter day was drawing towards dusk.

'*No*, Louise.'

'Oh, why not?'

'Because it's smelly and gipsies go there.'

'That's just what I like,'

'That's just what I like,'

said Jenny and Louise together. Meg had fallen asleep in an uncomfortable position and Alda paused to rearrange her head against the cushion.

'Oh, Jenny, do you remember that one with the yellow scarf? I expect he'd kidnapped *thousands* of children,' Louise continued dreamily, and began to wander back towards the café just as a lorry, narrowly avoiding the kerb, drew up with a rattle and a roar. A man jumped down, slamming the door after him, and hurried across to the café, where a girl's pretty, untidy head looked out laughing to welcome him. The door shut on them both.

'It's so lovely,' mourned Louise, with her nose against the window. 'Oh Jenny, there are pink cakes to-day!'

'Do come along, Weez, it will be dark before we get home,' said Alda sharply; she wanted her tea.

'Well, can we go there for my birthday treat?' asked Louise, reluctantly moving on.

'What a treat!'

'It's *my* birthday and *my* treat.'

'Even *you* said the cakes were nice and the tea was hot when we went there, Mother,' said Jenny with her judicial air.

'But it wasn't clean, Jenny. I do draw the line at dirty places.'

'And the ladies are all so pretty and nice. Even the old fat one was kind,' put in Louise.

'I give you all that, but I don't like gipsies and dirt. Now that's enough, come along.'

She hurried them away, down the long High Street which gradually ran out into fields. They left the village half in day-time business, and half in evening peace; curtains had been drawn across the bow-windows in some cottages, but in many of the small square houses of cream or grey stucco, built in the early years of Victoria's reign, the blinds were still up, and within, sitting in a room filled with strong gold light, was an old woman knitting as she listened to the wireless, a man lingering at the tea-table with the evening paper, a child bent over its homework. Evergreen bushes swayed and sighed in the evening wind, shutters were going up at the chemists and the butchers; it was that hour before winter dusk when the air clears and the sun sinks in purple mist even as the first star shines out in the icy blue.

'Lucky creatures!' said Alda, as three young women sailed past them on bicycles.

'Do you think we shall *ever* have bicycles, Mother?' asked Jenny.

'Of course we shall, darling. Next year, perhaps. As soon as Father comes out of the Army and goes back to the college.'

'We could go exploring.'

'And you could take Meg in a basket at the back.'

'Meg's nearly old enough to have one for herself. By the time we all have them, she will be,' said Alda.

'We could have super picnics.'

'And get to the sea, perhaps. It's only fifteen miles away.'

'It would be so lovely, Mother.'

This conversation had been gone over many times before but never lost its wistful fascination. Alda and Ronald had been enthusiastic bicyclists before their marriage, and had presented Jenny with a tiny bicycle almost as soon as she could walk, but they were only beginning to take rides as a trio when the Second World War broke out, and the bicycles had been destroyed with their home in Ironborough. Bicycles for all five was the family ambition, and had a good fairy given Jenny, Louise and Meg one wish, they would have unhesitatingly demanded in a shout: 'Bicycles!'

'When shall we give them the cigarettes, Mother?' asked Jenny presently.

'To-morrow, if they bring the letters.'

'Need we give them to the nasty one? I'd much rather give them to the nice one.'

'We'll give them to whichever one comes. Look, there's the camp.'

The low sheds behind the wire were faintly visible by the starlight—for it was now dark—and the glow from their own windows, while smoke from the kitchens indicated that the evening meal was being prepared. Alda thought that the bustle and animation pervading the scene made it seem homelike, intensified as it was by the lonely sighing wind and the black sky and leafless trees; indeed, really it looked cosy, decided Mrs Lucie-Browne.

6

She hardly noticed the presentation of the cigarettes to Fabrio the next morning, as her attention was immediately caught, after taking the letters from him, by one which had a black border addressed in Jean's writing. She tore it open and hastily read what she had half-expected; Mr Hardcastle had died some days ago after a short illness which he had lacked the inclination to resist, and he was to be buried that day.

Poor Jean, thought Alda, she didn't care much for her father, but it must have been a shock, and there will be everything for her to settle—the lease of the flat, all that furniture—the car—and what on earth will she do with herself afterwards?

Glancing again at the letter she discovered the answer to the last question: Jean proposed to come to Pine Cottage.

So I shall just leave everything to Mr Barrowford and beetle down to you for a week or two, darling. You won't mind, will you? I'll sleep in the coal cellar and go Dutch in everything, of course.

That's all very well, thought Alda, slightly dismayed, but what about——

'Yes, Jen, what is it?'

'He won't take them,' said Jenny in a tactful whisper, jerking her head towards the slender haughty figure in the porch, who was standing very erect and monosyllabically replying to the questions of Meg and Louise.

'Oh, what nonsense,' muttered Alda, and hurried down the passage.

'Don't you like cigarettes?' she demanded, bluntly yet sweetly, and smiling into his sullen face. 'The children bought them specially for you and your friend.'

'Yes, go on,' urged Meg, gazing up at him through her fringe, which needed cutting. 'They cost a shillun and two pennies.'

'Meg!' exclaimed Jenny and Louise, scandalised.

Fabrio looked down at her for a moment; then he swiftly stooped, put his hands gently about her plump body, and smartly squeezed her, twice, as if she had been a doll that squeaked, and she gave two loud, gasping laughs. Jenny and Louise laughed too; it was so funny; and Fabrio's face changed at the sound, becoming alight with friendliness. Louise pushed the cigarettes into his pocket, crying, 'Oh, you're going to take them!' and Meg danced up and down, shouting, 'Again! Again!'

'Thank-you,' he said, smiling, and Alda thought how much better-tempered his face looked when he smiled than did Emilio's face, which was always smiling.

'I would-a like a-book,' he said, turning to her. 'A—English book.'

'To read?' she cried. 'Of course! I'll see what we've got.'

'I—am-a learning to read English.'

'Yes—wait a minute—I've got one that will be just the thing for you,' and she hurried away.

In a few minutes she returned.

'There!' she said, holding out to him a thick volume in a battered green and gold cover. '*I Promessi Sposi, The Betrothed Lovers*, by Manzoni, you know—famous Italian writer. I'm sure you've heard of it. This is an English translation.'

Fabrio reverently took the eighteenth-century Italian classic, with its faded brown pages and end-papers stained by water splashes, in his strong hands, large in proportion to his frame and coarsened by years of work in the open air. Alda watched his face with growing sympathy and interest as he slowly repeated under his breath some of the English words on the title page.

'Is it any good?' she asked at last, choosing her words.

He shook his head dejectedly.

'Not-a much. I cannot read-a, much,' he answered without looking up. 'No good-a, this,' and he handed it back to her. The animation had died out of his face.

To her, it was strange to see the strong feelings struggling on eyes and lips and held back by his ignorance of her language, and then, suddenly, the dam burst, and Fabrio burst into a flood of Italian to which she listened; at first uncomprehendingly and then with increasing embarrassment, for although she could not understand a word he was saying it was perfectly plain to her that he was pouring it all out to her; his loneliness, his loathing of captivity, and his longing for his native land. She thought, too, from the expression in his blazing blue eyes that he was imploring her to be his friend.

What could she do? Only listen with sympathetic nods and murmurs that became increasingly mechanical, while the children stood round demanding, 'What is he saying, Mother? What's the matter? Doesn't he like the cigarettes?'

Suddenly he ceased. He turned away, shaking his head and making a downward, backward flinging of the hand as if condemning every word that he had uttered to a hell of hopelessness, and then Alda realised that Mr Hoadley was standing by the gate, calling sternly to him.

Fabrio went straight towards his master, and Alda, having returned Mr Hoadley's irritable 'Good morning,' went back into the house with *I Promessi Sposi*, and a little smile on her pretty mouth. All her relationships with men had been gay and triumphant, so why should she not smile?

But while she was getting through the morning's work with the help of Jenny and Louise, she decided (in spite of that smile) that all encouragement of Fabrio, beyond the barest courtesy, must now cease.

Any kindnesses in the form of talks, or books, or cigarettes would actually be unkindnesses, leading to the increase of that romantic admiration which he clearly felt for herself and to uncharitable comments from Mrs Hoadley, who was just the type to make them (in this opinion Alda was less than just to Mrs Hoadley). There would be rebukes from his employer; perhaps even a loss of the dignity, both private and public, of Mrs Ronald Lucie-Browne. She had the strongest contempt for married women who flirted, and never realised that her own eyes and manner were innocently inviting.

It would be easy enough to quell his admiration, for he was only a peasant; Mr Hoadley had told her as much; had he been a young Italian barrister or business man the task might have been more difficult.

Thus did Alda and her Dissenting ancestry dismiss Fabrio's manhood.

He, after hearing in furious silence some angry words of reproof for gossiping from Mr Hoadley, had gone on the farmer's orders down to the hay rick by the Small Meadow. This was a smallish rick garnered during the previous June, and where it had already been cut into for winter supplies, the surface of sombre gold looked good enough for a man to eat. He was ordered to get down fodder for the cows.

His feet ached with the cold inside his heavy boots and as he wielded the fork his hands gradually became numbed, but he did not mind the discomfort, for he was accustomed to hard work in the open air and took it for granted under blue sky or grey; what he did mind, what set his face in sullenness and made his eyes look savage, was the double wound to his pride.

The first he had inflicted upon himself, when he had lost control and poured out to the kind Signora (that comely, matronly mother of three daughters) all his hatred of the camp and his shame that he could barely read and write. He had not known this shame until he entered the Army, but since his captivity he had brooded upon it; sometimes in a dim, puzzled way, he believed that if he had known how to read and to write fluently, he might have avoided being taken prisoner, or escaped before he was brought to England, and his ignorance made him feel inferior to the other men in the camp, for the only other two who were similarly handicapped were a fierce vile-tempered Roman from the Trastavere, prematurely aged by vice, and a half-witted Sicilian lout from the hills of Calabria. Fabrio felt—he knew—himself to be the superior of both these creatures and he hated to feel himself linked with them in a common ignorance.

Then his master, that accursed man set over him whose very name he could not pronounce accurately, had insulted him in front of the Signora, with whom he had been getting on so well! He had shouted at him as if he were a slave!

And Fabrio did not feel himself a slave. How should he? in that unbroken pride of youth which is so strong that the young man or woman who experiences it feels: I shall never die, and this warm sunny wind blows into my face while I stride against it like a lord of the earth, and then (if she is a girl) she moves her rounded neck to see her gold earrings reflected in the window of the car and feels her power, right down to the very tips of her eyelashes. Fabrio, too, was still sustained by his former close contact with the earth and the sea, though month by month, as the life of the camp held him fast, the refreshing force declined in strength. In his own village and the nearby port he had been able to earn by his own hands enough to contribute to the family needs and to pay for his own needs and pleasures; pleasures strong and delightful to him, however simple and poor they might have appeared to over-civilised people. In San Angelo the young men had accepted him as their equal and the young women had been eager for his notice and he had not wanted more than this; he had been happy, like a bird in the woods or a cricket in the olive groves, never thinking, seldom unhappy except when a mood of melancholy (heritage and penalty from that drop of purer blood in his veins) drifted across his soul.

Holy Mother! he thought now, if I could drive *this* into him! and he struck the fork savagely into the bristling surface of the rick and shook it furiously to and fro, so that the misty shapes of the far-off Downs were momentarily veiled by a shower of dark fragments.

But as he worked, his anger gradually died away, driven down into the heaps of fodder and lifted into the air by his aching arms. This work was very different from driving the wedges into his father's olive-press in the courtyard of the ruinous stone cottage where the Caetani had lived for many, many generations; or trampling the scanty vintage in autumn with his sisters, but this cold, damp earth strewn with gleaming yellow straw was the same earth that he knew, crumbling under the lizard's flicking flight, in Italy (he could feel it now, hot between his toes) and that bird with the red bosom who perched on the gate and sang his sweet notes out into the still air lived in a wood even as did the nightingales of San Angelo. Fabrio looked meditatively at the bird and wondered if it were good to eat, and so his anger ran out and was lost in the vast, frontierless fresh air.

Mr Hoadley, having been to see what Emilio was up to and found it comparatively harmless, encountered his wife picking her way across the farmyard with a bottle of warm milk pressed against her white coat for the kids which were her especial care. Not a hair was out of place under her neat turban and her face expressed resigned disgust. She glanced at him, then asked:

'What's the matter, Neil?'

'Oh—Fabrio. I sent him up to the cottage with their letters and there he was, wasting his time jabbering away to Mrs Lucie-Browne. I've had enough of it; I'm going in to Horsham this afternoon to ask the Office' (Mr Hoadley meant the West Sussex Agricultural Board's office) 'to let us have a girl to train. We can teach her all we shall want her to know in the six weeks they allow, and if she's quick and willing it'll be well worth it.'

'Oh yes—if,' said his wife, but as she did not dislike the prospect of some female company, she did not put forward any objections to the plan, of which he had been talking for some time, and he went off.

She swung open one of the stable doors and five tiny kids rushed across the dim, clean place to greet her, white as snow and gleamy as silk, with bells of delicate flesh swinging from their throats. She shut the door and knelt among them, singling out the weakest and thrusting the teat of the bottle into his eager mouth to make sure that he received his share and was not crowded out by his stronger brothers. While he jerked and sucked and his yellow eyes shone with pleasure, she looked distastefully down upon the innocent heads of the others, who butted her sides and trampled her boots with tiny sharp hooves as they ravened for their turn.

Alda sat for a moment by the open window to re-read her friend's letter. Jean must be told candidly that she could not come before Christmas, because there was a chance that Ronald might come home on leave. After Christmas, though it would mean a complicated reorganisation of the sleeping arrangements she would be glad of Jean's company, her help with the housework and, frankly, of her contribution to the household expenses, for although it was possible to live more cheaply in the country than in a city, the rent of the cottage and other expenses came to nearly five pounds a week, and after Christmas the elder children's school fees would be added to the total. To meet it, there was Alda's allowance from Ronald's pay as a Major, and a small income from some investments made before the Second World War in various municipal undertakings in Ironborough which paid a low rate of interest. Alda occasionally received handsome cheques from her father, whose favourite she was, but

Ronald's widowed mother, of better birth than Alda's family, could not afford to do this for her son; indeed, he and his sister occasionally had to help her with money.

Poor old Jean, I expect she will find it lonely in that awful luxury flat without a tree for miles, thought Alda as she addressed her letter. And it did not seem strange to her that Jean, used to every comfort, should suggest coming to stay in a poky, dark, ugly cottage that was too crowded with people to be agreeable, for she had become used, in the twenty years of their friendship, to having Jean seek her company.

After Fabrio's outburst, the Italians came no more to the cottage with the letters, and Alda who rightly assumed that Mr Hoadley had forbidden them the place saw them only rarely. The children missed their visits, and something amused and mischievous in herself (which never seriously contended with the Dissenters but prevented them from having things all their own way) missed the sight of Fabrio's comeliness and the admiring glances of Emilio.

Jean had written to say that she would come down immediately after Christmas, but since her own letter Alda had sadly heard that the chance of Ronald's arriving for Christmas had vanished. Still, with a faint lingering hope, she had not sent this news to Jean.

'Mother!' exclaimed Jenny in her scandalised tone, on the morning of Christmas Eve, 'that poor man's books! Here they are still poked away in a cupboard and not read, and you haven't even thanked him for them yet.'

'No more I have, love. Look—will you paint him a Christmas card? and Louise can run down to the farm and find out his address? We'll post it this afternoon.'

There was a carol service at St Wilfred's Church in Sillingham that day at three o'clock, and Alda had thought it better to take the children to it rather than attempt Matins on Christmas morning.

'Do a golden bell,' said Louise, hanging over Jenny as the latter arranged her paint-box on the table.

'All right. (Don't loll on me, Weez, you know I hate it.) And we'll all sign it, shall we, Mother?'

'Meg can do *Meg her mark*, like people used to in the old days when they couldn't write,' said Louise.

'I can wite "Meg,"' said that person indignantly, looking up from her game with bricks beside the fire.

'Only copying, you can't really write. Shut up now, please. I want to do this,' and Jenny began to draw a large bell upon a square of stiff paper. She drew and painted neatly in a conventional style, but there was more life and originality in the scenes crammed with odd, stiff little figures with which Louise sometimes filled half an exercise book in a drawing fit lasting for days.

'I suppose there's no hope of Father coming at the very last minute, is there, Mother?' Louise now asked wistfully, letting her hair fall over her eyes which peered mournfully through it.

'Not a hope, I'm afraid. (*Don't* do that to your hair, darling, you look like a homesick Skye terrier.)'

'It is miserable,' said Louise, and sighed.

It is, thought Alda; and then she remembered the people— children—existing in cellars in Europe with not enough food and warmth to keep the life in their bodies, and felt heartily ashamed of herself.

'Ow!' protested Meg, finding herself suddenly pulled sideways and kissed in an access of thankfulness. 'What a howwid kiss. Wait a minute and I'll gib you a marbellous one.'

She had just concluded this ceremony, which she performed with tightly-shut eyes as if to concentrate her energies, when Jenny said proudly:

'There. Finished,' and held up the card.

'That's very nice, Jenny. Now, Weez, get your things on and run off to the farm and ask Mr Waite's address. You'd better write it down.'

Louise did not like going out of the warm parlour into the freezing air. She possessed less vigour than Jenny, and enjoyed warmth and solitude, and 'the wreathéd trellis of a working brain' employed upon reading or drawing better than running about in the open air; but after she had once or twice drawn her breath in gasps and pushed her chin down into her muffler to escape the fierce cold, she suddenly noticed that there was *ice* on the puddles; grey ice looking so solid that—perhaps one could stand on it with one foot (Louise stood so, for an instant)—and then with two! (she brought the other foot forward)—and still it did not break!

There was a chain of such pools leading towards the farm and along them she went; now sliding, now grinding her heel into the cat-ice at the edges, now glancing vaguely about her and enjoying the novelty, rather than the beauty of the scene. Behind the cottage the pines towered up, covered with heavy white frost and revealing the beautiful symmetry usually concealed by their own darkness. Louise had quite forgotten what she had come out for.

Mr Waite was returning along the track from the farm, where he had gone to telephone about some balancer meal for his battery birds which had failed to arrive. Walking slowly with his head down against the slight, wandering, icy wind, he was thinking what a beastly cold morning it was; the corn on the third toe of his left foot throbbed steadily and the one on the little toe of his right foot was quiet, biding its time. This meant that rain was coming; there would be a thaw; there would be impassable roads; breakdowns; burst pipes. These thoughts passed in gloomy, orderly procession through his head as he trudged along the causeway between the frozen lagoons, and on either side of his boots the round silver faces of billions of crowding air bubbles imprisoned in the ice looked up at him; the tideless winter air floated above, below and all about him, with its country sweetness frozen into an arctic freshness, and every grass blade had its mail-coat of frost and its miniature shadow, cast by the faint sunlight. *O ye Ice and Snow, bless ye the Lord.* A beastly cold morning and the pipes will probably burst, thought Mr Waite.

Had he followed his strongest instincts, which were to make himself comfortable and to disapprove of other people, he would have ignored Louise, but some other instinct prompted him, as their paths crossed, to address her.

'Where are you going to, my pretty maid?' he inquired. 'Fairyland?'

Louise gave him the polite smile with which properly-mannered children acknowledge whimsiness in grown-ups, and answered: 'No. I'm going to the farm to ask Mr Hoadley for Mr Waite's address.'

'Well, now, that's very interesting,' said Mr Waite, pausing and looking suspicious. 'And what do you want with "Mr Waite's address," if I may ask?'

'It's to send him something for Christmas.' Her large eyes, neither green nor blue and pale as those of the Ice Maiden, stared seriously up at him; pale curls of hair were sprayed against the dark fur that bordered her hood.

'Oh-ho, I see! I suppose I mustn't ask questions, then?'

Louise nodded. She was always so interested in looking at a new person that she never heard what they said, and this inattention, combined with her unwavering stare, frequently caused brisk young aunts and sharp elderly acquaintances to pronounce her half-witted.

'I *may* ask questions? What! so near Christmas?'

This time she shook her head, and, bored, produced a grubby handkerchief and thoughtfully made use of it. Mr Waite was repelled. He liked children to be neat, silent, polite, clean and admiring of grown-ups: in other words, he did not like children. Louise then went off into a trance, in which she waggled one foot as though she had lost her senses.

'Who do you think I am?' he demanded, as conversation seemed at a standstill and his corn was excruciating.

'Mr Waite,' she answered at once.

'Oh, you *know* who I am, then?'

She nodded. 'We can see you out of mother's bedroom window.'

Spying on me. Out of her *bedroom* window, too. Rather peculiar, thought Mr Waite; *and* inquisitive.

'Aren't you going to ask me for my address?'

She nodded again.

'It's Mr Phillip Waite, Meadow Cottage, Sillingham, Sussex,' he said impressively. 'Now can you remember that?' Here he observed that she was carrying a pencil: he made her produce the piece of paper from her pocket and write down the address, using his notebook as a rest, in her straggling baby hand. This took about ten minutes.

'What dreadful writing; I can hardly read it,' commented Mr Waite helpfully, when the task was accomplished. 'Why, do you know that when I was your age I won a prize for writing; a beautiful book about the St Bernard dogs——'

'They go and find people in the snow,' interrupted Louise, 'and they have lovely hot soup and brandy in a dear little bottle round their necks; a very good man called Saint Bernard invented it, he's in Heaven now, of course, but the monks still live in the place he invented, and they've built another place, in Tibet, up in the mountains and they have the dogs and the soup and brandy there too, in case anyone gets lost far away in Tibet. Isn't it a good idea? Saint Bernard was very clever and kind to think of it.'

Mr Waite had looked forward to imparting this information himself and furthermore had never heard about the hospice in Tibet. He said sarcastically:

'What a well-informed young lady! And where *is* Tibet?'

The Ice Maiden opened her lips, which were shaped like a small, full, pale rose, and replied without hesitation:

'In the north-east of India, between India and China; the highest mountains in the world are there. Father showed me on the map. And he cut out the bit about Tibet from the *Daily Telegraph* and I pasted it in the Commonplace Book.'

'You've forgotten my address!' cried Mr Waite triumphantly, finding the conversation unbearable.

'No, I haven't. Mr Phillip Waite, Meadow Cottage, Sillingham, Sussex. I must go now, good-bye,' and she slid away and did not turn round to wave.

Mr Waite walked on, convinced that her family must be an unpleasant one; ungrateful, inquisitive, tending towards indelicacy (or why peer at people from bedroom windows?) and priggish. I do like a child to *be* a child, thought Mr Waite, who did not like anything of the sort, and then his reflections took a darker turn as he thought of the Christmas posts, with letters and parcels from his family in Daleham, being delayed. Considering how he cursed the place when he was there, blaming it for lack of scope, dullness and narrow-mindedness, it might surprise those who do not know human nature to hear how deeply and persistently he longed for news of his mother and sisters at home in Daleham; small, prosperous, smug Daleham, untouched by six years of war, with its minster and its waters that relieved rheumatism, set in a valley amidst the Derbyshire hills.

'Well, lovey, did you get it?' asked Alda, on Louise's return.

'I saw Mr Waite. Here it is,' and Louise brought out the address from her pocket.

'Oh, did you? What's he like?' asked Alda, interested.

'He's got a miserable face.'

'Oh dear.'

'And he said my writing was awful.'

'So it is,' put in Jenny.

'And so is yours. Father says you "write a vile fist."'

'Yes, well, never mind that. Go on, Weez. Is he ugly?'

'I don't know. Yes, beastly.'

'About how old?'

'Oh, very old. About fifty-one, I should think.'

'You are hopeless,' said Alda, laughing. 'What did he say to you?'

'He called me a young lady and I told him all about Saint Bernard and the dogs. Is lunch ready?'

7

Saint Wilfred's, representing the Established Church in a village where the chapels of Free Christians, Brotherhoods of Holy Love and other small Dissenting bodies were to be found at the end of every back lane and bowery little close, had been the Parish Church since its first stone was laid in 1356. It had been twice badly damaged by fire, for its position on a hill exposed it to winds that fanned the flames, and only the shell of the building remained, while the interior had been mercilessly restored in the '80's. Innocuous stone faces, sexless rather than spiritual and crowned by the conventional stone diadem, stared out vacantly from every corbel, and all that was left of the ancient stained glass were some dim azure fragments in a small, ancient window in the chancel, which made the modern glass look insipid and suggested the life of that old, simpler world in which it had first been dyed to the blue of Mary's cloak. Within, the church was solemn and peaceful, inducing a devotional attitude of mind by its alternations of pale nave arch and soft dark shadow, but the outside—where yellow wallflowers grew in crevices of the stones fifty feet above the churchyard in summer and the buttresses set their shoulders and feet firm and deep against the weathered stone in their task—was beautiful.

'Hark, the herald angels sing——' sang Alda, standing with Meg beside her and Jenny and Louise on either hand. The church was fairly full and the service nearly over; the lancet windows showed the darkening sky and candles were beginning to gleam out in the dimness with a halo; laurel and fir and some great sprayed cedar branches, massy and close in their black green, were spread upon the altar steps and scented the warm air.

Somebody from one of the big houses in the neighbourhood had sent from their conservatories two pots of red lilies, and all the light in the dim building seemed to pour upon them; they glowed, their curved petals seemed so alive as to be listening to the singing, and Alda found her eyes wandering again and again towards them.

But she also glanced anxiously at the fading daylight visible through the windows, trying to see through clear spaces in the stained glass into the evening, for she feared that it had started to snow again. She had only the small pram for Meg, who did not seem so placid as usual and had shown some disinclination to come. A walk home through a snowstorm with Meg perhaps sickening for something would be very unpleasant, even dangerous, and Alda heartily called herself a fool for having brought her.

As the service proceeded, Meg showed increasing signs of distress; yawning; putting her head down on the front of the pew and even whimpering once or twice. Immediately after the Blessing was spoken and the congregation dismissed, Jenny said in a businesslike tone as they rose from their knees:

'Meg isn't well, Mother. Her hands are simply burning—you feel,' and she pushed Meg's ungloved hand into her mother's. 'I believe she's got a temperature.'

'Me face is burning, too,' said Meg, with some return of the grown-up manner which always deserted her when she was ill. 'Feel, Mudder,' and she lifted up a face unnaturally rosy, with heavy yellowish eyes.

'Never mind, love, we'll soon have you home,' said Alda with sinking heart, as they slowly made their way with the rest of the congregation towards the door. 'Mother will carry you,' and she lifted her up. Meg settled herself comfortably, sighed, and in a few moments was asleep. 'If only it isn't snowing!' murmured Alda.

But as they stepped out into the porch a shower of flakes

blew in to meet them, and then they paused to look down on the lights and roofs immediately below the hill upon which the church stood, all veiled in silent, steadily falling snow. Already the roads and distant fields were white, and the footsteps of those leaving the church were muffled as they set off down the paved pathway leading to the village, while their voices as they exchanged 'good nights' and wishes for a Merry Christmas were muted in that familiar and unmistakable hush.

Alda opened her thick coat and settled Meg more comfortably inside it. She was wondering what to do. The pram, which fortunately had not been stolen from the porch, was a light, completely open conveyance in which it would be the height of imprudence to wheel Meg home, for the heat from the little slumbering body already came up disturbingly against her own as she rearranged her scarf. Then she looked down, and met the solemn eyes of Jenny and Louise, waiting for comments and orders.

'We must try to get a car,' she said decidedly. 'Jenny, you know where Mr Bolliver's garage is; run down as quickly as you can and tell him what's happened and ask him to rescue us. We'll wait in the porch. Fly, now!'

Off ran Jenny into the snowy twilight, excited by its soft icy touch upon her face and lips and by the transformed world all about her. The rest of the congregation had hurried back to their homes to resume the business of Christmas Eve; through the half-open door of the church Louise peeped in and saw the verger extinguishing the altar candles one by one, and the pale arches, the green Christmas leaves, becoming dim in the dusk. Save for the old man, they were now alone.

Alda seated herself upon the wall-bench and stared unseeingly with troubled eyes at the list of vicars who had held office at St Wilfred's since 1356 which glimmered upon the opposite wall. Within the porch it was almost night, but outside it was still possible to discern the outlines of roofs and nearby houses. It grew rapidly darker. Meg was now breathing fast, and Alda began to feel a little frightened.

'Jenny is being ages, isn't she, Mother,' said Louise, shivering as she sat closely against her.

'I expect Mr Bolliver is out on a job He's sure to be busy on Christmas Eve.'

'Mother! I've got an idea. If he can't come we can telephone Pagets and perhaps the Friends will come and fetch us.'

'Oh Weez, what a good idea! I wish I'd thought of that at first. We'll telephone them at once. Look, here's my bag—you take fourpence in coppers—I hope I've got it—and——'

But here their exclamations and gropings in the gloom were interrupted by the sound of footsteps running up the paved path and Jenny's joyous voice calling:

'Mother! Good news! Good news! I've got somebody!'

In another moment she appeared at the entrance of the porch, her shoulders white with snow, breathing fast from her run up the hill. She was followed, at a slower pace, by someone else.

At first Alda could not make out whether it was a man or a woman, but then the figure made a gesture with its hat which indicated that it was a man.

'It's Mr Waite, Mother,' explained Jenny. 'You know—he lives near us. He was in the garage and kindly heard what I said. Mother, he says he'll drive us home in his car!'

'Oh, how kind.' Alda stood up, with Meg clasped closely in her arms, and smiled at the figure she could barely see. 'How do you do, Mr Waite.'

'How do you do,' he answered awkwardly, in a naturally unpleasing voice which he tried to make friendly. 'My little friend here says her little sister isn't feeling too good?'

'She has a temperature, I'm afraid, and I should be so grateful if you *could* take us home.'

'Oh dear. Nothing infectious, I hope?'

'I don't know yet.' Alda controlled her impatience. 'She was perfectly well this morning.'

'Ah, you can't be too careful with kiddies—or so I'm *told*,' on a wryly humorous note. 'Well, I think I can fit you all in, though it'll be a bit of a squeeze. Let's have some light on the subject, shall we?' and the ray from a torch suddenly shone upon Alda's shabby suède boots, and threw a reflected glow upon the children's excited faces. 'Can you manage, kiddies? Come along, then—follow Santa Claus,' and he set off down the path towards the village, shining the torch carefully behind him so that Alda could see the way.

The verger, hearing voices in the porch, slowly opened the church door and peered out into the snow and the night, then locked it behind him and, turning up his collar and lowering his head into the wind, set off for home.

It was not more than a couple of hundred yards down into the village street, and there was Mr Waite's car, an unexpectedly large 1937 Lagonda that had once been handsome, standing outside the shop that sold sweets and tobacco. What nonsense to talk about a tight squeeze, Alda thought with some indignation, there's room for an army in that thing, but she soon discovered that there was not, for the interior was full of sacks and boxes smelling of bran. Without waiting for an invitation she climbed over them and settled herself, tenderly clasping Meg, in the only unoccupied place, while the children fitted themselves between tins and sacks and Mr Waite took a rug off the engine. By the glare of the headlights Alda could see that he was dark and well above medium height; he was perhaps forty-three years old, his figure was good, and a woman who did not object to signs of discontent and obstinacy in a male countenance would have considered him handsome.

After one or two false starts by the cold engine and fussy apologies from Mr Waite, they got away, and soon left the village behind: spectral white fields glided by, the snow rushed steadily past the windows. Alda would have preferred to remain silent, but she guessed that Mr Waite was one of the touchy sort (from whom Heaven defend me, thought she) and would take it amiss if she did not prattle.

'You'll think us very rude, Mr Waite; we've never thanked you for the books you kindly left for us,' she began.

Mr Waite replied oh, that was all right, in a tone implying that ingratitude was all he ever expected or received in this world.

'I've been so busy getting ready for Christmas that I haven't had much time for reading. It's been——'

'I don't expect you've even opened one of them,' he interrupted, with what Jenny thought of as *a cross laugh*. 'It doesn't matter in the least, I only thought you might not find much to read at Pine Cottage.'

'It was most kind of you,' Alda repeated, thinking what a boor the man was. The children were next to him as he sat in the driver's seat and she herself had a large can, which smelt very vile, on the seat beside her, whilst her feet were confined by a stockade of meal sacks that made movement impossible. But home was drawing nearer every minute, and when once Mr Waite had conveyed them there, he could go and bury himself in his own sacks for all she cared.

Mr Waite, who seemed to have no small-talk, went on:

'Did you look at the one called *In Touch with the Transcendent* at all?'

'Er—yes. Yes, I did.'

'Wonderful, isn't it?' His tone of awe finished Alda, and left her struggling with a laugh. She had no use for any theories of The Transcendental beyond those of the simple theology she had been taught in her childhood.

'Well——' she was beginning, when he interrupted her gloomily:

'I tried Yoga at one time, but I had to give it up. It requires enormous concentration and perseverance and I simply haven't the time; these damned battery birds—I beg your pardon—the chickens take up nineteen hours out of the twenty-four.'

Alda made a sympathetic murmur. It struck her pleasantly that a man should apologise for saying 'damned' in her presence; it was the first sign of sensitiveness that she had observed in Mr Waite, whose social status was not easy to place. The apology might be old-fashioned, but it did imply that he came from a home where there were gentle women. What an extraordinary creature he is, she thought; he hasn't asked me a single question about ourselves or mentioned the weather or Christmas or shown any interest in anything except that dotty book . . . That's what comes of living alone with chickens.

'And yet, you know, if I *really* cared enough about it I should *make* the time,' he said suddenly. 'After all, what is reality?'

Alda controlled an impulse to ask him what on earth he meant, and occupied herself with rocking Meg, who was whimpering. Jenny and Louise were dividing their attention between the windscreen wiper and the conversation, with a distinct bias towards the latter.

'If I believe that other worlds are more real than this one, I ought to give up everything—the chickens—my work—everything, and concentrate on my spiritual development.'

'*Do* you believe that?' inquired Alda, trying not to sound incredulous.

'Of course,' he answered, glancing up for an instant at the little mirror above his head. In it he met her bright, amused eyes. He frowned, and pressed the car forward through the deepening dusk.

Bother, now I've offended him, she thought, but she was too concerned about Meg (who was now stirring restlessly and making little sounds of distress) to give the matter a second thought, and devoted herself to rocking and soothing her. She was bending over her, trying to see in the dim light how to loosen the strings of her hood, when Mr Waite exclaimed, 'Hullo, now what's the matter?' and put the brakes on hard. When she had recovered her balance from the jerk, she looked out of the window into the darkness and saw a figure standing in the glare of the headlights; a soldier in a greatcoat, laden with bundles. At the same instant the children began to dance up and down with delight and she saw that it was Ronald.

'He wants a lift, I suppose,' Mr Waite grumbled, 'a silly thing to do, stopping me like that, I nearly went over him,' leaning forward to open the door, 'can you make room there, Mrs— er——? (not so much *noise*, kiddies, *please*!).'

'It's my husband!' Alda said joyfully. 'What a lovely "Christmas present for the March family"!'

By this time Mr Waite (muttering that how they would fit him in he did not know) had got the door open, and was calling:

'Can we give you a lift?'

'Thanks very much; awfully good of you. Are you going anywhere near Naylor's Farm?' answered Ronald, stepping forward, and then Alda, shielding Meg from the inrush of cold air, called out:

'Hullo, darling! It's us.'

Louise and Jenny were leaning as far across the luckless Mr Waite as they could get in order to greet their father and the former, having grasped the situation, was fussily moving tins and the folding pram and sacks about in order to make some room. Ronald's exclamation of surprised pleasure was drowned in introductions, apologies, explanations and thanks, and some minutes elapsed while he was climbing into the car and crushing himself and his bundles down beside Alda, bringing the scent of snow and night freshness upon his rough coat.

'However did you manage it, lovey? We'd given up hope,' she said, clasping his hand as the car started again.

'I hadn't, Father. I still thought you'd come,' said Louise.

'I've got something lovely for you, Father,' said Jenny.

'Good. So have I for you. From Belgium.'

'Oh Father! For us both?'

'One for each of you! Is that Meg in there?' peering at the bundle in Alda's coat. 'What's the matter?' and his voice changed. 'Isn't she well?'

Alda explained, already feeling less anxious because of the comfort of his presence, and his daughters knelt on the seat with their backs to Mr Waite in order to join in the conversation, while the latter morosely drove on, wondering how long the springs would stand the weight of six people, a folding peram-bulator, eight sacks of balancer meal, four large tins of cod liver oil and luggage crammed with rubbish from Belgium.

Presently he stopped the car, and roused them with slightly sarcastic politeness from their family conversation by announcing that they had arrived at the gap in the hedge leading to Pine Cottage.

'Oh, thank you so much,' said Alda, hastily preparing to climb out, 'I hope we haven't brought you out of your way? (Come along children, hurry up.)' Ronald was taking out his luggage and putting it down in the snowy road.

'I shall have to turn her round and go back, my turning is just down the road, but it isn't far,' said Mr Waite. 'Glad I could be of any assistance. I hope the little kiddy will be better to-morrow. Good night. Good night, kiddies—a Merry Christmas,' and he disappeared into the darkness, which was less than total because of the widespread gleam from the snow and (for the clouds had now rolled eastwards and away) the brilliant starlight.

'Kiddies are baby goats. We aren't,' said Jenny in a quiet, impertinent undertone to her sister.

> 'Kind hearts are more than coronets
> And simple faith than Norman blood,'

quoted her father, pulling her hair. 'Can you manage Meg, darling?' (to Alda) 'I must have both hands for these cases and the pram.'

'Let me help, Father.'

'No, let go, Weez—I mean it—they're very heavy. You can walk with me and tell me all the news.'

Faint unearthly light and a deep hush lay over the fields; when a star glided out now and then from behind the scudding brown clouds its bright eye entered the scene as if alive and watching them, and the snow sparkling and crinching underfoot in the torch-rays seemed protesting as if aroused from cold, light sleep. Suddenly bells began to peal, faintly and far away; another tower in the night took up the sound; then Saint Wilfred's three miles off, and soon the air was filled with it. Strange, wild, rejoicing sound! untamed yet familiar, having nothing to do with any peace except that peace which comes after unimaginable struggle and *passeth understanding*, clanging and ringing out over the darkened earth to remind it of the unbelievable truth.

'How lovely,' said Alda, pausing for a moment and clasping Meg closer as she lifted her face to the starlit sky. 'Of course—I'd forgotten—it's Christmas Eve.'

Then, as the cottage came in sight, she exclaimed in astonishment: 'Oh—look, the lights are on! Someone's there!'

'It must be Jean, Mother,' said Louise, dismayed. 'Oh dear, and now father's here and we *did* want him to ourselves, what a nuisance.'

'She *is* tiresome,' said Alda, tired, worried about Meg, and now really annoyed at the prospect of a spoiled Christmas. 'I suppose she thought from my letter that there wasn't the faintest chance of your coming,' to Ronald. 'I've a good mind to send her packing off home again.'

Before he could answer, the front door opened and Jean, her fur coat swinging from her shoulders and her gilt hair swaying, hurried down the path crying eagerly:

'There you are, darlings! Come along in, you must be frozen. I've got a blazing fire for you and the kettle's boiling.' Then, as she saw that there were five dark figures instead of the expected four approaching her across the snow, her voice trailed off in dismay:

'Oh . . . oh dear. Is that Ronald?' peering into the dimness as she leant over the gate. 'I thought you weren't coming; Alda's letter seemed so sure. Oh, I *am* sorry—butting in like this—such a bore for you.'

'Don't be a goat, my dear girl, we're very pleased to have you, but Meg was taken ill in church,' said Ronald, 'and Alda's rather fussed.'

'I am not,' said Alda, between her teeth. 'Hullo, J. What a surprise. What time did you get here?'

'About half-past three. I'm awfully sorry, truly, Alda.'

'Can't be helped. Actually, I shall be glad you're here, when I've got Meg into bed and had some tea. Give me a hand with her, will you? the hot-water bottle's in the dresser drawer in the kitchen.'

'O.K.' and Jean hurried back into the cottage while the others slowly climbed the steep little path to the porch, the children pulling off their hoods as they came.

'Oh, what a *damned* nuisance,' said Alda very softly to Ronald as he shut the front door.

8

About half-past seven that same night a train, glowing with light and crowded with Christmas Eve passengers bound for the coastal towns and inland hamlets of Sussex, drew slowly out of Sillingham station, leaving a few people on the platform.

Most of these hurried away immediately as if on familiar ground and anxious to get home but one, who was tall and young and wore the Ayr green jersey and brief overcoat of the Women's Land Army, walked slowly and wearily out of the station and, having given up her ticket to the porter, stood gazing uncertainly about her as if looking for somebody.

The road and the few houses with snow-covered roofs bowered in leafless trees were dark and silent. The noise of the train could be heard diminishing steadily into the distance and overhead the red and green lights on the signal by the bridge shone amidst clouds and stars. After a moment or two, she changed her shabby, bulging suitcase over to her other hand and set off slowly up the long road leading to the village, keeping her small head bent before the rising wind; the Land Army's round hat was set well back to display a full pompadour of dyed golden hair and afforded her no protection.

When at last she reached the village and saw its one long street, slumbering beneath the snow but flashing and gleaming with Christmas lights from every curtained or shuttered cottage, she paused, and gazed again about her. As she did so, eight o'clock chimed from the church tower.

Sweet notes from the three old bells fell down through the dark air and spread away in ringing waves, and a few flakes of snow blew against her lifted face. This is the first snow I've tasted this year, she thought, as a crystal drifted between her lips, so I ought to wish, and then she shut her eyes. *Let me get a job on the stage very soon*, she wished, and walked slowly on.

The place certainly did look pretty; but corny, of course, like an old-fashioned Christmas card, she thought, and even the pub's shut—anyway, I'm not going to try muscling in there—and I suppose you could die in the street before anyone'd take you in and give you a cup of tea; gosh, a cup of tea'd be marvellous. Then, on the opposite side of the street, she caught sight of the Linga-Longa Café.

As usual, its windows were so steamy that it was impossible to see what was going on inside, but there were people, and they were moving about; and there was a notice hanging in the window that said OPEN. Hardly believing in her luck, she crossed the road and opened the door.

Immediately she encountered a stifling odour of stale frying that at any other time would have sent her straight out again, but she was so tired and hungry that desire for food and rest was stronger than disgust. She shut the door behind her and made her way between three or four tables crowded with raffish girls and loutish youths to a seat at the only empty one.

Resting her elbows among the stains and crumbs, she sighed and took off her hat, and a mane of rich healthy hair of a deep brown, contrasting with the dyed pompadour, tumbled in natural curls down her back, while she shook her head as if glad to be free of its weight.

'Yes?' inquired a slatternly girl a little older than herself, pausing at the table, and letting her spiteful, pretty eyes dwell upon the pompadour and the curls.

'A pot of tea and baked beans on toast, please.'

'No beans.'

'Bread and butter then—anything—I don't care.'

'Bread and butter's off. We got cakes.'

'Oo, yes. That'll do.'

'Tea and cakes for one. Right,' and the waitress made her way towards the reeking kitchen visible through a half-open door at the end of the room, but paused to exchange jokes with a tableful of young men. Once she tried to get away, but they detained her, and minutes passed while she lingered there, jeering at them. Sylvia Scorby sighed angrily, then took a book from her overcoat pocket and set it in front of her on the table, bending over it with her fingers in her ears as if she were learning. It was *Major Barbara*.

In a minute, however, she had let the book drop and was staring about her. What a dirty place, she thought, but it must have been quite nice once.

That was exactly what the poor Linga-Longa Café had been: with its white shelves adorned by blue Japanese pottery, its branches of palm in the spring and of beech in the autumn, its two lady proprietresses and its former title of The Blue Plate. In those days, nearly seven years ago, it had been frequented by nice people living in nice houses in the neighbouring villages and on the local bus routes; it had been *the* place at which to meet for a cup of tea while waiting for your particular bus to arrive; it had been as clean, as pleasant, as respectable as The Myrtle Bough in Horsham itself, but first the evacuees had come, and then the war had come, and then the Bomb, and the two ladies who managed The Blue Plate had been so much shaken, both literally and metaphorically, that they had sold the lease, fittings and goodwill of their business for less than it was worth; and then the Battle of Britain had come, and then the Canadians and then the Americans, and then the Italian prisoners, and then the flying bombs and—last of all, dirtiest of all, most familiar to the eyes of the Sillingham people and yet most exotic of all—the gipsies themselves had come; and they had all, every one of them, patronised The Blue Plate, renamed the Linga-Longa, and every year it had grown steadily dirtier, noisier and less nice, until only the large old settees covered with filthy ragged chintz, where gardening gentlewomen and golfing colonels had once chatted and drunk tea, and the white brackets and shelves where the Japanese vases had once stood, remained of the former elegance. Gipsies sucked up their tea at the tables with baskets of stolen kingcups resting at their feet, lorry drivers wrangled over their change on the settees, and that was the story of the Linga-Longa Café.

As Sylvia's eyes (beautiful eyes of a cloudy blue-grey, with heavy lids) moved slowly about the room, the door of the café opened and two Italian prisoners came in. The first swaggered forward with a knowing glance towards some girls at a table near the door, and Sylvia barely noticed the second one, because at that moment the waitress came up with her order, and she did not look up from arranging the teapot and her cup until a voice asked politely:

'May we sitta here, signora?' and the first of the two Italians stood beside her table, looking down at her.

'Oh yes, that's all right,' she answered in a loud, fresh, friendly voice, and pulled her book towards her again as she took the first grateful draught of hot tea. The two men, having thanked her, sat down.

But once more it was useless; she could not read; and after a moment she was gazing about the room as she ate and drank, with an air of not really observing it and a frown on her white forehead. She had the face of a child, small and pale cheeked with a deeply-dimpled chin and pouting lips like those seen in portraits painted during the eighteenth century, and a long throat and full bosom. Sensitiveness, intelligence, thought, were all absent from that face, but its bloom suggested some sturdy flower of the hedges and foreshadowed a type of looks—bouncing, hoydenish and healthy—that might one day become fashionable.

The tea and cakes were good and they refreshed her; each time she lifted her eyelids and glanced about the room with the placidity of returning comfort, there was an entrancing flash of dreamy blue against the pallor of her cheeks which naturally attracted the admiring attention of the Italian who had spoken to her. He stared at her continuously and boldly, but the other, whose eyes were blue as her own, sat lost in sullen thought and barely glanced at her.

Both men were subdued in comparison with the other occupants of the café, as if the gaiety of Christmas failed to touch them. They smoked and drank their weak sugarless coffee in silence save for an occasional quiet word in their own language, and all about them the noise and laughter grew louder as nine o'clock (when the Linga-Longa would close down for the four-day Christmas holiday) drew near.

Sylvia had nearly finished her meal when her book slipped from the table to the floor. Before she had time to stoop and pick it up, the livelier of the two Italians did so for her, and handed it to her with a polite smile.

'Thanks very much,' she said, smiling too.

He smiled again, with much display of poor teeth (for which the slums of Genoa were responsible) and exclaimed ironically, 'Merry Christ-a-mas!' at the same time jerking his head towards one of the livelier tables while his dark eyes glinted mockingly.

'Well, why shouldn't they?' she retorted, 'they've been through enough, god-knows.'

'Me an' my fren', we far away from our home,' said Emilio, doing a quick change from mockery to pathos while his eyes wandered over her shabby suitcase and handbag to see if she were good for some cigarettes, 'so we are sad-a, much, much.'

'That's your fault. You backed the wrong horse. Too much *Viva il Duce*, eh?' and she made a gay sign to the waitress to bring the bill.

'No, no,' protested Emilio eagerly. '*È finito*—all that. He was bad man, much, much.'

'You're right, comrade, he was,' she said, looking in her purse. 'Look here, I suppose you don't know the way to a place called

Naylor's Farm? Now let me guess the answer—you've never heard of it.'

The other Italian, who had been taking no notice of their conversation, glanced up, and Emilio exclaimed:

'*Si, si*, Naylor Farm—you want-a go there?'

'I do, comrade, and the sooner the quicker. Is it far from here?'

'Three mile.' It was the other Italian who spoke for the first time, and the words in that voice gave pleasure to the ear as if they had been two notes of music. Sylvia turned and stared at him while continuing to put scarlet paint upon her childish mouth.

'It can talk!' she exclaimed, 'I thought you were dumb, comrade,' and she grinned, for he certainly looked it.

Fabrio slowly lifted his eyes, and took a long look at her; her laughing mouth that displayed big white teeth, and the little round hat now replaced upon the back of her head, and finally he laughed too, and turned to Emilio, saying, 'What a monkey-face, eh?' for her rich curls, her skin, her eyes, were obscured to him by her uniform, which seemed to him, as an Italian peasant, the most ridiculous and immodest dress that it was conceivable for a girl to wear, emphasising her hoydenishness so strongly that he was only conscious of blunt features and a wide smile.

Emilio, however, made a flattering comment on her looks, and then the two of them had a little talk about her in Italian, wondering how old she was, and what her name was, together with other details, some of which were far from being their business. They knew, of course, that she must be the 'langurl' with whose prospective arrival Mr Hoadley had contemptuously threatened them, and they also knew that he had intended to meet her that afternoon at the station with the car. Where had she been (Emilio suddenly inquired of her, speaking English again) when the Signor Oadlie had been to the station and not found her? He had been angry; much, much.

'That's cheerful,' and Sylvia made a face. 'What's he like, anyway?' Emilio shrugged up his shoulders almost to his ears, and intimated a complete lack of interest in Mr Hoadley. Fabrio, who had now become silent again, made no movement, and the waitress came up with Sylvia's bill, which the latter paid.

The room had grown noisier as closing-time approached, and was now stiflingly hot and oppressive from cigarette smoke and fumes from the kitchen. Sylvia had been the object of steady stares from some soldiers, and of furtive regard from a gipsy, dark and dirty, who was seated at a table nearby, and she was relieved that she had the two Italians at her table. Their manner was not so respectful as she would have liked it to be, but there was nothing alarming in Emilio's frank stare of interest and the other one, the quiet one, she dismissed as just dumb (though had he been beautiful as a god he would not have attracted Sylvia, whose admiration was reserved for beings who were not men but shadows). She felt capable of handling both of them.

The fat elderly manageress now appeared at the kitchen door in a greasy blue apron, clapping her hands at the customers and good-naturedly beseeching them all to go home and give the girls a chance to get a rest, and everyone began reluctantly to gather their possessions together and make their farewells, Sylvia among them.

'Can you show me the way to Naylor's?' she asked of Emilio.

'It is long-a way. Three mile,' and he shrugged again.

'I know that. I'm not asking you to come too. I just want to know the way.'

'We come too,' nodded Emilio, buttoning his overcoat.

'Oh no you don't, thank you. I can manage,' she answered quickly, alarmed at the idea of dark roads, deserted and lonely, and these two on either side of her. Her confident assumption that she could deal with them departed abruptly.

'We come,' smiled Fabrio, not quite pleasantly, and picked up his cap.

'Didn't you get me the first time, comrade? I don't want you to come. *Nienty*. No can do. I'd rather go alone.' The three of them were now moving towards the door.

'She is a-fraid,' said Fabrio, his musical voice now mocking her, whereupon they both began to laugh uproariously, standing on either side of her in the snowy street, whilst around them people gathered in groups, bidding one another 'Good night' and 'A merry Christmas.' She looked angrily from one laughing face to the other, not understanding a word they were saying.

'Oh, very funny, very funny, ha-ha,' she interrupted at last. 'Now suppose you tell me the way and I'll be off—*by myself*, thank you.'

'We come-a with you,' said Fabrio, suddenly ceasing to laugh. 'We work there.'

'Me an' my fren', we work-a at Naylor Farm,' Emilio explained in his turn. 'We go back to *campo* this night, we go with you some tha way.'

'Oh, you *work* there?' she cried.

'You langurl,' said Emilio, nodding and touching the flash on her sleeve. 'We work all of us together there, sometime perhaps.'

'Oh, I get you. "Came the dawn." Come on, then, comrades, what are we waiting for? Let's go,' and she slipped one arm through that of Emilio and the other—after a glance at his face—through Fabrio's, and they set off.

Emilio was enjoying himself. He lived in the moment, and would have agreed with Lord Byron that old-fashioned pleasures were good enough for him; Sylvia's arm and side were warm against his own and an agreeable perfume breathed from her face and hair. From time to time, however, he glanced at the face of Fabrio, which he could faintly discern in the starlight, and saw that it was haughty, troubled and slightly averted from Sylvia. *Now* what's the matter with him? thought Emilio, irritated, for he loved his friend without understanding him.

Fabrio was annoyed at being unceremoniously seized by his arm, with never a hint of shyness on Sylvia's part beforehand or of pride and pleasure after she had got it, and he also felt ashamed of being seen walking linked with this noisy young girl in trousers.

He had seen 'langurls' on previous occasions, of course, cycling past the camp or working in summer on the surrounding farms and always he had thought how shameless and ridiculous they looked, and when they were pretty that only made it worse. Now he was striding along beside one, with her fresh young presence troubling him, and now—oh Holy Saints, she was singing! Mother of God, thought Fabrio, and winced, what a voice!

As the language difficulty made conversation constrained, Sylvia thought it best to sing, and what she chose to sing—as the untrodden snow rolled away before them in the starlight and keen winds wandered through the dusky leafless coppices—was *Jesu, Joy of Man's Desiring*. Even so might some Pagan seller of lupin-seeds in the Rome of Nero have bawled a good tune which he had overheard the Christians singing in the night watches from their prison above the Circus. Sylvia had heard this good tune on the wireless.

After listening for a moment or two, Emilio caught the air and joined in, but Fabrio uttered never a sound, sung or spoken, until the lights of the camp shone on the opposite side of the road, and then, as they all paused in their march, he abruptly shook off Sylvia's arm, barely nodded to her, and strode off towards the gates of the camp, where the sentry walked up and down with chin sunk in his collar against the cold.

'What's biting him?' she demanded indignantly, but a conscious expression in her eyes and colour deepening in her face betrayed that she was not completely insensitive, and the glance which she gave along the lonely road lying ahead was apprehensive.

Emilio only shrugged; he often found his comparative ignorance of English useful in embarrassing situations but in this case he did not know the answer.

'I come-a with you,' was all he said, trying to take her arm again. His face looked pinched and yellow and not attractive in the dim light.

'There's no need for that,' she said, hesitating between a little mistrust of him and a real dread of the solitary walk before her, 'You tell me the way.'

'No-o, no-a. Very difficult, much, much. I come-a an' show you.'

The sentry had turned his head and was watching the two of them with a weary ironical grin.

'All right then, if it isn't far,' she said, and let him take her arm again and lead her down the road.

Emilio calculated that he could walk with her for another quarter of an hour, for it was now half-past eight and he must be back in camp by nine; the last fifteen minutes must be spent in retracing his steps. Accordingly, when they had walked for some time in a silence made disagreeable by the fact that he had tried to kiss her and had been repulsed by a strong push and a loud indignant exclamation, he paused, and announced:

'Now I go-a back to *campo*.'

'Here, don't do that, comrade!' she said, dismayed, and set down her suitcase (which he had not offered to carry) with an exasperated movement. 'Where do I go from here?'

Emilio, a man of few words when he liked, sulkily pointed to a wide gap in the leafless hedge on their left.

'Down there? Thanks, I'm sure,' peering into the dimness. 'Oo, it does look dark!'

'Naylor Farm,' said Emilio, jerking his thumb at the gap. 'Go on, go on, go on. Then Naylor Farm. Now I go back to *campo*. See you some-a day, signora-mees. *Buona notte*,' and he sketched a salute and turned away.

'You are mean!' she called after him half-tearfully as his shape grew dim in the starlight.

'Merry Christa-mas!' he called back mockingly, and was lost in the snow-lit gloom.

Sylvia heard his footsteps grow fainter and finally cease, and stood there uncertainly, with her heart beating fast and lurid fancies engendered by the cinema, the wireless and the cheap bookstall rushing into her mind, assailing it with terrors as frightful as any imagined a hundred years ago by a peasant who could not write or read. She saw the front page of a certain morning paper with its heavy black headlines and on it her own name and the word Murder; she saw shapes in the white obscurity of the hedges buried in snow, motionless, watching her; she stared wildly about her and was almost ready to run, had she not been even more afraid that something would spring out of the shadows and run after her.

Suddenly a woman on a bicycle came round the corner, pedalling placidly along with a cheerful little red lamp throwing its ray upon the trodden snow. It was the District Nurse, returning home after her day's work, and she called a pleasant 'Good night' as she went by.

'Oo—please—is this right for Naylor's Farm?' shouted Sylvia, running a little way after her.

'First on the left; you can't mistake it,' Nurse called, as her tiny ruby light dwindled away down the road, 'then just keep straight on. Merry Christmas.'

Sylvia made her way through the gap in the hedge, and was soon slowly moving across the frozen morass of mud covered by virgin snow between the road and the farm. The lights from the latter's windows were still hidden by the dip in the meadows, and she could distinguish nothing beyond the dim blanched wastes extending on every side, broken here and there by the elongated white hump of a hedge or a large vague object, laden with snow and looming against the sky, that was a tree, and she soon became frightened again. The stars were hidden once more behind clouds and an icy wind blew into her face; she went slowly, doggedly on with her legs aching from the effort of lifting them at every step from two feet of snow; a tiny dark figure that was the only moving object between empty fields and vast sky. Had she been in company with a friend she would have been shrieking with laughter and enjoying it all, but she was not capable of laughing at discomfort while enduring it alone.

Meanwhile, Mr Hoadley was coming across the meadows towards her, carrying a lantern like a Shepherd or a Wise Man, and, unlike either of them, in a bad temper. As he was a good-natured man he disliked being in a bad temper, and he also felt that it was wrong to be in one on Christmas Eve, when even his wife's sharpness had been temporarily blunted by letters from home (Mrs Hoadley, like Dante and Mr Waite, was an exile; in her case, from Ironborough) and when there were a duck and a goose for the Christmas dinner to-morrow, and the farmhouse was full of his old parents from Amberley Wild Brooks and other relatives from out Pulborough way, including two little nephews of whom he, the childless man, was fond. But drat that girl! he had wasted the whole afternoon, when there were a thousand things to be done, in meeting three trains on her behalf; and finally he had had to come down here at nine o'clock at night in the forlorn hope that she might have come out on the eight o'clock bus from Horsham to Burlham and walked from there.

The rays of the lantern beamed along the glittering surface of the snow as his massive patient figure trudged on, and each of his steps made a hollow deep enough for a rabbit to shelter in. He swung the lantern impatiently, so that its ray flickered upwards upon his frowning face, and peered ahead, searching for a human figure in the dimness.

In the meantime, Sylvia had naturally taken the lights of Pine cottage for those of the farm, and was even now (though with some misgiving as she observed the smallness of the place and the lack of outbuildings and haystacks and that sort of thing surrounding it) knocking at the front door.

9

Within everybody was too busy to hear a knock at the front door, especially as they were not expecting one. Jean was undressing Meg and putting her into bed, while Jenny and Louise, with many whispers and grimaces, were moving their pillows and pyjamas into one bed in their room in order that Jean could sleep in the other. Alda was hastily preparing something more solid than the tea that had been awaiting herself and the children for Ronald, who had not eaten since early that morning, while giving him the latest family news.

'Is that someone at the front door?' he interrupted her, from beside the kitchen fire where he was warming his numbed feet.

'Oh no, darling, no one ever comes here at night. It's only the children bumping about. Here, drink this while it's hot.'

'Alda, I'm sure that is someone at the door,' he said again in a moment, when he had taken some soup.

'I'll go—it must be someone from the farm with a parcel,' and she was going out of the room when he stopped her, saying:

'Better let me go; we're living in the New Dark Ages, remember,' and he put down the basin and went down the passage, moving slowly because he was weary and stiff from travelling.

'Oo, please, is this Naylor's Farm?' inquired a loud, fresh young voice plaintively as he switched on his torch and opened the door. He looked down (for she had retreated outside the porch and was standing below its step) into a pair of blue eyes shining beneath a mop of dyed hair, dark and damp from the recent snowfall.

'I'm afraid not. This is Pine Cottage; the farm is about three hundred yards further on,' he answered.

'Thank goodness for that, anyway,' she said, cheered by the pleasant educated voice and the sight of a tall masculine figure. 'Sorry to have bothered you,' and she was turning away when Alda came down the passage to see who the visitor was.

'Oh,' she exclaimed, catching sight of the green jersey and Women's Land Army flash on the coat sleeve, 'Mr Hoadley will be glad you've come! He thought you'd got lost; he's been down to the station twice and we've just seen him go by here with a lantern; I expect he's gone down to the road to see if you've come by the last bus.'

'I simply can't go back across that field; I'll die,' declared Sylvia flatly, and sat down upon her suitcase. 'I'll wait here until he comes back and catch him,' and she gazed expectantly from one face to the other, obviously hoping to be invited to wait inside the house.

'Won't you——' Ronald was beginning, when a touch upon his arm from Alda silenced him.

Every human instinct of sympathy, of hospitality, of desire to feed the hungry and shelter the outcast, had been aroused in him during the past months in Germany, and every one of those natural instincts had been denied full expression. He now thought of a house only as a place into which so many *dispossessed persons* (as homeless people are now called) could be fitted with some prospect of relief, if not of actual comfort; and the sweet narrow walls of his own family life had not yet had time to rise about him once more and shut out the ever-present vision of that horde of starved, filthy, hopeless, almost nameless, fellow-creatures to whom he was father and judge.

But Alda felt the walls firmly and strongly about her, and she was certainly not going to invite another person into Pine Cottage that night, even though it was a snowy Christmas Eve.

'He should be back any minute now,' she said brightly. 'I'll leave the door open for you, shall I? I won't ask you in; you'd probably miss him. A merry Christmas! Good night,' and she went quickly back to the kitchen, leaving Sylvia sitting upon her suitcase in the snow.

Ronald followed more slowly. He did not like to see a girl sitting on a suitcase in the snow, waiting; it was too much like what he had been seeing at every station, all through Germany, all through Belgium, all through France, during his journey of the past forty-eight hours; nevertheless, he looked tenderly at the back of Alda's bright head as she bent over the stove, and loved her.

Meg immediately turned her flushed cheek into the pillow and went to sleep, leaving Jean with nothing to do but stand a shaded candle upon the mantelpiece, make up one of the fires which she had lit in a mood of Christmas Eve recklessness in the two bedrooms earlier that afternoon and tiptoe away into the next room, where she found Jenny and Louise bouncing up and down in a heap of bed clothes upon the floor.

'Hey, what's going on here?' she demanded.

'We're making the bed and all these pillows and things needed a good shaking.'

'I see. Well, now let's put them back on the bed, shall we? and then you pop into the bathroom and wash and I'll bring up your supper.'

The children had an indulgent liking for Jean which was unconsciously modelled upon their mother's half-derisive, half-affectionate attitude towards her, and although they barely regarded her as having a grown-up's authority, they consented to do as she suggested and were soon sitting side by side in the large, freshly smoothed bed, gazing at the two long black stockings hanging from the brass rail at its foot and waiting for their supper, while the firelight danced upon walls and ceiling, transforming the ugly room with cosy mystery. Both wore dressing-gowns made by Alda from an ample old white shawl printed with a Paisley pattern in red and green which she had bought for a few shillings at a junk shop in some country town.

There had not been enough of it to make a full-length one for Meg but all three children considered hers the best robe of them all, for it had a hem of green velvet a foot deep (discarded evening dress, Marion, vintage 1939) and Jenny called it 'absolutely princess-like.'

Jean was happy to be in this little house standing in the midst of the meadows, which, after the conventional luxury of her parents' box-like flat in St John's Wood, seemed to her a romantic place. All her journey had been romantic; the snow-storm, her struggle across the frozen fields with her suitcase, and finally, her entry, through the back door (which she greatly wondered to find unlocked) into a quiet, shadowy cottage where the fire burned in the parlour like a veiled garnet and all the clocks ticked peacefully through the afternoon hush. The recent bustle of her own life suddenly seemed to her blessedly remote. She had left behind her the documents to be signed and the relations to be consulted, the furniture dealers and lawyers and house agents and prospective tenants, and was now at rest, surrounded by the familiar atmosphere belonging to her oldest and closest friend.

'Jean!' Alda's voice came subduedly up the stairs. 'Supper.'

She had suspended branches of holly and yew with scarlet threads from the picture rail in the parlour, and these conspired with firelight and white tablecloth to fill the room with the mysterious innocent happiness of Christmas. Jean began to smile as she came down the dark narrow staircase into the light, and the other two, chagrined though they were at the spoiling of their family Christmas, smiled with her.

The remainder of the evening passed pleasantly, as Meg did not awaken, and sleep must do her good, and half-way through supper Jean remembered that she had a bottle of gin in her suitcase, intended as a Christmas present for her hosts. (The late Mr Hardcastle had known a number of wealthy, slightly mysterious men with hard faces who frequently sent him a bottle of this and a case of that, or gave him a tip in season about the other, and it was one of them, wishing to show respect to the dead, who had presented Jean with the gin.)

Sipping and gossip ended the day. At midnight she crept shivering into bed, having bestowed some sweets and Black Market oranges in the two sad, flat stockings hanging on the bed-rail; and in the shy and sceptical prayer which she murmured before she fell asleep, she asked a blessing upon her friend and her friend's husband and children.

When Sylvia had been sitting upon the suitcase for some ten minutes she saw a light coming towards her over the fields which seemed to her to be bobbing up and down in an irritable manner. However, she was now so hungry, cold and tired that she had ceased to be afraid of facing an angry farmer, and she therefore went down to meet the lantern, calling cheerfully:

'Is that Mr Hoadley? It's me—Sylvia Scorby. I say, I'm ever so sorry I couldn't get here before. I missed two trains from London on account of them being so crowded.'

Mr Hoadley was very surprised to see her, and also slightly annoyed, for he had by this time given up all hope of her and was returning to the farm resigned and ready to make the most of what was left of the evening's pleasantness. He also disliked having to jump abruptly from one state of mind into another, but he did notice with satisfaction that she seemed—from what he could make out in the dimness—to be a tall strong girl, and the cheerfulness of her voice was disarming.

'You've certainly given me an afternoon of it,' he answered gruffly, but putting out his hand for her to shake. 'I'd given you up for to-night. How did you find your way here? (This way—it isn't far, and we've kept some supper for you.)'

This was good news for Sylvia, who enjoyed eating better than anything in the world except shrieking with her friends and going to the pictures, and soon she was giving Mr Hoadley a lively account of her adventures on the journey—and she included Emilio's attempt to kiss her.

He let her talk away without making any comment, but the incident confirmed his personal belief that Emilio was the worse character of the two Italians, and it also gave him a favourable sidelight upon Sylvia herself. If she had displayed virtuous indignation even he, charitable and good-natured as he was, would have suspected its genuineness, for he was no fool and he took human nature for granted; but her robust mingling of impatience with laughter as she related Emilio's discomfiture convinced him that if there were to be any trouble 'in that way' later on, it would be started, not by this girl, but by the Italians.

Nevertheless—missing trains, picking up Italians in that Linga-Longa place, dodging kisses at nine o'clock at night on lonely roads—no, it was not what you might call a good beginning; she must be a scatter-brained creature, and, glancing at her as they went up the path leading to the door and light from the windows fell upon her eyes and hair, Mr Hoadley wished that the Board had sent him someone with glasses and a wig.

The next moment Sylvia stood in the kitchen of the farm-house, a long, low chamber running the whole length of the front of the building, with windows whose broad sills supported ancient shutters freshly painted grey, and a floor of narrow pale red bricks scooped into hollows by the tread of feet throughout two hundred and fifty years. The walls were washed in rose colour and divided at irregular intervals by wide oak beams richly blackened by smoke from countless household fires, and the ceiling was similarly adorned.

Mrs Hoadley could feel pride in entertaining a family party in such a room, and this evening she appeared at her best; flushed, complacent, hospitable, and pressing her light cakes and flaky sausage rolls upon the circle gathered about the fire. Supper proper was over, but the company was at the agreeable stage of sipping and smoking. Some had cigarettes and some had pipes, but the kitchen was so large that the air remained no more than agreeably warm, and tolerably fresh.

The inglenook was filled by an iron range which Mrs Hoadley seldom used, preferring the gas cooker installed upon the opposite wall, but to-night the whole top of this cumbrous object had been removed, converting it into an open brazier in which glowed a splendid mass of fiery cinders rendered fiercer by the frost outside, and supporting upon itself a massive log of oak up which climbed golden flames. Some eight people or so were gathered about the warmth; two little boys were reclining half-asleep against their mother's side and every now and then someone would remark that those boys really must go up to bed; and then the conversation would go on as before.

When Sylvia and Mr Hoadley entered, everybody looked up and exclaimed, and said that she must be cold, and they all drew aside to give her room by the fire except Mr Waite (whom she at once privately labelled Dirty Dick because of the cold look he gave her). Mr Waite was sitting in a corner sipping the mulled beer which Mr Hoadley had invited him to share on this Christmas Eve because he did not like to think of him alone up there with his chickens and his books. Mr Waite for his part disapproved of Sylvia from his first glimpse of her; a loud, provocative, painted young girl with dyed hair.

She was confused and made shy for the moment by the light and the heat from the fire and the many faces and voices after the darkness and silence outside, and only smiled nervously in reply to Mrs Hoadley's brisk pleasant questions, allowing herself to be installed in a retired corner with her supper on a small table, while the kettle was put on again for her tea and the company tactfully left her to herself.

But when she had finished her supper (which was a good one and promised hopefully for the future) she joined the circle about the fire and soon began to join in, and then to dominate, the conversation; telling them about her adventures on the journey and making them laugh, while her lovely eyes moved half-bashfully, half-audaciously, from one face to another and her voice grew louder, her laugh more frequent, as her nature expanded in the warmth of that general attention which was its strongest need.

From the darkest, warmest corner, where the shadow of the overhanging mantelpiece partly obscured the light, four eyes smallened by age yet still very bright watched her unceasingly, following every movement of her laughing face. A little old man and woman sat there side by side, both toothless, both past eighty years. They were like two small brown nuts, with all the satin smoothness of youth dried away. She had a dress of plum-coloured cloth, sewn with opal beads in a rich pattern round its high neck, the skirt carefully drawn up to show a black petticoat of crackling silk and a fairy-like foot in a tiny black boot; he wore a suit of thick cloth of the square cut of forty years ago, exhaling a musty odour. He was bald, but her thinning hair, parted and braided and coiled in a knot, was black as a girl's and showed off the earrings, shaped like cornucopias filled with roses and of a rich red gold rarely seen nowadays, that dangled from her tiny withered ears. These were old Joseph and Nancy Hoadley, the farmer's grandparents. They lived at Amberley, some seventeen miles away, and that morning he had driven over to fetch them from their home amidst the willow woods and marestail grasses of the Wild Brooks.

They, and the rest of the company with the exception of Mr Waite, found Sylvia highly entertaining, though they did not admire her so much as she thought they did and they all wondered whether Mr Hoadley would get any work out of her, for her small, white dimpled hands looked as useless as they were pretty. Mr Waite simply thought that she was a bold piece who ought to be smacked.

It was late when the party finally separated for the night. Mrs Hoadley, carrying a candle, took Sylvia up to the small chamber with sloping roof and tiny window that was to be her own.

There was barely room for the large young creature to turn herself about as she undressed by the soft light from the oil lamp, but this did not trouble her, for she was intoxicated by her social success during the evening and so prepared to be delighted with all the circumstances of her new life that she fell asleep with a smile on her lips.

'Well, what do you think of her, Molly?' asked the farmer, when he and his wife were alone.

'*She* thinks plenty of herself.'

'She looks strong, that's one good thing. We can do with all of that; we don't want any weaklings here.'

'Great lump,' said Mrs Hoadley, but not ill-naturedly.

'She might be a bit stupid at learning things; she talks too much, she'll never listen, I'm sure,' he went on.

'She made you laugh, anyhow; I haven't heard you make such a noise for months. And she keeps herself clean. That's something.'

'Girls mostly do nowadays, Molly,' he said mildly.

'Don't you believe it!' she snapped. 'Not as clean as that girl does.'

He had taken it for granted that Sylvia's manner and appearance would meet with his wife's strong disapproval, and was resigned to a series of scenes culminating at last in the girl's dismissal, but Mrs Hoadley's responses were not always calculable, and he now knew from her tone that she had decided to approve. He was relieved, and decided in his turn to suppress the story about Emilio.

In fact, Sylvia brought with her something of the nervous excitement and sense of quickened living that belongs to a city, and this was the salt, the flavour, for which the city-bred Molly Hoadley craved. She felt vaguely that Sylvia's opinion of country scenes and country routine, which she herself found so dull, would be like her own, and it was this that had really decided her in the girl's favour.

Mrs Hoadley would have been content to live in a suburb of some great city with a culture based upon the teapot rather than upon the fermented grape. Everything in the suburb would have been pretty, sensible, pleasant and orderly and run on electricity, and all the men would years ago have shot themselves or run away to sea. Because she was conscientious and fond of her husband, she did the work of two women on the farm: she scamped no detail, she forced herself to perform, to the last hairsbreadth and beyond, the duties she most disliked; but she dreaded the black icy winter mornings as much as she did the glaring summer ones noisy with crowings and cries; and shrank from the occasional necessary contacts with warm, hairy, unexpectedly strong animal bodies. Above all, she was depressed by the quiet, and the year-long lack of plentiful and frequent human company; she disliked equally the long hushed winter evenings and the long light summer ones when every flower in the hedge seemed to stare at her.

For the sake of having on the farm the company of another woman who shared her views (even if the woman was only a chit of eighteen) she was prepared to overlook dyed hair and a loud manner.

10

Ronald felt that he would return to Germany with an easier mind if he had heard a doctor's verdict upon Meg, whose temperature went up to a hundred and one every night without correspondingly alarming symptoms during the day. On the day before his leave expired, therefore, he walked over to the farm and, having with some difficulty traced and succeeded in talking to a doctor recommended by the Hoadleys, he arranged for him to visit Meg that afternoon.

The fields were still covered in snow, and the only moving objects in the white landscape were himself, and the smoke going up from the cottage chimney into the windless grey sky. He took off his snow-caked boots in the porch, and went down the passage in stockinged feet into the untidy parlour, now scented with balm from the Christmas tree and the metallic odour of tinsel decorations. Louise was there, reading a book in the clear glare of light from the snow with her elbows resting upon the table, and although she glanced up and said, 'Hullo, Father' and smiled as he entered, she at once returned to her book. He stood by the fire, supporting himself by one hand against the mantelpiece, and turned his numbed feet in front of the flames, and presently, as he gazed absently out of the window at the hushed landscape, he began to quote in a low tone—for the pleasure of speaking and hearing the French—a poem beloved by him in his youth:

> Qu'il est doux, qu'il est doux d'écouter des histoires,
> Des histoires du temps passé,

Quand les branches d'arbre sont noires,
Quand la neige est épaisse et charge un sol glacé!

Louise had raised her head from her book at the first sound
of the words and, after listening attentively, now took advantage
of the pause he made while recalling the next verse:

'What does it mean, Father? It's French, isn't it?'

'Yes. It means: *How delightful it is to listen to stories of the olden
days, when the branches of the trees are black, and the snow is thick
and covers a frosty earth.*'

'But it rhymes, I heard it. Is it a poem?'

'Yes; by Alfred de Vigny. It's called *Snow*.'

'Say some more.' She left her book and came over to the fire
to lean against him. He put his arm about her (how slender she
was, and her scanty jersey was darned on the shoulder—but the
children of the Homeless People were skeletons and their clothing
was rags) and went on, with an expression of pain that gradually
faded as the words performed their spell:

Quand seul dans un ciel pâle un peuplier s'élance——

Louise listened, with her eyes fixed dreamily upon the fire.
When he came to *Est-ce vous, blanche Emma, princesse de la Gaule?*
he broke off.

'There! No more,' he said, and gently kissed her. 'That's the
best place to end at.'

'Oh why, Father? Do go on. I like it so much.'

'Because that line is the heart of the poem. When I was
seventeen it summed up all the Dark Ages for me.'

He had forgotten that he was talking to somebody aged only
ten, but she, while only half-understanding what he had just
said, was charmed by the unfamiliar sounds and his air of
imparting a secret. She moved closer to him and murmured
again, looking up into his face:

'Do say some more.'

He was struck by the intelligence in her eyes, thirsty for what she did not realise as knowledge, and asked abruptly:

'Louise, do you want to go to school?'

'I shan't mind. Jenny's going too,' she answered, but her dreamy, eager expression was now replaced by a wary one, for all grown-ups, even father, had this habit of pouncing questions upon one which might lead to a row.

'Yes, but how do you, yourself, feel about it?'

'I shan't mind,' she repeated, a little uneasily now, and glanced towards her book lying on the table.

'You love reading, I know, but how about your arithmetic—tables, and that sort of thing?'

'I can do adding and subtracting and some multiplying. Jenny can do dividing, too. She was just starting on *long* dividing when we went away from Lyle Villas and didn't have Miss Leeper any more.'

'Let's hear your tables up as far as you know,' said her father.

She began confidently enough, but broke down half-way through six times, and he shook his head.

'High time you went to school, Weez.'

'You're cross with me,' she announced, in a voice of flat despair.

'Not a bit, dear; don't sound so miserable. You've got a good brain and if you work you're going to be a clever woman. Now run off and finish your book.'

He went into the kitchen to tell Alda what he had arranged with the doctor, aware as never before of the backwardness of his daughters in the elements of a thorough and solid education. He saw that he had allowed himself to be overcome by the difficulty of finding living accommodation close to a reputable school, by the long waiting lists for admission into the schools themselves, above all, by Alda's casual attitude towards the matter and he made up his mind then and there that whether Jenny and Louise were happy at the convent or not, they must stay there for as long as was possible.

He said as much to them before he left the next day, leaving them with rather long faces; for a word from him impressed them more, coming from such a grave, seldom-seen, revered source, than all Alda's frequent fireworks. The snow was melting under driving rain, it was impossible to play in the meadows, and the prospect of a long sojourn at the convent was rendered doubly depressing in their flat, after-Christmas mood.

'Cheer up, my Jen,' he said, and stooped to kiss her doleful face. His battered luggage was piled all about him; the taxi waited at the edge of the field, and beside him stood Alda holding up the umbrella with which she insisted on sheltering him although he protested that he would have to get wet sooner or later.

'Good-bye, darling, darling Father.' They clung to him, standing upon tiptoe to reach his neck, his waist, and hugging him with their thin arms. When he had disengaged himself, he glanced up at the window and there was Meg in her dressing-gown held aloft by Jean, smiling and waving with her fair mane floating about her face.

'Nothing much wrong with her to-day,' he said to Alda as they splashed across the field towards the taxi. The doctor had announced that Meg was suffering from a slight infection, not of a serious nature, of which there was A Good Deal About. England was full of such short, tiresome, nameless and apparently causeless fevers after the Second World War. Perhaps they blew across from Europe; perhaps they wavered up out of the dirty scarred streets in the towns, perhaps they were bred in bodies sick to death of pain and monotony and violence and grief. No one seemed to know, and of course the doctor did not express these picturesque views; he said that M. & B. was not necessary but might be tried if the temperature persisted, smiled at Meg and very gently pulled her hair, and went away. This morning, however, the temperature was slightly under normal, which was a favourable sign.

'Oh, I'm not worrying about her any more, but I expect we shall all get it—and in a house this size, in this weather——'

She had not meant to complain to him, but the words slipped out.

'Poor old girl,' he said. 'But Jean's here to help you, and I should get her to stay on for a bit, if she will.'

'Oh, she'll stay all right. The difficulty will be to get rid of her. Still, she will be a help. Here we are. Good-bye, my darling.'

They clasped each other close for a moment, with one kiss; then he turned quickly away and got into the taxi; the door slammed; she saw him sit back among his khaki bundles and suitcases, and he was driven off through the rain.

She furled the umbrella and went back across the fields. Each time he went away it was as bad as the first time had been; it never got any better, indeed, it got rather worse. Alda ignored her wet eyes and the ache in her throat and thought that the next time he came the primroses would be in the woods.

'Jean,' she said presently while they were making Meg's bed, with the invalid, swathed in a blanket, watching them from the other bed, 'when did you think of going home?'

'Not for ages, unless you want me to. I like being here.'

'I suppose you realise we shall all get this thing of Meg's? The doctor seems to think we're bound to.'

'Oh well—all the more reason for my staying. You can't cope alone.'

'Of course, if you *like* sick-nursing in the depths of the country in January——'

'My tastes always were a bit pecu,' said Jean placidly. 'No, honestly, Alda, I'd like to stay. I may have to run up to town now and then to see my lawyers or the house agents but no going back to the flat for keeps, thanks. I hope they soon let it.'

'They're sure to. You couldn't be trying to let it at a better time.' Alda lifted Meg back on to her own bed, unrolled her, and replaced her between the sheets. 'There isn't much wrong with you,' she said, gloating over her cool pink cheeks and the clear whites of her eyes. 'You're an old fraud,' and she tickled her. Meg chuckled.

'I do wish I could hear from my Mr Potter,' said Jean, sighing. 'He *might* have written when Dad died.'

'Don't they think it rather odd, your being down here?' asked Alda, not wishing to indulge this train of thought.

'Who? Aunt Alice? She doesn't know I am here. Aunt Daisy did say it was selfish of me but I pretended not to hear.'

'Good for you, the old monster. As for your Mr Potter,' said Alda gaily, struck by an excellent new idea as they went downstairs, 'don't give him another thought. I've found someone down here who'll suit you much better than your Mr Potter.'

'Oh, have you, darling? Do tell me. This place doesn't look as if there was a man for miles,' and Jean gave her silly giggle, which was not irritating because it was so infectious, but she felt disloyal towards the gentle woods and meadows that had comforted her during the past week; the bright green stems of sallows shining out in marshy coppices amidst purple thickets of blackberry and thorn, the sage-green catkins swinging in keen winds under hurrying grey skies. Of course this landscape did not look as if there were a man in it, or, indeed, marriages or kisses, for it lay in winter sleep, like the Beauty of the fairy story, dreaming.

'It's Mr Waite, who lives over in the next meadow,' Alda went on. 'He runs a chicken farm. He's awfully good-looking and he adores reading.'

'How marvellous,' said Jean; dutifully, but also slightly cheered by this picture, 'and if he likes reading he's sure to be—nice.'

She had intended to say 'intelligent,' but checked herself in time; Alda had more than once told her that she could not afford to be choosy, and who was she to demand intelligence in a prospective husband?

Alda herself had been slightly irritated by Jean's reference to her lawyer and house agent. Jean did not yet realise it, but when her father's will was proved, she would be wealthy; and when she was wealthy, and did realise it, she would become self-confident, as were all the other wealthy people whom Alda numbered among her acquaintance.

Alda did not like the idea of Jean becoming self-confident, after having been for fifteen years biddable and grateful for management and advice; and although her chances of marriage would increase when once she became known as a wealthy orphan, so would her chances of being married for her money. Years ago, Alda had sworn to herself that she *would* get Jean married, and when I make up my mind (she thought now) I do what I mean to do. She had decided that Mr Waite was just the type of desolate, gloomy male over whom Jean would enjoy fussing, while he would be only too glad to marry a pleasant, wealthy girl. Alda thought that it would all work out most satisfactorily.

11

In the harsh weeks of January, Sylvia learned what work is.

She had never read the Bible, and therefore she did not know that phrase about *hewers of wood and drawers of water* which contains the ache of bruised muscles and the sound of labouring breath; coming down through the ages and speaking in that language of the body which is the only language that has remained unchanged by Time, but with her own strong young body she now understood its meaning. In the dark freezing mornings when it seemed that light had gone for ever, in a silence pierced by the spectral far-off crowing of cocks, she staggered up out of a warm bed in which she seemed to have been lying for only a few moments, and by candlelight pulled on breeches and thick socks and boots still stiff from the wet of yesterday, wincing as each aching muscle reluctantly resumed its duties. She would be still dazed with sleep; she never had enough sleep, no matter how early she fell into bed, and her early morning work, the sterilising and milking of the six cows, was carried out as if she were drugged.

The icy air struck her face when she opened the yard door; the rays of her lantern glided outward, along the frozen ridges of strawy muck and the pools of foul liquid that would enrich garden and fields and send roses and lilies springing up into the sunlight in summer—summer! was there such a time? The sky was silent and black; all about lay the dark, silent fields hidden in freezing mist. Her boots crunched in the puddles and frozen mud as she trudged across the yard, and she would shout 'Good morning' to Mrs Hoadley, of whom she caught a glimpse through the half-open door of the stable where she sat among her goats, neat as ever in turban and white coat, resignedly staring down at her jerking, struggling pensioners. The lantern light threw Sylvia's huge shadow and its own golden rays against the black weatherboarding of sheds and barn as she plodded by, and then she would be pleasantly hailed by Mr Hoadley, who belonged in that half of the human race which wakes up alert and cheerful in the morning. (Mrs Hoadley belonged in the other half: this often happens in a marriage and it is no one's fault.)

The appetite for sensation and the instinct to display herself which Sylvia inherited from her father, who had been an actor, were outward symptoms of her inward shrinking from facts. The bull was a fact: when she cautiously pushed open the door of his stable and the light shone along his ponderous grey bulk as he crouched in the straw, and he slowly turned his black dewy muzzle and sombre eyes to gaze at her, she always experienced a thrill of fear which time and experience of his passivity did nothing to allay. She did not find the cows so alarming; the milky, straw-scented odour that floated out from their warm stable was sweet, and all was so calm there, when the lantern light fell on the faded gold of hay sprinkled with dried flowers and the brighter gold of the straw under their hooves. She would look up at the whitewashed ceiling where shadowy cobwebs drooped between the black beams, and listen for a moment to the silence and the little sounds in it; and she would feel comforted. Cows have been going on for a long time, she would think vaguely, standing with her hand resting upon the warm heaving flank of the Jersey; you dear old girl, you, and she would slide her hand along the silky, dove-hued hide.

Then memories of her friends at the Dramatic School returned to remind her that she was going to be an actress, that she was sleepy, aching, hungry and cold, and must have been crazy when she took on this job.

Yet in spite of the hardness and roughness of the work, and the scanty leisure, and the knowledge that she was getting older every day and no nearer to obtaining a start in that profession in which the early beginning is more important than in any other, she was not unhappy. Her strength responded to the demands made upon it, and something vigorous and energetic in herself accepted toil and dirty work, assimilated them, and transmuted them into entertainment, even into profit. She was afraid of the horses and the bull but she was not afraid of hard work; and she won approval from both her employers. The ample, nourishing food which the farm could provide maintained her health, and she bloomed; the ancient tarnished mirror in her bedroom reflected rounded cheeks and hair from which the dye was beginning to fade.

Sometimes the Hoadleys and Sylvia were still at breakfast when one of the lorries which conveyed the prisoners to work set Fabrio and Emilio down at the edge of the fields. The party at the table would hear the vehicle approaching, and often Mrs Hoadley would tell Sylvia to fetch two extra cups, and have tea waiting for the men when they put their heads round the door some moments later. Their brown faces would be chilled to blueness and sometimes their hair was silvered by floating hoar-frost but, unlike an English farm labourer in similar circumstances, they never stamped their feet nor slapped their hands together to warm them; they did not even comment upon the weather except by an occasional patient shrug of the shoulders; they slightly inclined their heads towards the group seated about the breakfast table, and sometimes the two of them together would faintly, gravely smile as they said, 'Good-a morning.' The tea was received with grateful mutters but in the same spirit of restraint, and it was speedily disposed of and the cup (in case it should be considered a presumption to rinse it in the scullery) set down again in exactly the place from which it had been lifted.

Sylvia was at first inclined to nickname them The Zombies, but this joke died for lack of anyone with whom to share it, and she knew from her first encounter with them that they did not always behave like Zombies. Emilio, indeed, soon developed a most un-Zombie like trick of pouncing out on her from behind hedges and ricks and kissing her.

What kick he gets out of it I'm sure I don't know, [she wrote to one of her friends at the Dramatic School] because I always crown him, and once I pushed him right over in some muck; he didn't half swear, at least, I'm sure it was swearing. The other one is very up-stage, thank God.

Indeed, Fabrio took no notice of her beyond the few words that were sometimes necessary when they encountered each other in the course of the day's work, and then he addressed her so curtly that she had more than once asked him what was biting him and who he thought he was talking to. Emilio always seemed very amused by these brief encounters, and after Fabrio had gone off, he would tap the side of his nose at Sylvia and jerk his thumb after the graceful retreating form of his friend as if he knew some secret about which he would like her to question him. But Sylvia never did question him, for she was a little shy of Fabrio. His silence, his gravity, his unfriendliness towards herself, made him unlike any other man that she had ever known and she could not bring herself to talk about him to Emilio.

One morning towards the middle of January the weather broke; there were two days on which the clouds drifted off in an ever-thinning veil until a sky of milky blue was revealed, in which gleamed a white sun whose faint warmth touched the wings of the robin, the storm-cock, the sparrow and other all-the-year-round birds which at this season possessed almost in solitude the leafless thickets and dripping hedges.

Mr Hoadley was just passing a pleasantry about them all being able to sit out in the garden if this weather went on, and Mrs

Hoadley was just receiving it in silence, when Sylvia looked up from her breakfast, exclaiming:

'Oo, who's that singing?'

A man's voice rang across the farmyard, in a gay and passionate song whose music seemed to be smothering its words in laughing kisses. Mrs Hoadley continued to study yesterday's *Daily Express* with the corners of her mouth turned down, and Mr Hoadley's face expressed only tolerance for the habits of foreigners, but the dog Ruffler, who was near the fire, lifted his head from his paws and thumped with his tail on the warm bricks, while Sylvia's eyes opened wider and wider.

'Is that Emilio?' she gasped at last. 'Gosh! fancy him being able to sing like that! Why, he ought to go on the air!'

'Emilio's singing too but I think it's Fabrio who's making the most noise,' retorted Mrs Hoadley, briskly folding the *Daily Express* into a neat packet and getting up from her chair. 'Now, Neil, if you want me to go into Horsham this morning will you please let me have that list; I've got my chickens to do before I go.'

Sylvia ran across the yard, with the sunlight falling warmly on her laughing, excited face. The song had now ceased.

'Fabrio!' she cried, waving the hat she had snatched up, 'congratulations! I didn't know you could sing like that—didn't know you could sing at all! You're marvellous—you ought to go on the air!'

She halted at the door of the little shed where the two Italians hung their overcoats each morning, and peered in. All was damp and shadowy within and for a moment she was dazzled; then she saw Emilio's face grinning up at her as he knelt to lace his boot. Fabrio stood and stared at her in haughty silence.

'I mean it!' she cried again, making an emphatic downward movement with the hat. 'I adore music and you can take it from old Maestro Sylvia, you're simply wizard!'

Emilio, who understood more English than Fabrio, turned

and said something to the latter which caused him to look haughtier than ever; then suddenly a quick, childish smile lit up his face, his eyes—even his hair, glossy as a chestnut, seemed to take on additional sheen from the sunlight and his own pleasure. But the smile went in an instant, and after one glance at Sylvia, he turned indifferently away and began to arrange his coat carefully upon its peg.

She, after repeating vehemently, 'I mean it, comrade,' lingered for a moment as if expecting him to speak, and, when he continued to be silent, turned away and walked aimlessly back to the house, feeling slightly annoyed that she had made advances towards him. What a sourpuss he is, she thought; I'm quite willing to be friends if only he would. I don't like him much but I don't see any point in going on like this; it isn't my fault I'm an enemy alien—and, come to that, what's he?

For she believed that his dislike of her was due to the fact that her country had defeated his own in armed combat. True, he was officially described as a collaborator and as working his passage, but that would not prevent him from expressing his hatred of the English by refusing to be pleasant to them, and this seemed highly foolish to Sylvia.

Before departing for Horsham, Mrs Hoadley put her head out of the car window and called:

'Sylvia, take their milk up to the cottage, will you? They won't be coming down this morning.'

The farmer's wife had encountered Alda on the previous evening and learned that her friend had succumbed to influenza just as all the children were well enough to demand perpetual entertaining but not well enough to come downstairs, and she knew that Alda would not want to spend twenty minutes in going for the milk and bringing it back again. Although she was impatient of 'that cottage lot,' her sense of justice compelled her to dispatch Sylvia.

Sylvia fetched the cans and went singing across the meadow.

She had not seen any of the inhabitants of the cottage since the evening of her arrival, and from that occasion she retained a sense of grievance because they had not asked her into the house; she also dimly resented the peaceful slumber in which the cottage was presumably sunk on those black dawns while she tramped about with heavy trusses and buckets, but these feelings were not strong, for her lively animal spirits made her ready to be friends with anyone.

She clashed the cans down on the step with a ringing 'Milk-o!'

Alda put her head out of the porch window and said: 'Oh— thank you very much. I couldn't have got down this morning: everybody's ill.'

This announcement left small impression upon Sylvia, who was never ill, but she made the face which she tilted up towards Alda look sympathetic.

'That's all right,' she answered vaguely, thinking how pretty Alda was, while Alda in her turn admired the eyes, the hair, and the complexion.

'How are you liking it at the farm?' Alda went on, with an interest half-motherly and half-inquisitive.

'It's beastly work but somehow I don't mind it, and the food's marvellous, only I'm crazy to get back to my real job, of course.'

'What *is* your real job?' indulging an obvious desire to be asked.

'Acting. The stage. Oo, I just can't wait to get started! I was training at the Canonbury Academy of Dramatic Art. My father was an actor.'

'Really? How interesting. I wonder if I know his name?'

'Oh—I don't expect you would, he was pretty ham, and only did tatty little parts in the provinces,' with an embarrassed laugh. 'He did play once in the West End, though, with Dennis Eadie, just after the last war, in *Milestones*, for sixteen performances. Before I was born, that was.'

'And you're very keen on it?' Alda ignored the slice of family history, upon which, indeed, no comment was possible.

'I adore it. It's my life,' solemnly. 'And I *know* I can act. I *feel* it.'

'It was bad luck your being called up,' said Alda sympathetically: she ought to have been carrying round washing-water to the invalids but she lingered, for the sun was pleasant and she found this hearty child amusing.

'Oh well, I wasn't exactly called up, but I was scared stiff I would be any minute, so I chucked up the Academy and volunteered for the land, so as to be sure of not being shoved into a factory.'

'This is your first job, then?'

'Yes—*and* my last, on the land. As soon as H.M. Government takes the irons off my legs, I've had it. Well,' she grinned and pushed her hat further on to the back of her head, 'I must get back. Bye-bye.'

'*Good*-bye,' said Alda—with emphasis: Ronald discouraged the translation of *God be with you* into the language of the nursery. 'Will you come and have tea with us when we are all better?'

'Oo, I'd love to. Thanks awfully. I do get one afternoon off a week,' and she strode away.

What an overwhelming young woman, but rather attractive, all the same, thought Alda. I will ask her for the same afternoon as Mr Waite. She's too young and crude to queer Jean's pitch; Jean will shine by contrast.

For the next week the invalids were occupied in recovering from influenza, languidly picking at the meals prepared by Alda (who mercifully did not catch the infection) and, in the case of Jenny and Louise, looking forward with apprehension to the day upon which they would go to the convent school.

The central-heating apparatus was being inspected and the mattresses from the dormitories were being hung out of the windows to air, after the custom at the mother-convent at Rouen in Normandy. The playground was emerging from the mantle of slush beneath which it had slumbered for the past month. There was even bustle in the convent; the airy, silent corridors with their tenderly smiling, life-sized statues in brilliant robes standing in every alcove and at every corner, were as peaceful on the day before the one hundred and fifty pupils returned as on any other day of the year, but perhaps the quiet pat-pat of slippered feet down the shining parquet floors was a little more frequent, and there were more conferences between the black-robed figures—'Yes, Sister. No, Sister. That would be it, Sister. Of course, Sister. That was what we heard, Sister'—in the hall and classrooms.

Sister Alban, the directress, was a sturdy middle-aged woman whose clear light eyes behind thick glasses were shrewd and secretive. She had a manner expressing great common sense and practical ability; she liked to lead the parents of prospective pupils through the large, light classrooms with their well-spaced modern desks, and to point out the view across the little lake and the groups of lime trees that in summer would waft down gusts of delicious scent and showers of creamy-green petals on the walks of the park. True, Sister Alban did not hold out these delights as an inducement to hesitating parents; she concentrated upon the advantages of spring mattresses and the lack of over-crowding in the convent, but such parents as were foolishly imaginative and open to the siren impressions of *atmosphere*, were ravished by those lime groves, those gleaming silent corridors with their fresh flowers and heavy curtains draped in graceful folds, that glimpse of the chapel with its snowy lace and crimson damask, and, beyond all, by the peace: the heavenly, refreshing, soul-sustaining and comforting peace breathed forth by all these objects, combining in harmony and united by the same spirit.

Alda was C. of E., with a very slight prejudice in favour of Low observances rather than High, due to those Dissenting forebears whom we have already mentioned. She was a little lax in her personal religious observances, as people described as C. of E. are apt to be, and she had never considered what might be the rewards of sacrificing the human Will; the rebellious, self-torturing, pride-scourged Will; but had she asked what were those rewards, the spirit that brooded in the convent could have answered her. There was the sacrifice: there was the reward. Side by side they existed, eternally opposed; the one perpetually struggling and the other perpetually incarnating peace, and if everybody on this planet liked peace, the conclusion would be foregone, but hardly anyone does like peace, most people preferring excitement, cigarettes, sex, drink, noise, danger, the pride of the body and fashionable hats.

'The children must be very happy here,' Alda observed to Sister Alban, in the course of the conducted tour.

Sister Alban replied, 'Yes, they are happy,' but in a voice which did not completely satisfy Alda. Her tone was not emphatic and her expression was blank; Alda received the impression that she frequently had to reply to such comments by parents and assumed this poker-face in order to conceal her sentiments. I expect she's wondering why on earth they should be happy, or thinking that if only they're good, they will be, thought Alda.

However, the building was spotless, the nuns' manner was kind, the fees were low and the teaching at convent schools, she had heard, was always excellent. She therefore entered the names of Jane Margarita Lucie-Browne and Louise Eleanor Lucie-Browne as day-pupils upon the register, having first warned Sister Alban that she might have to remove her daughters at short notice if her husband succeeded in persuading the local authorities to build a prefabricated house upon the site of their ruined home in Ironborough. In that case they would all return to Warwickshire to await his demobilisation.

Sister Alban was accommodating over the problem of school uniform, saying that while of course it was desirable that all the pupils should be dressed alike, many of the mothers found this impossible, and sent them to school in any plain dark clothes, but Alda had felt that Jenny and Louise, making their first entry into a large school, must have the help which a conventional appearance could give, and had at once sent an S O S to all the children's aunts, asking for green skirts or frocks or coats that could be converted into the necessary simple dress with plain white collar.

The Lucie-Brownes were at once pleased and dismayed when a large parcel arrived from Father's-Only-Sister-Marion containing two outsize (Marion was outsize) green dresses of fine wool, worn but far from shabby, and enough lawn to make each schoolgirl three collars.

> Lucky for you that this is a favourite colour of mine [wrote Marion]. The collars, I thought, could easily be washed and they could have a clean one three times a week. Jenny ought to have riding lessons this spring; John is getting along splendidly and is going in for a jumping competition on Bumblebee at the gymkhana here in March. I enclose a cheque to pay for twelve lessons for Jenny. I noticed how envious she looked when John and Richard were talking about Bumblebee the last time we saw you.

Alda put the cheque away in her handbag with a compression of the lips, even as did Mrs March under similar circumstances in *Little Women*. She thought that she would keep the promise of riding lessons a secret for the present; for, if days became very dark at the convent, a pleasant surprise would help Jenny to support them. Louise, of course, was sure to grumble and weep and despair over her first weeks at school because she always did over any kind of novelty or change.

12

'She likes your voice,' said Emilio to Fabrio, with his face alight with mockery, as the lorry carried them to work the next morning. It was eight o'clock and the sun had not yet risen, but brightness was mounting steadily into the sky over the flooded eastern meadows; black grass blades shivered in the wind across sheets of radiant water, and billows of yellow cloud were dissolving before the sun's approach. Fabrio sat among his brown-clad companions with his face turned towards the light, singing as loudly as the rest a chorus from a popular Italian operetta, and the driver, an English soldier with a resigned expression, bumped them along over the rutted roads.

Emilio felt refreshed and lively in the morning light and ready to tease, but Fabrio did not want to talk about that girl with a monkey's mug and shameless clothes; better not to remember her eyes wide with admiration of his singing; she made him angry; she was not like a girl at all; she was like a tall boy with a loud voice; a boy who was a little, a very little, taller than he was. So in reply to Emilio, he only nodded.

'I know something better, yes, much better, than tha-at!' he sang gaily in a moment, to the air from the operetta. 'I have had a letter, yes, a letter, from who? from who do you think?'

He slipped his hand into the breast of his overcoat and brought out one of the regulation envelopes sent to Italian prisoners of war, addressed in a neat pointed hand feminine as a silk stocking.

'A girl! Does it smell sweet?' and Emilio snatched at it but Fabrio held it just out of reach, smiling at his friend, while his face caught the golden advance from the rising sun.

'From a girl, yes! a girl. Twenty years old, with beautiful——'

Fabrio made an immemorial admiring gesture, 'and her name is Maria.'

'Well! and now I suppose you're happy?' said Emilio sarcastically. Emilio himself received copious letters from his wife every two or three days mostly concerned with such matters as boots, macaroni, the rent, and the misdoings and progress of the *bambini*, but Fabrio had no regular correspondents, and this made him exceptional among the prisoners: the Italian soldier is the most written-to combatant in the world, judging by the letters scattered over any battlefield on which he has fought, and fallen. Very occasionally did Fabrio receive a letter, and they were always short and laboriously written in a hand so clumsy as to be almost unreadable, and Fabrio, without encouraging comment, let it be known that the writer was his elder brother Giuseppe. Emilio, who had been born in the slums of Genoa and been forced to school by the *Fascisti*, had used his quick wits to master reading and writing thoroughly, and those same wits had long ago told him the secret that Fabrio was so haughtily trying to conceal. But he kept it a secret, and he, who loved to jeer at all the world, did not tease Fabrio.

His enormous, quarrelsome, dirty family at home in the Port had once, for a few days, housed a dog: a pedigree red setter belonging to a wealthy old Englishman living in the fashionable quarter, which a member of the Rossi tribe had stolen in hope of obtaining a reward. The dog had fascinated the young Emilio; it was the first creature with fine blood in its veins that he had seen, and in studying its behaviour and habits he had found endless occupation and surprise. He called it *Il Signor* (The Gentleman) and when it had been taken off to be restored to its owner, Emilio, alone of all the family, had seen it go with passionate regret.

Fabrio reminded him of *Il Signor*. He had the same reserve, and the pride softened by gentleness, the same flashes of gaiety and affection, even the same shining chestnut hair. Emilio thought that in many ways both Fabrio and *Il Signor* were fools; slow-witted, half-asleep; and he, the sharp one, the one who was never taken in, despised them both, but had Fabrio confided in him that he was descended from that beautiful *principessa* of the old days, Emilio would not have been in the least surprised, for *Il Signor*, the gentleman-dog (born, as his stealer swore, of a line of dog-princes) and Fabrio Caetano had the same air.

'She lives over the other side of the hills from our place,' Fabrio went on, while the chorus of another popular song soared tunefully all about him, 'but she has been away working in a shop in Santa Margherita,' (here he resumed a conversational tone) 'she is a friend of my sisters.'

'And of yours, no doubt, poor girl!'

'A little,' said Fabrio, and smiled.

But the smile quickly faded, as he remembered that last night before Maria had left her home to go to Santa Margherita. It had been during the grape harvest, and he and some of his brothers and sisters had walked over the hills to Maria's village, some eight miles away, to strip the blue grapes from their nestling places amidst the green-blue leaves, and pile them, snapped vines and foliage and clusters that were transparent gold where the bloom had been brushed away, into the deep baskets. It was a little harvest but merry, as such festivals always were; they had sung until midnight and laughed much and danced to the music from the wireless that was old Amato's pride, and then, with aching arms and hands still sticky with bloom and sap, the young ones had set out to walk home, still singing as they went, by the path that ran in and out of olive groves a hundred feet above the sea. In the warm moonlight they followed the narrow white path as it climbed or descended among the groves; the cicada hidden in the grass shrilled swiftly, and far below, between falling terraces of unstirring white leaves, moved and murmured the sea, dark between those leaves, but silver where it touched the cliffs. Now and again Fabrio's wet shirt lifted coolly against his breast as a faint gust of wind stirred the groves and died away; his arm was about Maria's waist and he looked down on her black head and felt her soft side warm against his own.

The lorry stopped with a jolt that flung the men forward in confusion. How wet and cold everything is! thought Fabrio, jumping down into the muddy road; even the sun feels cold in this horrible country, and in a minute I shall see her—she who has no proper feelings and does not appreciate me.

'And is little Maria going to write to you regularly?' asked Emilio as they tramped along the causeway through the marshy meadows.

'I am not quite sure what she says.' Fabrio felt in his pocket again and brought out the letter. He held it out, saying simply:

'Read it to me, my Emilio.'

Thereupon the sharp one, the one who was never taken in, Nature's nose-tapper, read rapidly and faithfully aloud:

'Dear Fabrio,

'How surprised you will be to see the name at the end of this letter—Maria Amato! For two years I did not know where you were and your sisters did not answer my letters, and I did not go home because of my stepfather. Now he is dead, and I am at home again to look after my mother, who is ill. I walked over to San Angelo and saw your sister Gioja and she told me where you were. Now I will tell you all the news. Your father walks with a stick now. They got three barrels of wine from your harvest last year. Your nephew Antonio is very strong and fat and last week your sister Elena had a girl, a niece for you. Her name is Giulia. I will write to you every week if you would like me to. I hope you are well. Our Lady bless and keep you.

'Your friend,
'Maria Amato.'

'Thank you,' said Fabrio, who had listened with bent head to every word, when Emilio had finished. 'I knew about the wine, Giuseppe told me. So I have a nephew! And Elena is married! And who to, I wonder? They never told me. And a niece, too!'

'That is nothing surprising. It is only surprising that there are not more. When once they start coming –' and Emilio spread his hands helplessly abroad. 'She's beautiful, you say, this Maria?' he went on.

'Yes. On Sundays she has a black silk dress with white lace round the neck and black silk stockings.'

'Is she little or big, eh?'

'Little; little and round.'

'Is she a blonde?' demanded Emilio; he knew that the girls in the northern mountainous regions, where Fabrio came from, often had fair hair. It is an inheritance, perhaps, from some Gothic ancestress who crossed the mountain passes with the barbarian hordes in the sixth century.

But Fabrio answered blithely:

'Yes, she is a blonde.'

'Ah, you lucky dog!' cried Emilio, looking at him with a new respect. 'And a fair complexion, eh?'

'Yes.'

'Ah-ha, I can just see her! And how do you feel about her?'

Fabrio smiled but did not answer. He never spoke of his thoughts: 'What an Italian thinks remains his own treasure hidden away in a safe, to the unlocking of which he alone guards the elaborate secret,'* and to the natural secrecy of his subtle race he added the inarticulacy of a peasant.

'You'll have to write to her, you know,' said Emilio not without malice: friendship was all very well, but now that Fabrio had a correspondent at home, and a blonde one at that, one could no

* Bernard Berenson.

129

longer pity him quite so much: one felt a little envy and one's feelings would have vent. 'You'd better let me do it for you.'

Fabrio shook his head.

'You're my friend,' he said, dropping his arm for an instant round Emilio's shoulders. 'But I will ask Father Francesco to help me.'

Father Francis was incumbent of the little Roman Catholic church at Sillingham. He heard the confessions of such of the Italian prisoners as attended the services there and administered the Sacraments to them.

'You'd better stick to me,' muttered Emilio, who was not devout, and they shouldered mattocks and spades in readiness for the day's work.

Sylvia had now determined to be friendly towards Fabrio, for her policy of international co-operation, her natural sociability, and an unconscious desire to break down his reserve all suggested the same line of behaviour. But she did not get much opportunity, because he avoided her. She would have approached him with comments on the weather and the work a dozen times a day, but he simply hid.

At first Mrs Hoadley had kept a sharp eye on the three of them. Her own chilly nature would not have suspected Goings On had not the frequency, indeed, the inevitability, of Goings On between men and women, of all kinds, and almost all ages, been so often thrust under her fastidious nose. But within limits she was a shrewd judge of character and she quickly discovered that Sylvia was innocent in mind and body. Her boldness was a child's boldness, and any coarseness of speech or forwardness of behaviour sprang from inexperience. There's no harm in her, the silly great lump, decided Mrs Hoadley.

And in Fabrio she detected sensitiveness. He was lazy, deceitful, insolent at times, but he was not gross, and she thought that he avoided Sylvia because she was 'loud.'

'She gets on his nerves,' said Mrs Hoadley to Mr Hoadley.

'Nerves!' was all Mr Hoadley said, and moved his big boot as though the toes itched.

Emilio was quite another matter; Emilio would be up to goodness-knew-what if he got the chance, but Sylvia did not give him the chance. Had not Mrs Hoadley herself, from an upper window, seen Sylvia give Emilio a push that sent him sprawling? That told you all you wanted to know. Quite right too; there were enough things a girl had to put up with anyway, later on, without horrible suggestions from low foreigners.

So they were lucky, she told Mr Hoadley, to employ a straight girl like Sylvia and an Italian like Fabrio, 'who didn't care about that sort of thing and had some self-respect'; between them, Emilio's low habits had no chance. Mr Hoadley, who was not such a shrewd judge of character, expressed agreement and, feeling that sufficient unto the day was the evil thereof, kept his intuitions to himself.

'Dear Mr Waite,' began a note which Mr Waite discovered in his letter-box on returning from Horsham some days later,

> I have now read all the books you kindly lent me and would like to return them to you. It would be so nice if you could come to tea on Wednesday afternoon about four o'clock. I hope that this is not an inconvenient time for you.
>
> We shall look forward to seeing you.
>
> > Yours sincerely,
> > Alda Lucie-Browne.

He carefully replaced the note in its envelope and arranged it on the mantelpiece before going upstairs to put on his slippers. His boots he had left in the porch.

Meadow Cottage, the house in which he lived, was another Prewitt perpetration, and even smaller, darker and more inconvenient than Pine Cottage. He had taken it partly furnished, and the peculiarly hideous pictures, and the ghastly shades (conjuring visions of vaults and crypts) of blue and pink favoured by Mrs Prewitt were strongly in evidence, but the cottage was not dirty, because an old woman who lived on the Froggatt road trudged out every day, wet or fine, to take up ashes, lay fires, dust, sweep and scrub, impelled by that Victorian spirit of devotion to the male, just as a male, which lingers on in most women over sixty. (Its gradual disappearance from domestic life is the cause of that silent, bewildered grief, that sense of aching loss, felt by many men who do not realise what is the matter with them.)

In his icy, neat bedroom, with the large photograph of Mother and The Girls on the mantelpiece, he thought over the invitation as he put on his slippers. He wondered what she (this Mrs Lucie-Browne) was Up To. She probably wanted something. Money? No, that was going a bit far; she looked a silly, excitable woman but she had, in spite of her shabbiness, an air of solvency. Advice? That was more likely; husband abroad, three kiddies to bring up, equally silly friend staying with her (oh yes, he knew about the friend; the man who delivered the groceries had told him); she probably wanted advice. What about? Might be anything from gardening to drains.

Eggs! Of course! Three growing kiddies to feed. Mr Waite surely can't want to send all his eggs to the packing station; he must have a few to spare for his friends. Let's ask him to tea and try and get round him. Well, she would find that he was not so easy to get round. He stood up and took off his jacket, replacing it by the shabbier one he wore in the house.

There is always a sense of surprise in the beholder when a shapely figure and handsome face produce an unpleasing effect. Mr Waite looked as if he walked perpetually in a cloud composed of suspicion, grievances and disapproval. The faces of Mother and The Girls, now looking out at the empty room through the lengthening spring dusk as their son and brother went heavily downstairs, offered no clue to the impression he gave. The girls were three in number; square, bonny women in the late thirties with cheerful faces and determinedly fashionable hair and surprisingly smart jumpers, while mother resembled a handsome rabbit. On the other side of the mantelpiece was Dad, a small but dynamic personality in horn rims.

Dad had been a self-made rich man, and when his only son was twenty-two Dad had lost everything; plant, capital, goodwill and all.

His son had expected to go into the business and had been trained for nothing else. He had had to leave Cambridge after only a few months there, and had returned to a home and a life in which there was no place for him. In the hearts of his mother and sisters there would always be a place, for he had been spoilt and loved from babyhood, but family life and some dull, badly-paid job naturally offered no attractions to him. His father died soon after the financial ruin, and while Mrs Waite moved into a small house with the choicest pieces of family furniture and china and the daughters energetically set about training as typist, nurse and masseuse, the son roamed the surrounding dales and hills in the car he must soon sell, raging at Fate and developing that sense of grievance which had never left him.

His sight was defective. During the Second World War he had served as a clerk in the R.A.S.C., without seeing foreign service, and after demobilisation he had expended his gratuity, the pay he had saved, and a small legacy from a relative, upon the chicken farm where we now behold him.

Between the Wars he had tried other jobs; as traveller for an old-established firm of publishers, the selling of insurance policies upon commission, a clerkship in a well-known and prosperous firm of house agents in Bristol. None of these posts had been poorly paid or degrading but in none of them had he been either contented or successful. He had always had a grievance, and he had always wanted to be his own master.

Now he was his own master—(or thought he was; actually, the chickens had him roped and tied).

He had left Daleham because he could not endure that the old family friends and neighbours should see him in reduced circumstances; but the place still held his affections, and anything that reminded him of his former comfortable, careless life there had a charm for him. Alda's invitation came in this category, and in spite of suspecting Mrs Lucie-Browne of being Up To Something (in which he was quite right) he immediately decided to accept her invitation.

'It'll be quite a riot for us, won't it, having two people to tea on the first day the infants go to school,' observed Jean to Alda, on Tuesday evening.

'Oh damn, I'd forgotten,' said Alda irritably. 'What a bore. Well, it can't be helped now.'

They were sitting beside the fire in the little parlour, Alda with her knitting and Jean with one of those apricot or rose-coloured silk undergarments in which she was for ever inserting fresh lace or repairing minute damages. Before the Second World War Alda used to see her making new ones, in elegant designs cut by herself from expensive patterns, and fashioned from the finest stuffs with exquisite tiny stitches, and it had always irritated her; she called it pussyish. Her own undergarments were shabby and fresh like those of a well-kept, gently-bred child, and except to swear when something wore out or snapped she never thought about them.

Jean had now been at Pine Cottage for almost a month, and Alda liked having her there, for the slight annoyance which she experienced when Jean went up to London to see 'the lawyers' or 'the agents' or 'a china-wallah' or 'a carpet-wallah' was coun-terbalanced by the usefulness of having a guardian for the children when Alda wanted to go out by herself, and cheerful, efficient help with the household and catering duties. There were several offers under discussion for the remainder of the lease of the Hardcastles' flat but so far nothing had been decided, and Jean hoped that Alda would put up with her until March, when Ronald would get his next leave.

'And to-morrow morning I'll beetle off into Horsham and get the cakes,' she said now, glancing at the clock, yawning, and beginning to put her work away in tissue paper. 'Isn't it a relief those frocks are done!' She glanced at a side table where the two green dresses with their white collars made by herself were displayed for the benefit of the schoolgirls.

'Yes. You really are a brick,' said Alda, also putting away her work. 'I'm sorry I've been snappy all day. The fact is, I don't want them to go to school. I know they've got to, but I just don't want it.'

'Oh, I expect they'll adore it when they've got over the first shock. Infants all seem to love school nowadays. It's different from when we were kids.'

'I didn't mind school but of course the holidays were the thing.'

'I hated the holidays, except when I stayed with you.'

'Mother adored school,' said Alda. 'She was a boarder at the North London Collegiate in the nineties. It was a jolly good school but they had no end of a time; it seems to have been a cross between a comic opera and a concentration camp.'

'All boarding schools are,' said Jean, who had been to five of them before settling, at twelve, in the school attended by Alda and her sisters. 'It's foully cold. Should you think the snow's coming back?'

'I hope not. I don't like the idea of those nuns driving a car on frozen roads.'

But the next morning it was snowing fast.

13

'Here she comes.'

'Shut up, Ann, leave me alone.'

'Yes, be quiet, everybody, we don't want a row *before* prayers as well as after.'

The car, competently driven by the chilblained young hands and feet of Sister Benedict, slowly drew up opposite the group of children standing on the corner. The door opened, and a fresh and worried face framed in white and black looked out at them.

'Good morning, Sister!'

'Did you have nice holidays, Sister?'

'Good morning, Sister!'

Jenny and Louise kept to the back of the group, pale and silent.

'Good morning, children. Och, the roads are like glass this morning,' lamented Sister Benedict. 'Now in ye get, quickly. Don't ye begin the new term with pushing, Ann Cotter. And who are *ye*?' fixing her eyes, with this Biblical inquiry, upon the Lucie-Brownes.

'Jenny Lucie-Browne,' said Jenny, slightly encouraged by a smile, 'and this is my sister, Louise. We're new.'

'Och yes, ye're in Sister Matthew's form, I remember. Now don't dawdle, in ye get,' and Ann slammed the door on Louise.

The trees and hedges were veiled in frost and the road slippery and treacherous under the ice, and Sister kept up a soft perpetual lament in her Irish voice: 'Och, it's nothing but glass, it's terribly dangerous unless I go slowly and I don't want to be after being late to school with ye all, och, it's shocking, the snow and the ice.'

Alda had left her daughters to await the convent's car, thinking that they might be embarrassed by the presence of their mother. But Louise and Jenny were not yet of an age to suffer this particular shame, and they were not yet schoolgirls; they were still children, longing for their mother when she was absent and delighting in her presence. Her departure was the last straw; Jenny was defiant and already in deadly feud with the lively Ann, and in Louise's throat there ached a large lump which made her dread being spoken to in case she found that she could not reply.

Jenny, who was not shy, had been encouraged by the liveliness of the waiting group, but the other two had instantly banded themselves against herself and Louise and crushed snowballs down their necks with furious excitement, and their attempts at polite conversation had been met with giggles and whispers. They were bewildered and angry. These children were rough and horrid. The convent would be horrid too. It was all horrid.

Then, as soon as Sister Benedict appeared, a hush had fallen upon the other two. Long faces, lowered eyes, arms and legs well under control, transformed them. When Jenny ventured to pipe out a remark four eyes were turned upon her in exaggerated surprise and horror and Sister said absently:

'Ye must not talk, Jenny Lucie-Browne.'

Ann made a triumphant face at her, and as the car turned in through the iron gates, Jenny felt despairingly that it was entering a prison.

Bless them, they'll be all right, thought Alda as she walked homeward; that nun looked so serene and kind.

Sylvia had only one idea about a party: you made yourself look as smart as you possibly could. Therefore, a full hour before the time she was expected at Pine Cottage, she might have been seen in her low chamber under the roof, earnestly rubbing rouge over her full pale cheeks and elevating the pompadour (freshly re-dyed the previous week in Horsham) to new and fearsome heights. Below this erection her blood-coloured mouth suddenly popped out at the beholder like a small piece of raw steak, but her lovely eyes, blue as love-in-a-mist, smiled out at the world, ready to enjoy anything and anybody. Some people find this attitude disarming. When she had zipped herself into a black dress with a high neck and much drapery over the hips and skirt, she looked ready for a cocktail almost anywhere. It was a nuisance that rubber boots had to be drawn over her only pair of silk stockings, but that was what life in the country was like.

Over at Meadow Cottage, Mr Waite was frowningly replacing his black tie with red spots by a dark blue tie with grey spots. This duty to the conventions paid, he set out, glancing searchingly at the chickens as he passed between the coops. They in their turn glanced as searchingly back at him. This is all very well, my boy, they seemed to be saying, but how about our tea and supper? Off you go; enjoy yourself; we understand as well as anyone; but no forgetting Us.

'What are you doing, ducky?' Jean demanded mildly of Alda, coming down from her room to find her apparently engaged, half an hour before the party was due, in turning out the parlour.

'Can't bear this beastly furniture another minute,' said Alda, lifting a flushed face as she steadily pushed an armchair down the passage. 'I've taken down all the pictures and just put that enormous marmalade jar full of ivy trails on the mantelpiece and oh—you go in and look. It looks heaps better.'

Jean, whose taste ran to the amply curtained and upholstered, looked round the transformed parlour, forlornly bare in the spring light, and did not agree. The parlour was the type of room which looks the better for being filled up and covered up. But there is a lovely fire, she thought, and it was a good idea to cover the settee with that Persian shawl, it's such a rich silky blue.

Jean was one of those women whom the rationing of clothing does not seem to affect. She was so slender, light on her feet, and conventional in her activities that she was not 'hard on her clothes'; she always seemed to possess silk stockings; and in the winter she appeared, and had steadily appeared throughout the war years, in dresses made of the finest, lightest wool, occasionally even Angora wool, in soft hues of orange or turquoise or dove; materials and colours which ordinary women had simply forgotten about or only remembered in fevered dreams. With these, she wore diamonds: a diamond clip shaped like a feather, a diamond ring shaped like a smaller feather, and diamond earrings shaped like two smallest feathers of all. That was how she was dressed this afternoon.

'Are you going to change?' she now asked Alda, who was taking some ivy out of the marmalade jar.

'Shan't bother,' glancing down at her old tweed suit, 'besides, there isn't time.' She suddenly cast a glance over her friend.

'You look very nice,' she said approvingly, and her eyes, her mouth, all of her, seemed to light up with mischief. 'Good hunting,' she said, and dropped a light kiss on Jean's cheek.

Jean returned the kiss with a quick embrace, but although her manner had the usual mingling of shy excitement and amusement which she had displayed during the past fifteen years, whenever Alda had introduced her to a new man, for the first time on such an occasion, she was neither excited, shy nor amused. Instead, she felt slightly bored. Upstairs on her bedside table there was Ethel Mannin's new story and an unopened packet of cigarettes, and she would sooner have passed the afternoon in their company.

Precisely at four o'clock there came an impressive knock upon the front door. With some vague thoughts of Mr Waite and military habits of punctuality, Alda went to answer it, and there, shining down upon her from a great height, was the pompadour.

'Oo, am I too early?' asked Sylvia, but obviously the question was rhetorical; it was not possible to be too early for a party.

'Of course not, do come in. I'm so glad you could come,' and she was leading the way to the parlour when at the foot of the stairs Sylvia paused.

'May I just run up and change my shoes? *Look* at these awful things!' displaying her boots.

'Of course. I'll show you the way.'

After some eight minutes of powdering, patting and peering in front of Alda's mirror, she disposed her coat and scarf upon the bed, changed into shoes with extremely high heels, and rustled (how does she manage to rustle? thought Alda, catching the unfamiliar sound) downstairs after her hostess. As she went, she breathed forth perfumes.

After being introduced to Jean, she sat down upon the edge of the settee, very upright, and smiled dazzlingly; she more than smiled, she wrinkled up her small nose in a monkey's grimace as if the excitement of being alive were suddenly too much for her.

'Oo, it is lovely to be at a party again!' she cried, glancing round the room and then at the two ladies. 'That's the one thing I *do* miss down here, parties!'

'You look very nice,' said Alda, greatly amused, and attracted, as ever, by cheerfulness.

'Oo, this is my only really smashing dress. I bought it from one of the girls at the school, ever so inexpensive, it was. And look!——' she slid up her skirt and revealed, first a large leg tightly covered in silk and bound by a blue garter, and next the crisp, shelly ruffles of a blue taffeta petticoat. Alda and Jean exclaimed with genuine admiration, and both were favourably impressed by the perfect freshness of the exhibits.

'My mother made it. Out of a piece she had by her.'

'It's beautifully made,' said Jean, recognising the hand of an expert.

'Mum is a dressmaker, that's her profession. She's wizard at it. Dad died about four years ago and ever since then she's done everything for us.'

'Are there lots of you?' smiled Alda. 'I thought you came from a large family. So do I.'

'Eight,' said Sylvia, and laughed outright.

'There are six of us. Are you the eldest?'

'No, Bob, he's the eldest. He's twenty-six. Mum was married twice, see, and her first husband left her a little bit of money (of course, I don't approve of that, being a Communist, but it came in very handy) and then she married Dad and had me and Shirley and Alan. Then there's Hugo, and Iris, Lily, and Sybil, she's the baby. All Communists,' she ended, beaming.

'What, even Sybil? Poor little Sybil!'

'Oo, she loves it. She's nine. She goes out selling the *Daily Worker* on Saturdays. Not for money, of course; just to help the Party.'

Alda and Jean, who were hugely enjoying all this and congratulating themselves upon having secured such an entertaining guest, were here recalled to more sober thoughts by a deep, melancholy dab upon the front door; it had a distinct suggestion of the tolling bell, and they glanced at one another with the same thought: how would Sylvia go down with Mr Waite? Well, it could not be helped now. I hope he isn't a Blimp, thought Alda, as she hastened down the passage, but judging by that evening in the car, he may well be.

'Good afternoon, Mr Waite, I'm so glad that you could come. Oh—let me take that,' seeing him glancing doubtfully about for a place to put his hat, 'there's nowhere to put it here, I'm afraid, we must take it into the sitting-room. Do come in,' and she led him towards the parlour, his own contribution consisting of mutters and gestures with the hat.

A room cannot look completely unattractive when it contains three pretty young women and a bright fire, and even Mr Waite, who had come prepared to be wooed into amiability, felt amiable sooner than he had intended as he surveyed the scene. After the presentations were over he seated himself in the most comfortable chair, and prevented a silence from falling (not that he noticed the threat) by staring round the room and exclaiming:

'What's happened to all the furniture?'

'Oh, I suddenly couldn't bear it another minute, so I moved it into the woodshed,' said Alda cheerfully, holding out the cigarette box, 'but it's all coming back this evening.'

'Into the *woodshed*? But from what I remember of the size of the woodshed here, and the amount of furniture there was in this room, you could hardly get it all into the woodshed. (Thank you.)'

'It was rather a squeeze, but I managed. (Have you a match?— Oh, Jean—your lighter—thank you.)'

'There were some heavy pieces, too,' pursued Mr Waite, having acknowledged the offer of the lighter with a shake of the head at Jean, a mutter, and the production of one of those extremely large, heavy military lighters in yellow metal which suggest to the nervous the possibility of explosions.

'Not very heavy, if you made up your mind.'

'Quite nice pieces, as I remember them,' said Mr Waite, reprovingly.

'Oh no, definitely nasty,' said Alda, who was beginning to feel slightly hysterical.

'"*Something nasty in the woodshed,*"' said Jean. 'Alda darling, shall I go and make the tea? The children will be in any minute.'

'Please, J. Er—are you lucky enough to have your own possessions at Meadow Cottage, Mr Waite?'

'I took it partly furnished. There are some nice pieces there too, but not so nice as here, as I remember them.' (He talks as if they were all dead and I wish they were, thought Alda.) 'Well, if you are going to move them all back in here this evening, I must help you.'

'Oh no—it's most kind of you—but really——'

'You cannot possibly move those heavy pieces of furniture by yourself,' said Mr Waite sternly. 'I must help you.'

'That will be kind of you; thank you very much,' said Alda brightly.

She opened her mouth to introduce the subject of her daughters' first day at the convent school, when Sylvia, who had all this time sat in silence staring at Mr Waite, said loudly:

'I don't expect you remember me, do you, Mr Waite?'

'I remember you perfectly,' answered Mr Waite at once, turning upon her a disapproving look which proved that his ignoring of her presence had been deliberate, 'but for the moment I did not recognise you.' His handsome gloomy eyes took in the raw steak, the pompadour and what Alda now only saw by the bright afternoon light: a sheen of blue upon Sylvia's eyelashes.

'I expect I look a bit different from the way I do every day,' she said, colouring and looking annoyed. 'You can't make yourself look anything in those awful duds they make you wear, it's a treat to get out of them.'

'It is not a becoming dress for a lady,' said Mr Waite, and his audience felt that neither were mucking out cowsheds nor moving heavy pieces of furniture becoming occupations for ladies. He implied that somewhere there were ladies who did dress and behave becomingly; who wore tightly-buttoned, pale gloves and knots of sweet peas among their laces while they poured out the tea and listened to the gentlemen talking.

'Of course, I'm only doing this work temporary,' said Sylvia defiantly.

'Miss Scorby is going on the stage as soon as the Government releases her,' said Alda, now feeling that there were few things she would enjoy better than shocking Mr Waite.

'A very hard life,' was Mr Waite's contribution.

'Oo, I shan't mind that. My father was an actor—Sylvester Scorby—you may have heard of him.'

Alda glanced at her, then glanced away, remembering those remarks about 'pretty ham,' but if the child wanted to glorify her father's memory, that was touching and right.

Mr Waite shook his head.

'A very hard life—especially for a lady,' he repeated, then stood up as Jean came in with a tray.

'I must help you,' he said with an awkward smile.

I wish he wouldn't say he *must* help us, as if it were a sort of curse laid on him by Heaven, thought Alda, carefully not catching Jean's eye, and observing that Sylvia had leant back and crossed her legs and was not going to help anybody except by displaying four inches of the petticoat.

'Oh, thank you,' said Jean, smiling up at him and letting him take the tray. All her diamonds, large and small, glittered in a late gleam of sunlight that had found its way through the screening laurels, and this accounted for his first definite thought about her: *she must have money.*

Soon the cups of tea were distributed, and everybody was eating bread and butter or a sandwich and Sylvia was dominating the conversation, as she always did where more than three people were present; only a *tête-à-tête* with someone who enjoyed eating, talking and showing off more than she herself did, could force *her* into the part of listener.

'——where I was trained, the Canonbury School of Dramatic Art, it's three big houses; you know, regular mid-Victorian mansions, all knocked into one. Oo, we did have a wizard time there! I'd give anything to be back. On V.E. night, do you know what me and a lot of others did?'

Pause, while the eyes, positively darting sapphire sparkles of joy and mischief, roved round the circle of faces. Alda and Jean were sparkling a little themselves but were trying to look merely pleasant and entertained and Mr Waite was looking extremely severe.

'Well, all us girls put on our trousers so's not to spoil our good clothes (I had an awful old Lana Turner, too, *miles* too tight it was, it looked simply *awful*, so I pinched one of the boys' coats, Benjy, a Jewish boy he was) and then we all went down into the West End. Crowds! You never saw anything like the *people*! And everybody dancing and singing and letting off crackers——'

'Highly dangerous,' put in Mr Waite in a tone of melancholy satisfaction. 'Easily blind anyone or cripple them for life.'

'——Oo I know, but that was part of the fun. Me and my friend Marie, she's a Polish refugee, her people are rolling in money, not that that makes any difference to me, of course, I'm a Communist——'

Here Mr Waite gave a sardonic nod. I knew it, said the nod; I was expecting it. Necromancy and the Black Mass to follow.

'——and she never has a dime anyway, they lost it all when Uncle Joe liberated Poland, she and I, we believe in *living dangerously*, you know, like Nietzsche said. Oo, we did have a lovely time! Do you know what we did? The boys got hold of one of those wooden carts the roadmen take round, and all us girls climbed on to it and the boys began to pull it downhill and it went quicker and quicker, and the boys couldn't stop it, it was so heavy with all of us on it, and it began to *run away*! And did we scream! Oh boy, oh boy, we sounded like all the werewolves in Germany! And everybody was looking at us! Oo, it was lovely! And then what do you think happened?'

'The police arrived, I hope,' said Mr Waite.

'No—I tore my trousers! They caught on something on the cart and I pulled and tried to get free and the next minute there was a r-r-r-r-r! and I nearly fell off the cart. It was simply flying down the hill now, the boys couldn't keep up with it. And me with this awful hole in my trousers! Right on the seat!'

'Do have some more tea, Mr Waite,' said Jean, holding out a white hand and a slender arm draped in a soft orange-coloured sleeve, for his cup. He gave it to her and noticed that her eyes were brown, rather unusual, he thought, dark eyes and fair hair.

'And then what happened?' asked Alda, feeling that it was time that someone beside Mr Waite commented upon the tale.

'Oo, we all jumped off before it got to the bottom of the hill. I didn't half bruise myself. One of the girls lent me a safety pin to pin up the tear and I was all right. Oo—and then Benjy and me got on the back of a lorry! (It was ever so late by this time, nearly one o'clock, but there was still crowds of people about.) Well, this lorry'd slowed up for the traffic lights, and me and Benjy got on the back! The driver never saw us, and next minute he really got cracking and we simply flew off down the road! Ever so dangerous, it was!'

'It must have been fun,' said Alda, and meant what she said. Jean, in whom no tomboy had ever dwelt, merely looked amused.

'All the others screamed when they saw us go off, but we soon left them behind and there we were, flying along the deserted roads at one in the morning!'

'I thought you said there were crowds of people about,' said Mr Waite; said it with actual disagreeableness, without a smile, and then he turned right round to Jean, so that Sylvia could see nothing but his back, and said loudly: 'Do you know this part of the world, Miss Hardcastle?'

The snub was so crude that Alda felt ashamed for him and sorry for Sylvia, but the latter only made a lightning and completely unembarrassed grimace and, turning to Alda herself, went on with the tale, which grew more alarming as it progressed; Benjy nearly fell off; I nearly fell off; me and Benjy hung on to each other like mad; we didn't half shriek, and so forth.

With the other ear, Alda could hear the decorous exchanges between Jean and Mr Waite. All seemed to be progressing easily enough, but she did not detect a trace of that mutual absorption and discovery which means that two people are attracted. And what a lot she's telling him about herself! thought Alda, slightly disturbed. She really ought to be more discreet. She certainly will be married for her money one of these days unless she and I are both very careful.

'It's nearly dark,' she interrupted Sylvia suddenly, 'the children ought to be in by now.'

'There they are!' exclaimed Jean. 'I'll go and let them in,' and she hurried off to the front door, where the loud, fierce, despairing attack upon the knocker seemed to indicate that someone was in a bad way.

'Well, duckies?' she cried, opening it wide, and there looked up at her two faces, one crimson and indignant and bearing traces of tears, the other pale and solemn and similarly marred.

'It's *awful*!' burst out Jenny. 'It's been the most absolutely beastly day I've ever had in all my life. It's like *Occupied Europe*! And the food's simply *filthy*! Oh, what a *heavenly* smell of toast! *Could* we have some *at once*, we're simply *faint* and *starving*!'

'Of course, you poor sweeties, in you come. Weez, you're cold—let me take your hood off. Was it really so awful?' she asked in a lowered tone as Jenny flew off to find her mother, for in the family it was generally realised that while the practical Jenny was sometimes swept away by her feelings, the unpractical Louise was capable of taking a more detached view.

'Bits of it weren't so bad but it's not *nice*,' said Louise, standing within the circle of Jean's arms and gazing seriously up at her. 'The Sisters were quite kind to me but they were beastly to Jenny. They didn't seem to like her.'

'Never mind them, the old trouts, they'll get over it and so will you,' comforted Jean, leading the way to the parlour. 'Here's lots of hot toast and some of your favourite pink horrors from the Linga-Longa. So cheer up!'

Jenny was already seated by the fire eating steadily and holding the attention of the room, though Mr Waite looked more disapproving than ever (he belonged to that small and fast-disappearing rearguard which holds that children should seldom be seen and never heard) and Sylvia looked bored. She had already smugly asked Jenny whether she had been a good girl at school; having herself so recently attained grown-up status, her rare assumptions of its soberer mannerisms were still largely imitative.

Alda was listening to her daughters with mingled satisfaction and dismay. But was the place really as bad as this? What would Ronald say, if it was? He had been so determined that the children must remain there for as long as possible.

'Where's Meg?' demanded Jenny, interrupting herself to gaze round.

'Gone to spend the afternoon with the old lady at Pagets, they're bringing her back at six. Go on, Jenny,' said Alda. ('You will excuse all this, won't you?' smilingly to Mr Waite.)

'——and we had four lots of prayers. And no sooner was the praying over than the bullying began.'

'What sort of bullying?' demanded Alda. 'Now, Jen, don't exaggerate.'

'I'm *not* exaggerating, Mother. They speak to you in such an unkind voice and they won't let *you* speak at all. The child next to me knocked a book off my desk and Sister Peter accused me of doing it, and when I tried to say I didn't, she got red in the face and said—"You mustn't say it—you mustn't say it"—and simply glared at me.'

'That seems very unfair,' said Alda, trying not to sound pleased.

'Old cat,' said Jean placidly, in exactly the same tone that she had used of her own form mistress twenty years ago.

'Oh, but Roman Catholics are like that,' broke in Sylvia loudly, 'I wonder you sent them to the place. Beastly holes, convent schools are, teaching the kids to be deceitful.'

'All forms of organised religion are the same,' said Phillip Waite. 'Teach a child to recognise The God in Every Man and to keep In Touch With The Transcendent, and that's all they need.'

'But that won't teach Jenny and Louise French verbs and long division,' retorted Alda rather sharply, 'and the education at convent schools is always excellent.'

'I'm in a *very* low form, with people of *eight*,' mourned Louise, 'and Sister Paul said that my writing was like *spiders*, and she held it up so that everyone could see and all the children laughed.'

'I simply hate it there,' Jenny said, drawing a long sigh, 'and the lunch was wet mashed potato and icy beetroot.'

'I thought it was rather nice,' said Louise, looking up from her place by her mother's knee, warmed by the fire and cheered by much toast and three pink cakes. 'The meat was rabbit.'

'Cat, more likely,' put in Sylvia with her noisy laugh.

'And we've got *piles* of homework to do; all about Henry the something; it will take hours,' sighed Jenny.

'I'll help you with it later on,' said Alda soothingly, deciding that she would also defer the inquiry about those tearstains. 'Go in the kitchen now, darlings, there's a nice fire there, and get your books ready.'

No sooner had the door closed than Sylvia burst out:

'I say, Mrs Lucie-Browne, you aren't having them taught religion at that place, are you? all that stuff about the Virgin Birth and the rest of it?'

'Sister Alban, the head, said nothing about their being taught religion,' Alda replied coldly, 'I suppose they teach them Bible history; all schools except the National Schools do, I believe.'

'Oh, well, the Bible's different,' said Sylvia tolerantly.

'There *is* quite a lot in the Bible, and I don't mind admitting it, I'm capable of seeing both sides of a question, I'm like that, but I do draw the line at all that Jesus stuff.'

'A great Teacher,' put in Mr Waite approvingly, 'perhaps the greatest that ever lived.'

'Jenny and Louise and Meg have been brought up as Christians and when they are old enough they will be confirmed,' said Alda with some irritation. Then she glanced at her watch. 'Meggy should be here any minute, J.; will you put the oil-stove on in her room?'

'Honestly, though, Mrs Lucie-Browne, are you bringing them

up as Christians?' Sylvia went on. 'It sounds awfully queer nowadays, sort of old-world. Absolutely no one does. Why, *I* don't even *know* any Christians.'

'I can well believe that,' snapped Alda—very severely, but her patience was exhausted. Sylvia looked surprised and hurt.

'It's both interesting, and beautiful, the old faith, if only it were not marred by such hideous bloodshed and superstition,' said Mr Waite. 'And what are *your* views on Christianity, Miss Hardcastle?' suddenly pouncing upon Jean.

'Oh, help,' murmured Jean, who, not wishing to miss any of this conversation, had lingered to pile some plates upon a tray. 'I'm bothered if I know,' and she went out of the room.

'Ah, there's Meg,' exclaimed Alda, hurrying to the door. 'Excuse me.'

When she returned she found Mr Waite and Sylvia united in an unholy alliance against Superstition and Dogma, rolling the Pope in the dust, shoving the Church of England into the grave which its narrowness and timidity deserved, biffing the Saints and Martyrs all over the place, and hurling the missionaries into an outer darkness black as the converts whose primitive innocence they corrupted. She was just in time, had her irritation permitted, to hear them sailing off in separate clouds of glory, Mr Waite towards The Transcendent and Sylvia towards the Classless World State.

'I must get the furniture back into this room, it's beginning to snow again,' she interrupted smilingly.

'Can I stay and help wash up?' implored Sylvia, suddenly looking young and woebegone, 'I haven't got to be in until nine and it's so deadly boring in that place.'

'Oh I daresay we can put up with you for a bit longer,' said Alda, exactly as she would have spoken to Louise. 'Run along, the others are in the kitchen.'

Sylvia cheerfully blundered off, and Mr Waite said that he must help her to get the furniture back.

'That *is* kind of you, this way, then,' she said, and led him down a dark passage smelling of coaldust. It was time that Mr Waite came to somebody's heel. If ever a man needed a woman's touch, he did. Let him bump himself and starve his chickens while he helped her to move back the furniture, thought Alda; it would do him good.

'It's only the sideboard and the bookcase and that little cabinet,' she said cheerfully, opening the door upon the chaos in the woodshed. A confusion of large, dark objects confronted them with a hopeless air. Snow blew in Mr Waite's face and settled upon his best necktie.

'Can you see?' she asked.

'Well enough,' replied Mr Waite, without any of the inflections that might have been expected, and for the next twenty minutes he pulled and pushed and steered the furniture round awkward corners, while Alda, in silence except for an occasional laugh or brief comment, helped him at critical moments. When at last he stood in the hall, dusting his hands and looking down at her, she was surprised to see that he did not look cross. He buttoned his overcoat, still looking at her; he seemed absent.

'There!' she said, surveying the orderly sitting-room. 'Now if Mrs Prewitt comes back in the small hours, she'll find everything all right.'

'Are you expecting Mrs Prewitt?' in a startled tone.

'Of course not, it was only a joke,' soothingly. 'Thank you so much for helping me. Oh—your hat.' She held it out to him and he took it. She opened the front door. 'I'm so glad that you were able to come. Ugh! Summer seems years away, doesn't it?'

Together they peered out into the night. Snow drifted glittering into the beam of light shining out from the hall and vanished again into darkness.

'But it isn't cold,' he answered, still with that absent air; then seemed to recollect himself.

'Good-bye, Mrs Lucie-Browne, thank you for a pleasant

afternoon—oh, I nearly forgot.' He felt in his pocket and brought out some chocolate. 'For the kiddies. They oughtn't to have them to-night; too heavy; keep them till to-morrow.'

'You *are* kind!' exclaimed Alda, in a voice of genuine and unflattering surprise. 'Thank you very much indeed; they will be so pleased.'

'Not at all. Er—you must all come and have tea with me one day soon, only,' laughing ruefully, 'I can't promise to move all the furniture in your honour, you know! Good night.'

'We'd love to. Good night.'

And she shut the door.

Oh, what a relief it was to rush into the kitchen, where washing up was in its last stages, accompanied by gales of laughter and jokes about the Sisters, who were rapidly being transformed by Sylvia and Jean into harmless funny old cats and who would remain so until twenty minutes to nine on the following morning when Jenny and Louise again saw Sister Benedict approaching in the car! Men can be bores, thought Alda, scooping her daughters into an embrace, and honestly believing that she preferred the society of women.

'What did you think of him?' she could not help asking of Jean, in a lowered tone.

'Wasn't he awful?' said Sylvia, standing by the draining-board with a teacloth draped round her ample hips to protect her dress and glancing delightedly from one face to the other. 'He didn't half tick me off, didn't he? But I soon bobbed up again; you can't keep a good woman down. He's a regular masochist or monagonist or whatever you call a woman-hater, isn't he?'

'Misogynist—if you must call him something,' said Alda. 'Meggy, my love, come along—bed.'

Meg was leaning with her elbows on the seat of a chair and sucking her thumb (a gesture she only used when she was sleepy), while her eyes, which were already heavy under her pale gold fringe, moved interestedly from one grown-up to another and then back to Jenny or Louise. She wanted to go on watching and listening, but something—a warmth, a deliciousness that came nearer and nearer inside her—kept breaking over her, plunging her each time a little deeper and making her open her eyes slightly wider against its drowsy waves. When her mother lifted her up, she said indignantly, 'Meg will stay up to supper,' but as no one took any notice, she inclined her head gratefully upon Alda's shoulder, sighed, and was borne away.

Alda came downstairs and found Sylvia patronisingly helping Jenny and Louise with their homework, her loud voice, giggles and dictatorial manner adding to their already considerable confusion.

'Off you go, Sylvia,' said Alda crisply. 'It's half-past six and these two have to be in bed by half-past seven sharp.'

'Oh, must I, Mrs Lucie-Browne? We're having such a lovely time, aren't we, Jenny and Weez?' and she grinned at the children, who did not respond.

'Mother, I'm in an awful muddle and we really must get it done,' said Jenny, who now looked exhausted and inclined to tears, while Louise was pale and yawning.

'J., can you just start them on whatever they've got to do?' said Alda, 'and I'll take Sylvia up to get her things on,' for she perceived that Sylvia was not going to leave the cottage unless she were firmly ushered out.

'It's not much fun at that place, I can tell you,' said Sylvia when they were in the bedroom. 'Mr Hoadley's all right, but *she's* very funny, you never know how to take her, and that girl they have in three times a week's bats, if you ask me. As for the Italians, the little one's always trying to paw you about, it makes me sick, and the red-haired one——'

'Fabrio? What about him?' asked Alda with some impatience as Sylvia paused to paint her mouth.

'Oh, he'll murder me one of these days, I should think, he hates the sight of me.'

'Much more likely he's in love with you and frightened that you'll guess, young men don't hate the sight of attractive girls,' said Alda, with the gay authority she used for such announcements, and looking at her with renewed interest. 'How do *you* treat *him*?'

'It's not my fault, Mrs Lucie-Browne, I'm quite willing to be friendly. After all, we were all victims of the Capitalists' War, weren't we? Him just as much as you or me or anybody. *I* haven't any Fascist hatred for Germans or Italians or Japanese.'

'Yes, I know all about that, but do you like him?'

'I don't get the chance. He never speaks to me and if I speak to him he slaps me down.'

'Well, you offer to help him learn English. I happen to know that he's mad keen to learn, and he couldn't slap you down for a friendly suggestion, could he?'

'Oo, no, he couldn't,' said Sylvia doubtfully. Then, suddenly realising what Alda had said earlier, she cried out, '*In love* with me? He'd better not be! I hate all that sort of thing, it just makes me laugh.'

'You're a very unkind little girl,' said Alda, who at eighteen had done her own share of private jesting at scars because she had never felt a wound, and who indeed was one of those Eternal Fifth Formers, most common in England, who are capable of inspiring the subtlest pangs without understanding what on earth it is all about.

Nevertheless, she was too kind-hearted to enjoy the thought of Fabrio sighing in vain. 'He is a prisoner, and far away from his own country and I expect he gets very lonely sometimes,' she went on. 'He's not married, by the way, is he?' for she was not going to promote a friendship that might end in a sordid tangle.

'Emilio is, but not Fabrio, Mr Hoadley says.'

'Well, you take my advice. I'm sure he'll be grateful, and teaching him English will be good for you, too.' She did not say why; indeed, she did not know. Behind her towered Mother Nature, blindly, blandly, inexorably pressing forward these suggestions with her pitchfork from which drooped wheat and olive sprays.

'All right, I will. He can only push my face in, can't he,' said Sylvia amiably. As she went down the stairs she giggled and added:

'Oo, I know you'll think I'm crazy, but I do wonder if there'll be a letter for me to-morrow? I've written to Alan Ladd telling him his last picture was corny.'

'What was that? I haven't seen him in anything since *This Gun for Hire.*'

'Oo, wasn't he *smashing* in it?' (Alda remembered a boorish young man shooting his way in and out of railway sheds.) 'I made the letter ever so critical, and I was just wondering—of course, he won't—but he might write back, and send me a signed photo.'

'Would that be so wonderful?' asked Alda, smiling as they paused at the front door.

'It would be *marvellous*,' and she sighed ecstatically. 'I'm simply crazy about him. You'll think I'm quite bats, but I was wondering if he'd send for me—you know—to go out to Hollywood and give me a part in his next picture.'

'But I thought you wanted to go on the stage?' said Alda beginning to open the door.

'Oo, so I do—but a part in an Alan Ladd picture—only of course a film star's life is awful really, isn't it? and they're all awful, too—so uncultured.'

Alda only laughed and said 'Good night' and gently edged Sylvia, earnestly thanking her for a lovely time, out into the porch.

'You take my advice about giving those English lessons,' she called after her, as she shut the front door. She thought that Sylvia would make a better wife for Fabrio than she would an actress, and if Fabrio was the son of a prosperous peasant farmer, as no doubt he was, she would enjoy considerably more comfort and authority than her own social setting could provide in England; she was also better educated than Fabrio and would improve his mind.

All of which would have delighted the young man who had once been in love with Alda, and who had made her indignant after a long silence had fallen between them at a dance by taking her hands and saying adoringly: 'Promise me that you will never try to think.'

She found that the children's homework was not so difficult, as they had led her to suppose. Jenny had a short chapter to read and digest on the religious, economic, and social changes brought about in England by the Norman invasion, and Louise had the future tense of *faire* and *aller* to learn by heart, Sister Paul having discovered (without showing any of the surprise and approval which she felt) that 'my father' had taught Louise the other tenses of these verbs when he was on leave at Christmas. Whereupon Sister Paul had quelled any tendency towards complacency in Louise by comparing her writing to spiders.

'Is that why you cried?' asked Alda, sitting by Louise's bed while Jenny was in the bathroom.

'No, Mother. As a matter of fact' (lowering her voice) 'I rather liked it. The Sisters were quite kind to me; but they were so beastly' her eyes suddenly filled, and she gulped 'to Jenny. I do *hate* it when people are unkind to people.'

'But what did Jenny do to make them unkind? (don't cry, darling).'

'Well, nothing, really, it was the way she spoke to them—sort of loudly and looking straight at them while she talked. She wasn't *respectful*.'

Alda muttered something; then said: 'Children aren't brought up nowadays to be respectful to grown-ups. It's an old-fashioned idea, and so long as they aren't rude it doesn't matter. Was Jenny rude?'

'Oh no, Mother, truly. But you should be respectful to the Sisters, they're so good. They give up their whole lives to God.'

'Is that what they told you?'

'No. Damaris Bernais told me. She's one of the big girls. She's nearly fifteen. She's half-French and she stays there all the time. She saw me crying and she *was* so kind, Mother. And she's so pretty, she's got natural curly hair, not permanently waved at all, and a lovely long necklace of little black beads and pearls with a little crucifix on it. She said Jenny was *rebellious*.'

Alda thought this the greatest nonsense and took a dislike to Mlle Bernais from that moment. Who was this chit, with her rosary and curls, to criticise Alda's Jenny and win the admiration of Alda's Louise?

She gave them their chocolate, with a caution not to awaken Meg, and went thoughtfully downstairs.

'Jean,' she said while they were at supper, 'you could go out with Jenny while she has those riding lessons, couldn't you? I'm afraid they're going to be necessary.'

'Love to,' said Jean cheerfully. 'I'll probably fall off, but who cares. Would you let me stand Weez some lessons, too, darling?'

Alda gratefully but absently said that of course she would.

14

Sylvia walked back across the snowy fields, determined to follow Alda's advice. Alda had taken her measure at the first meeting and adopted towards her precisely that mixture of kindness, amusement and bossiness which Sylvia unconsciously expected from elders and betters, and she respected Alda, though of course the word itself never entered her head. She also thought Alda very pretty (though she could have looked much smarter if she had used make-up) and she had been impressed by the sight of Ronald's books lying about; Mallock's *The New Republic*, Sartre's novel (in French) and Toynbee's *A Study of History*. She imagined herself asking Alda if she might borrow them, especially the French one. If only she could read French! But she would; she would learn to.

Indeed, the world of ideas did attract Sylvia, but only because there might be drama therein. Her father had possessed strong vitality and it had been transmitted to his children in varying forms. His eldest son could play any tune by ear; the girls were expert dancers, well known at the dance-halls of North London, and Sylvia had been from childhood 'the mimic'; she could 'take anyone off; isn't she a yell!' All were voracious readers of any book, newspaper or magazine that came to hand, which they would afterwards discuss for hours in their loud young voices, sitting over the untidy tea-table and waving their hands about in the cigarette smoke, while the mother (who was fat but still beautiful, and the only one among them who possessed a sense of direction, and the will to drive herself and others towards a goal) moved about the big kitchen of their house near the Nag's Head; tidying, managing, sometimes pausing to put an emphatic word into the conversation or to nod sardonically over some piece of wisdom from a sixteen-year-old.

Drama was what these Scorbys desired: clash, the strong tension between black and white in colours, between extreme Left and Right in politics; the exhausted sweetness of extracts from the works of classical composers plugged on the screen and afterwards sold in simplified versions in Woolworths as 'The Concerto from the film'; the acerbities and generalisations of the Brains Trust; they wanted nothing that was slow, quiet, patient, subtle, or humble, nothing that required listening to in silence, nothing that was noble.

This family of nine people living in North London in a working-class setting and neighbourhood used the names of Nietzsche, Marx, Darwin, Beethoven, Wagner and other men of genius every day in conversation, and were familiar (in a highly distorted form, thanks to the film and the wireless) with the chief events of their lives. History itself had to be floodlit and telescoped in order to hold their attention and if they read biographies they were in the form of vivid easy novels.

They knew no dates, referring to all historical events or costumes as 'Elizabethan' or 'Jane Austen style' or 'Naughty Nineties touch.' Beyond the reign of Elizabeth their knowledge, such as it was, stopped abruptly, and there was a blank until they reached the Ancient Greeks and the Ancient Romans: behind these, the background was 'Prehistoric' and, of course, funny. They spoke with hatred of the rich; they despised as fools such educated people as they encountered who had no glamour and did not get into debt in order to buy smart clothes, a car and a steady flow of alcohol; yet, had they known intimately an educated family which did, they would have disapproved even more bitterly, because (buried deeply in their minds and by them unsuspected) there lingered on the ancient *noblesse oblige.*

A fascinated scorn of the film stars drew the Scorbys three times a week or so to the pictures. As Communists, they despised these luxurious lives, yet the personal beauty and dazzling success of the latest favourite aroused their bitterest envy and almost silenced the voice of their hard working-class common sense, which told them that such triumph could only be purchased very dearly.

Sylvia was entranced by the world of the cinema: she would suddenly fling aside the part she was learning, rush upstairs to the bedroom she shared with her sister Shirley, and reappear with cheeks painted like peaches and—if it were summer—a rhododendron blossom in her hair stolen from a neighbour's garden. Off she would go to the local (which can mean a cinema as well as a public house) and sit there, dazed and adoring some 'curled Assyrian bull' of a young man or one with a face like an amiable sponge, if he happened to be the star of the moment, for two or three hours, creeping home at last sullen and yawning, with all the world about her seeming slow, colourless and lacking in ro-mance.

She preferred American films, because their pace was faster, their violence more blasting, their morals and contrasts easier and sharper, than those in British ones. Such films as *The Rake's Progress*, *This Happy Breed*, *I Know Where I'm Going*, took a story from everyday life and touched it with poetry, and the Scorbys did not notice everyday life; they were too bemused with words and drama and half-baked theories. In these films the soul of England shone tenderly; and the Scorbys did not know about tenderness; they were too busy, poor little things, trying to be tough. Here hovered the spirit of small gardens, of the Caledonian Market with its white tower above and its Indian or Regency junk on the stones beneath, the kitchen dozing in the afternoon hush, the lawns and orangeries of lordly mansions that have become resting places for ordinary people. But the Scorbys dismissed British films as corny.

And all these young people, except Hugo the eldest, were disturbingly inept with their hands. The girls sewed clumsily when they impatiently tried to mend a tear or make the simplest garment, the boys could not put up a shelf and they never noticed the garden unless they rushed out into it to snatch in some dabbed-out washing or chase away a cat. Mrs Scorby occasionally arranged a pot of flowering plants upon a window-sill which she herself had painted blue, and Hugo's fingers were quick and intuitive upon the keys of a piano, but even he was not capable of the concentration necessary to learn to read the simplest music. He had been apprenticed before the Second World War at one of the numerous piano factories in Camden Town, and had returned to his work after being demobilised. He was warmly welcomed, for piano-making is a craft which does not attract young workers to-day and serious observers are wondering what will happen when the sixty-, seventy- and even eighty-year-old craftsmen are dead, and he liked his work. His sisters and brothers drifted in and out of jobs, a way of living which increased their restlessness and lack of concentration. While they had the tall, ugly old brown house to come home to, with copious meals cooked by their mother and no regular ways to interrupt their smoking and talking, the Scorbys enjoyed life and they did no harm. Only in the company of quieter, older or more solid people did their shallowness become apparent, and to such people they were the most dreadful bores. There was an old man who lived with his old wife in two top rooms of a house overlooking the Scorbys' garden, and how he did long to get his hands upon that thirty feet of neglected, trampled earth! To him the dramatic Scorbys, ever gesticulating behind the windows in the smoke-filled rooms or screaming to each other above the noise of the wireless, were objects of strong disapproval, distaste and weariness. He described their activities to himself as Always At It.

When Sylvia was sixteen, her passion for displaying herself took shape in an ambition to go on the stage, and her mother (who despised her children for their lack of will, but was also ambitious for them) exerted herself to find the money for training. She imposed a tax upon the elder Scorbys who were in regular work and herself made a batch of the gaudy, dashing dresses and hats which she designed and executed for local girls and occasionally for small local shops. She had a marked talent for such work but did not make a regular income from it because she was bored by steady application to one task.

Sylvia went to a cheap dramatic school at Canonbury, a neighbourhood of large trees and mouldering, once-elegant mansions that was a short distance from her home, and there she stayed for eighteen months; greatly enjoying herself, impressing some of the pupils, causing the flamboyant, knowledgeable old actor who ran the place to raise his eyebrows and grit his teeth, and perfectly willing to stay there for evermore.

She actually paled when she heard stories of the bullying and brutality which the beginner must endure; she dreaded the plunge; she wanted to prolong her training indefinitely in this small, absorbing world where everyone laughed or cried or raged all day, and where everyone, except the teachers, was young; the two stately, crumbling stucco mansions with their furnishings of dusty mahogany and threadbare velvet were enchanted places to her, and while one half of her cruel young mind mocked at the tattiness, the other half transformed the scene.

But when the elder students began to be taken into the Services and the factories she became frightened; on one side loomed the harsh and terrifying yet infinitely desirable world of the real stage, and on the other loomed the equally terrifying and very undesirable world of the A.T.S. or the war factory. Acting as always upon impulse, she left the dramatic school and joined the Women's Land Army, because there lingered within her, not yet destroyed by adult urban life, a child's longing to be in the open air. Her mother was angry and called her a fool and told her that she had had her chance and lost it, and her brothers and sisters laughed at her. Other people's opinions had no effect upon Sylvia and she went down into Sussex, prepared to shriek and giggle over whatever might come and utterly unaware that her action proved that she would never be an actress.

She paused for a moment now, and gazed at the farm in its hollow; the landscape lay under faint light from a young moon reflected dimly in the welling pool before the house, and the dark fields were streaked with melting snow.

To-morrow I'll speak to Fabrio about teaching him English, she thought.

Mr Waite spent the ten-minute walk between the two cottages in thinking what a peculiar woman Mrs Lucie-Browne was. He simply could not understand her behaviour with the furniture. The idea of the Waites turning out a room half an hour before the arrival of people to tea was unthinkable. It would simply never occur to any of us, thought Mr Waite. And putting it in the wood-shed! So bad for it; a damp, dirty place like that; putting it there simply because—what was it she had said?—'I couldn't bear it another minute.' She must be both silly and uncontrolled. And then she had a peculiar manner; at one moment she was being downright with that painted piece of a girl, and the next she was soft and smiling. Soft and smiling, repeated Mr Waite to himself. Her costume was shabby, and the thick white jersey under her jacket was shrunk; noticeably shrunk, thought Mr Waite. The Lucie-Brownes could not have much money—unlike Miss Hardcastle, who had been nicely dressed and had worn some good diamonds. But how foolish to wear them in the country—how foolish to wear them at all, for that matter, in these dangerous times! The proper place for diamonds was in the bank, not upon female ears. Miss Hardcastle seemed a nice girl.

He did not waste much thought upon Miss Blue Eyelashes, whom he had summed up and dismissed at their first meeting.

In spite of his hostess's queer ways, it had been a pleasant afternoon and had made a change, thought Mr Waite, glancing at his watch as he lit the lamp in the kitchen and seeing to his dismay that it was seven o'clock. Good heavens, those birds would be starving! and he hurried into the lean-to where he mixed the battery birds' food, and began to measure and mince vegetable scraps and scoop out grey, gritty, oily goo from a large tin. Each time he did this (and he did it twice every day) he thought disturbedly about his fifty battery chickens, sitting day and night in cages so small that they could barely turn round and with their every natural faculty, except that of egg-producing, distorted and controlled. There they sat, glossy and plump, showing no excitement except when he approached with their food. The pamphlets explaining the Battery System emphasised that it was not cruel. Mr Waite always wondered what Buddha would have said about it.

The soft brilliant light from the lamp shone upon the dusty shelves and ancient, odorous stone sink of this little outhouse, built by some past occupant of Meadow Cottage, and upon the dark worried face of Mr Waite as he scooped and mixed and chopped at the table while his giant shadow loomed and dwindled upon the whitewashed wall behind his back. His thoughts had returned to Mrs Lucie-Browne and he decided that he would invite them all to tea in ten days' time.

Then he hurried out to the row of cages where sat the battery birds, who greeted him with fierce rattlings of the zinc bars of their huts and starved, reproachful shrieks. He went from cage to cage, doling out food and fresh water, a little figure moving within the feeble circle of light from the hurricane lamp under the vast black sky. The birds ate with insane voracity; their hard golden eyes gleamed in red sockets and the sheen on their copper plumage ran down into the rich fluff on their legs. They looked the picture of health. All the same, he kept wondering whether Buddha—and Mrs Lucie-Browne—would think him cruel

The morning was rainy and fresh; the snow had vanished and water-globes slid down the bowed grasses on to Sylvia's boots as she went down the garden path carrying a pail of food for the Hoadley fowls. All the sticky and shelly creatures were abroad; slugs curled on the wet black mould and fully-exposed snails travelling their fragile horns and brilliant slime across the drying flags. The air was scented with rain and with the tiny faint odours from these dwellers under stones and roots, and with the faded wet grass.

While she was scattering the grain among the birds in that graceful gesture which must be one of the most ancient performed by man, she glanced down the garden and there, crossing the yard at the end of it by the gate, she saw Fabrio. It was the first time she had seen him alone for a week; he had as usual been avoiding her.

She hastily poured the last of the food over the chickens, dropped the pail amidst the grass, and ran down the path towards him—lightly, on the tips of her rubber boots. He had paused to make some adjustment in the harness he was carrying over his shoulder and did not hear her until—smiling, eager, her hair lifted by the wind—she was upon him.

'Fabrio!' she cried. 'Hullo! Good morning! I say, how about me teaching you to speak English?'

Fury flashed into his face; his nostrils distended; he dropped the harness he carried; the very blue of his eyes deepened with rage and his lips worked. He *is* going to crown me, thought Sylvia, afraid, and even stepped back a pace, but suddenly the fury vanished; and his face lit with mockery. He put one hand on his heart and swept her a low bow (she caught the faint breath of stale clothes as he moved) and began to make her a speech in Italian. She gathered from the tone that it was a bitingly sarcastic speech, but she did not listen to it for long; she rode it down with impatient friendliness.

'Oh, cut it out, comrade! I'm not trying to insult you, I really mean it. I *want* to teach you to spik-a da English,' and she held out to him her hand.

It was no longer white, but it was still dimpled and pretty. It would never—that little hand—seem instinct with knowledge of life's hardness, or look worn from acquiring some expert craft, or become thin and sensitive because its owner's spirit had filled it with her life. But it was so friendly, so pretty, so small; it was a young girl's hand.

Fabrio stared at it. Sylvia patiently kept it extended. He had avoided her; he accused her of insulting him; never mind; she would be really friendly towards him—and she would get her way.

Suddenly Fabrio put out his own hand, big and coarsened and young, and clasped hers within it. Again, for an instant, she felt afraid. It was one thing to offer friendship to Fabrio; it was another to touch him, and she wanted to draw her hand away but she controlled the impulse and slowly, deliberately, gave to his warm hand (she could feel the dried earth from his early work upon it) a friendly pressure.

He did not return the pressure or look at her but when she exclaimed: 'There, comrade, that's swell!' he nodded slightly and his expression had less than its usual reserve. She went on talking, and presently he slowly raised his head and looked at her without a guard upon his face. Wonder at this lively, chattering, feminine creature, this woman dressed like a boy, who was so pleased and excited because he had taken her hand, showed in his eyes. She must like me, after all, thought Fabrio, and his head went up into its usual easy, proud pose, and he looked at her with conde-scension. (He could not look down upon her, because she was as tall as he.)

'We'll have a lesson every day,' she was saying. 'I have to have my lunch with Mr and Mrs, but I'll finish by one. Where do you have yours?'

He shrugged his shoulders. 'By Big-a Rick, in room, any place.'

'Listen, I'll meet you by the Big Rick every day at twenty minutes to one and we'll start to-morrow. How's that?'

'Good-a,' he said, nodding, and for the first time he smiled. He liked the shed called the granary, where straw and chaff filled the cool dark air with snufflike scents, and when he said that he had his lunch 'in room' he meant in the granary. Sometimes Emilio went too, but more often Fabrio ate there alone; lying full-length against the plump sacks and slowly chewing through half a small loaf of stale bread and a small piece of hard cheese, and an onion when he could get it, and gazing at the rain drifting past the open door. The granary stood in a remote part among the scattered farm buildings, and the inhabitants seldom went there, so that he was almost sure of being undisturbed. He did no harm there, except to take twenty minutes over his time for lunch in sleep, and it was the only place, in the camp or in the farm, where he felt at home. It is like San Angelo, he would think, lying alone in the dusk, with the thick grey swags of cobweb above him and the rusty disused objects that had collected in course of time upon natural shelves formed by the massive oak wall-beams all about him, and the sacks of living grain warming his body; it is like home.

They parted with amiability, more marked upon her side than upon his: she returned to her chickens and he trudged on, past a grey pond brimming to the straight banks that he had helped to clean, with a grey beech sweeping down over it, towards the stable where lived the plough horse Admiral (whom Fabrio did not much like).

'*La Scimmia* is going to teach me to speak English,' he shouted gaily to Emilio some time later.

(The Monkey was their private name for Sylvia. It should be remembered that hers for them had been The Zombies.)

'Oh yes, that's a good one!' Emilio called back, pausing with the large bundle of hazel-wands for kindling that he was carrying up to the farmhouse.

'It's true. She asked me if I'd let her, and I said yes,' and Fabrio began to whistle. Admiral, whose stable he was sweeping out, slowly turned his head and fixed a large velvet eye upon him.

'Oh-ho-ho-ho!' cried Emilio with a ribald intonation. 'And when do we begin?'

'To-morrow after dinner.'

'And where? I'll be there, you see.'

'That's a secret, and you keep your ugly nose out of it.'

'I'll be there, you'll see,' repeated Emilio, and went on towards the house, pleased that his friend was happy but resentful that he should be going to spend time alone with a girl.

'I am going to teach Fabrio English, Mrs Hoadley,' said Sylvia brightly, when the two of them were seated at lunch that morning. Mr Hoadley had taken the car into West Mewling to see a man who had some wire netting to sell and Sylvia knew it; if he had been present, she would not have made her announcement, for she knew his opinion of the Italians.

Mrs Hoadley, who was eating roast pork as though rebuking it, glanced up from her plate.

'I don't envy you,' she said, but without disapproval.

'I thought it might make things a bit easier for him—must be awful, not knowing what people are saying all round you.'

'Oh, he understands a good bit more than he seems to, only he can't talk.'

'I'm not doing it in Mr Hoadley's time,' said Sylvia earnestly. 'We're going to meet at twenty to one by the Big Rick every day and I'm going to give him a lesson until one o'clock.'

'It's kind of you, Sylvia, but I don't envy you,' repeated Mrs Hoadley, casting a shrinking eye over a very large dish of the fine dark green winter spinach which was Mr Hoadley's favourite vegetable at this time of the year as Sylvia took from it a majestic second helping. 'Still, I expect he'll soon pick it up, he's quick enough when he wants to be, and it'll be an interest for you both.'

Not the faintest smile, not even a lurking echo of a teasing note, showed on her face or sounded in her voice, as she discussed the prospect of a fresh girl of eighteen and a comely man of twenty-three spending twenty minutes alone together every day. Blessed are the cold in heart, for at least they do not put ideas into other people's heads.

'He needs brightening up a bit,' said Sylvia meditatively, biting at a hunk of bread. 'They're a low type, those Italian peasants. It's lack of civilisation and education, isn't it? Do you know, Mrs Hoadley'—and she leant across the table and her chicory-blue eyes looked wide and shocked—'Fabrio *smells!*'

'A good many people do,' said Mrs Hoadley resignedly, 'but you shouldn't say that, Sylvia, it's vulgar. It can't be very bad, I haven't noticed it, and I should have.'

'Oh, it isn't so bad as all that, it's only sort of earthy, and his clothes aren't very clean.'

'Poor man, I expect he doesn't get much chance to wash himself or his clothes either in that camp. When the weather gets a little better and Mr Hoadley's grandmother at the Wild Brooks sends us another batch of her soap, I'll tell him he can wash his clothes here.'

'Yes, do!' cried Sylvia, putting a potato into her mouth and talking through it. 'We'll soon civilise him, won't we, between us!'

'What a lot you do eat, Sylvia,' said Mrs Hoadley—adding hastily in answer to a surprised and reproachful glance, 'I don't grudge it you, but I don't know how you *can*. Half a slice, and I'm done.'

'Oo, I love eating. Food—I could go on for ever!'

'You'll get fat,' said the farmer's wife, with a not unkind smile.

'Oo, I'm fat now,' glancing down at her shirt, 'they said at the School I'd have to lose a stone if I wanted to look right on the stage.'

'I like a nice slim figure myself,' said Mrs Hoadley, stroking her sides. 'It shows off your clothes.'

'I want to wash a few things this evening, could you let me have a loan of your soap powder?'

'I will, but you use such a *lot*, Sylvia, and we're a bit short until next month's ration comes along. Can't you use old Mrs Hoadley's soap?'

'Doesn't lather like the powder. Whatever's it made of, anyway?'

'Wood ash and pig fat—I don't know half what she puts in it.'

'Ugh! The first time I heard you talking about her sending you some soap I thought she kept a shop or was in with the Black Market.'

'There's nothing like that goes on here, as you know,' said Mrs Hoadley sharply. 'The old lady and her husband keep pigs on their bit of land just outside Amberley—Amberley God Knows, as they call it round here—and she can always manage to get hold of a bit of fat, in spite of the Pig Board, to mix up with her wood ash. They've got a regular wilderness all round them too, hazels and willow and all that stuff that grows so quickly and the old chap cuts that down and burns it for the ash. You seem to have eaten all the pudding, it's just as well I've put Mr Hoadley's by. Come on, there's just time for our tea before we start again,' and a faint note of satisfaction came into her voice with the words.

'That's nice,' she said, when she had drunk some tea, and she sighed.

'I'll have to get it a bit earlier for you to-morrow, if I've got to be there by twenty to one.'

'You needn't trouble, Sylvia, I don't want it hustled,' said

Mrs Hoadley, decisively. 'If I can't drink it in peace and quiet I don't enjoy it.'

Sylvia sucked up her own tea and looked apprehensively over the top of the cup.

'I could manage to get it before I go, really I could.'

'It's kind of you, but I'd rather not. I don't want you banging and clattering about like a young elephant getting the tea.'

'Young elephant! Thank you!' The last drop of tea went down, and Sylvia set her cup on the saucer.

'Don't bang it down like that, you'll break it, next thing.'

'Sorry. Well,' she stood up, 'I must get cracking. Thanks for a smashing lunch.' She slowly stretched her arms out, straining the coarse shirt over her bosom, then vigorously twisted her hair into a knot and secured it with two large black hairpins. Over this she tied a faded scarf.

'The way *I* like your hair done is low on your neck,' said Mrs Hoadley, poking the fire.

Sylvia made a face. 'It makes me look so *corny.*'

'Don't be silly, it's a refined style and it shows up your eyes, that side parting.'

'Perhaps you're right,' said Sylvia, pleased, and she strode away whistling, thinking that perhaps she would dress her hair like that when she met Fabrio.

15

Part of Jean's nature belonged to a sentimental slave. Had it grown to the power over her whole character which it had threatened in her early youth it would have made of her a different person; morbidly, helplessly wandering in that labyrinth which ensnares those who are both timid and chaste yet longing for love, and from which few find their way out into the fresh air, for the lamp they carry has long ago been quenched and become a tear-bottle. But she was saved by her sturdier qualities and the varied nature of the novels she read; had they been only love-stories, all the voices in her nature (laughing or sharp or ironical) might have been muted in sighs and tears. But from the age of fifteen, when she found *Tom Jones* and *Three Men in a Boat* and *Quo Vadis* in the attics at Alda's home, love in novels was to her only one of the novelists' themes, and not the most absorbing; and although that *sick, true-hearted slave* in her soul continued to run forward to meet and recognise Love before Love had made any movement towards her, side by side with the slave dwelt her other selves, who took a different view of life, and who had lately taken to criticising the slave's habits.

During the days that followed her first meeting with Mr Waite, she thought her usual thoughts about a new man; his figure was good, his eyes were handsome, that severe manner was exciting, and so forth, but the incantation refused to work, the fumes did not rise, and the slave remained sober. I am not thrilled with him; he isn't quite my type, decided Jean.

She and Alda had not discussed their new acquaintance as exhaustively as they might have done, because their attention was at this time fully engaged with the children and the convent.

The first weeks there were so unhappy that Alda seriously thought of taking them away, and as she knew that if she wrote her intention to Ronald he would certainly forbid her to do so, she was almost as miserable as her daughters. In listening to Jenny's shuddering accounts of the unappetising lunches and the severity of the nuns, she had no previous experience in disentangling such tales to help her to distinguish truth from the exaggeration due to violent distaste, for, until now, she had always known the backgrounds against which Jenny and Louise had moved. She did not realise (though she might have, from remembering her own years at a boarding school) that children always grumble about school food, just as they always praise food served in the shoddiest restaurant or tea-shop; and she did not understand that, to little girls brought up in a home where virtue was assumed unless wrongdoing had been proved, the system of assuming wrongdoing, and not believing even in the *desire* to do right, appeared terrible in its harshness and injustice.

Day after day Jenny came home with those marks of tears upon her face or flushed and defiant with the recent recollection of some conflict with authority; yet, when Alda caught a glimpse of Sister Benedict in the mornings when she waited for the children in the hushed, gleaming, flower-decorated little room with the statue in blue cloak and white robe, and they were ushered in to her by a nun whose businesslike manner did not prevent her from smiling, it did seem difficult, indeed, it was not possible, to reconcile this clean, peaceful orderliness and these calm pink faces with Jenny's tales of uneatable meals and those same faces purple and snapping with fury.

'That's only their cleverness,' Jenny assured her, sitting up in bed in shabby pyjamas which were a hand-on from her cousin Richard. 'They always put that on when the mothers are there. Egg says so.'

'*Who* says so?'

'Egg Peers. Her real name's Eglantine. She lives at that

enormous house just outside the village. Her people are awfully rich. She's got a pony.' And Jenny sighed. The clarity of her expression had already been destroyed: at one time it had been so clear as to suggest that nothing went on behind her eyes that was not spoken by her lips. It had gone, and it would not come again, but mothers must make up their minds to see that expression 'fade into the light of common day.'

So Eglantine had a pony, had she? Well, thought Alda, at least I can do something about that. The moment was certainly ripe.

'Jenny, would you like to have riding lessons?'

'Oh Mother! Super! But—we can't afford it, can we?'

'Marion sent the money to pay for twelve lessons for you just after Christmas. I've been keeping it for a surprise.'

'Oh Mother! How lovely! Oh, it's something to look *forward* to,' and Jenny slid beneath the bedclothes and ecstatically danced her feet. 'I've always wanted them,' her voice came up, muffled by blankets, 'only I pretended I didn't because I thought we couldn't afford it.' She emerged, with ruffled hair and a joyful face. 'Where shall I go for them? Carina Smith——'

'*Who*, Jenny?'

'Carina Smith. She's in my form.'

'What perfectly extraordinary names they do have there— Damaris, Eglantine, Carina!'

'Their parents like them to be different, Carina says. She doesn't think Jenny's an unusual name at all. I suppose you wouldn't let me call myself Janina?'

'I would not, and neither would your father. I've been talking to Mr Hoadley about riding lessons and he thinks Mr Mead down at Rush House would be the best person to go to. He says those people who run the school at Burlham are more expensive and not so good.'

'Egg goes to Burlham.'

'I daresay.'

'Mother darling, will you come out with me?'

'I will the first two or three times perhaps, then Jean can go out with you. She's going to treat Weez to some lessons, too,' she added.

'Oh good.' Jenny was her mother's daughter and it did not occur to her that anyone could be afraid of a horse.

Communications were accordingly opened with Mr Mead and Jenny's first lesson was arranged for the following week, which was the third in February.

The children had been at the convent for nearly a month and as the days went on, with their undiminished catalogues of misfortunes from Jenny, Alda began to notice a slight change in Louise. She had never been so passionate as her sister in her complaints of the convent discipline and Alda had always known, from the reports of the children's various haphazard instructors and from Ronald himself, that she was the cleverer of the two. These qualities now began to work for her greater comfort, for although the Sisters never praised those patient efforts to improve the spider-writing, it did begin to improve; it straightened, the blots dwindled and finally, like the last flying drops of a rain shower, ceased altogether; the simple verbs and tables and dates, at first stumblingly repeated under a fire of sarcastic comment, gradually became fluent and accurate and were received in silence but with full marks and, above all, the submission and obedience with which Louise received every reproof or irksome instruction earned the affectionate approval of those among the nuns who loved children and cherished in their souls the image of that heavenly Child whom they believed that human children should aspire to imitate.

In these mornings of earliest spring, which were gradually growing brighter as the sun came up earlier across the fields and sent low rays between swelling willow buds and catkins, Fabrio would see the group of children setting out for school as the prisoners' lorry paused at the crossroads to set down Emilio and himself, and sometimes, if he did not feel morose, he would wave to them. Should Sister Benedict happen to arrive in the car while the lorry was there, all the prisoners would shout 'Good morning!' to her and receive in response a smile and a movement of the lips which those of them who were Christians knew meant *God bless you*.

Fabrio drew from the presence of the convent among its spinneys that same sense of familiarity and home which dwelt, for him, among the rafters and sacks of the granary, and sometimes as he worked his mind would vaguely dwell upon a picture of the Sisters, at prayer before the altar or moving amidst flowers and holy images. On Sundays he went to early Mass with a few other prisoners, and once a week he went to Confession but there, to him, it was an awesome, confused impression of words muttered in an unfamiliar tongue whose sound had yet been familiar to him almost from babyhood, the severe colourless face of Father Francesco above the shining curve of the Cup, the scent of burned-out incense steeping the air, the glow of flower colours and the glimmer of stars upon Our Lady's mantle; and these, though they were dear to him and he would have missed them strongly if they had been taken away from him, were less dear than that sense of home breathed out by the granary and inspired in him by the sight of the Sisters' black robes.

Father Francis had sharply and severely discouraged his timid wish to perfect his knowledge of reading and writing. Faith of a sort among the Italian prisoners committed to the priest's charge was not uncommon, but unquestioning faith and regular observances such as Fabrio practised were not common, and Father Francis, who felt for this ignorant and devout soul a harsh pure love, was not going to risk its being delivered over to hell by the questioning and discontent often induced by reading. It was also as well, Father Francis decided, that Fabrio could not speak much English. He would soon be returned to his own country, where the Faith was national and not practised as a mission among heretics, and there, among a peasantry which was still devout, his soul would be safe.

On the morning of his first lesson with Sylvia, Fabrio lay on the sacks in the granary, finishing the lump of hard cheese which he had been sharing with the dog Ruffler, who lay at his side. He looked sulky; he resented the plan and the fact that she had made it, and he dreaded the coming lesson in which she would discover that he could spell out only the simplest words and barely write his own name. She will make fun of me, he thought; that's why she offered to teach me. I wish it were Maria who was coming instead, and he pulled out the cheap worn wallet where he kept his identity card and a few other papers and glanced proudly over the lines of Maria's last letter, which told him a little about affairs at San Angelo and a great deal about how much your friend, Maria Amato, misses you. It had that morning been read aloud to him by Emilio. There is a girl, thought Fabrio, returning the letter to his pocket, not a half-boy with a voice like the *pavone* in the gardens up at the great Villa at home.

'Yoo-hoo!' cried the voice of that same peacock, and her head came round the granary door, 'Oh, there you are, I thought you might be. (Hullo, Ruffler, good boy.) You ready, Fabrio? Come along, then, let's go and sit on the rick, it isn't going to rain after all,' and without waiting for his answer she strode off. Ruffler glanced inquiringly at Fabrio, then went away on his own affairs.

Fabrio got up leisurely, with the grace that no one at the farm had noticed, and followed her out into the daylight. She had seated herself upon the heap of straw at the foot of the rick, which looked across a field of brilliant green winter wheat to a marshy coppice, already yellow with catkins; the wind was from the west and blew into their faces fresh odours from grass and wet straw and brimming pools hidden in the woods; all the sky was hurrying and confused with low clouds grey as pearls, and clear spring light lay over the scene.

She was smiling and holding out a packet of cigarettes, invitingly opened but as yet unrifled.

'Will—you—have—a—cigarette,—Fabrio?' she said in the voice of an affected schoolmistress.

Fabrio accepted one and muttered his thanks in his own language, for he was too embarrassed to attempt English. He lit it and inhaled a few puffs without making any movement to seat himself by her side. He glanced down at her; her hair was almost concealed by her cap and a little smear of chocolate from the recent meal was on her chin. He glanced away again, thinking Holy Mother, how white her skin is.

'Sit—down,—Fabrio.' She made room for him and brought a book out of her pocket. 'Here—is—a—book—for—you—to—learn—from. I—bought—it—in—Horsham. It—has—a—funny—name. Look!' and she held it out to him.

This was the second time in a few weeks that a woman had held out a book to Fabrio, as if it were the apple from the Tree of Knowledge, and the familiar feeling of reverence, interest, humiliation and rage which he always experienced upon seeing a book began to invade him. But there was no look of amused, superior interest upon Sylvia's young face to make him long to assert himself as a man, there was no Mr Hoadley here to shout at him, and the feeling subsided. He swallowed once or twice, and then read slowly aloud in the beautiful voice which nervousness made slightly less deep than usual:

'Re—re-ad-ing—redd-ing wi-oout——' He broke off, and impatiently shook his head; then suddenly glanced at her, smiled shamefacedly, and sank down by her side.

'Why—that—is—very—good!' cried his governess approvingly, moving a little away from him. '*Reading—Without—Tears.* Look—at—the—pictures,—aren't—they—corny—(old-fashioned),' and she turned the pages with their woodcuts of chubby children in crinolines or round jackets gathered about their mother's beflounced knee.

'*Anticamente*,' nodded Fabrio, his face expressing deepest interest.

'We—will—not—start—reading—to—day,' pronounced Miss Scorby, shutting the book upon an exciting picture of some little boys having a fight. 'To—day—we—will—have—conversation. Good morning, Fabrio,' leaning towards him and nodding and smiling. 'Now—you—tell—me—in—Italian.'

Fabrio wanted to go on looking at the pictures, in which he took a child's pleasure, and his expression became sulky again as he muttered:

'Buon giorno.'

'Now—say—it—like—this—Good morning.'

'Good-a morning—good-a morning, gooda morning!' and he added impatiently, 'I know it—I can say it for a long-a time.'

'Yes, but you don't say it *correctly*. You've got to get a good accent, It's important. Now say it again; not good-*a* morning; good—morning.'

Fabrio did not say it. He continued to stare obstinately down into the straw and was silent. Sylvia waited with slightly compressed lips and eyes sparkling with mischief, and in a moment he glanced up, said explosively, 'Good morning!' and burst out laughing.

'That's grand!' she exclaimed, laughing too. 'I am hungry. I want my lunch. Now tell me in Italian, like you did before.'

This time he obeyed at once, but she lingered so long over the next few phrases in Italian while repeating the words after him, and he was so pleased to become teacher instead of pupil that the short time allotted to the lesson passed very quickly, and it was fortunate that the question 'What is the time?' caused her to glance at her watch. She exclaimed, and jumped up, saying, 'Gosh, it's just on time. You've done very well to-day, Fabrio——'

'Fa*brio*,' he corrected, standing a little way off from her and gazing at her from under his brows; now that the lesson was over he seemed sulky and withdrawn into himself again.

'Fa-*brio*, then—but I can't stay here all night saying it. Bye-bye. See you to-morrow, same time and place,' and she ran off, repeating under her breath *I want my lunch* in the Ligurian coastal dialect in which Fabrio had naturally taught her to say it, while he went in the opposite direction muttering *I want my lunch* in the muted Cockney used off the Camden-road.

She had not thought of herself as learning Italian from him, but although she took no interest in the language itself she liked to think of *me jabbering away in Italian, it's not so common as French, everybody knows French*, and she was also intelligent enough to realise that a knowledge of languages is useful. She did not, of course, conceive of them as instruments which could give her pleasure. In the same way, her family dismissed both the knowledge of history and history itself as *dates and kings and fascist battles and all that stuff*, and had no idea of the richness and solidity which even a limited knowledge of history can bring to everyday life.

Yet, if compared with a London family of forty years ago, how kind they were! and their kindness extended far beyond their immediate circle and embraced, at least in theory, all the millions of people living in all the countries of the world. It was as if the Christian law *Love thy neighbour as thyself* had at long last, after centuries of misunderstanding and abuse, begun to flower side by side with the fiercest and most despairing materialism the world had ever endured and as if those who were loudest in their denunciations of the Christian Church were compelled, by one of those superb ironies in which we detect, or imagine that we detect, the humour of God, to practise one of the chief virtues upon which that Church had been founded.

However, Sylvia had no intention of letting the lessons develop into Italian lessons for herself. The small red book was soon in use and Fabrio was struggling with *Bet Sells Buns* and *He gets on his nag*. He tried to assert himself by producing a copy of *Post* and demanding to be allowed to read the captions under the photographs, but she made him put the paper away and continue with the longer sentences (*Ned was rude. He plucked a trumpet from the tree*) at the end of *Reading Without Tears*. She explained each word to him with vehement pantomime after he had read the sentence aloud, telling him that it was good practice for her as an actress, but Fabrio did not enjoy looking at *La Scimmia's* face when it was distorted in mime; he preferred the Conversation, in which she sat quietly beside him, with her eyes fixed upon his own as she gravely or laughingly spoke the simple sentence, and then it was his turn, having guessed what she meant or had it explained to him, to tell her what it was in Italian.

She soon insisted that he should use her Christian name, which he thought very pretty, too pretty for its owner, whom he continued to regard with disapproval, though after a time as he became more used to her noisy ways and frank manner he ceased to notice them. He grew to look forward to the daily lessons and to enjoy laughing with a girl, whose woman's laugh was so different from that of his comrades at the camp. But she seemed to him, despite her boldness and her education, a silly young creature, towards whom he could feel superior and indulgent. Sometimes, on days when it rained, he would lounge beside her on the granary sacks, chewing a straw and looking at her out of half-shut eyes and thinking how feeble was her strength compared with his own; that she talked too much; that she let him see what was in her mind; that her voice was too loud; and then Sylvia, not liking the half-contemptuous expression in his eyes and on his mouth, would sharply tell him to sit up 'properly' and pay attention to the lesson—and, smiling, he would lazily obey.

'Does he behave himself—not rude to you or anything?' Mrs Hoadley asked her, at the end of the first week's lessons.

'I should hope so! He'd better.'

'No, but does he? because Mr Hoadley's only letting him

have the lessons as a favour to you, you know, Sylvia, because he's pleased with your work.'

'Is he? Goody. No, honestly, Mrs Hoadley, Fabrio's no trouble at all and he's getting on ever so well. He's quite intelligent, really, when you get to know him a bit, though he doesn't say much.'

'I don't expect he gets a chance, with you about.'

'I do talk a lot, don't I?' laughing and grimacing. 'Oh well, I must get cracking—*a rivederci!*' and she bounced away.

Mrs Hoadley, whose instincts as a respectable matron and an employer of female labour under the age of twenty-one had only been aroused by some sharp inquiries from her husband, was satisfied that all was proceeding respectably, and said no more. Fabrio continued to smile enigmatically at the bawdy jokes made on the subject by Emilio, and Emilio continued to try to kiss Sylvia whenever the opportunity occurred, and to be pushed away as vigorously as her small hands could push.

And it was the second week in March; red rays of sunset pierced between lilac clouds in the lengthening evenings, shining through the hazel coppice where Alda and the children moved from cluster to cluster of primroses, pulling the long stems of the flowers from their nests of cool leaves; thrushes sang in the budding elms and cold scents breathed up from the freshening grass and were blown across from distant fields; even on days when there was no rain the pools and ditches gave out their faint watery odour, and the hedges were dimly green above thick mats of budding violets.

16

Jenny had received and greatly enjoyed her first hour of instruction upon a sly, stout, wilful pony named Blackberry who realised that in Jenny she had met her mistress; and on this fine Saturday afternoon Louise was to go out for the first time with Jean. At four o'clock the party from Pine Cottage was to present itself at Meadow Cottage to take tea with Mr Waite.

'Can I come too?' implored Jenny, standing at the gate as Jean and Louise came down the path; Jean in jodhpurs and jacket made by a house famous for sports clothes, and Louise in some which had been given her, against Alda's wish, by Eglantine Peers.

Alda had written a markedly formal note, thanking Mrs Peers for the jodhpurs and adding that she would have preferred to buy them or to make an exchange with some of Jenny's clothes. She had heard no more of the matter beyond a vague remark from Eglantine to the effect that 'Oh yes, Mummy did get it.' It appeared that Eglantine had been evacuated to America for the first three years of the war and 'gets all the clothes she wants from there.' Alda set her lips and did not try to feel grateful. Jenny herself wore riding breeches that had belonged to her cousin Richard ('As if it weren't bad enough to have to wear his beastly pyjamas').

'I should like you to,' Jean now answered in reply to Jenny's request. 'The more the merrier.'

'It won't be a lesson, it'll just be me on Strawberry, so I shouldn't think he'd charge as much as he would for a proper lesson, would you? I have got four shillings saved up.'

'Forget it, infant. This is my treat.'

'Thanks *awfully*, Jean darling, it is kind of you. Egg gets *five shillings* a week pocket money, don't you think it's a terrific lot for a girl of her age?'

'I used to get ten shillings when I was twelve.'

'And you could buy more, too, in those days, before the war. Tell me about what you used to buy.'

As they walked down the road under the airy shadows cast by the giant elms Jenny and Jean gossiped cheerfully but Louise was silent. When they reached the stables they found Mr Mead leading out two ponies.

'Will it be all right for Strawberry and Blackberry to go out with Socks?' inquired Jenny. 'Do they like each other?'

'They're old friends,' smiled Mr Mead. 'There you are. That'll be better for you,' to Louise, as he shortened Blackberry's stirrups. 'Not nervous, are you?'

'Of course she isn't,' said Jenny haughtily. Louise swallowed and said nothing.

'Oh, you beauty,' exclaimed Jean. A long golden head with a white mark upon the nose suddenly reared over the gate of a nearby stable; and a great eye like a jewel rolled round at them.

'Ah, that's Shooting Star,' said Mr Mead, glancing up. 'He is a beauty, you're right. He needs exercise but there isn't anyone round here that's good enough to ride him.'

Jean was advancing to caress Shooting Star's nose but thought better of it when he flung up his head and neighed; she heard his hoofs striking the stones, not in anger but in pettish boredom as he retreated from her, and all the force and fury of the life in his body seemed to ring in the sound. People always imitate a horse's neigh as if it were funny, she thought, but when you actually hear it, it isn't funny in the least.

'That's right. Now I'll go and get Socks,' said Mr Mead.

Strawberry and Blackberry, who were sisters, stood side by side, saddled and ready, and Jenny and Louise respectfully patted them and commented upon their looks.

'Strawberry looks gentle,' said Louise. 'Is Blackberry gentle too?'

'Oh, she's got a will of her own when she likes, they both have,' said Mr Mead, 'but you mustn't let her get away with it; you show her you're the mistress, see? Be gentle with her but have your own way. Now—up you go.'

Meanwhile, Jean had been inspecting her own mount, Socks. He also was black; a young-middle-aged horse lacking in personality, with two white socks on his forelegs. In a few minutes they moved off down the track leading from the stables, into the rough open meadows and paddocks where the horses were exercised and the less experienced riders came for canters and gallops.

Jean had a good seat, but did not ride so well as she appeared to do, for her power over the horse sometimes failed her just when it was most necessary, and this afternoon she did not feel quite at ease; the air was wild with that floating spring sweetness, rising from the earth and breathing out from woods under the changing sky, which dizzies and intoxicates human beings and horses even when encountered on a chance wind in the streets of a city, and how much more so when it sweeps unrestrained over open country! Jenny rode upon one side of her, completely at ease upon Strawberry although she had never ridden her before, and on the other side sat Louise, holding on to the pommel of Blackberry's saddle and smiling constrainedly.

'Now,' said Jean, when they had ridden through a marshy coppice and halted in a meadow enclosed on three sides by hedges from which burst puffs of white blackthorn bloom, 'we'll tie Blackberry up to this gate, Louise, and you can watch while I give Jenny a lesson. Then it'll be your turn.'

Louise smiled faintly and nodded. Jean thought it wisest to ignore this lack of enthusiasm, and dismounted and led Blackberry to the gate, over which she slipped the rein. Jenny sat picturesquely upon Strawberry the while, and Socks stood like a horse made of wood staring dully at the distance. Jean remounted, took Strawberry's rein and led her out into the middle of the field, where she began to put pony and rider through their paces, gently criticising the position of Jenny's hands and heels and forcing Strawberry (whose one desire was to fill herself with moist grass and who brought home to Jean the meaning of the words 'eating like a horse') to lift her head from her banquet, and trot.

The field lay upon a slight incline, and overlooked another wilder field streaked with dark belts of coarse reeds and water, and bearing thickets of old thorn trees here and there. It was separated from the meadow in which they were riding by the hedge to which Blackberry was tethered, and lower down it was not easy to see if this hedge remained unbroken, or if there were gaps in it. Suddenly there sounded a high, shrill neigh. Jean glanced across to the wild meadow and there, running along with mane flying and looking like a steed from a fairy tale, was a young white stallion. He was coming down towards the hedge.

Strawberry pricked up her ears and eagerly lifted her head towards the sound, and neighed in answer, and at the same instant Socks started forward, plunging and rearing. Jean reined him tightly in, speaking to him in a low soothing voice which she interrupted only to say quickly to Jenny, who was struggling to rein in Strawberry, 'That's right—grip with your knees and shorten rein—it's all right, they're only saying "hello" to each other.'

The stallion had halted a little way from the hedge and now stood gazing towards them. He lifted his head and neighed again. Jean, still struggling with Socks, who was trembling all over, gazed anxiously at the hedge. Could the stallion get through? Her heart was beating fast. She had never realised how immensely strong a horse is. It was all that she could do, by exerting her utmost strength, to rein Socks in.

'She's going to run away,' gasped Jenny, almost crying. 'Oh

Jean—I can't hold her!' At that moment Jean saw a confused movement by the gate and there came a scream from Louise:

'Jean—Jean, it's running away!'

She turned her head, and was in time to see Blackberry in agitated movement and Louise falling to the ground, screaming as she fell.

'*God,*' said Jean and, crying to Jenny to hold on, urged her horse forward.

In a few seconds she had reached Louise's side and dismounted. It was not so bad as she had feared. Blackberry had shaken her rein loose from the post and was feeding apparently undisturbed at a little distance away, and Louise was crouching in the grass hysterically crying. She seemed unhurt.

'It's all right, ducky, you're quite safe. Don't make such a fearful noise—you're frightening Strawberry,' said Jean, putting her arm around her shoulders. But Louise continued to cry in a sobbing scream, while tears poured from her eyes. Her face was distorted with terror.

'Oh—oh—don't make me get on her again—please, please, don't!'

'Are you hurt anywhere?' asked Jean, and Louise sobbingly shook her head.

'Then get up and do stop that awful noise,' said Jean, even with sternness. 'Look, here comes Jenny to see what on earth's the matter.' But Louise continued to shudder and wail.

Jenny had now controlled Strawberry and came trotting up, with a frightened face. The stallion's neigh came shrilly to them again, and Jean glanced across and saw him scouring backwards and forwards along the hedge as if seeking an entry.

'It's all right, he can't get through, there's no gap,' said Jenny, following the direction of her look, 'I've made sure as I came along.'

'Thank goodness,' muttered Jean.

'Is Weez hurt?' asked Jenny anxiously.

'I don't think so—only frightened. Weez, ducky, *do* pull yourself together—they'll hear you at Horsham.'

'I want to go home,' wailed Louise.

'Yes, do let's go home, please, Jean,' added Jenny. 'I don't feel like riding any more.'

'Neither do I, heaven knows,' said Jean feelingly. 'All right, then. Jenny, you just stay where you are, if you feel you can manage Strawberry. Now, Weez darling, I'll catch Blackberry, and——'

'Oh, don't make me get on her again, *please* don't!'

Jean glanced helplessly in Blackberry's direction and was dismayed to see that she had strayed down to the hedge towards the stallion and was wandering about cropping the grass with the reins tangled about one of her forelegs. Jean knew from experience that she would not be easy to catch. Then, she looked back at Jenny, who was frowning and shaking her head, mutely imploring that she should not force Louise to remount.

'All right—if you really feel you can't,' she said cheerfully, taking Louise's hands. 'Now up you get—that grass is wet—and I'll catch Blackberry, and Jen and I will take the horses back to the stable while you stay here. All right?'

'It can't get through the hedge and get me, can it?' and Louise cast a fearful glance towards the stallion.

'Of course not, but even if he could, he wouldn't hurt you. He's only feeling good because it's a lovely day.'

'I hate him,' sniffed Louise. 'Oh, must you both go? Can't Jenny stay here?'

It was plain that Jenny would have to. Louise was still trembling and her face wore that peculiar, pallied greenish hue which only follows deep terror and shock, and all the while she was speaking she convulsively grasped and ungrasped Jean's hands.

'Of course she can,' she comforted, and gave to Jenny, who was gravely watching them, a meaning look which meant '*Take great care of her.*' 'Now I'll go and catch Blackberry.'

Jenny dismounted and led Strawberry, who appeared perfectly docile, to the gate, and tethered her. Then she took off her jacket and spread it upon a sandy bank and made Louise sit down, and as Jean walked down the slope towards the pony, she saw out of the corner of her eye that Jenny had found a dirty handkerchief in Louise's pocket and was carefully (but without so much tenderness as to increase the patient's self-pity) wiping her eyes. What a gem the child is, she thought, but, of course, she does happen not to be afraid of horses. Thank goodness Socks is behaving himself (Socks was peacefully eating grass near the gate where Strawberry was tethered). I misjudged him.

She had, indeed.

Upon seeing her approach, Blackberry gave an impatient toss of the head as if to say, 'Oh lord, there's no peace nowadays,' and absently moved a few paces on; then, as Jean ran down towards her, she broke into a trot and made for the hedge. There was the quick sound of hoofs on turf, a squeal, and the stallion's head reared above the frail wall of greening thorn, full eye glittering, nostrils distended, the white of muzzle and forehead shading and rippling under the light as if dull velvet changed to shining satin, and all proclaiming such wild innocent joy in the spring day that Jean cried out, 'Hello, you lovely boy! I hope you can't jump that hedge!' as she ran forward and triumphantly caught Blackberry's rein.

The stallion restlessly watched while she disentangled the pony's reins from between the hoofs; it took some time, because Blackberry would not move when she was told to, and once or twice she trod on Jean's feet, bruising them with her solid, immovable, frightening weight. But at last she was freed, and Jean led her back to the children.

'It's no use, she won't ride again,' said Jenny in a lowered tone, coming to meet her. Louise was still sitting upon the jacket, looking sulky. 'And she won't be left, either. What shall we do?'

Jean judged that she had been giving her sister a lecture on cowardice and horsemanship, for she was glowing with right-eousness and bustle, but in spite of this, when Jean suggested that Jenny should ride each pony in turn back to the stables while she herself rode Socks, Louise refused to let her go.

'I want Jenny,' she said obstinately, trembling and pale.

'Oh Weez, do pull yourself together! I can't ride Socks back and lead both the ponies too. I'm not experienced enough.'

'Can't you ride them all back one at a time?' suggested Jenny.

'That would make us so late at Meadow Cottage; it's half-past three now. Well, I shall just have to make two journeys, that's all. You are a trial, Weez ducky,' she added mildly, as she went off to catch Socks.

'Sorry,' gulped Louise and began to cry.

Jean thought it best to take no notice. She mounted Socks (who surprised her by jerking his head away with bared teeth as she caught at the reins) and called to Jenny to bring Blackberry. Then, holding the pony's rein, she called cheerfully, 'Shan't be a moment,' touched Socks with her heels, and rode off.

The track ran beside a meadow bordered by chestnuts, those trees whose bounteous lower branches sweep groundwards and in summer form a level roof of green above meadows hazy with light.

As they drove near one of the lowest-drooping boughs, Socks swerved towards it and increased his pace, and Jean, taken by surprise and hampered by Blackberry, only succeeded by an exertion of strength which she did not know that she possessed in pulling him up short immediately in front of the tree. He snorted, and stood still.

'Trying to sweep me off, were you, my beauty,' she muttered, trembling unpleasantly as she turned him round and forced him back to the track. 'All right, now I know what you're like. I only hope we get home safely.'

The next few minutes passed uneasily; she felt that something was going to happen; however, nothing did; Socks continued at his natural awkward pace that was neither canter nor gallop and Blackberry ran at his side, keeping well clear, Jean noticed, of his hoofs. The stables came in sight; she turned Socks towards them, and with Blackberry following they rode past the sheds on either side into the yard.

Immediately ahead was an open doorway with a low lintel; beyond, in shadow, she caught a glimpse of gold seeds spilling down from a heap of sacks and a graceful gold and white pony tethered beside a black mare. The pony lifted his head and whickered; Jean caught the coarse, exciting odour of fresh grain; she dropped Blackberry's rein and let her go free, and the next instant Socks sprang forward and charged through the doorway.

She just had time to lower her head. Had it struck the lintel she would have been killed. As it was, when Socks suddenly stood still, she raised herself, confused by the speed with which this had happened, and struck with her scalp the low roof of corrugated iron. It clanged loudly, and Socks snorted with terror and started backwards through the doorway. She was swept from his back by the doorpost and fell on her side into some straw beside the entrance. She sprang up instantly and ran after him; he had halted outside in the yard and stood trembling and glancing wildly from side to side. Of Blackberry there was no sign. She caught the bridle and patted and soothed Socks, but she did not know what she said; she only felt that she was bruised all over and that her hands were scratched; then she saw the head and shield-like breast of Shooting Star, ready for any mischief, rear itself half-way above his stable door.

Socks's stable door stood open. She coaxed him across the yard towards it, every inch of the way, for he was still uneasy and unwilling to move, and just as they reached it Shooting Star, who was still pressing eagerly over his own stable door, flung up his head and neighed. Socks shied violently and plunged towards him with bared teeth. Jean's grasp was jerked from the rein, and for an instant she did not know what was happening. Then someone came behind her and gripped Socks's head over her shoulder, and a man's voice said fussily:

'What on earth's the matter?' It was Mr Waite.

She thankfully retreated and stood at a little distance, rubbing her bruised arms and side and trying to calm the thudding of her heart, while she watched him force the horse into the stable. Socks did not want to go in, and before he got him in Mr Waite was red in the face and his lower lip stuck out and when he did shut the stable door he slammed it very hard indeed. He looked as if he were going to shake his fist at Socks and cry, 'There, my lord!' but instead he turned to her and said crossly as he set his jacket and sleeves to rights:

'Can't you manage a horse, Miss Hardcastle?'

'Yes, of course I can, usually, but he's such an extraordinary horse, he seemed so quiet, and we've had a spot of bother down in the meadow with a stallion—oh and where's the pony?—the children! My goodness! I must fly—thanks awfully——' and she was already hurrying away, ignoring her trembling legs and stiff aching arms, when he came after her, saying:

'Are you all right? What happened? Where are the children? I'll come too. I must help you.'

This last remark, now a favourite joke between Alda and herself, upset Jean into a silly laugh which she stifled in her handkerchief. He looked at her more tolerantly, pleased that she was feeling hysterical.

'Thank you very much,' she said, and explained what had happened.

'Are they down there now alone with the ponies?' interrupted Mr Waite. 'Can they manage them?'

'There's only one; the other's wandered off somewhere and they aren't trying to manage anything; they're both sitting on Jenny's jacket, and I expect they're both howling by now,' she retorted, annoyed by his hectoring tone.

'I'd better get down there at once,' he muttered, and turned back.

'What are you going to do?' staring.

'Ride. It'll be quicker,' explained Mr Waite, who did not believe in leaving anything to the intuitions of his listener, 'I'll bring the ponies back with me. You just go quietly on; I'll overtake you.'

In a few minutes he did. Far off she heard the exciting, joyous thud of released hoofs flying over turf; the next instant there was a gold flash, a streak of white, a whirlwind, and Shooting Star flew past, carrying Mr Waite to the rescue.

He rode superbly; she had often read in novels old and new of that harmony between horse and rider which makes them look like a single being, and now she saw it, and very beautiful and impressive it was.

A scene of pastoral peace dawned upon her as the meadow came in view. Mr Waite was conversing with Jenny and Louise, who were both eating something which presumably he had produced from his pocket. Shooting Star was tethered to a gate, eating. The ponies were tethered to other gates, eating. The stallion was at the far end of the wild meadow, eating. Even Mr Waite had a cigarette in his mouth, and Jean suddenly sighed aloud:

'Oh, I do want my tea!' and remembered that at this very hour they were all supposed to be drinking it in Mr Waite's cottage.

'You've managed them all!' she said, smiling at him as she came up to the group. 'I don't know what I should have done with Socks if you hadn't come along. What a horse! Well, Weez, are you all right now?'

Louise nodded, lifting a face still pale, but comfortably touched with chocolate about the mouth and ready to smile.

'Mr Waite does ride marvellously!' burst out Jenny. 'You should have seen him come up on Shooting Star, it was like the pictures!'

Mr Waite did not smile. 'It's all a question of letting the horse know who's master,' he said austerely. 'Now, you ladies are supposed to be having tea with me this afternoon, you know; I met Mrs Lucie-Browne in the lane and she told me you were here and I thought I'd come up to meet you. It was a good thing I did, wasn't it?'

They all meekly agreed that it was.

'Well, then,' looking at his watch, 'we'd better be off.' He turned to Jenny. 'Can you ride Blackberry back to the stables?'

'Alone or with you?'

'With me.'

'Of course I can,' she said confidently, and it was arranged that Jean and Louise should walk back with Strawberry.

They rode off, Mr Waite again godlike upon Shooting Star, and Jean wondered that the force of will necessary to subdue the fiery horse had not gained for him a fuller life than that of a chicken-farmer living in the middle of a damp meadow. She also thought that it was as well that her *first* sight of him had not been when he was on horseback, or she would certainly have fallen in love again.

17

Alda leant against the gate of Meadow Cottage, delighting in the afternoon sun and hoping that Mr Waite and Jean were getting to know each other better while strolling home from Rush House.

She had been struck by the impoverished appearance of his home: it was shabbier and uglier than even bachelor habits could account for, and indicated a freezing lack of money in its owner, yet he never spoke of money; the rueful, contemptuous or envious references to the tiresome stuff which most people, in most classes, make from time to time never came from Mr Waite. Alda neither thought that this showed a pleasant nature nor a peculiar one; she merely thought that Jean had enough for them both. (And indeed, no one would have suspected that Mr Waite's silence upon money resembled the silence with which an experienced lover shrouds the name and habits of his mistress: he loves too much to speak her name: if he did, he would betray himself.)

She was just firmly dismissing Meg's suggestion that they should go into the cottage and explore when he came in sight. He was alone.

'Hullo!' called Alda. 'Couldn't you find them?'

He did not answer until he was almost level with her, and she waited, gazing at him curiously. He was carrying his hat and his appearance somehow suggested that he was on his way to a funeral. He said gravely:

'Now there's nothing to worry about, Mrs Lucie-Browne; the little girls and Miss Hardcastle have gone back to Pine Cottage, but they'll be here any minute. There's been a little accident, but it's nothing——'

'What happened?' Alda neither paled nor started and her tone was only impatient. Her nerves were healthy, her imagination just active enough to redeem her from the accusation of sheer insensitiveness, and her immediate answer to alarming news was usually amusement or anger. Mr Waite was shocked.

He looked at her, as she stood by the gate with the sunlight shining on her hair and her old jersey, the colour of thick cream, showing up honeysuckle tints in her skin, and he was shocked. How pretty she was, but she lacked femininity.

'The little girl fell off her pony,' he said severely.

'Weez? Poor old goose!' said Alda, and burst out laughing. 'Was she hurt?' But she knew that Weez could not have been hurt, or Jean would have sent Jenny with Mr Waite: Jean would never have let a stranger break bad news.

'She was very much upset, poor little mite,' said Mr Waite. Here Meg, who had been listening with eyes fixed first upon his face and then upon her mother's, broke in with the demand:

'Is she goin' to die?'

'Of course not, dear,' said Mr Waite very kindly, smiling down upon her upturned face, which expressed an interest that he interpreted as anxiety for her big sister, 'she isn't even scratched or hurt at all.'

'Was there any blood?' persisted Meg.

'Shut up, you little ghoul,' said Alda, gently touching her with her knee. 'Weez was only frightened.'

'Oh, oh, poor Weez, oh! oh!' roared Meg, bursting into tears, 'oh, oh, I shan't shut up, Meg wants tea.'

'Yes, and I am sure poor mummy could do with a cup, too,' said Mr Waite. 'Allow me,' and he bustled past Alda into the house. 'The big kettle is boiling, and by the time the tea's drawn the others will be here.'

He was ready to forgive her if she would only be Poor Mummy, but Alda, who had never felt herself as Poor Mummy in her life and who did not relish being cast for the part now, only answered cheerfully, 'That would be marvellous,' and, picking up Meg and giving her an angry kiss that silenced her, carried her into the cottage.

Tea was arranged in the parlour, which was even worse than Alda had expected. The walls were distempered dark acid green, the carpet was grey with beige angles, and there were more pictures of those old men with churchwardens, depicting some jolly incident in their carefree Georgian lives. The curtains were faded blue cotton. There was nothing pretty or attractive in the dark little room except the tea-table, which was spread with a dazzling white cloth of finest lawn inlaid with bands of exquisite drawn-threadwork; the cups were a smiling, open shape with elaborate handles that delighted the eye, made from thin china and coloured a clear pink deeply banded with gold. The smooth silver milk jug flashed blue in the afternoon light; the sugar basin repeated its bland surfaces and narrow fretted bands. Bang in the middle of all this elegance, as if Mr Waite's resources and energy had suddenly failed, was a hideous Prewitt vase stuffed with primroses.

'Pink cakes,' said Meg, in a hoarse whisper, pointing.

'Please make yourselves at home,' came Mr Waite's voice from the back of the house. 'The tea's just coming.'

'May I see your kitchen?' said Alda, and strolled down the passage followed by Meg.

'Mr Waite, who stood beside a filthy old gas stove, warming the teapot, looked embarrassed. He said nothing.

'Why, it's much nicer than the sitting-room!' exclaimed Alda, looking round, 'and what a lovely view over the fields! Why don't you have meals out here?'

'I do occasionally,' he said, arranging teapot and hot-water jug, 'but when ladies come to tea the proper place is the dining-room. Allow me,' and he went out carrying the tray.

You're rather nice, decided Alda, loitering after him with hands in her pockets; pussyish, but nice.

Voices and footsteps were now heard in the porch and Jean and the children arrived, freshly washed and brushed and wearing everyday clothes. Louise looked pale but complacent.

'Mother, Weez *will* say she was "*thrown*"!' burst out Jenny. 'She wasn't, was she?'

'How on earth should I know, ducky? I wasn't there. Well, Weez, did you fall on your seat?'

'She didn't even fall!' said Jenny indignantly. 'Blackberry just walked on a little way and Weez slid off.'

'You're all right, aren't you, darling?' Alda caressed Louise's hair, with a keen look at the child's face.

'My back aches,' said Louise, not without pride.

'It's bound to, for a day or two,' said Jean. 'I'll rub it with that stuff of yours to-night, Alda, and it'll be all right in the morning. I say, is there any tea? I'm collapsing for mine.' She looked pretty, for the walk across the fields had given her a colour and ruffled her fair curls and her diamonds winked against the yellow, green and blue flecks in a suit of soft tweed.

'Ah, there you are.' Mr Waite appeared at his front door. 'We were beginning to think you had got lost,' and he laughed. 'Come along in, tea's all ready.'

He might be seventy-three and old for his age, thought Alda, as they trooped after him back into the house.

Having directed his guests to their allotted seats, he surveyed them in silence. There was a pause. They gazed back at him. Jenny's lips were shaping the words, 'Can we begin? I'm starving,' when Mr Waite, whose gaze had come to rest on Alda, said:

'Will you be mother, please?' and moved the tea-tray towards her.

'I was just going to; it's second nature to me by now,' she said, and began to pour out.

There was not enough to eat on the table, a fact which the children saw from their first mouthfuls and which caused Jean and Alda (who were also hungry, the one after the afternoon's

adventures and the other because of a delayed tea hour) to limit
their own intake so that Jenny, Louise and Meg might have the
more. Mr Waite neither noticed what they ate nor thought about
it, being too busy eating his own share—which was large—and
curbing his impatience over the account, which now took place,
of the events at Rush House. Alda listened with deep interest,
for she had that strong interest in the discussion of everyday
events, especially when they admit of some technical analysis,
which is felt by practical women who lack the poetic or specu-
lative streak; her faculty of Wonder was slightly underdeveloped.
What she relished was anecdote, or information lucidly and
lightly conveyed, or the shrewd entertaining dissection of people's
characters, but she disliked scandal.

As soon as his guests had finished commenting upon the
behaviour of the horses and their riders, Mr Waite took advantage
of their faces being temporarily buried in their cups and mugs
to launch into a lecture upon the folly of ladies and kiddies
trying to ride horses at all; adorned with sombre illustrations
drawn from the fate of ladies known to him and his family who
had attempted to ride horses in Daleham and its neighbouring
districts.

His audience listened politely for a while, but at the third
account of a female coming to equine disaster, Alda broke in
impatiently:

'But that doesn't prove anything. Thousands of women ride
horses every day and are all right. I shan't let this afternoon's
affair make any difference to the children's lessons.'

'Oh Mother, *need* I learn any more?' burst out Louise imploringly. Mr Waite fixed reproachful eyes upon Alda. There, you see,
his look said.

'But, darling, it's such fun! and later on you'll be so glad that
you started when you were quite young.'

Louise projected her lower lip and looked down at her plate.
Her eyelids quivered and she was silent.

'It's super,' said Jenny, giving her a scornful glance.

Louise muttered something that no one could hear.

'You'll be all right, now you've fallen off,' said Jean, soothingly. 'Everyone has to fall off once—I don't know why,' and she giggled.

'Oh *yes*!' exclaimed Jenny, suddenly; she had been talking in lowered tones with Louise. 'Bicycles,' she added, turning to her mother.

'Yes, but that's a long way off, if we ever do get them, and you can ride every week for twelve weeks *now*,' said Alda shortly. She was annoyed with Louise at displaying her timid, over-feminine aspect before Mr Waite (who needed no confirmation in his view of The Sex), and making herself appear as an unsympathetic mother.

'I'm not frightened of bicycles,' explained Louise, and Jenny's mutter of 'It's a wonder you aren't' was lost in the general laugh. Alda took advantage of this happier turn to lead the conversation on to the pleasures of bicycling and tea ended—though Mr Waite more than once compressed his lips or shook his head—on a cheerful note.

The children ran out to see what Meg persisted in calling 'those poor chickens,' and the ladies lingered over a cigarette with their host in the dark little room where one late ray had found its way through the shaded window and the primroses glimmered green and yellow out of the golden dusk.

Six o'clock from the village church chimed slowly across the fields. A silence had fallen in the casual talk: the three figures seated about the table looked very distinct in the soft dim light. Mr Waite happened to be gazing at Alda.

'Blackbird!' said Jean suddenly and softly, lifting her head so that her hair slid back, and she got up and wandered over to the window and thence out into the garden. The blackbird was singing near at hand but she could not see him.

'We'll help you wash up,' announced Alda, determined that

she would leave Jean alone with him, thus employed, while she went out to find the children.

'I can't allow that,' said Mr Waite gallantly, but Alda was already stacking the cups.

'What beautiful things you have,' she said civilly: she could never admire any objects, except those made by God, without a slight feeling of envy.

'These are my mother's; they come from The Old Home,' said Mr Waite and the faithful negro servants, the porch fragrant with mint juleps, the family portraits and the Federal hordes were all contained in his tone.

'Aren't you afraid I'll break them?' asked Alda, giving him one backward glance as she went out of the door. It was bad of her, but she could not help it; in another minute she would have flung open a window and shrieked.

'Of course not!' he protested eagerly, hurrying after her with the milk jug. 'Ladies never break things.'

'Don't you believe it,' she muttered, looking round for a dishcloth. 'I'm the world's champion smasher.' She pushed up her sleeves and took a steaming kettle from the horrid little stove.

'Oh, I can't believe that, you know.'

'It's true, all the same. You know,' she continued, beginning vigorously yet carefully upon the cups with a little mop, 'you have mistaken ideas about women, Mr Waite.'

'Have I?' He was standing still, with the tablecloth in his hand, looking at her.

'Yes. You're old-fashioned about them.'

'I prefer to be,' he answered stiffly, taking a cup and beginning to dry it.

'I daresay you do, but it isn't fair to all the women that you know personally.' She raised her voice. 'Jean! Come and give a hand with the washing up!' But Jean had wandered away into the fields.

'That business about women riding, for example,' said Alda. 'If everybody had those views none of us would ever do anything at all. Women aren't always remembering that they're women, you know.'

'Aren't they?' Mr Waite held the teacloth suspended while he gazed at her.

'Of course not! I don't go creeping about all day thinking *I'm a woman—I'm a woman.* Do you go round thinking *I'm a man—I'm a man?*'

'Well—yes, I do, on the whole, I think,' he confessed. 'Quite often, anyway!'

'Well, I don't,' said Alda emphatically, setting down the last cup on the draining board. 'I'm too busy enjoying or hating things and being a *person.*'

And she wrung out the miserable little dishcloth so hard that it tore.

'Oh, you are a feminist, then?' said Mr Waite, but more in a tone of caution than in the one of righteous horror that might have been expected.

'Indeed I'm not; I think they're crashing bores who can't get their own way by natural means,' and she smiled: a smile which seemed an emanation from her hair, her eyes and her delightful nose. 'Besides,' she went on more vaguely, 'who would *want* the things they do? Oh, there you are,' to Jean, who now strolled in with hands in her pockets, 'where have you been? It's all done.'

'Looking for the blackbird,' Jean answered. 'Look,' and she held up between her white forefinger and thumb a dark spike of bluebells in bud, 'Isn't that very early? They usually aren't out until late April. I say, can I help you put things away?'

It was now Alda's turn to wander away after the children while Jean and Mr Waite made journeys between the kitchen and a beastly little cabinet lined with dirty plush in which the cups were stored. Jean said nothing, and he too was silent at first. Once or twice, when he was not looking, she glanced at him and thought how good-looking he was: Alda would have approved of this, but not of the thoughts which accompanied the glance. He, for his part, completely approved of Miss Hardcastle; her clothes, her placid silly manner, the casque of gilt hair that slid obediently as she moved her head yet never became untidy, her lack of disturbing qualities.

He also liked the aura of money which surrounded her. He was used to this type of girl at home in Daleham; the only daughter of wealthy parents, dressed in the height, but not the extreme, of fashion, with an ingenuous manner that did not match her sophisticated clothes and hairdressing. Such had been the provincial belles with whom he had danced and motored in his early youth, before the loss of the family money, and he felt much more at ease with Miss Hardcastle than he did with Mrs Lucie-Browne. Presently he was making a mild joke or two, to which Jean, always ready for a laugh, cheerfully responded.

'Want to see the chickens hab their tea,' announced Meg threateningly, bustling into the room. She halted, lowering at them from under her fringe.

'Little girls should ask nicely and say "please",' retorted Mr Waite, slowly rising to his full height after tucking away the last cup, and looking down gravely upon her.

'I'm afraid there won't be time for the chickens, it's after Meg's bedtime now,' said Alda, and thereupon what Mr Waite, with sudden irritation, thought of as *the whole tribe* swarmed into the parlour. 'Say good-bye to Mr Waite, children.'

Did Mr Waite shut the door upon them and turn back into his quiet room, in which the last light now lingered, with a feeling of relief, or did he loiter in the porch, watching them go across the meadow until they were out of sight, and then reluctantly re-enter his lonely bachelor abode? Reader, we have to irritate you by saying that he did both; he lingered a little at the door, and yet he was satisfied to take up the morning paper and sit down in the silent room to glance over it before going out to feed the chickens. But a strong impression remained with him; a shape, a face, certain intonations in a voice, presented themselves to him over and over again, against his will, until at last he pushed the paper aside and went out to his evening's work.

'Oh, doesn't the fresh air smell lovely—it's like a present!' cried Jenny, as soon as the garden gate had shut behind them.

'Be quiet, Jen, he'll hear you,' said Louise, glancing back at the cottage. 'Mum,' taking her mother's arm, 'can we have a high tea when we get back? I'm starving.'

'So am I,' called back Jenny, who had run on ahead. 'Those cakes! Ugh! I bet they didn't come from the Linga-Longa!'

'Meg could peck a bit,' remarked a cross voice from below Alda's waist, as if to itself. Alda silently stooped and lifted her up: the intonation meant that she was overtired.

'Poor man, he did his best, he just isn't used to women with our appetites,' said Jean.

'He isn't used to women at all,' muttered Alda. 'All right, we'll all have sardine sandwiches for supper when we get in.'

'Jean, does your side still hurt?' she went on.

'I can feel it, thanks, but it isn't bad.'

'Try rubbing it with that stuff of mine to-night, it's marvellous. You probably won't know you've got a side to-morrow.'

'My botty still hurts,' sighed Louise. 'Mother, need I have any more riding lessons? I do hate them.' She looked pathetically, but without real apprehension, at her mother. Alda's bark was worse than her bite and her daughters knew it.

'Well——' Alda hesitated, then glanced at Jean.

'Don't make her learn any more if she doesn't want to,' said Jean cheerfully.

'Oh, thank you, darling, darling Mother!' cried Louise, dancing about to express her gratitude and relief.

'Now don't go telling everybody at the convent that you were *thrown*,' said Jenny severely, but also beginning to dance. 'Come on, let's go on ahead and lay the supper ready for the sandwiches.'

The evening hush led Jean's thoughts on towards evenings of high summer, and she remembered seeing the lights of Paris sparkling in blue-grey August mist as they glided past the windows of the train which bore herself, a child, towards the mountains: awakening in the hour before dawn and drowsily hearing, to the hollow rumbling of milk churns rolled along the platform, the far-off, sonorous voices of porters chanting, 'Lyons, Lyons': awakening again—in the ghostly light before sunrise—the hour of the Resurrection—and turning her face towards the air blowing in through the window of the carriage where she lay and feeling it cold: becoming aware of effort trembling through all the train's length and realising that it was now climbing: creeping into the corridor through the greyness and leaning out of the window: breathing the chill air fresh with dewy scents: looking out over dim green hillocks and fields and vales under a sky clear as water, with blossoming fruit trees standing like white clouds come down to earth: rubbing her eyes as smoke from the engine drifted across them for a moment and then, when the smoke drifted away again, suddenly seeing something far off on the horizon; an unsubstantial vastness heaving itself solemnly up into the colourless sky and touched with a spectral light, something which at one glance transformed all the scale of the land over which she was gazing: oh! it must be, it was, a mountain crowned with snow.

Her parents had at least given her holidays abroad, she thought; lonely holidays spent dawdling about in French and Swiss and Italian hotels while her parents were off ski-ing or sun-bathing or gambling, but never dull while she could look about her, and had money to buy a Tauchnitz edition of an English novel, and could exchange shy remarks in halting, execrable French with chambermaids and waiters and concierges. Years later, when she came to read Proust, she had thought that her own holidays had been not unlike those passed at Balbec by the delicate, morbid 'I' of that story; she knew it all; the evening light on the white napkins laid on empty tables awaiting the hour of dining; the sharpened sense of life and importance given to fellow guests, who would have seemed ordinary in an uncoastal setting, by the brilliance and sting of sea air and light. Oh *yes*! she had cried to herself again and again in recognition when 'I' fell in love with a girl he had never spoken to or had seen once through the window of a tram: and she remembered the page boy at the Miramar, the young life-saving attendant at the Bristol, and the waiter at the Floraison, and how she had silently loved them all. I have been in love so many times since I was eleven, she thought, but now something seems to be happening to me. Of course, he (this was Mr Waite) is good-looking and he does ride marvellously but I don't seem to be able to get thrilled about him. Of course, I still am very thrilled with my Mr Potter.

'Somebody ought to get that man out of that place, he's wasted there and I don't know how he stands it,' said Alda suddenly, with a glance at her friend. 'What do you think of him, Jean?'

Jean considered. 'I'm sorry for him,' she said slowly, at last.

'Jean,' Alda said abruptly, 'could you pull yourself together about him? Make up your mind to marry him *and do it*?'

Jean surprised her by answering, 'I don't suppose so,' in a tone different from any she had ever heard from her; it was both reserved and dry; but even as Alda, startled, turned quickly to look at her, she went on in her usual voice:

'He's marvellously good-looking, of course, but, darling, I do think he's the least bit dreary, don't you?'

'He's very dreary,' admitted Alda handsomely, 'but he's also kind. He is really, J., underneath all that pussyishness, and that's what you want in a husband.'

'Pussyishness?' Again the dry, unfamiliar tone.

'No, kindness. (At least you would want it; Ronald is very kind, of course, but I could probably get on with him if he weren't quite so kind, I'm tougher than you.) And Waite only seems dreary to us because we're both used to other kinds of men. But most men, even dreary ones, are nice, if you get to know them,' concluded Alda.

Now this opinion, with all that it implied, contained the secret of such success as a woman as Alda enjoyed. To *like* men: their company, their conversation, their approval, and sometimes to challenge them a little—that, for a woman, is the passport to men's affection and the love that leads to marriage. If she can also be prettily dressed, kind, and gay in the middle of an earthquake occurring on a Monday morning while she is doing the week's wash, there is absolutely nothing to stop her from marrying as often, and whom, she chooses. (These remarks are addressed to all women who would like to be married, not to those straying outside the ring of domestic firelight who prefer children or music or even dogs to men.) We would add that the liking must be genuine, and not feigned to conceal rapacious or parasitic intentions.

'Are they?' said Jean, wonderingly.

To her, men meant love, and since the age of sixteen she had seen all men through that amethyst haze. It had not occurred to her to decide whether she truly preferred their company to that of any other, because she had been so feverishly sure that she did, but now, living down here in the country with no masculine society save occasional encounters with Mr Waite, she was beginning for the first time to muse about what and whom she really did like.

'Of course they are,' said Alda carelessly, 'and if you *concentrated* on him you'd soon get to like him.'

'I don't *dis*like him, Alda. It's only——'

'You can't afford to be too fussy, J. They always seem to slip away from you somehow or some witch gets them at the last

minute—I don't know how it is—but down here there's absolutely *no* competition. And he'd soon get to—see your point of
view.'

They both laughed, and Meg stirred on Alda's shoulder.

'He approves of you, and that's a good beginning,' said Alda,
as they went up the path to the cottage.

'Oh, does he, darling? Do tell me how you know; I never
can tell, myself.'

'By the way he looks at you. But he does *not* approve of me,'
and she chuckled.

Jean was silent. It had suddenly occurred to her that Captain
Ottley and Michael Powers, two elderly men whom she had
first met at Alda's house, had approved of herself and slightly
disapproved of Alda. And the more she thought about concen-
trating upon marrying Mr Waite, the less she liked the idea, for
she knew that she would never be able to keep to a plan of
campaign, no matter how skilfully Alda mapped one out for her.

She began to talk in an amused, protesting tone:

'It's so difficult, darling, having him living so near. I shall
always be barging into him——'

'All the better,' said Alda. They were now in the cottage, and
she turned to shut the door on the twilight fields.

'Yes, but *rather* embarrassing, darling. Besides, he hasn't any
money.'

'He's got more than he seems to have, I expect,' said Alda
(who thought that he surely could not have less). She did not
add that Jean had more than enough for both.

A wail came from the kitchen:

'*Do* buck up, we're simply starving.'

'Start without us, then, I'm going to put Megsy into bed,
she's asleep,' Alda called softly in reply, and went upstairs.

Jean was relieved by the interruption and went into the
kitchen, where she found Jenny mourning because she could
not manage the key of the sardine tin. It seems a pity that the

people who are always trying to fly their repulsive aeroplanes at seven hundred miles per hour do not turn their colossal intellects on to simpler problems.

Later that evening, while they were sitting over their sewing, Jean said to Alda:

'Darling, I've been thinking about what you said, and I do agree with it, only, if you don't mind and won't misunderstand it, I don't think I want to *concentrate* on doing anything. I would rather things just came about *naturally*, if you know what I mean.'

'Just as you like, of course, J., only your affairs do have a habit of going wrong when they're left to Nature and I'm all for taking the practical view and making a definite plan. French marriages are always arranged, and this idea of letting anyone just drift into marrying anyone else is only about a hundred years old, you know; in England, at any rate. In your case, I'm sure it would be better to try to run the whole affair in a practical way. But of course, if you want romance——'

'It's not exactly that, darling——'

'By "practical" I mean—never letting the idea of marriage with him out of your mind; not getting vague and sloppy or letting him see you're attracted by him, keeping him guessing but not frightening him off—oh—it would be so easy!' and her eyes sparkled as if she saw herself stage-managing the affair.

'But—Alda—' Jean said hesitatingly—'there is his point of view—and besides, one hasn't the right—I mean, don't you believe that every human soul has a value?—and it may be really *wrong* to try to use other people for one's own ends, as if they were *things*, not souls—oh, I can't express myself properly—but——'

'Of course I believe people have souls, I'm not a heathen,' said Alda, staring, 'but I'm bothered if I see what the fuss is about. Surely it's better for the poor man to marry you and get out of that dim life and perhaps develop his brain and be of some use in the world, and for you to have a husband and a home and probably children, than for both of you to stay unmarried because of some extraordinary idea about souls? The fact is, ducky,' she said more gently, 'I don't want to come the Old-Married-Woman over you, but *honestly* you don't know what you're talking about.'

She was silent for a moment; she gazed down at her work but did not see the little sock she held, for she seemed to be casting her inward eye over the rich varied fields of her possessions, the family of human lives growing and flourishing about her with ripened sheaves or young promise of harvest.

It's no use, you don't understand, thought the virgin sadly. I *do* want all the things you have; I know how beautiful they are; but it's like that Victorian picture called *More Heavens Than One* where the nun is watching the cottager bathing her baby, only in my case the idea is reversed. You're telling me about your heaven, and I want—or I'm beginning to think I want—quite another kind.

18

'Sylvia,' said Mrs Hoadley, a week or so later, 'a nice day out on Sunday would do you good. There's this chicken I want to send to the old people at the Wild Brooks. How about your taking it over?'

'How about your posting it?' retorted Sylvia, showing her kitten's teeth in a grin. The two were lingering over the tea-table, amid a dazzle of late sunrays falling on the crystal jam dish and the rich brown cake.

'Last time I posted one some miserable thief stole it,' snapped Mrs Hoadley. She did not look well; her face was sallow and bore dark rings under the eyes.

'Next Sunday's your day off, isn't it? I think you'd better go. The old lady likes to see a new face now and then; and you'll make a change for her,' she went on.

'I hate going places by myself.'

'Take your boy friend then,' and she got up and began half-heartedly to clear the table.

'Who—Fabrio?' Sylvia let out a screech of laughter and clasped her hands round her knees. 'What a thought! Still, him and me don't get on too badly nowadays. It's an idea. He'd make a change for the old lady, if you like.'

'Take him, then.' She sat down again. 'Here, you can clear these things away, and earn your keep for once.'

'But he isn't allowed out of that monkey cage on a Sunday, is he?'

'He can go anywhere within twenty miles of the camp, all the Italian prisoners can, now the war's over, only they're on parole. The Wild Brooks is only about fifteen miles from here.'

'All right, then, I'll ask him. There's no harm in asking. We can practise our lessons in the bus.'

'You don't go by bus, you go by train. And, Sylvia, you'd better dress yourself a bit quieter than you usually do on your Sundays off. I expect you'll get stared at, an English girl out with an Italian, and the ignorant sort might pass remarks. Take my advice and do your hair in a bun, too. I shouldn't like to tell you what the old lady said your hair looked like, the last time she was over here.'

'I know; a tart,' said Sylvia defiantly; she cast down her eyes, but her mouth twitched with mischief.

'S'sh!' with an expression of distaste.

'It isn't a bad word, Mrs Hoadley, it's only short for sweetheart.'

'It means a bad woman, and that's enough. It's a pretty old word, come to that,' she went on drearily, 'but it's been spoilt by men, like everything else,' and suddenly she put her hands up to her face and began to cry.

'Why, whatever——! Here, cheer up, have some more tea, do,' said Sylvia, nervously moving the cups and saucers about and keeping a half-frightened gaze upon her, 'Do you feel bad?'

'I'm all right; leave me alone, thank you, Sylvia,' indistinctly from behind her hands. 'You go and mix the chickens' food. I'll be better in a minute.' She made no attempt to explain what was the matter. Sylvia, after aimlessly moving the crockery for a little longer, went away.

She spoke precisely the truth when she said of Fabrio and herself: 'Him and me don't get on too badly nowadays,' although Fabrio never expressed interest or pleasure in their lessons together, or showed disappointment when owing to some mischance they had to be missed; never answered or displayed anger when Emilio leered and hinted and tapped his nose as they passed Sylvia in the yard. He only worked silently and diligently at his reading and his English, sitting apart in the crowded hut at night while the other men gambled or sang or gossiped, with his fingers in his ears and his eyes fixed upon the book before him, while his patient peasant's lips repeated a score of times the craggy English consonants so different from his own cooing, liquid Italian vowels. Sometimes he would push the book angrily aside and join his companions in whatever was going on, but he always returned to his studies, and every day, almost every hour, his English became more fluent.

Sylvia had been very shocked to discover that he could barely read. She had believed that everybody could read except the Indians, who were forcibly prevented by British Imperialists from learning, and Spanish Republicans who were Kept Under by the Church. However, her strong sense of the shamefulness of Fabrio's case prevented her from expressing surprise or making inflammatory comments; she would as soon have thought of lecturing him upon the odour from his unwashed clothes as upon his ignorance, and she taught him to read without once jeering at him or becoming impatient with his slowness. She truly pitied this fellow-being sitting in intellectual twilight, and her pity silenced her boisterous tongue and softened her didactic impulse.

And for his part, Fabrio now pitied her—*La Scimmia*—Monkey-face. Heaven had bestowed upon her a head of hair glossy and brown as the chestnuts of Italy, and a white skin, and what use did she make of these gifts? Dyed the one, like the women who flaunted their sin in the streets, and painted the other as they painted their cheeks. And yet, he felt that *La Scimmia* was not like those shameless girls: she was not even like his own elder sisters, who had slept with strange men when the times were hard and there was no money in the house: that had seemed to make little difference to Nella and Maria, when once they had confessed to Father Domenico and received absolution and done their penance, and they had been cheerful and gay until the next time; and yet she was not like his little unmarried sisters either; she was not like any woman or girl he had ever known; *La Scimmia* was *La Scimmia*, and only like herself, and he pitied her.

He accepted her invitation to accompany her to the Wild Brooks with complacence, for Sylvia told him that the old people had taken a fancy to him and wanted very much to see him again. She made the proposed visit sound like a kindness from two gay, important young people towards two poor old geezers who might not be here long. He liked the idea of the day's outing, too, and he even liked the idea of spending a holiday with *La Scimmia*, but oh! how he hoped that she would not wear the trousers and that faded rag upon her head! Everyone would pity *him*. And if she cast off the rag, if she bared that high brass roll of her terrible hair, so harsh and conspicuous, then everyone would stare at her and say that he was out with a loose woman.

The situation was difficult. However, dawn on the Sunday morning was windy and bright; light sped swiftly up into the sky instead of creeping up as it usually did here, and the crimson clouds turned to gold; heaven was full of them; and in the woods surrounding the camp Fabrio heard the cries of birds as he dashed his face and breast with icy water and blinked his stinging eyes beneath the veil of wet. All around him were his fellow prisoners, naked to the waist, laughing or sullen or shouting to one another as they splashed and shuddered when the cold April wind blew on their dripping bodies. He dressed carefully, and thoroughly blacked his boots, and went off with the others to Mass. Holiday, pleasure, freedom: the words rang in his ears and made his blood dance with joy.

He was to meet *La Scimmia* near the railway station at eleven o'clock and the old people were to give them their dinner. He remembered Mrs Hoadley's golden earrings shaped like baskets of roses, which he had greatly admired, and wondered if she were rich. Perhaps she might die soon and leave him her money, enough to buy a piece of land of his own (for his father's farm would go to his elder brother Giuseppe) and a wireless and some books. Then, when he was set free from this accursed country— where it was not even possible, because they were kind, to take comfort from hating the people—he would go home and marry Maria, who would be only too pleased to have him, and begin to save money for their children.

He walked on down the road, under the tall budding hazel bushes and by the blackthorn now fading as the may came on, between pools of fresh water, for it had rained last night, it was always raining over here. He wore his long brown overcoat closely buttoned against the wind and the black gloves issued by H.M. Government, but no hat, for he had lost that whilst stalking rabbits with Emilio, and his face was grave but his eyes danced, like the eyes of a child going off to a treat.

The shop near the station was open for the sale of newspapers, and in passing he caught sight of a little card of small bright objects in the window. He went up and peered in; they were brooches made of tiny flowers in white, blue and yellow, and they seemed to him very beautiful. He had one and ninepence halfpenny in his pocket; he jingled it thoughtfully, then he went into the shop.

As he came out, he saw a figure coming down the road towards him who must, by her height and the colour of her hair and the fact that she was waving to him, be *La Scimmia*, but he did not recognise her. No, at first he did not recognise her; for this was a young lady who was coming to meet him, wearing a grey silky dress under a plain black coat, and gloves, and her golden hair parted at one side and smoothly rolled low at the back of her head. Her broad white brow, her blue eyes— how innocent they were, how young and girlish she looked, how good! And he went forward to meet her, smiling and holding carefully in his hand the little box containing the brooch.

He was so set upon giving it to her at once, and so relieved at her quiet, elegant appearance, that he did not observe that she looked defiant and cross; also, the spring sun was in his eyes as they met. He bowed to her.

'Good morning,' said Fabrio. 'This is for you,' and he held out the little box.

Sylvia was surprised. She was on the defensive: she had only put on her quietest dress and rearranged her hair after a sharp reminder from Mrs Hoadley before she set out, and this had meant re-dressing in a hurry. She had been prepared to vent her annoyance, and also her self-consciousness at appearing in this corny get-up, by an even louder manner than usual. She felt that the soft curve of her hair, the white daisies scattered over her sober dress, drew attention to a part of her nature which she preferred to ignore, and which she did not want to display to Fabrio. But she was only nineteen, and it was a lovely morning, and he was offering her a present, and she was not an ill-tempered girl. Her irritation vanished. However, the amazed admiration in his eyes embarrassed her, and she lowered her own as she held out her little gloved hand to receive the box.

'In my country when a man take a lady out,' explained Fabrio slowly, drawing himself up, 'he should give her the flowers. But there are none in this country' (casting a glance of peasant scorn at the hedgerow which was the natural place whence to procure flowers; no one *bought* flowers except silly rich foreigners), 'so I give you this-a flowers in case.'

She exclaimed with pleasure, thanked him, and after some posing of the brooch against her coat, pinned it on her bosom. They set out on the short walk to the station in amiable conversation. When they came to take their fares an embarrassing moment threatened because Fabrio now had only threepence halfpenny in his pocket; he had been so ravished away by the brooch that he had forgotten the fares, for which in any case he would not have had enough; but Sylvia quickly produced money which she assured him was a present from Mrs Hoadley, a contribution to the day's pleasure, and although he was at first inclined to be haughty, he unbent when once they were in the train.

He did not smile all the time, but it was plain that he was enjoying the excursion. He eagerly watched every change of scene from the window and sometimes he glanced at her for confirmation that she had seen what had amused or interested himself. Once or twice she caught his eyes fixed upon her, but there was nothing in their grave blue gaze to embarrass her, and she did not see their expression when he watched her unconscious profile. She was enjoying the change of air, and beginning also to enjoy the change from tough land girl to quiet young lady. There was pleasure, as if she were acting, in subduing her voice, in keeping her hands at rest in her lap, in smiling instead of screaming with laughter. Even the paint upon her mouth was a deep rose hue, soft and fresh and in keeping with her part.

But while she joked with Fabrio and commented upon the scenery, her mind was busy with a fairy story in which the film star Van Johnson, happening to be in Amberley that day, saw her in the village and immediately chose her to play opposite him in his new film. She saw his face; she smiled up at him, and he moved towards her; he held her preciously, tenderly in his arms and swept her person up and down with his eyes, and then they were locked together in a long, thrilling, crazy kiss: his job forgotten; her job forgotten; everything forgotten but love, love, love.

An unconscious sigh passed between her parted lips as the dream faded: then she looked up to meet the gaze of Fabrio. He leant towards her.

'You feel cold?' he inquired politely. 'You would like-a the window to be closed?'

She looked at him for a moment in silence; it always took her a little time to emerge from these daydreams, and while the miasma was slowly drifting away from her she saw, not the face of the young man sitting opposite to her, but the face of the shadow-lover.

She blinked, then gently smiled.

'It's all right, comrade. I guess I was just . . . dreaming,' and she finished off with another sigh. But Fabrio only smiled, and folded his arms and leant back comfortably. *La Scimmia!* There she was, sitting opposite to him, transformed into exactly the kind of girl he liked best: big and strong and able to bear many children and work hard, but also modestly and prettily dressed, and looking soft and kind. *La Scimmia!* but no; he would not call her that name any longer or think of her by it either: he would use her own pretty name, Sylvia, and now, from this day onwards, everything between him and this big, beautiful, gentle Sylvia, who looked like the statue of Our Lady in the church at Santa Margherita, would be quite changed, quite different. How surprised, how very surprised, Emilio would be when he saw that they no longer jeered or spoke roughly to one another! He would say that they loved each other, perhaps. Well, he, Fabrio, would not mind. And the summer was coming: soon they would all be harvesting, standing by the blue-painted waggon amidst the wheat in the hot sun, binding up the sheaves. Fabrio suddenly felt the heat, the glare, the summer scents, all about him, and began to whistle. The train stopped; they had arrived.

In the distance amidst bright green meadows he saw a castle. It was not very large; it did not stand on a high hill as did the one at home in San Angelo; but it was undoubtedly a castle, towering above the village that clustered at its feet and looking out ever the level fields towards the big hills a mile or so away. He pointed, exclaiming:

'*Castello!*'

'Yes, Amberley Castle, it's nothing but an old ruin,' she said carelessly. 'There's a much better one at Lewes, you must have seen that.'

He nodded, but did not take his eager gaze from the castle as they went down the platform and out of the station. The ancient stones were pale brown, and he could plainly see the slit windows and irregular outline of the battlements. The day had now clouded over and all the landscape lay under a clear melancholy light, in which the far-off details were distinct; the sky was packed with low violet clouds but behind them light seemed about to burst through and flood the strong dark blue of the distant hills, the lowering grey-green of those near at hand, the shining river banding along the water-meadows, with brilliance. Everywhere the great delicate elms guarding cottage or farm in their shade were smothered in buds; veil-like, dazzling. And there swept across this vale of water-meadows surrounded by hills that scent which is to the nostrils what music is to the ears; a scent made up of countless odours from grass and earth and stone and water and, at this season of the year, primroses and budding bluebells and violets.

They set out along the road towards the village. Sylvia glanced brightly from side to side and admired her own feet in their country shoes. The peasants' heritage of large extremities had been spared her, and her greedy little hands and stubby little feet were her pride.

Fabrio had been glancing over the landscape as they went and now observed:

'Sad, all this. Not cheery.'

'What do you mean, sad? It's ever so pretty, it'ud be a regular beauty spot if everybody knew about it.'

Fabrio shook his head and vaguely waved his hand over the clear sunless prospect spread before them.

'There is no farms, there is no fields with the corn growing. There is not-a any trees with the apples or the pears.'

'It isn't the right kind of land for growing things; it's only fit for grazing,' and she pointed to a large meadow in which some thirty cows and fatting cattle were wandering. 'It's all the water makes it so good, Mr Hoadley says.'

'Yes, it is sad,' he persisted, gazing about him. They had turned aside down a narrow lane winding between iron railings and lengths of low hedge, then beside a hayrick now, in the shadow of a stone wall repaired with brick. They were amidst scenes made by man, and the poetic light, the sense of slumber, that lies over this valley was slightly lessened, but still there was the impression of a beautiful decay.

'Oh well, just as you like,' she muttered, skirting an expanse of fresh black mud. 'It's a funny thing, I *can't* get to like the country. It's very interesting on the farm, I give you all that and I don't mind the work and I love the fresh air, but I don't feel,—oh, I don't know, I just like it better in London. 'Course, it may be better when the summer comes. Do you like the country, Fabrio?'

He was looking with interest at the vegetables in a little garden they were passing, and answered with a shrug:

'What do you mean, Sylvia? I have live there for ever.'

It was true: he did not know whether he liked the country or not, because he took it for granted. Those questions of the country's beauty, its quiet, its slow tempo compared with the city's haste, which interest and concern a townsman had no meaning for the peasant. Sylvia thought, he's dumber than he looks; half the time I don't believe he's thinking about anything at all; and at that moment they came out into Amberley.

The two pairs of young blue eyes gazed curiously up and down the silent street; the two heads covered with youth's shining hair turned quickly, impatiently, as if in search of movement and life.

But there was none. The houses were built of time-greened stone thatched with old silver straw and were taller than those in most Sussex villages. They were shadowed here and there by a lofty tree, but the light that came down through the branches was clear and unreal as the light in a picture. There were many pheasant's-eye narcissus, most poetic of all the flowers of spring, in the garden plots, and they dreamed motionless in the dreaming light; the cool, swooping April wind which had blown against the cheeks of Fabrio and Sylvia on the way here had died away or did not fully penetrate to this winding place, and all the windows of the cottages, large and small, were closed and dark. There was nothing pretty or bustlingly comfortable about this village. It was beautiful.

'Everybody's at church,' said Sylvia at last, and at that moment they did see some people making their way across the large churchyard which lay beside the castle as if on their way out from the service, while a bell began to strike twelve.

'Cigarettes!' exclaimed Fabrio, slapping his bosom distractedly, 'I go in a pub to buy some!' and he was hurrying away in search of one when he paused, glanced at her, and retraced his steps.

'I beg-a your pardon, Sylvia, you can no come in a pub. It is not nice. And——' but he checked the confession that now he had not enough money for cigarettes.

'Well, I don't like them, as a matter of fact,' she confessed, 'but I could wait for you outside.'

He shook his head. 'No, no.'

'Never mind. Old Mr Hoadley's sure to have some, he smokes like a volcano.'

'Ah-ha! Napoli!' exclaimed Fabrio, delightedly recognising a word, and seized her arm and broke into gay lilting song, lifting his face to the sunlight that suddenly, majestically poured down through a cleft in the clouds.

'Oo—lovely and warm!' she cried, also looking upwards. 'Do let's sing—never mind all those old sourpusses!' and she glanced at the homeward-bound churchgoers. Their faces were completely wooden; nevertheless, in a moment she gently withdrew her arm from Fabrio's, and when the Sunday hush and the dreamy peace caused his song to falter and die away she made no attempt to revive it. She felt that singing arm-in-arm with a foreigner did not suit a young lady on her way to visit a poor old couple.

At Fabrio's request they went into the churchyard and wandered through its long grasses until they came to the walls of the castle towering above it at the end farthest from the village, but he abruptly rebuffed her suggestion that they should go into the church in case there was anything historical to be seen there.

'Why not? There's nobody in there now; they've all gone home.'

'*Protestante*,' said Fabrio, casting down his eyes.

'So what?'

They had paused beneath that part of the castle where a closed door is set in the massive wall; above their heads little green plants that had lodged themselves in the crevices waved in the light wind and now a looming cloud-shadow passed coldly over the vast worn fabric of stone and then a burst of sunlight warmed it; all about them were tombstones tilted sideways in the long deep grass.

'What!' she cried, suddenly comprehending, 'you mean to say you mustn't go in there because you're a Roman Catholic?'

He nodded, but absently; he seemed to have lost interest, and was straying onwards.

'I never *heard* of such———' she was beginning violently, when the sight of her own gloved hands, flung out in protest, checked her. Their pretty neatness did not harmonise with the strong words which had been about to pour from her lips; while the clear, still air, the sombre beauty of castle and church towering above her, and the green gravestones at her feet, also hushed her vehemence. But she gave a loud, impatient sigh and tossed her head.

'Will we go in the *castello*?' said Fabrio, who had turned again to gaze up at the walls. 'There is the door,' and he pointed.

'We can't. The owner won't let us.'

'Who say so? Why not?'

'The Duke of Norfolk,* I expect; he owns most of the land round here.'

Fabrio nodded, satisfied: of course Dukes owned land and of course they kept you out of their *castellos*.

'He live in there?' jerking his head at the castle.

'No; trust him, he's got a castle in Arundel as big as half Sussex.'

'Another *castello*?'

'Yes, a huge one. Come along, Fabrio, it's getting on for one

* Sylvia was mistaken; the owner was an elderly lady.

o'clock and I expect the old lady will have lunch all ready, we don't want to keep them waiting. It's a pretty old place, we'll have another look at it on the way home if you like.'

He shrugged his shoulders and smiled with eyes half-closed against another burst of glory from the sun.

'Now I have seen old *castello* I don't want to see it again, Sylvia. I like better to look at you,' he ended in a murmur, but she had walked round that part of the churchyard wall which overlooks the village road, and did not hear.

'Quite a nasty drop,' she exclaimed, peering down. 'We can't jump it, we'll have to go round by the gate.'

Then, as one o'clock struck from a clock in a nearby house, 'We shan't half be late!' she cried, and they hurried on.

They went down a hill enclosed by ancient cottages, and then, with the wall of the castle looming immediately above them and a row of budding willows immediately in front, she paused at a gate and pointed.

'There's the Wild Brooks,' she said.

He saw meadows overgrown with dark coarse reeds amidst gleams of water; large ancient willows overhung the open pools, with weeping foliage now covered in light green buds, and along the far end of this expanse, which bore a trace of fainting-sweet marsh odour among its fresh scents, ran a thick barrier of willows and hazels, agitated as the fitful wind streamed along their length and looking like emanations from the silver water and green grass.

Fabrio did not like the look of this at all. Where was the comfortable little farm, the orchard of the apples or the pears, which he had expected? and the *porcelli*, those interesting and valuable animals about which Sylvia had laughed so much in the railway train? He had greatly looked forward to seeing the *porcelli*, for he had gathered from remarks made by the Hoadleys that they were animals of which every part could be eaten or sold; and this recommended any animal to Fabrio's respectful interest. But there was no sign of a house; nothing but grass and water and that little forest of waving trees. What, then! did the rich old grandmother with the gold earrings live in a swamp?

'Where is the house?' he demanded disapprovingly.

'Over there,' pointing to that very barrier of unpromising green. 'Come on, let's get cracking, we're late now.'

But it was not so disagreeable as he had expected, for there were continuous winding tracts of solid land over which they could make their way and Sylvia shrieked as she balanced herself between the expanses of mud trodden out by cattle and more than once he had to grasp her hand and pull her—how easily!— to safety. No, it was not so bad.

'What is this?' he asked curiously, when they came to the first of many dykes intersecting the fields, and he peered down into the brown gliding water.

'It's something to do with draining the river off when it floods—I don't know,' carelessly. 'Do come on, I'm starving, aren't you?'

He would have liked to linger by the dyke, puzzling out why and how it had been made, but she hurried him on; through mud, past pools fringed with the dark green marestail, by shining scatters of celandine and buttercups and yellow iris with roots in the water, until they stood below the willow forest.

'Ah-ha! *Treno!*' exclaimed Fabrio, startled by the surprising sight of a train leisurely making its way across this marshy wilderness.

'Yes, the railway runs right through here. Here's the bridge— come on,' and she ran out on to a perilous projection of planks and old tree trunks which spanned the dyke.

They entered the wood of hazels and willows and made their way along a well-defined path into its heart; the ground here was higher and covered by thin bright grass and primroses and white and purple windflowers and Fabrio was reassured to see some low buildings between the trunks of the trees, with smoke issuing from a rickety tin chimney. It is like a beggar's house, he thought, staring with all his eyes at the open glade which they now entered, where the grass and flowers were trampled down, and old rags and stained newspapers lay scattered about. The house consisted of three or four ancient huts, huddled together and joined by clumsy passages made from old doors and sheets of tin and deal planks. Some of the windows had curtains and others were stuffed with rags and one of the sheds had a porch of rotten wood before its closed door, and towards this Sylvia went. She too looked slightly dismayed, for although Mrs Hoadley more than once had resignedly warned her that 'the old people live very rough,' she had not expected anything so rough as this.

She smiled at Fabrio and lifted her eyebrows with a grimace as they stood side by side in the little porch. The noon air was silent except for the distant chattering, scattered all over the landscape like the light, of the nesting birds. Suddenly a thick contented grunting broke out near at hand. Fabrio's eyes opened wider and he smiled.

'The pigg-as!' he said. Sylvia wrinkled her nose.

'I can smell them, too,' she said in the softest possible whisper. 'Don't think much of this, do you? I hope there's some lunch,' and she raised the knocker of thick worm-eaten wood which was nailed crookedly upon the door, and knocked. There followed a silence. They gazed about them and waited.

19

They waited a very long time, it seemed to the hungry Sylvia. The birds chirruped, the hidden pigs grunted as if they, at least, were eating their Sunday lunch, and Fabrio gazed intently through a gap in the nearest window curtain; he had caught a glint of gold in the darkness of the room. What could it be? Sylvia frowned down at some large sky-blue polyanthus and yellow wallflowers rising serenely out of a wilderness of weeds. The fineness of the flowers surprised her; she glanced round for further evidence of Mrs Hoadley's remark that 'the old lady has got green fingers, anything will grow for her,' and saw a peony in luxuriant bud and a distant sheet of yellow flowers which she took to be wild daffodils, but there was no recognisable attempt at a garden.

They had been waiting perhaps ten minutes when a small figure in a long skirt, black jacket and flat chip hat came briskly round the corner of one of the huts, carrying a pail. It caught sight of them, and paused.

'What do ye want?' called old Mrs Hoadley in a small voice soft with age, shading her eyes to look at them. 'What are you up to?' The words 'Girls and soldiers—no good, I'm sure,' followed, in a sufficiently loud, if absent, mutter, to cause Sylvia an angry blush.

'It's me—Sylvia, Mrs Hoadley,' she said, going forward, 'and here's Fabrio—from the farm, you know. You remember—you asked us over for the day.'

'Never did anything of de sort,' retorted Mrs Hoadley, stooping her doll-like body to scrape the mud from her boots with a twig. 'I like my Sundayses to myself, same as I do my weekdayses.'

'You *did*, Mrs Hoadley,' protestingly, glancing at Fabrio, who

226

was politely standing at attention. 'We've got a chicken for you,' and she indicated the basket he held.

'I'm middlin' sure I never did, but now you're here you may as well come in. Dere's no dinner but some cold pork, but *you*,' pointing a tiny brown finger with a hooked purple nail at Fabrio, 'can go and pick us some wet-de-beds, and I've got potatoses, yes, we'll manage. Here,' she held out her little arms in their rusty black sleeves for the chicken, which he, after a glance at Sylvia, handed to her. 'Mr Hoadley and me'll enjoy dat for our supper.' Then she kicked against the door with her boot.

'Mr Hoadley's still abed with de papers, I expect,' she said, after a lengthy pause. 'We'll go round de back.'

The back proved to be hardly distinguishable from the front in its litter of yellow newspapers, shreds of rag, rusty tins, and shards of white or blue china in the young grass. The door of one shed stood open.

'Joseph, Joseph,' called Mrs Hoadley briskly, stepping over the bricks which formed the rough threshold into a little room beyond, but to her soft ancient voice (its sound also muffled by the rags and newspapers bursting out of an old green dresser, and the trays of seeds, and pots of mouldering beans half embalmed in salt which stood about on tables and chairs and floor) there came no reply.

'Still abed. He's just-about lazy,' she said, and set down the bucket, upon which Sylvia's horrified gaze now became fixed—as anybody's would be, if they saw a pig-bucket which had not been scraped out for some eighteen months. Mrs Hoadley's own eyes, filmed with blue over their former velvet black, followed her gaze.

'Don't you mind dem, dey won't hurt you,' she said soothingly, but with a mischievous cackle. 'Girls are always worrying about something,' she added to Fabrio, who was staring about the room with the deepest interest. 'De fresh scraps go on top of them every day and de pigs don't never get a taste of them.

It's high time Joe cleaned it out but he's bone lazy. Now you go out and pick me some dangylions,' to Fabrio, 'and we'll get a page of de paper off Joe and us'll have our dinner.'

'Dang——?' he repeated inquiringly, turning to Sylvia.

'Dandelions, she means, don't you, Mrs Hoadley?' but Mrs Hoadley had gone through into a smaller room, whence came a stuffy odour as if a kettle had boiled over on old rags, and was raking out the range.

'Here, I'll come and show you, there's some yellow flowers over by the wood, they may be dandelions,' said Sylvia, glad to get into the open air again, but Fabrio was enjoying the warmth from the oil-stove and reluctant to leave these interesting rooms.

However, the flowers were not dandelions or wild daffodils and Sylvia had never seen others like them.

'It's an unpretentious little flower, isn't it, but quite pretty,' she said, holding the deep yellow blossom, whose lower lip was spotted with scarlet, elegantly between her gloved fingers and twisting it about. 'Look, there's some dandelions, over there; you just pick the green leaves, not the flowers. The old girl wants them for a salad, I saw about it in one of those Ministry of Food recipes.'

He smiled in recognition when he saw the dandelions and she left him plucking the young leaves with a peasant's ruthless closeness of touch: indeed, they were as familiar a food to him as bacon and eggs used to be to an Englishman, and many a salad of them had the Caetani enjoyed in the bright evenings of the Italian spring.

'You can do the potatoses,' announced Mrs Hoadley as Sylvia entered the tiny kitchen, which was dark, despite the brilliant light outside, because of the rags stuffed in the windows. 'Dere's de bowl, dere's de water, dere's a knife, dere's de saucepan. Dey won't take more'n an hour. Now you get on. I'm going away.'

She nodded up at Sylvia, like a female gnome standing before some tall goose-girl whom she had enslaved but of whose docility she was not quite assured. Her mouth was firm but her eye had a gleam of doubt.

Sylvia was annoyed; she had not put on her good dress and painted her fingernails in order to peel potatoes. However, such a service was in keeping with her temporary assumption of gentleness, and as she was also as good-natured as a young carthorse, she set to work with no outward grumbles, and Mrs Hoadley did go away. She disappeared completely into the low rooms of the tiny ruinous cottage to which the old husband had added shacks and outhouses until there was ample room for the junk which they collected and hoarded like two old magpies, and Sylvia peeled potatoes in silence unbroken even by the ticking of a clock. It must be after two, she thought despairingly, and am I hungry!

However, the kitchen was warm and peaceful, and beautified by the red and gold china of which Fabrio had caught a gleam between the curtains. There were at least forty pieces of a dinner service, arranged upon the green dresser: red grapes and golden birds twined and flew all over the generous surfaces. It must be Oriental, I bet that's worth something, Sylvia thought, and in spite of her hunger and her unsuitable employment, she felt cheered, and decided that the old Hoadleys could not be as poor as their hovel implied. She enjoyed the thought: and a conviction that The State ought to look after all old people and that No One Ought to Have Savings and Property existed comfortably side by side with it in her half-baked little brain.

The knife which she was using was worn down to a stub and as sharp as a razor, and while she was gazing at the china, it slipped and cut her finger. She stanched the brilliant blood as best she could with the sacking apron which she had put on to protect her dress, and managed to get the potatoes on to boil without much of it dropping into the water. She was looking about for a rag to bind the cut when Fabrio came in.

'You've brought half the garden!' she exclaimed, surveying his fistfuls of sappy leaves. 'Here, find me something to bind this up, I can't do a thing,' and she held up her finger.

He was inclined to tease her gently rather than to show

concern, and they soon found a piece of comparatively clean cotton in a cupboard below the dresser, but the water had been heating on the little range while she peeled the potatoes, and they were now boiling much too fast.

'They'll be a mash,' she said, peering at them. 'Oh, give me modern amenities every time! There's no way of slowing them down, that I can see.' Then a hand gently clasped her wrist—surprisingly gently, for it was an unusually large hand—and she turned quickly. But it was plain that he was thinking of nothing but binding up the cut; he looked compassionate and was frowning slightly as if considering the best way to begin. She stood quietly, studying the thin young face close to her. He's got a nice face, she thought, though he isn't exactly good-looking. Her heart did not beat faster; she felt no embarrassment. She felt towards him as she did towards her own brothers or the young animals at the farm.

Suddenly there sounded a soft cackle; the old woman had come in noiselessly behind them and now stood surveying them with her brown face screwed up in sly laughter. Sylvia quickly pulled her hand away and took the rag from him.

'Here, I'll do it,' she said sharply, furious to feel a blush coming up into her face, and she began to wind the bandage clumsily round her finger. Fabrio looked delighted, which increased her annoyance.

'The potatoses'll be just-about boiled to mash, tearin' away like dat,' said Mrs Hoadley. 'Can't you move 'em on to the cool?' and she pulled the saucepan sideways.

'Sorry. I'm not used to cooking with these old—with a coal range, Mrs Hoadley.'

'Dey do middlin' well; and better dan a 'lectric one when it goes on strike, and we've all got to learn,' darting a mischievous glance from one youthful face to the other.

Sylvia tried to look haughty but her anger vanished. The old girl was quite a character in her way. She glanced at Fabrio's face and burst into a giggle in which he joined.

Then the old woman attended to the finger, making no comment upon it, but dragging a chair across the room and standing on it in order to reach the tall mantelshelf, where a silent clock stood among other dusty objects. She fumbled in the space behind it, and at last brought out a round thing resembling a bun. Sylvia exclaimed; it was covered in mould.

'Take off dat rag,' Mrs Hoadley commanded, stepping down from the chair with a scornful look, 'and we'ull put a bit o' dis on de place.'

'Put blue mould on my finger? Not if I know it, you won't!'

'Yess, yess,' the old woman insisted, 'dat's good for it, dat 'ull heal it up an' make it sweet, won't it?' appealing to Fabrio, but with an increasing contempt in her black eyes. Fabrio shrugged his shoulders and politely smiled. He had the peasant's respect for a Wise Woman, and although the little cake did not look like a medicine, its recommender did look very like a white witch.

'It'll poison it,' said Sylvia resignedly, beginning to unroll the bandage. She thought it best to give way, for further objections would delay the serving of dinner.

'No, it won't,' Mrs Hoadley snapped. 'I don't go for to poison girls. Dis is a cheese bun, like my granny used to use for us liddle children. Hold it out.'

Sylvia held it out, and watched in disgusted silence while a piece of mouldy bun was put upon the cut and bound in place.

'Dere!' said Mrs Hoadley, when the operation was completed. 'Now you leave dat alone for three days, and den take it off. De cut'ull be just-about healed up so's you won't know dere's *been* a cut.'

Sylvia earnestly promised that she would do so, resolving to fling off the dressing as soon as they should be out of sight on their way home.

Dinner passed off gaily. True, the tablecloth was two sheets of the *Sunday Pictorial* and Sylvia's plate rested upon a photograph

231

of a large pair of naked female thighs while Fabrio was interested to see the words *God* and *Murder* glaring up at him from between the cups (for they drank strong tea with their meat), but the pork was rich and sweet and the potatoes eaten with big dabs of butter. The talk was anecdotal, reminiscent, teasing, and they all began to like one another. Old Mr Hoadley came in, wearing his best suit, and devoted himself to Sylvia, passing her the bread, the pickles, with slow politeness. He was a silent old man, seemingly much older than his wife, and she sometimes became impatient with his halting movements and spoke roughly to him, but he did not seem to mind. They had spent all their lives together (Mrs Hoadley told Sylvia that they had married from the same village when she was fifteen and he nineteen) and had grown so close together in body and habit that words between them had ceased to mean much to either.

They all enjoyed the strong tasty food, the sunlight pouring into the room and gleaming on Mrs Hoadley's grand collection of china pieces and busts that was ranged all round the walls, the sweet fitful cries of birds ringing in through the open door. Summer is coming, thought Fabrio, leaning back with a little black cigar, produced by Mr Hoadley, between his teeth and stirring the treacle in his tea, and this summer she will be here too; I shall see her every day, my Sylvia, my girl. He smiled at her gently, across the untidy table. Every shade of coldness, of sullenness and suspicion, had vanished from his face, leaving it frank and happy. His mother and sisters would have seen him, at this moment, as if the war and his captivity had never been. The two pairs of blue eyes met, and Sylvia smiled at him in return: for the first time she saw him as a comely, friendly young man, with a sweet, lazy ardour in his eyes that she did not resent.

Then three o'clock struck hastily from an ancient grandfather clock wedged amidst the mugs and the pottery busts of Victorian statesmen. It seemed in a hurry, which is never a good state for a clock to be in. Mrs Hoadley glanced at it, and briskly got up.

'Can't sit here all afternoon, dere's the pigs to be fed,' pronounced Mrs Hoadley, 'Sylvia, you come along with me and have a tidy-up and Mr Hoadley'll take Albert' (early in the proceedings Mrs Hoadley had said that she could not bother with Fabrio's name, and as he minded her of a Belgium who had worked with Mr Hoadley in the last war-but-one whose name was Albert, she would call him Albert). Fabrio's eyes followed Sylvia as the two women went out of the room and her last glance as she passed through the door (like that exchanged between two children who share a secret) was for him.

'The pigg-as!' exclaimed Fabrio eagerly, as soon as the door had shut, 'I will like much, much to see them, please.'

'Dey won't run away,' said Mr Hoadley placidly, blowing out smoke. 'We'll put these scraps,' indicating their plates, 'into the bucket and take 'em along in a minute or two. Haven't you ever' glancing at him in mild surprise 'seen pigses afore?'

'Only when I was far off. I would like much, much to see pigg-as close to me.'

Mr Hoadley nodded as if this were a perfectly understandable wish, and presently—he having silently indicated to his guest on their way out to the sties a little black shed with a door lolling off its hinges—Fabrio joined him at the sties, having found the way there through a tangle of blackberry bushes and hazel wands by the sound of grunts.

The sties were large and unexpectedly clean in such surroundings and there was an enormous sow with fifteen piglets. Fabrio's respect for the old Hoadleys, which had been shaken by the poverty of their home, was partly restored. He remembered Giulio Ferraro at home in San Angelo, whose miserable existence in the hovel where he had starved himself to death had not prevented the legend of his wealth persisting, and when Father Mario had entered the den after Giulio was dead, holding his nose and gathering up his cassock from the floor, had he not found bundle upon bundle of lire hidden in the walls? No, a poor house did not always mean that its owners were poor; they might be clever and he, Fabrio, would be courteous to these old people.

It was easy for him to be, for he was happy here. He liked the grunting, and the birds' cries, and the faint scents from flowers and woods, and the strong odour of pigs; he liked the huts, with the warmth from the oil-stoves, and those beautiful plates, and the cushions made from thousands of tiny gay rags; he liked the tales (but half-understood by him) about her young days and the scandals about her neighbours of to-day that Mrs Hoadley had related at lunch, and he was full of rich pork and strong tea. And over all his bodily happiness, like a sweet scent, floated the thought of Sylvia.

He leant his arms companionably upon the wall of the sty beside Mr Hoadley, and complimented him upon the fatness and strength of the *porcelli*, and began haltingly to ask questions about them to which Mr Hoadley slowly but willingly replied, for he had taken a fancy to him.

The air in the bedroom was warm and close. Sylvia wandered over to an old dim mirror that stood on the dressing-table and saw her young face looking greenish and twisted, as if reflected in a pool. The tiny window was shut, and dead flies lay along its sealed frame. The beds were unmade; a rank odour came from the stiff, ancient clothes that stuffed the cupboards; from worn slippers and huge muddy boots lying amidst the grey fluff on the bare boards. She saw an overflowing hair tidy, a china tree laden with brass rings and the cornucopia earrings, a tray scattered with rosebuds and filled with huge iron hairpins worn shiny with age, curlers, burnt-out matches. She turned quickly round; she did not like it here; she wanted to get outside into the air. In the dim light Mrs Hoadley was pottering about, opening a drawer, pushing a dirty garment under a pillow. Now she turned round too, and as she saw Sylvia's disturbed face, a smile stole over her own. She sat down upon one bed and leant forward and patted the quilt upon the other in invitation.

'He's a very nice young man,' she began soothingly. 'And so Molly's in de family way at last? About time, too.'

Half an hour later Fabrio heard Sylvia's voice calling, 'Hullo, you there! Where on earth are you?' and in a moment she blundered out through the hazel thickets into the glade. She was followed by Mrs Hoadley carrying the pig bucket, with eyes brighter, fuller, younger than they had been at lunch; bright and black as a snake's in the shade of her chip hat.

'Thought you'd gone home,' she said roughly, and shook back her curls, which, unaccustomed to lying low upon her neck, were beginning to come loose. 'I hate my hair this corny way, I'm going to put it up,' and she gathered the whole mass in her hand and with a pocket comb scraped it back from her brow and up into a knot upon her skull, revealing the pompadour once more. The two men stared at her, the old one placidly, Fabrio in bewilderment. Her face was flushed, her mouth sullen, her very voice was harsher. She was *La Scimmia* again; her graceful clothes did not seem to belong to her.

'Hideous things, aren't they, really,' she said, turning from the spectacle of the sow and her sucklings, 'I shan't fancy pork again for some time,' and she gave an angry laugh.

Mr Hoadley continued to draw at his pipe and to show no surprise. Mrs Hoadley was emptying the bucket into the trough and laughing at the squeaking and scurrying and gobbling.

'Come along, you give us a hand,' she called to Fabrio. 'They's just-about starving, you'd think,' and he took the bucket from her, still in bewilderment, and emptied it, then emptied another smaller one which she handed to him. Sylvia took no notice; she had wandered off towards the edge of the coppice and was staring away into its clustering green stems. A sheet of the unfamiliar yellow flowers spread itself at her feet but she did not see them, for she was so angry, so disgusted, so ashamed—she could have smashed something.

235

'Dey's a pretty flower,' said the old man's voice behind her. 'Musk, dat is.' He slowly stooped, and with his trembling brown hand covered with swollen purple veins pulled up with some difficulty one of the full yellow blossoms with scarlet-spotted lip. 'But dey don't smell sweet no more, like dey did when I was a boy. I heerd on de wireless dat's de same all over de world; de musk-flower's given up smellin' sweet. I lay it's because of all de muck dey puts into de ground nowadays, all de chemists' muck. But my son over at Hayward's Heath, he says dat's as good as de old stuff. Here, put it in your coat, missy,' and he held out to her the posy he had laboriously gathered.

She accepted it with sulky thanks, but she would not accept the invitation to have a cup of tea which Mrs Hoadley casually extended to them both a little later. She insisted that they must go home, that they were expected at the farm before evening and that it was half-past four now. Fabrio did make one attempt to make her change her mind, but she turned on him so roughly that he was silenced.

So in a little while they set off, Fabrio carrying a bag of homemade soap, and Sylvia striding ahead of him, with a sullen look and the sun shining full upon her brazen hair.

'What's de matter with her?' asked Mr Hoadley, when their visitors had passed out of sight between the dazzling sunrays and the budding bushes.

Mrs Hoadley gave her soft old laugh, and turned away, jingling the oddments in her apron pocket.

'Girls—dey's always worryin' about something,' was all she would answer.

The other two hurried on in silence. Fabrio kept his anxious eyes fixed upon her back as she walked ahead of him through the copse and over the plank bridge, hoping that when they came to the marshy meadows she would turn to him for help. But she did not; she made her way across the patches of drier ground swiftly and in sulky silence. What was the matter? A week ago he would have dismissed such conduct with a shrug; she was *La Scimmia*, and that explained any peculiar behaviour, but to-day—until an hour ago—she had been Sylvia, a friendly laughing girl with lovely eyes that met his own loving look without mockery; he could not feel angry with her, even now, although the terrible hair-style had returned and her very walk was different. Poor little one, he thought, something has upset her. I will ask her what is the matter. And with a few easy strides he caught up with her.

'Why are you angry, Sylvia?' he asked, trying to take her hand, and his voice sounded deeper, more musical than usual, just as a bird's is sweeter in the mating season. 'Are you angry with me?' But he did not believe that he was the cause of the trouble, for what had he done? Nothing.

'No, of course not,' she retorted, snatching her hand away with a cross smile. They had paused on a little expanse of firmer ground; the glory of the declining sun flooded the wide sky, the ancient willows in their sweeping bud veils, the pools of golden water where dark reeds were mirrored, and the distant hills, now a wise golden-green and filled with tender shadows in their mighty hollows. The air was growing cooler but as yet there was no feeling of approaching night. He stood in silence, with his hands in his pockets, gazing gravely at her.

'I'm hungry, I want my tea, and it's that disgusting place—the pigs and everything,' she went on petulantly, smoothing her hair. 'I expect I look a sight, too. I loathe that sort of thing—meals off of newspaper, and outside sanitation, and those old-fashioned ideas——' here she tore the dressing off her finger and tossed it into a pool. 'Well, they're disgusting, really. Of course, Fabrio,' condescendingly, beginning to move on, 'you wouldn't realise how bad it was because——'

(She checked herself; she had been going to say *You come from that sort of home.*)

'——because you haven't seen really nice working-class homes

237

where the people are progressive and have some self-respect,' she went on, her loud angry voice ringing across the hushed, wide, radiant meadows. 'When you see that sort of place you can understand why people are Communists.'

He listened attentively, straining to understand the long, un-familiar words and why she was so angry, with his anxious eyes fixed upon her face.

'My God, it burns me up, those poor old people living in shacks without any proper amenities and the big industrialists like B.I.C. and Rank and all those other bosses, and Lord Nuffield (I'd give him *Lord*; what's *he* done to be a Lord, except have a lot of money that other people have earned for him?), the workers ought to control the means of production *and* the raw materials, same as they do in Russia, my God, this country makes me sick!' she ended, and began to climb the gate leading out on to the road, irritably waving aside his eager offer of help. All the time she was clambering over the rails she was talking; such words as 'democracy,' 'industrialisation,' 'nationalisation,' 'freedom,' 'commu-nity,' 'socialism,' 'fascism,' 'communism' poured from her rosy mouth and utterly bewildered him; he began to feel cowed, beaten, ignorant, under this hail of words.

He glanced back once across the meadows. They were all one glory of gold, and the willows sat among them like wise long-fingered old Chinese men, gazing down into the water. I can't understand, I wish she would tell me what's really the matter, he thought; and then his unhappy eyes wandered unsee-ingly to some half-dismantled haystacks of last summer near at hand, their grey straw weeping down over their shapelessness, and vaguely they reminded him of something, some figure. Yes, it was the straw images that the ignorant people set in the fields at harvest time far down in the South, near Naples; the Straw God that blessed the harvest, and died and came again next year. He felt a strong need for comfort at that moment, from something older, wiser, bigger than himself, and the towering shapes of the budding elms, the willows by their pools, the shapeless harvest-figures crouching in haystack shape, all vaguely consoled him. Then his thoughts turned to Our Lady, and he uttered a silent prayer to Her. She was so beautiful, so kind, she must know what was the matter with Sylvia because She too was a woman, and perhaps She would help him.

All the way along the road through the village, across the short cut through the fields, and down the hill to the station, Sylvia went on talking, brushing aside his timid questions, turning upon him angrily when he tried to tease her out of her ill-temper, striking her clenched fist upon her palm as she told some tale of injustice to the poor or privilege of the rich, and quoting figures to prove what she was shouting.

His English was still so imperfect that he knew only one way to interrupt her—by some sharp army blasphemy or foulness: but that he could not do: for only this morning they had been so happy! the Sylvia he had loved only a few hours ago was no longer there, but she *must* be hidden inside this angry, violent girl who seemed to hate the whole world, she could not have gone for ever. This other girl wore her clothes, the modest black coat, the dress coloured like a *colomba*, she still wore the beautiful little brooch he had bought for her, clasping some fading flowers.

No, he could not shout bad words at *La Scimmia*, because she was still dressed like Sylvia, but he began to feel very wretched: her loud voice beat upon his ears and soon he heard references to God, to the Holy Catholic Faith, which horrified him, and he began to feel angry. By the time the station was reached and they stood waiting for the train, he had been silent for some time and his face was as sullen as her own. Our Lady had not heard his prayer; and in a little while he would be back in the *campo*.

The train came in, and they entered a carriage. It was empty; Fabrio had moved towards it with some vague instinct not to expose their mutual unhappiness to other people's eyes, and

STELLA GIBBONS

Sylvia was absorbed in what she was saying about the Bevin Boys. He slammed the door on them, and the train moved off.

They were journeying into the sunset and the carriage was filled with blinding brilliance; they could see nothing clearly. She exclaimed pettishly, interrupting herself, 'What a glare! it's sickening, can't you pull the blinds down or something?' He glanced at her, then obediently fumbled with the blinds and under her impatient instructions pulled them both down on the sunward side. Sylvia leant back and was silent at last; she frowned at the celandines going by, already shut against the evening chill and the dew on the shadowed banks. Presently she burst out again, turning towards him where he sat beside her with his arms folded and a heavy frown on his face:

'You can say what you like, and I daresay having been brought up in it you can't even understand properly how other people feel about all that superstitious rubbish, it's holding back progress, that's what I hate about it, the Church always has, and you Roman Catholics are the worst of the lot, why, they won't even let you read the Bible properly, of course, I don't believe in the Bible but it is great literature, everybody's got to admit that, and I don't see why the working classes shouldn't have the privilege of reading it, well, it's only justice, isn't it, the Bible is only myths from a scientific point of view but——'

Suddenly he turned towards her; his hands gripped hers, gently, but with such strength that she could not move; his bright chestnut head came down swiftly to her own, and he silenced her parted lips with a tender, voluptuous kiss.

She sat still, so astonished that she could not move. Delight sprang to meet that kiss: then she denied it, and let herself be overwhelmed with disgust and rage.

'Here, what do you think you're doing?' she demanded furiously, thrusting him from her with all her strength. 'Leave me alone. I hate you,' and she sat back in her corner, breathing fast. Her eyes sparkled with rage.

Fabrio had given way to her thrust because he loved her, not because his great strength had felt any force from her own. He said nothing, but moved over to the opposite seat and sat quite still, almost crouching, his imploring eyes fixed upon her face.

She vigorously drew her hand across her lips as if wiping his kiss away, and angrily jerked her collar, her hair, into place, then she turned away from him and stared out at the fields going leisurely by in the yellow afterglow. Presently he turned up the collar of his coat and put his hands in his pockets, for the air in the carriage was growing chill, and then he too stared out of the window and neither spoke.

His anger and misery would have kept him silent if his pride had not. All of him suffered: he felt bruised, he ached with wretchedness and baffled tenderness. He continued to feel the thrust of her arms against his breast and as he remembered the happiness of the morning, tears did come to his eyes and he kept his head turned away so that she should not see.

She was wishing only one thing: to be back in London. In London there were no ignorant old women to poke their noses into what did not concern them and make disgusting remarks; and there were the Movies, thrilling, always changing; there were the Stars, playing those parts which she knew in her secret heart she could play too, if she only had the chance. Oh, how she longed to be at the Movies! now, at this miserable moment, and to forget everything except the figures on the silver screen! She never cried, unless Mr Smedley-Porter at the Dramatic Academy was imploring her to squeeze out a tear for Art's sake; but now she turned her head away so that Fabrio might not see how much he had upset her. She had been getting to like him, but— never again, comrade. He had had it.

They alighted at Sillingham and set out on the short walk to the camp. Had they been married, Fabrio would have stalked ahead and Sylvia would have trailed after him, thus proclaiming to everybody that they had quarrelled, but the pride of unbroken youth kept them walking side by side, step in step, in a haughty silence, through the yellow dusk. Presently the thought came into Sylvia's mind that they must look a couple of fools, and in a minute or so her lips twitched. She glanced at him, but it was very plain that the thought had not occurred to him, and she hastily glanced away again. At that moment they heard a car approaching behind them and its horn sounded. It was a large handsome open car, travelling fast; as it passed them, the women and children in it turned back and waved, and they saw their faces distinctly.

'Why, that's Mrs Lucie-Browne and Miss Hardcastle and the kiddies!' she exclaimed, addressing no one in particular, 'I didn't know they ran a car.'

He did not reply, and the next turn in the road brought them to the gates of the camp. The yards looked lonely in the twilight and the sentry stood outside his box, staring at an aeroplane passing across the afterglow beneath the evening star. The barbed wire enclosing the low buildings was invisible in the dimness. Fabrio sickened at the sight; he felt such a strong impulse to go on down the road at her side that he had actually to force himself towards the camp: and he wrenched himself round, turning slowly away from her.

She did pause and glance at him; she had the impulse to exclaim, 'Oh, for goodness' sake snap out of it!' but the impulse passed, and she only tossed her head and walked on. When he reached the gates he turned and stood gazing after her as she rapidly disappeared into the dusk.

20

We now have to invite our readers into a public-house, and no doubt some of them will be glad.

Mr Waite was not a Regular at The Peal of Bells in Sillingham, but he did look in there once or twice a week to drink a pint or so and exchange cautiously gloomy views with local acquaintances, and he drove his car into the yard there on a fine evening some weeks later. He had passed an extremely trying afternoon in Horsham, arguing with the Egg Board over a matter that fortunately need not be described in detail here; he had been, of course, baffled, and was now tired and depressed. He was also, although he did not know it, in need of sympathetic company.

He arranged the car with his customary niceness, locked it, cast an eye over all its boring doors and windows and things to see that nothing was likely to go wrong with them, and entered the saloon bar.

He caught sight of several other acquaintances, the place was quite crowded, and he nodded to several people and said, 'Good evening.' However, he did not feel like talking just yet. He bought himself a pint of mild and, having exchanged a few remarks with the barman, he retired to a seat by the fireplace, which was already banked up with green branches as though summer had come. It was about seven o'clock and bright evening light poured in through the low windows.

He swallowed his first draught of beer and took out his cigarette case. He began to feel better, as he leaned back in the wide-armed old wooden chair, worn smooth by the sitting patrons of the past hundred and fifty years, and when Fred Lowe, who owned the big garage and petrol station at the north end of the village, came up to his table, he welcomed him. They got into a satisfying conversation in which the names of the Egg Board and the Ministry of Fuel and Power frequently re-occurred; but, as their tones became more emphatic and their faces more lowering, the words 'Ministry' and 'Board' were replaced by other, older, simpler names, and Mr Waite and Mr Lowe became so interested in their conversation that they did not notice a crash and other confused sounds in the yard outside, followed by feminine laughter as two more customers entered.

Mr Waite vaguely saw the backs of two handsome fur coats as their owners moved towards the bar, and then he really had to interrupt Fred Lowe again to tell him how the Egg Board had done exactly the same thing to him, only with eggs instead of petrol, and he forgot the new arrivals until, on going up to get two more pints, he heard a woman's voice say with a nervous laugh, 'Hullo, Mr Waite,' and he turned to see Miss Hardcastle.

Her fur coat was hanging loose on her shoulders in a most untidy way, and she seemed upset. She had just put down two glasses for two more short drinks; and just for an instant (but it was only for an instant, and the suspicion had gone immediately) Mr Waite did have a suspicion.

'Good evening,' he said gravely. He did not like to see ladies in pubs. His sister Marjorie could laugh if she chose, but nothing could ever make him approve of the sight.

'Two more of the same,' said Miss Hardcastle to the barman, smiling troubledly. Mr Waite glanced at the corner where her companion waited; he did not want to look but he had to; he knew whom he would see; he knew just how she would look and it was like her to come here, too, unfeminine, frivolous, peculiar creature that she was. And then, after all, it was someone else who sat there, blinking out of her furs at the crowded smoky room; someone with a white face and huge eyes.

Miss Hardcastle was beginning to steer her way between the groups, carefully guarding the two little yellow glasses. He felt sorry for her because she seemed worried, and he did not like the look of that friend of hers. Even from a distance, she looked—well, he did not like her.

'I must help you,' he said, coming behind Miss Hardcastle, and reaching over her shoulder for the drinks; and you would have thought he had said something funny by the way she was laughing as she quickly turned her head to thank him, but she looked grateful too, and, he thought, relieved.

He set the glasses down on their table and nodded politely without looking up as he heard Miss Hardcastle murmuring introductions—'I don't think you know each other—Mr Waite—Mrs Peers———' and he turned away at once, only anxious to get back to Fred Lowe and the Egg Board, but as he went he heard Mrs Peers laugh and caught the word 'Christ.'

Jean sat staring down at her little glass and slowly twisting it about, and now and then lifting her eyes, as she listened, to those eyes opposite that were like huge dim jewels. She remembered them when they had been clear and full of light, for this was Nancy Burnett, now Nancy Peers, with whom she and Alda had been at school, and when one's chief memories are of someone wearing a gym tunic with amused disdainful elegance, and when one still sees their cheeks and lips as geranium-red, it is difficult to replace that memory by grey massaged flesh, and dyed hair, and spots.

Some days ago, she and Alda had walked up to the school to meet the children, and had been hailed by a hoarse sweet voice from an enormous car standing outside the gates. There had been mutual recognition; amusement that Alda had written to Mrs Peers without knowing who she was, and some exchange of news (Mrs Peers's contribution consisting of the remarks, 'Yes, I've taken it for six months, it's lousy,' and 'No, ducky, it's the other one I'm married to now, not Clive, and I've had that, too'). Since then the family at the cottage had seen a great deal of the family at Hampton House; which consisted of Mrs Peers, some servants, and the pale, self-willed, pretty Eglantine, whom her mother called Egg. ('Eglantine was Robert's touching idea.') They gathered that Robert had followed Clive and was Eglantine's father. The present encumbrance was Mrs Peers's third husband; she had been married at seventeen. It was, as Jean observed, another world.

Every morning the car, containing Eglantine, stopped at the crossroads to pick up Jenny and Louise, sometimes driven by a chauffeur and sometimes by Mrs Peers herself. It also took the children home in the afternoons, and in the lengthening evenings Alda and Jean would be interrupted at their gardening by a figure in fur coat and black sweater who sat down on the roller announcing, 'You're coming into Brighton with me for a drink.' Then, because the children could not be left, one of them would stay behind, and one would go in with Nancy, because they used to be at school with her and because they were sorry for her.

All the same, it was a bore. The smoke in the bars of the expensive hotels stung Alda's eyes, and she felt out of place in her shabby clothes amongst the black suits and the jewelled clips, and she grew tired of listening to the curt sentences and the blasphemy and the oaths; she grew confused, as the evening wore on, between the men that Nancy talked about, and as the bill for the drinks piled up, Nancy became confused too. Alda's head ached, she never really wanted more than two drinks, her mind wandered away to the children and she wanted to talk about them instead, and she felt that Nancy both despised and envied herself. Nancy soon preferred Jean's company to Alda's, and Alda settled down again to her gardening, and knitting, and listening-in.

Jean now accompanied Nancy into Brighton and sometimes to London, and although she liked the excursions even less than Alda did, she could not get out of going. She never could think of an excuse, for her clothes were right, she had a stronger head, and she was a better listener. But she told Alda philosophically that at least her sufferings would not last long. 'Don't you remember,' she said, 'how she used to take people up at school and give them a marvellous time and then suddenly get bored and drop them completely? That's what she'll do to us.'

'Roll on the day, say I.'

'Me too. Poor old Nancy,' she ended, as if all her complaints had been only leading up to that remark.

This evening she was a little frightened. They had been at Hove all the afternoon, drinking in a flat belonging to one of Nancy's casuals, and now Jean was thinking about the drive home.

Her head had been aching violently when they came out from the stuffy flat; into the wide, quiet, evening streets of Hove, where the last sunlight was shining high up in the air along the balustrades of massive houses soaring against the luminous blue. There was no one about, and a cool wind wandered down the Palladian avenues. Nancy had had words with her casual and come away in a black mood.

She drove superbly, but that was not what one wanted in someone driving a car: one wanted them to be sober. So far there had been risks but no disaster, but now Nancy had started drinking again.

Jean glanced at Mr Waite. His usual disapproving manner and his help with the glasses had been very welcome, like a stodgy but familiar face seen in a nightmare and as for disapproving, how right he was! Drink was all very nice when you were cheerful but when you were miserable it was dreadful.

Then she glanced at Nancy. At that instant Nancy's eyes swept up to hers with that flash of colour which never failed to startle Jean, and she grinned. She knew how Jean was feeling. At school, she had always enjoyed teasing until it hurt, and Jean was so dim, she asked for it.

'Shall we ask him over?' Jean suggested, too eagerly indicating Mr Waite. He now sat alone with his half-finished beer, surveying the room as if about to sentence it.

Nancy slowly, dazedly moved her lovely head from side to side.

'Who darling?'

'Mr Waite. He's over there. He's—he's a friend of Alda's.'

'Is he good? I mean is he any good, darling?'

'I'll go and get him,' and Jean was getting up when a long hand in a black glove came over the table and the fingers waved her down with an imperious gesture that was miserably familiar. She used to do that in class when you tried to stop her fooling about, thought Jean unhappily. Oh Lord, this *is* beastly.

'Someth' wrong?' said the sweet hoarse voice, loudly and dangerously.

Jean could feel the eyes of the room suddenly fixed upon them, and although she did not look at him, she knew exactly the shocked, embarrassed expression that the barman had. A lady, Mrs Peers from Hampton House, drunk in his bar! But contempt and amusement lurked under his look too, and suddenly Jean hated them all—except Mr Waite. He, at least, was not furtively grinning.

Nancy was standing up.

'Something's the matter,' she insisted quietly, reasonably, leaning on the table with her slim height stooping over Jean.

Jean stared up at her, trying to think of what to say, what to do, when there was a purposeful stir among the people behind her, and someone crossed the room and stood at her side.

Mr Waite took her arm and spoke in a low decided tone.

'Mrs Lucie-Browne asked me if I would see you home, Miss Hardcastle. I have my car outside, and we can be there in ten minutes,' he said.

Nancy sat down so abruptly that her chair rocked, and shook her head.

'May be outside but can't use it. I ran into it,' she said, an enchanting smile beginning to creep over her face. 'I *couldn't* be sorrier. You must let me know wh—wh—wh—you must let me know.'

Mr Waite became flustered. The smile was so intimate, so

almost tender, that for a moment he wondered confusedly if he had met her somewhere before? But his car—the car—what was this about the car?

'Jean *said* it was yours,' said Nancy loudly and indignantly, and flashed the eyes on to Jean. Everybody was staring amusedly.

'I'm afraid it is, but I don't think it's much hurt,' said Jean quickly, pulling on her coat. 'Come on, let's go and see,' and she made her way rapidly through the crowd followed by Mr Waite.

In the yard the air was fresh and silent, with a yellow afterglow lingering in the remote west. The cars stood about on the pale stones like obedient slumbering monsters, bulky and solid and neat; all except Mr Waite's, which was knocked sideways with a shocking effect. One mudguard was smashed in. Mr Waite uttered low cries in which 't't' (a noise which Jean had supposed occurred only in old numbers of *Punch*) mingled with indignant gasps, and hurried to examine it.

She said: 'Thanks awfully for coming to the rescue, Mr Waite,' but he was too busy to notice. She did not mind, for it was so delightful, such a relief, to be out in the fresh air and away from Nancy. A faint breeze moved the branches of the budding lime trees and fanned her forehead and already her headache felt easier. She leant against one of the other cars and silently watched him for a while; then her gaze wandered across the road to the Linga-Longa Café, whose brilliant lights during these lengthening evenings were always the first to flash out along the village street. Some of the girls there had had the idea of cleaning the windows only that afternoon, and she could see plainly into the interior. A tower of yellow hair caught her eye; it was familiar; yes, it was Sylvia from the farm, sprawling at a table and waving her arms about as she related some tale. The girls were flinging their heads back, nudging each other, roaring with laughter. They're having more fun than Nancy and I do, thought Jean.

'I do hope it isn't badly damaged?' she said to him, at last.

'I can't tell in this light, that's just the trouble,' he sighed, standing upright from an inspection of the engine, 'and my torch is nearly exhausted. I am anxious about you, too. I want to get you home. You shouldn't be hanging about here after being in that stuffy place, you may catch a chill.'

'Oh, I'm perfectly happy. Don't worry about me.'

'Mrs Lucie-Browne will be anxious about you,' he said, and said no more.

So that's it, thought Jean, putting her hands in her pockets. Oh well.

But when he tried to start the engine it would not move. It uttered not a sound: it would not even make the painful noise that means a car is at least *trying*. He became agitated, darting from dashboard to engine and back again, but in vain. At last he said sombrely:

'I am afraid the damage is serious.'

'Oh dear.'

'It's too bad,' burst out Mr Waite, wiping his face. 'I use the car every day and all day—I don't know what I shall do—it may take weeks to mend. And how am I to get you home?'

'She didn't mean—at least—she wasn't——' said Jean awkwardly. But she knew that Nancy had run into his car on purpose. She liked smashing things.

'All the worse,' he retorted, slamming the door and peering closely in order to insert the key. 'I could see that you didn't like being with your friend in that state, and I was glad of it.'

'She isn't really a friend, she's only an acquaintance. She was at school with Alda—Mrs Lucie-Browne—and me.'

'It's a dreadful sight, a lady in that state,' he said, sighing and dusting his hands. 'I can never get used to it, never.'

'She's had an awful life,' said Jean, standing upright and taking her hands out of her pockets. She shivered slightly; she felt a little chilled but her headache had vanished.

'That's no excuse,' said Mr Waite severely. 'A great many people have had hard lives; I have myself, but I haven't taken to drink.

It's a good thing she didn't drive you home, there might have been a dreadful accident.'

'When she was sixteen she was simply lovely,' said Jean absently. 'Poor Nancy.'

Mr Waite ignored this, for sounds from the passage leading to the yard now indicated that some patrons were coming out. He said quickly: 'I am sorry, but we shall have to walk home. Do you feel equal to it?' She nodded, and he went on quietly:

'Please take my arm,' and she was so surprised that she did so without comment.

She was afraid of seeing the white face, the huge eyes, looking out at her from the door of the saloon bar; she only wanted to get home as quickly as possible, and he also seemed to fear an encounter. They walked quickly out of the yard and across the road.

She found that her step fell in comfortably with his and that his height matched well with her own; there was no bobbing or bumping or apologising; they walked on easily together through the spring dusk, along the dim road bordered by shadowy trees in bud. Unnoticed, the moon in its second quarter had risen over the dark fields and was now shining behind the elms and casting their shadows upon the road. The mildness, the gentleness and freshness of the air and scene soothed Jean's senses, and she was trusting that they had done the same for him when he said, so explosively that he made her start:

'Yes! That's what I must do. Telephone Fred Lowe (he keeps the garage on the London road and does my repairs) to pick up the car to-night. I can do that from the farm, they won't mind, it isn't late.'

'I'm giving you a lot of trouble, I'm afraid, Mr Waite. I'm so sorry. I *could* have gone home by myself——'

'That would have been quite impossible,' he answered firmly. 'You have had an unpleasant experience and I am happy to have been of any help.'

He suppressed a sigh: he was still very angry, and he wanted to be quiet to think about the car: the probable amount of damage, what the repairs would cost, whether he should send the bill to this Mrs Peers, and so on. But to walk with Miss Hardcastle arm-in-arm in silence would be embarrassing to them both; besides, he wished to distract her attention from the evening's disagreeable events, and he began determinedly:

'Do you drive, Miss Hardcastle?'

'I used to, but I never was much good. I——'

She suppressed the confession that she had several times run into things (not people), and concluded not quite truthfully:

'I never could get the knack, somehow.'

'Ladies seldom can,' replied Mr Waite, feeling better disposed towards her and glancing down at the gilt, turbaned head level with his shoulder, 'and yet it is perfectly simple. I don't suppose you fully understand the principle upon which the combustion engine is constructed, do you?'

'Not quite, I'm afraid. I'm not bright about that sort of thing.'

Mr Waite was now at ease (or nearly so; he completely relaxed only in company with Mother and the Girls) and he at once began.

On they walked, at a pace neither irritatingly slow nor tiringly fast, and myriads of clouds, in hue a bright, tender grey and in shape curved like shells, gradually covered the sky and veiled the moon, and the only sound was the pacing of their feet upon the road and Mr Waite's slightly harsh but not unpleasing voice explaining the combustion engine. His earnest wish to make all perfectly clear to her added a gentler note to its usual dictatorial or disapproving tones, and Jean, glancing from time to time at his regular profile, wondered why she was not thrilled about him, for he was better-looking than Captain Ottley and far, far kinder than Mr Potter. Still, it was pleasant to walk peacefully thus, enjoying the night, and comprehending not one word of what he was saying.

She glanced again at Mr Waite. He was without charm, he was narrow-minded and not always polite; he fussed; he was always taking thought for the morrow and he never even glanced at the lilies of the field, but no one could deny that he had been exceedingly kind. He had shown no especial desire for *her* company, no personal concern for *her* (and that was not flattering) but he had rendered, through her, homage to that remote, gracious Goddess of Womanhood enthroned in his mind. Jean wondered whence he got his ideals about Ladies. Not from his mother and sisters, she felt sure, for he had dropped remarks which indicated that they were bustling, practical, active women, making Christmas presents in July with one hand and nursing sick cousins with the other. Perhaps some Sunday School teacher or elegant young stranger seen at a party had set the standard years ago when he was a boy. Women were no longer like Mr Waite's Ideal Lady; perhaps they never had been; but there was a lingering irritating fascination about her charms and her code.

They had now passed the camp and in a little while they would be home. Mr Waite broke a silence by hoping that she was not tired.

'Oh no, not a bit, thanks. But I am wondering if I've had it so far as Nancy is concerned. She's very touchy.'

'Alcohol has that effect upon people, in time,' said Mr Waite in his stiffest voice. 'Your friend has no right to be annoyed with you; you only did what was right. I hope it will make her ashamed of herself.'

Jean gave a tiny shake of her head, unseen in the dim moonlight. Mr Waite did indeed live in a world of his own.

'Where is her husband? Not demobilised yet?' he went on. 'I heard from the milkman that she is not a widow.'

'Er—he doesn't—they aren't together any more. He is her third husband, as a matter of fact.'

Mr Waite gave a movement of the head, a compression of the lips, that Alda would have called pussyish.

'Married for her money, I suppose. She seems to have plenty.'

Jean gently withdrew her arm from his in order to make an unnecessary adjustment to her turban.

'I don't know about that. She's always been very attractive to men.'

'But the money helped them to make up their minds,' with a little laugh.

'I expect so,' answered Jean, and then she was silent. She was remembering that the solicitors had assured her of an income of three thousand pounds a year clear, after death duties had been paid and annual income tax met, from her father's business. Mr Waite's little laugh, combined with the knowledge of her own wealth, had started an unpleasing train of thought and one which was unfamiliar to her, for she had always been so blinded by her romantic longing for marriage that it had actually never occurred to her that it might be possible to buy it.

Unfortunately Mr Waite seemed in a moralising mood, and went on to deplore Mrs Peers's frequent marriages, pointing out that the more often you were married the more were the opportunities for failure. Some people, of course, were sensible enough to avoid marriage completely.

'Like me,' concluded Mr Waite, with another laugh. 'No, Miss Hardcastle, I've seen too much of married life to want to tie *my*self down; I've had married friends; I've seen them worried almost into their graves over school bills and rent and doctors' bills and holidays, no peace, no opportunity to put a little bit by for that rainy day we're always hearing about (it's been raining for the last thirty years, it seems to me) no time to realise the Highest in your Self; no thank you, I'm not having any.'

This was not pleasant hearing; it never is, even if you are not in love with the man who says it, but Jean's spirits did not sink as they would have if Mr Potter or the Blakewell boy had uttered such words. She only thought *Poor Mr Waite*, and answered cheerfully:

'Oh, I think you're so right. I shan't marry, either.'

Indeed, the only thought in her head at the moment was *Thank goodness I haven't got to marry, what with poor Nancy's example and Mr Waite being so depressing.*

But Mr Waite at once became grave; he shook his head, he turned to look down at the face smiling up into his own, and he said:

'I don't like to hear a lady say that, Miss Hardcastle. You're doing some poor chap out of a happy home.'

She laughed, but the laugh covered some exasperation. She was tempted to exclaim, 'And they call women illogical!' but refrained. His speech was illogical, but it was also pretty, and she believed that he meant it. *I like him,* she decided.

A light shone in the window of Pine Cottage and it was only nine o'clock, but Mr Waite, halting at a distance of some two hundred yards from the gate, declined Jean's invitation to come in and have a cup of tea. She said she was sorry that it would only be tea, and he replied austerely that surely they had seen enough that evening of what alcohol could do? standing, as he said it, with his hat in his hand and his eyes carefully not wandering towards the light in the window. He then explained that he had a letter to write to the Egg Board, cut short her thanks, said good night and walked quickly away.

Alda was listening to a snarling voice telling her how awful everything was in America. She switched it off when Jean entered, and sat upright, eager for all the news, and listened with great interest to her account of the evening's events. When at last she heard of the moonlit walk home, her face sparkled with approval; she cast an anxious eye over her friend to see how she must have appeared to Mr Waite by that transforming light, then nodded approvingly, and was not at all dismayed when Jean repeated his views on marriage, assuring her that men always talked like this when they were attracted by that particular subject, and adding firmly, 'It's like moths.'

She told Jean that everything between herself and Mr Waite was going well: he had rescued her, he had taken her arm, and he had begun to fulminate against marriage. She ended by reminding her again that down here there was no competition for his interest, but Jean, who had emptied her handbag on to the table and was tearing up bills and bus tickets and rearranging her purse, a cigarette case, a lipstick, and a tiny New Testament, thought to herself that there was Competition, only it did not know that it was competing.

The personal excitement, the sensation of herself as heroine, which had always accompanied these discussions with Alda like a chorus of violins, had ceased: the violins were silent and she felt only weariness and some distaste, but Alda seemed to enjoy her own part as much as ever.

The next morning Nancy's car drew up at the crossroads as usual to take up Jenny and Louise, but the driver was a pale girl in bright clothes, with that oversweet manner which, as Miss Berta Ruck has wisely observed, invariably conceals bad temper. She informed Alda that Mrs Peers had suddenly got sick of the country and gone to a hotel in town, leaving herself in charge of the place and darling Egg. Alda received this information with relief, and when at the end of two days Jenny and Louise announced their intention of walking to and from school 'because it's fine weather now and Magda is so beastly to us,' she gladly agreed.

In what precise way Magda was beastly, she never found out; questions only drew forth the answer 'Oh—I don't know—she's so unkind,' and she was content to leave it at that, knowing that while a child is still a child, kindness is the only quality which it finds irresistible: wit, authority, imagination, personal beauty, even a real love of children, are nowhere beside a simple, even a stupid, person who is unfailingly kind. In a week the convent heard that Eglantine had been whisked away to join her mother; the unkind Magda vanished too; and the Peers incident was over.

But it had served the purpose of making Mr Waite feel that Alda and Jean were ladies permanently in distress and in need of his protection, and he made this clear to them, in a reserved manner, whenever the two households met, which was more frequently now that full spring, with bluebells and may, had arrived. Once or twice they even found five eggs sitting upon the cottage doorstep; large, unallocated, unstamped eggs whose smooth brown countenances were so different from the pallid visages (blurred with purple letters and smeared, like hopeless tears, with heaven-knew-what) of the allocated eggs that they seemed to belong to another egg-world: eggs of a primal vigour and bloom; eggs before the Fall.

This gesture impressed Alda and Jean with a sense of his growing goodwill towards them the more strongly because, ever since their first days at the cottage, the Hoadleys had indicated that it was no use hoping for presents of stray eggs from Mr Waite; what the Egg Board did not demand as a natural right, he himself needed for his private customers, among whom the family at Pine Cottage was not included. After these warnings of course, they would all have bitten their tongues out before hinting about the eggs, admiring the eggs, or even mentioning the eggs (though Meg had sometimes turned large-eyed looks upon her mother when they met Mr Waite crossing the meadow carrying two baskets filled to the brim with them). In these circumstances, they felt that the eggs upon the doorstep were profoundly significant.

21

Just as Alda had promised the children in December, life at the cottage now became pleasant, for it was possible to spend hours in the open air. Two or three times a week she and Jean met Jenny and Louise at the convent gates with Meg in her pram and high tea packed in a basket, and off they would go to the nearest wood and settle themselves under the rosy foliage of young oaks, exclaiming at the profusion of primroses (now beginning to retire, rather than fade, so gentle was their decline down into their leafy cradles before the advance of the bluebells) and the occasional drifts of dying violets and the bluebells themselves; gentle, limp and cool, with their heavenly odour wherein water and wine seem blended and their dim, thick purple-blue petals.

Long after tea was over, and the children were beginning to ask what there was for supper, they would linger on, while day radiantly declined behind trees not yet fully leafed enough to break the light into rays but revealing it as one glory, and Jenny perhaps told some story of a little boy stricken with leprosy and declining intercession for his recovery on the part of his confessor because he longed to go to Heaven, which had that day been related to the children at the convent. Louise listened in silence, and if she joined in the laughter which followed, it was constrainedly and with a troubled look. Alda noticed this, though she made no comment. Ronald would be home on leave again in a week or so and she was determined to have a long talk with him about Louise and the Roman Catholic Church.

On one of her free afternoons Sylvia accompanied them on a picnic and at first added to everybody's pleasure by her own pleasure in the sights and sounds and scents of the woods; she loudly declared, more than once, that she must come here again, she must bring Mum, and so forth; and she helped Jenny and Louise to light a fire to boil water for tea (for it transpired that she had once been a Brownie).

But when she wanted to turn the fire into a bonfire, casting excited and covetous glances at the young branches hanging low enough to tear down and burn, and imploring Alda to go home with Meg and let the kiddies stay on with her until the moon came up and have a real gipsy-fire and a sing-song, Alda firmly said no, and then Sylvia turned sulky. The afternoon was not spoiled, for she soon became good-tempered again, but the kiddies themselves were disappointed because they had been excited by her suggestion, and the next time there was a picnic they seemed to find the woods, lacking Sylvia's shrieks and her thirsty quest for thrills and her stories about murders and vampires and zombies, rather dull.

Jean and Alda agreed with some amusement that she would have felt herself deeply insulted if they had compared her with the 'ignorant nursegirl,' the 'skivvy,' of papers and magazines published fifty years ago, for she was a Communist, an ex-dramatic student, and heir to the Humanism of four hundred years. Yet here she was, coming from the same class as the skivvy of the '90's and over-exciting and frightening the gentry's children exactly as the skivvy used to do whenever she got the chance, and lacking the skivvy's unanswerable excuse of ignorance.

Alda was not one of those people who excuse every human fault, from rudeness to murder, by saying that the offender has been badly brought up, and she told the children that Sylvia was stupid and vulgar and had not made the most of her advantages. But as Jenny, Louise and Meg now had a passion for Sylvia as a source of excitement and fun, these remarks made no effect.

Alda herself could not refrain from asking her a teasing question or so about Fabrio, to which Sylvia replied that he had gone all haughty again and was always coming the old acid over her, and that she was getting browned off with him. She added that she supposed he had just made a convenience of her to learn English off of, and now he could speak and read it a bit he thought he could drop her. 'And that suits me, so we're both happy,' she ended, with her ploughboy grin.

Indeed, she drew a gleeful, malicious pleasure from his imploring looks, instantly withdrawn when she glanced towards him, his miserable silences, his sullenness under the jokes of Emilio; all this amused and delighted her and fed her vanity. It made a good story to tell the girls down at the Linga-Longa, where she had quickly found company greatly to her taste: three or four girls who had managed to evade the Services and the factories on pleas of old mothers or delicate health, who now earned a scanty but more or less cheerful living as waitresses.

All were pretty and all were pining to get work in London or Brighton, but they stayed in Sillingham because the work was not so hard there and because they liked Ma, who managed the café and was easy-going. Boiling coffee and pretty faces attracted plenty of casual male custom, and at the Linga-Longa there were always current love affairs to discuss. Bette and Pat and Pam slopped and shuffled about, with paint peeling off their nails and their curls half-way down their backs in fuzzy blonde or dusty brown tangles; they were always ready to stop work and slip arms round each other's waists and stand with heads close together, murmuring and giggling: they never thought about the past, they never thought about the future, they lived completely in the present and were interested in nothing but tales about other people and their own looks.

They found Sylvia amusing and welcomed her visits, and she enjoyed every moment that she spent at the Linga-Longa and on her one half-day a week she was usually to be found there, gossiping and laughing with the girls and sometimes helping with the work during a rush of custom.

Once or twice she went with the three into Brighton and walked arm-in-arm rapidly along the front; past the pale, curved houses gilt by the spring sunlight and the closed, dusty little shops which had once sold luxuries, while a cold wind blew steadily in from the vast, dim grey sea and the old Jewish men and women sat huddled in their furs and thick clothes behind the glass of the shelters, showing now and then a gleam of gold against a wrinkled neck. In Brighton her rough innocence served to check some grosser instincts in her friends, and the outing took on a schoolgirlish flavour which none of them were sufficiently worldly or corrupt to find dull: they usually ended by going to the pictures and eating a large tea in the restaurant attached to the cinema before catching the bus back to Sillingham.

These excursions and the improving weather made her life much pleasanter, and had it not been for the increasing gloom at Naylor's Farm she would at this time have been thoroughly enjoying her work and her circumstances.

But the news had now been mysteriously allowed to circulate that Mrs Hoadley was to have a baby in December, and depression crept over everyone. Mr Hoadley was silent and timid in manner towards his wife and she herself went about looking martyred. White and pink wool (for Mrs Hoadley was of course going to bear a daughter) appeared in odd corners, and knitting needles and work were whisked away when men appeared, and the farmer's wife began to make occasional resigned references about the coming event to Sylvia. Her appearance remained as neat as ever and her health was apparently unimpaired save for an increasing fear of burglars and tramps. One day she abruptly announced that the baby's name was to be Joyanna, looking resigned when Sylvia heartily agreed that *Joanna* was ever such an uncommon name.

'I'm very glad to hear it; it's what she needs and that poor man is so fond of children,' said Alda decidedly, when Sylvia told her the news.

'Well, I wish it was here and done with. It gets me down, the way we all have to creep about the place,' Sylvia grumbled. 'It was bad enough before, but it's awful now. If we weren't all so busy, I don't know how I should stick it.'

'Oh, she'll get over that. We all go through it,' said the matron.

They were very busy, so busy that the lengthening days were not long enough to hold all the work that had to be done as the spring advanced, and Sylvia found amusement in her frequent encounters with Fabrio in the open air, as their duties took them about the farm.

The English lessons had ceased without a word on either side. When they met, she shouted a casual 'Hullo!' or '*Buon giorno!*' and he either ignored her or answered roughly without looking at her. There was embarrassment between them, rather than anger. She remembered that kiss with extreme vividness, which did not lessen as the weeks went by, and she was sure that he remembered it in the same way. Men had tried to kiss her before now and been repulsed, but not one of them had been so serious about it afterwards, avoiding her, and not looking at her, and going about the place with such a miserable face. She made up her mind two or three times to ask him what on earth was up with him: and each time, on meeting him, she had suddenly found that she could not.

She enjoyed Alda's teasing and she did not deeply resent Emilio's nods and winks, while she revelled in boasting and complaining to the girls at the Linga-Longa about Fabrio's behaviour; but when she actually saw him, when his sturdy graceful body shrank aside to let her pass him in some narrow way, and he stood in silence, pale, with downcast eyes and trembling mouth, as she hurried by with a laugh, then she did not find him in the least funny and she could not ask him what was the matter: she was furious, and she would have liked to give him a good shaking, and sometimes she believed that he was doing it just to annoy her, but she could not bring herself to question him.

And Fabrio spoke of his feelings to no one. Emilio had met him with eager questions after the excursion to the Wild Brooks, assuming in the face of all improbabilities that what used to be known as The Worst had happened, and Fabrio had allowed his friend to think what he liked. He neither boasted nor denied. He kept a haughty smile upon his face and answered Perhaps and Maybe and Who Knows? for his manly pride would not let him deny a conquest, and yet his true love for Sylvia, the lost girl, the gentle maiden imprisoned within the blundering body of *La Scimmia*, would not let him lie about their happy hours together. Let Emilio think what he chose to think.

Emilio was much taken up by letters from Genoa, where the eldest of his *bambini*, aged nine, had just embarked upon a promising career of American lorry-robbing, armed with a razor blade to slit tyres or canvas, and commanding a band of eight followers younger than himself. Giulia wrote that the family had twice enjoyed tinned meat within three days! the first meat of any kind that they had tasted for two years! Emilio's fatherly heart glowed with mingled envy and pride.

Fabrio spoke of his feelings least of all to Father Francesco in the confessional box. His faith resembled some sturdy bright flower of the hedgerows with a winding, accommodating habit, and he had even suppressed the fact that Sylvia was teaching him English, for had not the Father sternly discouraged his wish to learn? and would he not be even sterner if he heard that Fabrio had been taking lessons after all, and lessons from a young *protestante* girl? Fabrio did not want anyone to be stern with him: he had had quite enough of that in the army and the prison camp, and now he wanted only to be loved and admired. It was difficult to conceal his increasing fluency in English from Father Francis, but he pretended to be stupider than he was.

Fabrio was also troubled over Sylvia's soul, for her wild words at Amberley had revealed to him that she was a victim of *ateismo*, atheism, a state of darkness terrible in its implications to this believer. He believed that if only he prayed earnestly enough to Our Lady, She would work a miracle and show Sylvia the truth, and he did pray exhaustively for her on Sundays at Mass, but during the week there was so much to do, and no proper place to pray in, so he resolved to utter a prayer for her every time he passed her in the fields or the farmyard, but the light shone on her hair, her blue eyes glanced smilingly up at the blue sky while she scattered the grain, and he forgot his prayer in human longing.

He was very miserable and increasingly homesick, with a thirsty, passionate longing for San Angelo that the coming of fine warm weather did nothing to slake. He noticed the flowers, but they were not the flowers he knew at home; and the shade of these great trees, that had towered so gloomily over him in the winter, was not as grateful as the sharp black shadows of the olive grove, because the sun was not so hot; it was hardly hot at all; it was always being shaded by some cloud or cut off by one of those same enormous trees that dripped down his neck when it rained; and this year, more painfully than in any other spring during his captivity, he missed girls and love.

Regularly once a week, as regularly as Mass and the lifted golden Cup with the white face of Father Francesco behind it, there came a letter from Maria. At first Fabrio had not taken much notice of it, except to feel flattered and to wave it gaily in front of Emilio (whose letters from home were more and more concerned with the alarmingly successful prowess of the gangster-*bambino*) but as his reading improved, and he became able to master the contents without asking his friend's help, he began to enjoy the letters; then to look forward to them; and at last, when April came and the woods below were filled with bluebells and the blue sky above them went on for ever, Maria's letter had come to be the one happy thing; the only thing he

looked forward to, in his week. It became his comfort, his link
with home, giving him the warmth and peace which he had
once dimly felt at Mass, and now felt no longer.

The letters were not long but they were filled with news.
(There was never anything about thoughts or feelings in them;
Maria would have regarded such a use of the difficult art of
writing as a waste of skill and time and so would her correspondent.) She told him that his brother Giulio had cut his hand
while planing posts for a gate; that there had been a fall of rocks
on the path leading up to Santa Maria and one had to climb
round them with one's basket of three eggs for sale or one's
letter for the post because there was no one to clear the rocks
away, as most of the men of the village had not yet returned
from the war; Luigina had had a bambino by an Americano;
Emma Tommasi was to marry her Americano; Giuseppina Cappa
was to be married at Easter. Maria's mother's new white chickens,
saved for during four months and bought at last, were laying
well. Andrea and Paolo Montanari now had six children.

His letters to her were in a similar style, telling her of his
work at the farm and doings at the camp; what he ate, where
he went, but never what he felt. He boasted a little about the
pleasures to be found in that fine large town Horsham, where
there were many cafés and cinemas; he gave her the impression
that life was not at all bad in England, and never once did he
write 'I am longing to come home.' Now that he could write,
he shaped his letters with the natural grace and ease that he put
into any small job, and Maria admired the bold regular lines and
full curves of the 'a's and 'o's; it was quite a picture, Fabrio's
handwriting, and she looked up to him more than ever.

She was now living at home, she wrote, and doing most of
the work on their smallholding. She did not tell him, poor Maria,
that after months and months of blunders and excuses and tears
and exasperated forgiveness in the shop at Portofino, her employer
had at last rapturously welcomed a young man home from the

wars who had offered his services as assistant. Maria had been
sent home the same afternoon. I am very stupid, she thought
humbly, and if I tell him that I was dismissed it will only make
Fabrio despise me. At first she missed the sweet smells and the
pretty combs and other trifles in the hairdresser's shop, but soon
she became used to weeding their small plot of ground in the
hot dust of summer and hoeing it in the bitter mountain spring,
with her head muffled in her old shawl and bowed before the
wind, and she was content. There was almost enough for herself
and her old mother to eat, and one day her brothers would
come home from the camps in Austria and that other place, far
away, down almost as far as Russia, and once a week the postman
brought his old mule up the narrow path, round the fallen rocks,
past the stream that dwindled every day as summer advanced,
with Fabrio's letter.

Very rarely, Fabrio received a letter from his eldest brother,
but he only told him the family news which Maria had already
heard from his sisters in her weekly visit, and Maria wrote a
clearer hand than Giuseppe and at greater length. Fabrio's father
was ill. He was now too ill to sail the boat; he sat all day in the
shade, in the stone yard where the olive-press stood and the
doves rustled and cooed among the broad leaves of the chestnut
tree, and Fabrio knew, though Giuseppe did not say so, that
presently his father would die. Then Giuseppe would have the
house and the land.

After he had read the letter giving him this news, Fabrio
thought for a long time; and when the hour for dinner came,
he bolted his lump of hard bread and his little cube of cheese
and went to look for Mr Hoadley. The farmer often took his
dinner out into the fields nowadays and ate it while he worked,
for Molly was no company at the dinner-table, picking at her
food and sulking, and that great mare of a girl never stopped
talking.

'What is it?' he asked shortly, looking up as Fabrio hesitatingly approached him. He was in one of the open sheds, removing rust from the mould-board of the plough.

'I want to save my money,' said Fabrio, and he took sevenpence from his pocket and held it out to the farmer. 'Please keep it for me, signor.'

Mr Hoadley straightened himself from his stooping posture and dusted his hands on his trousers. This seemed to him the first sensible remark he had heard from either of the Italians.

'Why, are you going home?' he asked, not ill-naturedly.

Fabrio shrugged his shoulders and smiled broadly.

'Some day perhaps,' he said.

'All right, I'll keep it for you,' and he pocketed the sevenpence. 'It'll soon mount up, you'll be surprised. But why pick on me?'

'I will not give it to Father Francesco, because he will tell me to put it in the church box,' Fabrio answered candidly, 'and Emilio will want me to buy the cigarette and beer.'

'I see. *Capisco*. All right. And now how about you two learning to use a double handsaw on that oak down by the rue' (he meant a narrow ditch below a bank, bordering a coppice) 'instead of wasting my time using an axe?'

This time Fabrio's face sparkled with conscious mischief.

'Cannot,' and he shrugged.

'Cannot my foot. Will not, you mean. All right, get on with your work now. Your money's safe.'

'Thank you, signor,' Fabrio answered, and went off.

His mind was more at ease. His eldest brother would have the land and the house and all the other brothers in between would have privileges before himself, who was only the youngest son, but he would return with some money saved, and what with that, and his knowledge of the English tongue and English ways he would not be a person who could be completely ignored and overruled in the family councils.

Mr Hoadley presently started to whistle. It was a pity that Molly was so sulky nowadays and of course he was sorry for what she would have to go through later on, but it was the natural thing, after all; and it was the best piece of news *he* had had for years, and in spite of her resigned looks he had to express his satisfaction.

Alda had been prepared to give Mrs Hoadley advice if it were asked for, but she had no intention of offering it if it were not, and when she perceived with surprise and some contempt that it was Sylvia who was to be the confidante, if anybody were, she lost her small patience with Mrs Hoadley and referred to her as 'that ass,' not realising that the farmer's wife, still a girl in outlook and temperament, preferred to make her few confidences and complaints to another girl, rather than to a matron, however youthful.

Alda herself was not very content, for Ronald's latest spell of leave had been delayed by more than five weeks and there was still no definite date for his arrival, and Father's-Only-Sister-Marion had suddenly opened a sharp pincer-movement on the young Lucie-Brownes' education, combined with an interrogation as to their political views. Were they being trained to take their place in the New Democratic World? Marion herself had a surprise for Alda: she hoped one day to stand for Parliament as Labour candidate in the very Ironborough constituency for which Ronald had planned to stand as a Liberal. It was at present held by a Conservative who was old and in feeble health. Should there be a by-election, Marion would stand.

'Beast!' cried Jenny, on hearing this news. 'Why, that's father's constituency! Her own brother! She ought to be ashamed!'

'Sneaking it away from him while he's abroad doing his duty!' Louise joined in hotly. 'She *is* a beast!'

'Poor father,' mourned Louise. 'Mother, he'll be fearfully disappointed, won't he?'

'I'm afraid he will, but not very surprised,' answered Alda, who had gathered from Ronald's recent letters that something of this sort was brewing, 'and as she's got the money and the ambition and the brains, she'd better do it.'

'Father's got brains!' cried Louise, shocked.

'Much better brains than Marion, lovey, but a different kind. Oh well, it can't be helped. You must all be extra loving and good when he comes home next time, that's all. And he might find another constituency later on,' she ended.

Although she honestly regretted Ronald's disappointment, her own disappointment was not deep but she did resent the tone of Marion's letter, which was so exultant and dictatorial as to seem insulting. There was a reference to Jean, whose orphaned, idle and prosperous condition now rendered her peculiarly fitted to take up some public work. She might Speak or Write (political writing, of course, not useless writing) or take a course of instruction in Socialist political theory. In any case, she certainly would not want to waste much more time down in the country doing nothing, and Alda was to let Marion know if she could help with introductions or advice. And how was Jenny's riding getting on?

Alda was hurrying up the cottage stairs, waving this letter and muttering and intending to show it to Jean, when the latter came out of her bedroom. She wore her coat, and on seeing Alda she looked conscious.

'Jean, you must hear Marion's latest. Your future is all arranged. Do listen! Really, she *is*——'

'I'm so sorry, darling, but I've got to beetle off. Terrific hurry,' and she was smilingly slipping past when Alda caught her waist.

'Where to? No, but do listen——'

'I will when I come back; I'm only going to the station.'

'Why? Are you meeting someone? Jean! It isn't Ronald?' and Alda suddenly sat down on the stairs and gazed up at her with a face full of hope.

'Of course not, idiot. It's just something I've got to collect.'

'At the station? I'll come too.'

'No, Alda. I'd rather you didn't. You'll see what it is—them, I mean—all in good time,' and she began to laugh, 'only I don't know how on earth I'm going to bring them home!' and still laughing she hurried down the stairs and out into the sunny morning.

'Meg will go for a walk,' observed a determined voice. Alda glanced down and saw that Meg had crept up unobserved and was now standing just below her in the steep shadowy well of the stairs, bending forward with plump hands supporting her weight upon the tread, her plain, cheerful little face lifted to her mother's.

'All right, Megsie, we'll go down and meet Jean. She's gone to fetch a surprise.'

There was nothing to do in the cottage, so they went.

When we say 'there was nothing to do,' of course we know that there is always some necessary and pithering work to do in a house, but Alda bothered herself little with such details in Pine Cottage, because it was such a dark, cross, dusty cottage, always managing to look, even in the midst of a Sussex meadow, as though it lived in Pimlico. We must confess that neither she nor Jean did much; but there was always the mending, and it is a fact that days in the country do glide past with a mysterious ease and calm; there always seems plenty of work to be done yet there is never a feeling of haste; something of the endlessness of childhood's days returns to the grown woman and she can delight in it without a sensation of guilt. And as every woman in England nowadays is overworked, we thought it would do no harm to present a picture of two who were not.

When Alda and Meg had strolled perhaps half-way to the station, they heard voices and laughter approaching and then, round a curve in the road came—first, Jean, wheeling a new bicycle that spun and glittered in the sunlight; next, Mr Waite, also wheeling a new bicycle that flashed in silver and scarlet; after him, Emilio and Fabrio in that order, each guiding a smaller bicycle of the same shiny newness and, last of all, came one-of-the-little-Dodders, belonging to an enormous family, reputed to be half-witted, which lived in extreme poverty, dirt and smiliness in a capacious cottage at the lonelier end of the Froggatt road.

The sex of this particular little Dodder was at first not clear, as it was very pretty but wore tattered knickerbockers, and it was wheeling a charming little tricycle.

Upon seeing Alda, everybody except Mr Waite broke into exclamations and laughter, and they all stopped short and waited for her to come up. She herself had coloured deeply; with excitement and pleasure and resentment. What a present! They must have cost a small fortune! No one but Jean would have done such a thing; so lavish, so kind, so certain to be welcomed, such a store of pleasure for months—years—ahead! Nevertheless, Alda preferred to give presents rather than to receive them. It is the commonest human failing and the one by which Man fell.

Emilio was smiling, the little Dodder was smiling (without one trace of envy, for when your toys are pebbles and sticks you cannot imagine owning a top, much less a tricycle), even Fabrio's pale face was alight with admiration for these beautiful shining new machines. Only Mr Waite was not smiling, for Mr Waite saw in this action of Miss Hardcastle's yet another example of how casual she was with her money, and he was thinking how very much she needed a man to look after her and prevent her from spending her late father's hard-earned fortune so lavishly. And now Mrs Lucie-Browne would go flying down the lanes, attracting attention and perhaps falling off.

'I've been expecting them for weeks, darling; I went up to town and ordered them right back in January, I'm so glad you like them, they do look rather smashing, don't they?' Jean was saying, while Alda brought out her warm and slightly embarrassed thanks. 'I thought I'd better get a trike for Megsy,' she added in a lower tone, as the *cortège* moved on, Mr Waite walking beside the ladies, 'because she really is too small to come out for rides with us yet. Oh, it will be fun, won't it!'

'Can the elder girls ride?' inquired Mr Waite, not in a damping tone. It was impossible to sound damp while looking at the women's happy faces, and while he was sure that those two Italians (who had happened to be at the station fetching a crate of ducks that had not arrived) ought to be at work, that was Hoadley's affair, not his. As for the little Dodder, it was a disgrace, but apparently harmless.

'Jenny used to, but I expect she's forgotten,' Alda answered, turning her smiling face to him. 'Why? Will you teach them?'

'There's that bit of flat road by the crossroads. I was thinking, I've got an hour to spare after tea. I might give them a lesson this evening—if you like.'

'That *is* kind of you! I *should* be grateful, because it really needs a man to hold them up. For some reason, everybody feels twice as heavy on a bicycle.'

'All right, then. If you're there by six o'clock I'll try and come along.' He hesitated. 'Do you ride?' he asked.

'Oh yes, thank you, and so does Jean,' she answered laughing, and he looked relieved.

While Emilio and Fabrio were discussing the bicycles in their own language, Meg and the little Dodder had walked along in silence, Meg keeping one hand jealously upon the seat of the tricycle while the little Dodder wheeled it. Suddenly the little Dodder, who had been glancing smilingly down at her out of beautiful slanting brown eyes, remarked huskily:

'Goinridin.'

'I beg your pardon, I din' hear what you said,' answered Meg, ceremoniously.

'Goinridin. Onna bike, I says.'

'It's mine,' replied Meg softly. 'Jean gabe it me. It's a pwesent,' and she stroked the glossy leather seat.

The little Dodder's smile became wide.

'Name's Evie,' she remarked presently. 'Wass yours?'

'Alda Meg Lucie-Bwowne. I were cwisten Meg, not Margarwet.'

THE MATCHMAKER

The little Dodder did not understand, but she smiled even more widely and presently she put out a dirty hand, red and chapped from helping Mum with the washing which she took in, and gently pulled Meg's plait. Her own short hair was the rich colour of dead leaves and dull with dust.

When they came to a gap in the hedge she made off through it, and her broken rubber boots and torn knickerbockers were seen no more. Mr Waite remarked that Those Dodders Are a Disgrace, but everybody was busy talking about the bicycles and no one answered him. Soon the opening leading to the farm was reached, and the Italians and Mr Waite, having wheeled the machines to the cottage gate, went off in pursuit of their various duties.

Alda thought it her duty to reprove Jean for her extravagance but only very briefly, for she felt that strong protest would have been ungracious. Meg was already proudly pedalling up and down in the garden, and Alda herself riding in imagination along lanes canopied with blossoming may.

In the middle of lunch a telegram arrived. Ronald would be home by tea-time on the following day, and Marion's public-spirited letter was thrust into Alda's handbag and forgotten.

22

Jenny emerged at ten minutes past four with a fiery, stained face as the result of a sharp battle with one of the Sisters.

She was surrounded by a sympathetic circle, comforting her and anathematising her accuser, for she had made a large circle of friends at the hated convent and in spite of her *loathing* of the Sisters, the lessons, the rules and the food, she eagerly looked forward to going there every day. There were others who said they *loathed* it too, and it was fun to *loathe* things with a lot of other people: all her friendliness, her liveliness and her deftness at games were finding eager expression.

Louise walked slightly apart, with her one best friend. She took no notice of Jenny and her group: it had been Jenny's fault; it always was; and she would hear quite enough about it when they got home.

But when they did get home every word about Jenny's misfortune was forgotten in the amazing sight of the bicycles propped against the porch. Tea was forgotten; homework was forgotten; even the news that father would be home to-morrow was for the time forgotten in the glorious surprise, as Alda and Jean and Meg hurried out, and there were cries of rapture and exclamations of delight and Jean was almost stifled by embraces. Alda watched them with a smile of pleasure; she could not help wishing that the bicycles had been her own present, but the children's delight gave her so much delight that all envy was swept away.

After tea they all went down to the crossroads for the first lesson. The evening was calm and the setting sun changed the colour of the fresh leaves to gold: the weather was not yet hot enough to draw up scents from the earth as evening came on and only coolness, scented with new grass, pervaded the air; buttercups and daisies were beginning to bud but glittering celandines still covered the ditch-banks and shone out in the meadows. The gaze wandered on, beyond coppices and spinneys that had not yet attained the full opulence of summer and still showed the brown shades and angularities of early leafage, past distant hillside meadows of emerald wheat and those low jewel-blue summits in which all horizons in this part of Sussex seem to end, but always it returned to one point: Chanctonbury Ring, beckoning the imagination towards its woody shades, high and far off in the clear air, against the rosy sky.

The children marched along, wheeling their bicycles and chattering, while Alda walked with Jean, who she was pleased to note looked particularly well that evening. She hoped to hear her friend and Mr Waite upon Christian name terms by the end of the bicycling lesson.

Suddenly she exclaimed in dismay. Sylvia was coming towards them wearing her civilian clothes, with her hair loosened, and looking pleased and excited. She hailed them and proposed to join the party: Emilio had told her about the bicycles, and he and Fabrio (worse luck, added Sylvia) were also coming to see the fun.

'The more the merrier,' said Jean, as Alda said nothing. 'But I thought those boys had to be back at the camp by half-past six?'

'Emilio says they've got a late pass this evening, Miss Hardcastle. Oo, I do wish Fabrio wasn't coming, he gives me the willies.'

'Has he proposed to you yet?' demanded Alda.

'Mrs Lucie-Browne! He hardly ever utters, since that time he got fresh with me in the train.'

'What will you say when he does?' teasingly.

'Mrs Lucie-Browne! What a question! He comes from ever such a poor home, you know, no electric light or running water or anything like that; I asked him; and his sisters, well! They don't seem to be much better than you-know-whats. He was always shooting a line at first about the ancestral mansion and its extensive grounds (ahem!) but I soon found out it isn't much bigger than a dog kennel. Probably looks like one, too. Of course,' she ended, recollecting her politics, 'the Italian peasant has been ruthlessly exploited, hasn't he?'

'Has he? I wouldn't know,' and Alda came to a halt, for here was the crossroads and there was Mr Waite, looking unusually athletic in an old sweater and grey bags. He wore an earnest look as if about to go into training for a welterweight champion-ship and Alda and Jean were slightly dismayed at the sight: would he get irritable with the children if their progress were slow? Alda rather wished that she had left their first lesson to their father.

But he proved to be a painstaking teacher, and if he were annoyed by Louise's clumsiness and Jenny's impatience, he controlled himself. Up and down he went in the failing light, while the sunrays faded off the hedges and the air grew chill. An old horse gazed over the edge and the two Italians strolled up and lolled on a gate to watch; and presently Emilio was instructing Louise, leaving Jenny to Mr Waite, but Fabrio leant his arms on the gate in silence.

A last beam of sunlight shone between the leaves and touched his cheek and his russet hair; his blue eyes sternly, sadly gazed anywhere but at Sylvia. She, of course, was soon riding unsteadily on Alda's bicycle, screaming with laughter and clutching at anyone who happened to provide support, and presently (for she had ridden before and was only a little out of practice) she sailed away down the road, and her exclamations of pleasure died off into the evening hush.

Fabrio at last let his eyes follow the young figure in the black dress with gold hair flowing free. From a distance, now that he could no longer hear her voice, she was again Sylvia, his kind love, and he could send his passion flying after her in one long, thirsty gaze.

The evening was so quiet and beautiful that it seemed to him made for love, but no one here thought so: the English signoras, the children, that man whose face always made him think of the taste of lemons, even Emilio (who was an Italian and should therefore have known better), they all treated this budding, flowering, dreaming twilight as an opportunity for running up and down on bicycles and loudly laughing. A bicycle-lesson provided opportunities for embraces, but none of them seemed to be taking advantage of this fact: all was hearty, rough and bustling as a game of *footaballa* in the camp. Fabrio turned his comely head away and sighed, resting his cheek against the ancient wood of the gate as if against a comforting shoulder.

Back came Sylvia, hair flying, eyes sparkling, round young legs pedalling like mad, white teeth glimmering between her red lips. She darted a glance at him as she went by and it proved fatal: her machine swerved, she shrieked and lost control, and it fell sideways, sending her sprawling in the road.

Before she could pick herself up, while she was still crouching there lamenting, 'My stockings! I bet they've had it!', before the wheels of the bicycle had ceased to spin, two big hands, strong yet gentle in their touch, encircled her and drew her to her feet, and Fabrio, kneeling, was tenderly dusting her skirt, keeping his head bent so that he need not meet her eyes.

All the other riders glanced in their direction with anxious cries of inquiry, and Alda, strolling up to see if her bicycle had been damaged, found Sylvia laughing ruefully over her ruined stockings.

'What happened?' Alda asked, glancing from one to the other. 'Sylvia, you don't seem very experienced! Fabrio had better give you a lesson.' For Fabrio's pallor quite went to her heart.

Sylvia tossed her head and said that she was perfectly all right but he could if he liked, and presently Alda had the satisfaction of seeing them set off down the road; Sylvia now much quieter, and Fabrio resting his hand upon the carrier of the machine with the lightest of guiding touches and a good three feet between himself and the shapely back of the rider. Not a word had he said while Sylvia was uttering all her impatient requests and comments, but the expression of pain had gone from about his mouth, and Alda congratulated herself.

I wish she'd mind her own business, thought Sylvia. *I* don't want to be friends, if he doesn't. But he was ever so nice, helping me up like that, I can't make him out. Oh dear, it is a shame about my stockings.

My love, thought Fabrio, my love with shining hair like chestnuts in the woods at home. We would have a little house together and go on Sundays to Mass with all the *bambini* and you in your black dress. My Sylvia, I love you.

Suddenly she called in a friendly voice:

'Fabrio, my knee's hurting where I grazed it. I'm going to get down,' and she cautiously did so. 'There!' shaking back her hair and smiling at him. 'Thanks for your help, Fabrio. Let's walk back, shall we?'

He nodded gravely, still without a word, and they began to retrace their steps. Occasionally he glanced at her, and once she met his glance with a smile that was kinder, perhaps, than she intended, for his graveness embarrassed and even frightened her a little and she felt that she must placate him. And gradually he began to feel happier. He praised the bicycles and she eagerly agreed; he remarked upon the fineness of the evening and she expressed the hope that there would be a good harvest; soon they were talking together, still with some reserve, but as they had not talked for weeks. No reference was made to the unfortunate excursion to Amberley nor to Fabrio's sin in the train; even the English lessons were felt by both to be a dangerous subject and were therefore avoided, but when Sylvia and Fabrio rejoined the rest of the party both were smiling.

During all this time, Meg had been steadily riding up and down a miniature lane leading off into nowhere which she had found for herself. She was now actually drowsing as she rode, but would have gone on until she fell off the saddle fast asleep, had not her mother suddenly exclaimed, 'Megsy! Just look at that child! It's nearly eight o'clock. We must go home at once!'

The Italians said good night and went off to the camp, and Mr Waite rolled down his sleeves and held the bicycle for Louise to dismount, telling her encouragingly that she had done well for a first lesson. Then Alda picked up Meg and they set off across the dusky, dewy fields under the rising moon. Not a cloud was in the darkening sky and all was still; the last blackbird had ended his song and gone to roost. The children's voices as they chattered with Sylvia sounded very clear in the hush.

'Careful,' said Mr Waite, putting his hand upon Jean's arm to guide her. They were walking a little behind the others.

'It was a mole heap, I think, I can't see.'

'I am sorry I can't offer you my arm.'

'That's all right. Isn't this fun?'

Mr Waite gave a short laugh and said that nothing was worse for rheumatism than dew. He added irritably:

'May I use your Christian name? Hardcastle is such a mouthful.'

Well——! thought Jean.

'Oh, please do!' she answered pleasantly. 'And may I use yours?'

'It's Phillip,' he said stiffly, 'but my mother and sisters call me Pip.'

'I like Phillip best, but that's rather a mouthful, too, so I'll call you Phil.'

She glanced up at the face a little above her own in the dusk; it looked dark, rigid and disapproving. But I shall think of you as Mr Darcy, she decided; you're almost as rude.

She knew now why he had never stayed long in one job and why he lived this lonely life of drudgery, for during their recent casual encounters he had let fall some facts about his past life.

He had been formed by Nature and by his own expectations to step into the shoes of an older man who had founded and developed a successful business: he would have been admirably fitted to carry on old traditions or cautiously expand them to the needs of a new age; to give orders, yet to rely upon a background built up by one more decisive, more courageous, than himself. He could not take orders: he was independent without being ambitious, and when the career for which his character and upbringing alike had fitted him was snatched away from him, it had meant that there could never be a successful or contented career for him. That was why he preferred to live this poor and lonely, yet orderly and independent, life as a chicken farmer. He took orders from no one except the Egg Board, and his battles with that gave zest to his days; while the chickens (at least in theory) took orders from him.

'Well, summer's nearly here,' he said, breaking a rather long silence.

'So it is,' lifting her face to the immense gentle vault of the darkening heavens. 'It's the first of May to-morrow.'

'Then we shall have the Longest Day and before we know where we are the evenings'll be drawing in and there'll be next winter to think about.'

'Oh please don't!'

'Don't what? What's the matter now?'

'You've left out the summer altogether!' and at that moment she stumbled again and he put out his hand and caught her arm. His next remark was made while firmly holding on to her.

'Well, why not?' he said, and that was all. But she felt very sorry for him. He had no money, he had no passion for reading, he led a life without pleasure or hope or imagination, and he had carefully confined his conversation that evening to herself and the children. Poor Mr Waite—poor Phil.

'Well——' she began, but found it difficult, and then impossible to continue. She wanted to tell him what pleasures and joys lay all about, even for the poorest, even for the most unhappy and how the deepest joy of all, the joy that outlasted all the others, was always spread silently in front of everyone, like air or light, like a delicious feast. But she was quite unable to say this to him or indeed to anyone, and so she kept silence, and he went on to make one of his stock remarks about life nowadays giving you no time for Higher Things.

She still kept silence, but, walking there beside him in the dusk and listening to his harsh discontented voice, she felt more and more sorry for him.

Alda had gone ahead of them and laid Meg down in the parlour and was now lighting the lamp in the hall. The soft glow slowly brightened until her face and hair were brilliantly illuminated, while her two sheltering hands holding the lampglass seemed made from transparent coral; she looked as if she were within a shrine, and all at once the dusk seemed chilly and lonely, and the two watchers felt shut out.

'Mr Waite?' she called, standing upright and dusting her hands. 'Come in and have some tea after all that hard work?'

'Yes, do, Phil,' said Jean warmly, but both women were surprised when he accepted. They were also slightly dismayed, for as was usual in the country within two hundred yards of a herd of cows in the nineteen-forties, the household was short of milk.

When Alda had put Meg to bed she came down to the parlour and found the tea ready and Mr Waite sitting in the only comfortable chair explaining something to Jean. Alda let it drone past her ears as she contentedly poured out tea; to-morrow was undoubtedly going to be a fine day and Ronald was coming.

'J.,' she said suddenly, 'you won't mind taking the children out on the bicycles for the next few evenings, will you? Megsy can stay with Ronald and me, but I know the others will be wild to be off.'

'They won't be fit to ride after one lesson!' exclaimed Mr Waite, who seemed unusually at ease and undisapproving tonight, and then he took great draughts of tea and promised his evenings to the Lucie-Brownes for the next few days, and on being thanked, said that the light evenings always meant he had less to do.

'Don't you garden?' asked Alda, glancing out of the window at the narcissus she had planted in December glimmering in the dusk.

'Only vegetables,' said Mr Waite.

'Oh, but vegetables are thrilling!' exclaimed Mrs Lucie-Browne, and Jean surprised a most sardonic look upon his face; how silly women are, it said, but there was something else in it that seemed to excuse one particular woman.

'Jean and I have put in thousands of radishes but I'm bothered if I'm going to plant anything *serious* and I shall jolly well take my bulbs with me when we go,' Alda went on.

'Why, do you think of going soon?' he asked, after there had been a little pause.

'My husband has been trying for the past year to get us a house in Ironborough, where we used to live and all my people and his people live, and we may hear at any time that he's got one. It may have to be a prefab but we shall be thankful even for that.'

He nodded and passed his cup for more tea. Jean thought that his manner was less easy and friendly, and wondered why. Had he realised that the Lucie-Brownes and their friend Jean were only temporary residents at Pine Cottage, and decided to repress all amiable feelings towards them so that he might not miss them after they had gone? Or was the change caused by references to 'my husband'?

In fact, Mr Waite's sudden reserve had nothing to do with sentiment. He was no novel reader and he was not given to self-analysis. He had never faced certain emotions that sometimes invaded his heart at the sight of one face and the sound of one voice; he ignored them; nor had it occurred to him that when

Pine Cottage was empty once more his life would again be very lonely. But when Jean had remarked to Alda that next week she must go up to London to see her father's business manager; and had gone on to explain to Mr Waite that the management of the glass and china exporting firm was still in the hands of the very capable man who had been Mr Hardcastle's chief adviser for the past thirty years, Mr Waite had simply not been able to resist deciding to propose to her.

The opportunity was too tempting; it was more than a man situated as he was should be called upon to refuse: a pleasant girl, alone in the world, emotionally unattached, owner of a prosperous business about which she seemed to know nothing, and plainly longing to settle down (Mr Waite believed that all ladies longed to settle down, as if they were feathers that had floated about until they were tired). For his part, he could not understand why she had not been snapped up before, though that she had not was a piece of great good fortune for him.

He asked for nothing better than a pretty, docile wife with money. And such money! Not an income depending upon investments, to which anything in heaven or earth might happen and usually did, but money flowing in from an established and prosperous firm dealing in glass and china; cups and saucers, jugs, basins, plates—objects that everybody wanted, all over the world; and an *export* firm, too! at the time when 'export' was not only a part of the National Consciousness but was also encouraged in theory, if not in practice, by the Government!

She had let slip the first time they met that she was an orphan and her father's heir, but he, Mr Waite, had supposed her to have merely some snug investments that bought diamond feathers for her, not a Business! a Business that would go on expanding and providing a ceaseless source of interest and comfort to herself and her husband for a lifetime!

Mr Waite did not often experience vague, uneasy sensations, for his mind and character were almost uniformly practical, but on this occasion he did have a faint feeling that there was *some-thing* that should have prevented him from proposing to Jean Hardcastle. However, it was not possible to think the matter out in detail amidst the chatter of the women, so he dismissed it from his mind until he should be walking homewards.

No sooner had he shut the garden gate than Alda said:

'He's made up his mind. He's going to ask you.'

'Alda, *how* do you know?'

'Oh, I can tell. I know the symptoms.'

Jean did not want the conversation to continue, but Alda went on:

'You see what an advantage it is, to carry on a courtship in the country. You really get to know each other; you see each other with 'flu and falling off bicycles, and out in the rain, and washing-up—oh, I think it's heaps better than in town, when you're both dressed up and on your best behaviour. Well, ducky, by June I shall be scratching madly round for my matron-of-honour dress. Can the children be bridesmaids?'

'Oh Alda—I don't know—really, darling, I do think you may be mistaken, truly.'

'Not me. I've seen too many of them on the brink.'

Jean was silent. Alda took it for granted that she would accept the man. But shall I? thought Jean rinsing cups in the kitchen while Alda went round the house whistling, locking windows and bolting doors. No doubt it was *better* to see Mr Waite in all sorts of dreary and useful occupations; draped in a sack and feeding the chickens or tramping through the mud in his Wellingtons to pick a cabbage, but it was not *romantic*. I should like to see if he *has* a best behaviour and if he *could* dress up, thought Jean. Besides, I am not thrilled about him. Now if it were only my Mr Potter——

'You aren't worrying about Waite, for goodness' sake, are you?' demanded Alda, coming back into the room and catching a glimpse of Jean's face.

'Not exactly, Alda, only I don't feel thrilled about him.'

'Well, honestly, J., you can't have *everything*, you know. The man's definitely not glamorous but he's honest and kind-hearted and as near a gent as makes no odds. What more do you want?'

Jean was silent. Alda moved vigorously about the room, banging cushions into place and straightening newspapers with a crackle. She pushed back a chair against the wall; then glanced at her friend, and came over and put an arm about her shoulders.

'Truly, ducky, I do know what I'm talking about. Thrills are very little, you take my word for it, compared with all the real things,' and she gave her a little shake that was also a hug.

Jean stood still, within the firm, kind, impatient embrace of that round arm. Then she said, in a low voice:

'Don't you think he might be trying to marry me for my money?'

Alda hesitated, then answered: 'Well, I expect he sees all the advantages. He'd be blind if he didn't. But I'm sure he isn't trying to marry you *only* for that, J. He isn't the type; he's too honest. I expect he'll say something about it when he asks you. And now come along, let's get off to bed; I want to be up extra early to-morrow.'

She always was up early; her brisk step and thrush's whistle were heard about the cottage before anyone else's, and lazier people, lying in bed listening, knew that she had dashed her face with cold water and looked eagerly out at the morning before they were awake. This is not an endearing habit, but it seems slightly unfair that people who enjoy early rising should be so roundly condemned by those who do not. The latter have only Doctor Johnson on their side, and even he *tried* to get up early.

Jean lay long awake with her book and cigarettes, and the pleasantest hour of the twenty-four was spoiled by confused thoughts, and doubts, and indecision. Now that she was to be proposed to, she experienced none of those emotions which she had always anticipated she would feel in such a situation.

She thought of Mr Waite (it was still difficult to think of him as Phil) with slight alarm. Honesty, kindness and a high standard of morals might make a man an excellent husband, but what if he had no sense of humour, and no indulgence for other people's failings, and a silly religion? (It was all very well for modernists to tell you that you should 'respect' other people's religion, but where would Saint Paul have got if he had done that?)

She had always hoped to marry a man that Alda and Ronald would like, so that the old friendship should continue uninterrupted, but had Alda considered the prospect of dining with Phil, drinking-at-six with him, picnicking and bridge-ing and lunching with him, for the next thirty years or so, and he without one clue to their particular kind of joke?

Jean was sure that Alda had considered nothing of the sort, for she was so anxious to bring off her scheme that she had looked no further than the wedding-day. I should be left alone with a strange man, thought Jean, sighing, and shutting up the book in which she had read not a word for the past twenty minutes, and if I did refuse him, she would be so cross.

Walking homeward across the meadows, Mr Waite gave his full attention to his decision. If he did not marry Jean, some fortune-hunter would; he had feared this since the day of their first meeting and, from a casual remark once made by Alda—Mrs Lucie-Browne—he knew that she feared it too. He had not felt so strongly upon any subject but the Egg Board for years: Jean needed protection from prowling males, the firm needed a man's guiding hand, and he would supply both.

She herself presented no difficulties. Her nature was gentle and attractive, and unspoiled by silly ideas about a woman managing her own affairs. It was a long time since he had met a girl who approached so closely to his Ideal, and owing to the extraordinary but fortunate circumstance that no one had so far succeeded in Snapping Her Up, she was fancy-free (at least, he presumed that she was fancy-free; she wore no ring; she never dropped hints or blushed or anything) and his for the asking! He would wait for a few weeks, until their acquaintanceship had ripened into a solid friendship, and then he would speak.

Owing to his rapid pace across the grass and his confident thoughts, Mr Waite's expression was unusually cheerful as he entered his dark and chilly cottage, and even the look which the chickens gave him when he brought their food half an hour late could not sober him. The vague sensation that had troubled him earlier in the evening, that there was some obstacle in the way of his proposing to Jean, some reason why he should explain something at length and carefully to her, had passed completely away.

That night Fabrio lay upon his side in his hard bed, wide awake, and staring into the dimness that was less than completely dark because of the light from the spring moon. It was nearly midnight: the uneasy quiet of the long hut, filled with tainted air, was broken by snores and sometimes the heavy movements of a restlessly sleeping man. Fabrio's heart beat fast, and now and again he sighed, but it was with joy. He had decided: he would ask Sylvia to be his wife. She did not hate him; she would not have smiled at him so kindly only this evening unless she liked him; perhaps she even loved him, and that coldness, that rough way of talking, that fury when he kissed her, had been assumed to hide her love. Girls often did that. And she would be glad when he asked her; girls always were. And prisoners often married the women of the country where they were held captive: had he not seen half a dozen such cases in the newspapers?

It was true that he had no money beside the four and eight-pence halfpenny guarded for him by Mr Hoadley, but, Mother of God! he was young, he was strong, he knew how to work, and when he returned to Italy there would be work for everyone. It was a pity to disappoint Maria, who had no doubt begun to hope, after all these letters, that he would marry *her*, but a man had to marry the one he wanted, and he wanted Sylvia.

He would creep about no longer, quiet and wretched; he would sing as he worked and show her that he was one to be admired, and when the time of harvest came, and they worked side by side in the fields under the hot sun, he would ask her to be his wife. He sighed tremulously, and muttered a prayer, and fell asleep at last with his tousled chestnut head thrust into the pillow in a way that would have stifled anyone but a foreigner.

A young man lounged in a great basketwork chair in the gardens of a club on the other side of the world, his eyes shaded by a linen hat from the fierce sun of a South African morning, a tall icy drink by his side, and an unopened copy of a newspaper, whose wrapper bore English stamps, on his knees.

He had slightly prominent greenish eyes, a big nose, a wide mouth that often laughed to show good teeth, and an easy, casual, gay manner that might make a sensitive heart doubtful of *holding him down*. Presently he began to read the newspaper, and presently he saw in it a piece of news that he re-read. When he had finished with the paper, he yawned, and pushed it aside, stretched, and pulled his hat further over his eyes, then opened a writing-case and dashed off a letter.

We must now return to Sussex.

23

Alda contrived to have her talk with Ronald about Louise and Roman Catholicism, but she found him so agreeably impressed by what he called 'this improvement in the children' that he was inclined to make light of Louise's enthusiasm, and when Alda admitted that she had not noticed any change for the worse in the child's character, he advised her not to take the matter seriously. He broke the good news that he was actually in negotiation for a house in Ironborough which might be theirs by the autumn; a secret that he had kept until now, when the arrangements had reached a hopefully advanced stage, and he pointed out that when the family left Sussex the influence of the convent must disappear.

Alda was left with a sensation of slight bafflement. She was pleased, of course, that he was pleased, and of course she liked Louise and Jenny to be cheerful and busy and progressing, but she wished that they could have been equally cheerful and busy without going to school. School had undoubtedly taken them away from herself. They still loved her dearly and liked to be with her, but she was no longer the foreground and the background too; the Sisters, and Damaris Bernais, and a convent wit and daredevil named June Wilson, were the foreground, and had been for weeks. Alda resented this; refused to admit her feeling to herself; and took to making much of Meg, who received her attentions placidly.

They made of the unexpected fortnight's leave a second honeymoon, even going to Ironborough for some days to visit Alda's people and inspect the house for which Ronald was negotiating. Fine weather and the knowledge that the children were safe and happy in Jean's care sent them off on their journey content.

Jean was relieved to see them go. Ronald had insisted upon the same old creature who slaved for Mr Waite coming in three times a week to clean Pine Cottage, and Jean felt it tiresome that at this time, just when she wanted to take a detached view of Mr Waite, she should have to listen to a highly undetached running commentary upon him from old Miss Dodder (no relation, as she was careful to explain, to the feckless half-wit Dodders before mentioned); the trouble he took with they birds, up half the night with they; his kindness to Miss Dodder herself, paying her half-wages when she had the sciatica; so pleased with anything you done for him; so well-spoken; not like some people; and so on. Even so, thought Jean, did Mrs Reynolds, the house-keeper at Pemberley, praise Mr Darcy to Elizabeth Bennet, but the latter knew (or thought she knew) just where she stood: she did not have to make up her mind whether to accept the man or not, for she had already refused him.

Jean's own indecision had the effect of presenting Mr Waite to her in a more romantic light: she now coloured when she saw his tall form at a distance digging in the rough vegetable plot surrounding his cottage, or coming down in the lane to give the children their evening's lesson, and sometimes a glance from him or his casual touch would cause her heart to flutter.

Mr Waite observed the colour and suspected the flutter, and was pleased. He had started upon his courtship, and as the days went by he made his intentions plain; he did not intend that she should misunderstand him. He sought her out at unexpected times with a present of four eggs or a colossal cabbage; he waylaid her as she was crossing the meadows with her basket of small purchases and offered her *In Touch with the Transcendent*, which she had not the courage to decline, and more than once after the children were in bed he strolled across on some pretext of lending a newspaper or returning an electric torch and lingered by the gate (too careful of her reputation to enter the house) chatting with her and smoking a manly pipe and looking, in his rough country clothes and tall boots, an attractive figure.

If only his nature had been warmed by laughter and rashness! if only he had not been so solemn, so careful, so disapproving, so conventional, so stiff, how easily she could have loved him! But she was a little afraid of him. In what kind of a house would she have to *settle down* with him if she accepted him? What orderly, trim, organised establishment in which no one ever thumped on the piano or sprawled or rearranged the furniture? She felt like a small sheep being rounded up by a large, handsome, purposeful sheepdog.

He, for his part, found it easier to pay her attentions because he was not in love. He had never, to his knowledge, been in love, but throughout his forty-odd years there had been certain women of whom he had strongly disapproved, and when he thought of these women, who all belonged to the same type, he always congratulated himself upon having avoided 'getting caught,' and that was as far as his thoughts ever carried him. Mr Waite, in short, was a Sleeping Beauty: upon such sleepers of both sexes the awakening kiss often has unexpected results.

He was relieved that Major and Mrs Lucie-Browne were away just now, for he preferred to carry out his courtship as far as was possible in private. And it was progressing favourably: she showed emotion at his presence and yet she welcomed him; she had returned *In Touch with the Transcendent* with the assurance that it was *a marvellous book*, and she was suitably grateful for the cabbages and the eggs. It did occur to him once or twice to invite her out, but there was nowhere in the neighbourhood that suited his own solid yet rich tastes, formed in a wealthy provincial town during the boom years of the '20's; the pictures he scorned, Brighton he considered sordid and flashy and he did not choose to spend several pounds on taking her to dine at a roadhouse. Such an action would have seemed to his standard of behaviour slightly insulting; like bribery, like scattering grain before a chicken to lure it into the run. No; she must accept him as his everyday self; and then no one would be able to say afterwards that he deceived her or made out that he was richer or gayer or livelier than he was.

He took the same attitude about compliments. He had always told himself that what he approved in a woman's appearance was Neatness and No Paint, and he certainly was not going to praise in Jean what he did not approve. He sought about for some part of her to praise; she was always neat; yes, he could truthfully praise that, and so the first compliment he paid her was a grave: 'You need not do that; you are always perfectly tidy,' uttered one evening as she glanced in her handbag mirror. A few days later he remarked, in a slightly uncertain tone, that her hair was a pretty colour.

'Gosh, that isn't its real colour,' answered Miss Hardcastle cheerfully, suppressing a slight impulse to ba-a-a, 'it's brown, really.'

'To match your eyes,' keeping his own fixed steadily upon her. 'Why dye it?'

'For fun,' she retorted firmly, determined, on her side, that he should not be *completely* deceived as to her true nature. 'Don't you ever feel you'd like to dye yours?'

She was relieved to hear him give his short laugh, but she knew, as well as if he had told her, that if she married him she would have to give up dyeing her hair.

And all this—her lack of ease with him, her suspicion that he might be proposing to her for her money—was unimportant compared with the fact that he did not come first in her feelings. *There*, Mr Potter lingered.

Easter fell while Ronald and Alda were still away. Jean bicycled in with the children to Sillingham Church on the morning of Easter Sunday, with Meg seated upon a little carrier at the back of her own machine. Their ride was a joyful progress along roads white with the dust of a week's sunshine, through the radiant light of full spring, and on every side such companies and troops of flowers!

The ride began a period of some sixty hours, during which her imagination was invaded by all the blossoms of spring and her nostrils were never empty of their confused exquisite scent, while their curved or hollowed or pointed petals and their stems, supporting round hearts packed with seed, presented themselves in her mind's eye just before she fell asleep in patterns and single devices of marvellous beauty.

In the afternoon she went out with the children to pick flowers. They roamed across the meadows and entered the woods that covered the low hills; the sunlit slopes left bare by the soldiers who had felled the trees were now high in young bracken, and they pulled up a few stiff fronds, but mostly they picked bluebells and windflowers and daffodils; their hands became stained with saps and juices from the leaves and roots; they picked white and dark violets and tied them in little bunches and tucked them in amidst the bunches of larger flowers, and Meg filled a miniature basket, made for her by Emilio, with orchids and celandines on a bed of dark moss tipped with gold.

They strayed for hours, it seemed, through the woods and by the hedges under the cloudless blue, and when they got home, intoxicated with fresh air and freedom, the sun had set and the fields were growing dim. On the doorstep, staring stolidly at the rising moon, sat a perfectly enormous cabbage. Oh bother, thought Jean, stepping round it, we haven't got through the last one yet.

On the following day the two elder children were invited to tea by a school friend living near while Meg had been asked to spend the afternoon at the farm, because Mrs Hoadley, with Joyanna in mind, thought that she would like to see how a baby girl behaved. She went off hand in hand with Sylvia, politely replying to the latter's condescending questions and plainly forgetting Jean the minute the garden gate had closed upon herself and her guide.

An hour later Jean was coasting down a hilly road towards the village of Sedley, whose square church tower she had seen long since among the trees. Her cheeks were already burning with sun and the warm wind, the sleeves of her white blouse were rolled up, her jacket was off, and a bunch of wilting flowers trembled on the carrier. Each time the thought of Mr Waite came into her mind she thrust it away, for she did not want to think about anything except the warm lazy beauty of this first day of summer.

The church stood on a little hill and looked across water meadows to Chanctonbury Ring, fifteen good miles nearer here, and no longer dark and mysterious. It was so near that she could see the bloom of young green upon its trees, and the hill blowing with summer grass. The church was very small, with a low square tower bursting out in tufts of wallflowers and some thick silvery plant she took to be houseleek; the porch was of oak, so ancient that its very lines and seams were shrunken, and of the same ghostly grey as the plant waving from the stone roof. The list of vicars (beautifully written, and adorned with gold and crimson capitals) began in 1145. She padlocked her bicycle to a stout oak bench, tied a scarf about her head because, in spite of the Bishops' permission, she never felt quite comfortable in church with an uncovered head, and pushed open the massive door.

She expected dimness, silence, chill. But the church was filled with colour and light. The walls were distempered in apricot, and against them the unpainted leaden pipes of the organ looked a heavy blue green. There was barely room for the seats, the altar and pulpit and lectern; all the space seemed filled by the glowing amber curves of the low, sturdy, Norman arches whose heavy shoulders upheld the stone roof and above it the stone tower, and which were dashed with gleams and melting rays from the lustrous red, blue and amber glass in two minute lancet windows. The other windows were clear, and let in the burning sunlight. And the altar, the altar steps, the pulpit, the lectern, the font, were smothered in flowers from hothouse and garden and meadow; white lilies, amber lilies, yellow lilies; rows of humble glass pots supporting the dove-like heads of white violets mingled with crimson-tipped daisies; bowls spilling over with orange primroses; and winding among all this white and golden splendour, dark trails of ivy like traces of tears. Delicious fragrance floated across to her, drawn out by the heat and freshened by the cold ancient walls, but she saw that all these flowers were just, and only just, past their prime: on Easter Day they had been offered to God and soon they would be thrown on to the huge healthy heap of leaves, sweepings, mown grass, that she had noticed at the back of the church.

Entranced, she stood perfectly still, letting the joyful silence fill her ears. The impression of light and colour and happiness was so powerful that the stonework seemed transparent and all the heavy, ancient little building, sunk into its hillock for eight hundred years of time, nothing but a shell filled with light and sounding with praise. The sweet sacramental scents filled her nostrils and all at once she felt a longing, the strongest desire she had felt in all her life, to love and serve God.

The colours and light struck with fresh joy upon her senses. She went over to the lectern and mounted its little steps; she felt an obedient pleasure in being here, a delight in lingering in God's house and examining all its furnishings. Slowly she turned the stiff pages of the old Bible, so thick that they seemed to retain some of the heaviness of the wood from which they originally came. She paused at the last chapter of Saint John the Evangelist:

15. So when they had dined, Jesus saith to Simon Peter, Simon, son of Jonas, lovest thou me more than these? He

saith unto him, Yea, Lord, thou knowest that I love thee. He saith unto him, Feed my lambs.

16. He saith unto him again the second time, Simon, son of Jonas, lovest thou me? He saith unto him, Yea, Lord, thou knowest that I love thee. He saith unto him, Feed my sheep.

17. He saith unto him the third time, Simon, son of Jonas, lovest thou me? Peter was grieved because he said unto him the third time, Lovest thou me? And he said unto him, Lord, thou knowest all things, thou knowest that I love thee. Jesus saith unto him, Feed my sheep.

She shut the book gently, and covered her face with her hands and stood for a moment in silence. *Oh dear God*, she prayed earnestly and humbly, *I don't know whether I love You, I long to love You but I don't know if I can, but, oh dear, dear God, I will feed Your sheep.*

That is a thing I *can* do, she thought, stepping down from the lectern and slowly walking across the cool hallowed flagstones to the door, and I'll begin to-morrow with those Dodders on the Froggatt road.

On the ride home she was still slightly dazed; and the joyful silence, the light, in the church returned again and again, each time with a cooling breath, into her spirit. She rode on in a kind of trance, avoiding the crown of the road by instinct and keeping well in to the hedge, and fortunately the byways by which she went were not much frequented, as everyone with a car had on this lovely day gone roaring into Worthing. Her mind was occupied with plans for equipping the little Dodders with undergarments and opening their small souls to the Christian faith.

She was so busy with all this that she was nearly at the gap in the hedge leading across the pastures to the cottage, when Mr Waite came out through it with a chicken under each arm.

She put the brake on just in time, but he fatally wavered from side to side, his grasp upon the chickens loosened, and they at once squawked and fluttered away into liberty. He uttered an exclamation of annoyance and gripped the bicycle, causing her to dismount hastily and almost on top of him.

'I'm awfully sorry,' she gasped, looking up at him confusedly. 'I didn't see you, I was thinking.'

'It's all right. I am sorry, too; I startled you, I'm afraid.'

They were standing so close together that she caught a breath of some severe and nameless unguent with which he dragooned his hair. She became uncomfortable, and (as his expression slowly became purposeful) very anxious to escape.

'I'm longing for some tea,' she said bluntly, making a movement as if to pass him, 'or I'd stay and help you catch the chickens.'

The chickens, wild with unaccustomed freedom, were now legging it down the lane as hard as they could go, amid peals of hysterical chicken-laughter. But he ignored them. His face slowly deepened in colour and became embarrassed, but he also looked determined, as his well-shaped lips parted, and he said firmly:

'Don't go yet, I have something to say to you.'

The two pairs of brown eyes, the light ones still filled with lingering joy from Heaven and the dark that had gained their bitterness from looking on Earth, gazed questioningly at one another, but Jean's only wish was to get away from him, to be once more alone with her happy thoughts.

'For some weeks now, since the last time I had the pleasure of having tea with you, I have meant to ask you to marry me,' he began, 'and I—I think we should get on together. I think you need a husband to look after you, and—and to help you manage your late father's business. I am not in the habit of saying what I don't mean,' he went on gloomily, 'and I admire you. You are almost my ideal of what a—a woman should be. I don't know exactly what your feelings about me are, but I have given you every opportunity to show if you disliked me, and I am sure you don't, do you?'

'Oh no,' said Jean—faintly, hanging her head and wishing wildly that she were running away with the chickens, whose maniacal cackles now sounded faintly round the curve in the lane.

'Then, that being so, I suggest that we should become engaged at once,' he said decidedly, looking relieved, and put his hand in his pocket and brought out a plump, heart-shaped case of worn red leather. He pressed the gilt fastening, and then and there displayed to her despairing eyes a ring of pale Victorian gold, carrying a heart of fine garnets. She gave a sigh of dismay. Poor little old-fashioned ring! It was the last straw. How could she refuse him now?

'It was my Aunt Janet's,' he said, regarding it with satisfaction. 'She always intended it for my wife. I wrote to my mother for it last Wednesday.'

And he took it from its bed of faded rosy velvet and held it out to her. She swallowed, and forced her dry lips to say faintly:

'But I haven't said anything yet!'

The words came out in a protesting squeak.

He immediately looked dismayed. The garnet heart withdrew an inch or so and he frowned.

'You said that you—didn't dislike me?' he said, and suddenly Jean understood that, by her admission, she had implied love to this extraordinary man.

Violent agitation now confused her. She remembered her disappointments in love—so many, so fruitless, so painful! How lonely she had been—how lonely she was! Her complete happiness of an hour ago was forgotten. She only saw, in the dark face gazing down at her, a companion for life, and a home, and perhaps children as lovable as Alda's children. Alda's advice—every word that Alda had ever said to her upon the desirability of the married state—sounded in her ears. She told herself that romance did not matter. She told herself not to be a fool, and she wanted to take away the puzzled and slightly hurt expression from his face. She held out her hand, saying in a low tone:

'Yes. Yes, I did. I do like you, Phil. I think we should get on together too, and I'm very glad you asked me. Please put it on.'

The garnet heart fitted perfectly upon the third finger of her left hand, that finger upon which she had so often been tempted to slip a ring in order to provoke Mr Potter to ask leading questions. She held out her hand, gazing at it. It looked unexpectedly well; quiet yet romantic, generous in colour, graceful and elegant in shape. Yes, she liked her engagement ring. But did she like her betrothed?

After he too had looked at the ring for a little while, he suddenly took a step forward and clumsily bunched her into his arms. The kiss he gave her was determined rather than ecstatic. Still, she thought, at least I didn't shudder, like people in Victorian novels (no one ever shudders in modern novels, or if they do they only enjoy it, her thoughts went on irrelevantly).

She glanced up at him inquiringly. Now would he insist on coming back to tea with her? The thought of the cool dark cottage and a cup of tea and a book in solitude amidst the bowls of silent flowers was so attractive that she could hardly refrain from going off at once to enjoy them. Oh, if only he would not want to come too!

But she forgot that he had a bachelor's habits. He said nothing about coming to share her tea. He drew out the large silver hunter whose chain was looped across his middle and announced that he would go home and have some tea and change his clothes and look in at the cottage for an hour about seven o'clock.

'Oh yes, do,' said Jean amiably, thinking *That's nearly two hours to myself—hooray.*

'I must go after those birds!' he exclaimed suddenly. 'I'd forgotten all about them—they must be half-way to Horsham by this time.

When you get home, Jean, run cold water on your wrists for three minutes, and make your tea a little stronger than usual. You look as if you'd got a little overheated riding—that'll cool you down and act as a slight stimulant. (Not *too* strong, the tea, mind you.) And keep your jacket on in the house until you are cool; otherwise you may catch a chill. Good-bye, I'll be over about seven.'

And he pulled his hat over his eyes and hurried after his chickens without another glance at his betrothed.

Jean wheeled her bicycle slowly homewards. Rings and Dodders and kisses and Alda and Phillip went round and round exhaustingly in her head. She tried to recall that breath of coolness and peace from another world, but in vain; only the memory, not the breath itself, remained. She continued to tell herself that she was engaged, but she could not believe it, and when she looked down at her ring it did not help her to realise the fact.

Meg was sitting placidly upon the doorstep as she came up the path, playing with three ants and a cockleshell from the garden border. Beside her lay a letter.

'Hullo, darling, had a nice time?' Jean asked, stooping down to her. 'Who's this for?' picking up the letter.

'Mrs Holey did gib Meg a special cakie for her tea. It's for you, Sylbia said.' And she went back to her game of scooping the wretched ants into the cockleshell.

Jean was staring at the letter. She knew that writing. The stamps were South African. It had been forwarded on from her parents' flat in London. Her heart beat as it had not beaten for Phillip's kiss as she tore open the envelope.

The letter expressed sympathy at her father's death; it said that the writer would be in England again in three weeks' time; that one of the first things he would do then would be to call her up and arrange a meeting; it breathed warmth, kindness, and affectionate concern for her welfare, and it was signed hers always Oliver Potter.

24

Alda and Ronald returned on the following day, and heard of their friend's engagement with somewhat absent interest and pleasure, for arrangements were nearly completed for the acquisition of the house in Ironborough and they could think of little else. It was a small double-fronted house covered in ivy, with large light rooms and a garden and orchard, standing on the outskirts of the city but not inconveniently far from the university, where Ronald would resume his duties after being demobilised. Alda was very sensible of their good fortune in securing it. This was due to the fact that house and land were owned by the university, which preferred to see its property occupied by a member of its Faculty. She and Ronald talked of furniture and wallpapers and hot-water systems and permits, and neither of them noticed that Jean lacked the radiance of a newly betrothed young woman. They asked Mr Waite in to share the liqueur which Ronald had brought from Germany, and Ronald observed after he had gone that he seemed to possess excellent solid qualities, at which Alda made a face, and they both wondered how soon the wedding would be, and then returned happily to their staircoverings.

Jean had often read of letters lying in people's bosoms like serpents. Now she knew what it felt like. Mr Potter's letter lay in her handbag like a serpent, and every time she opened the bag to take out a cigarette it crackled at her as if it were hissing. She had not dared to tell Alda about it, because she feared a command to ignore it, or a sharp reminder that Mr Potter meant nothing to her now because she was engaged, or something of that sort. And she had not answered it, because feverish calculations upon her fingers had showed her that Mr Potter would arrive in England any day now; indeed, she lived in almost hourly expectation of a wire from him or even his appearance at the cottage door. Between these apprehensions and settling herself into her new part as an engaged girl she soon became confused and troubled and not very happy.

Romantic love can make the choosing of a gas cooker into a romantic ceremony but Mr Waite was not romantically in love and nor was Jean. He discussed what type of soil their house should stand on, and whether they should have a geyser or an Aga cooker or one of those electric things you put into the water tank; there was even an exposition upon the desirability of little mats at the foot of the stairs, while his fancy plodded, as if upon a treadmill, round and round the coal cellar and the bathroom and the kitchen.

Every evening they met for a walk along the lanes, or drove in to Sillingham for a drink (he advised her to drink only ginger ale and she did) and at ten o'clock she would come wearily up the path to the cottage door with her shoulders drooping and her simple fifteen-guinea hat swinging in her hand. The murmur of voices would be floating out on the warm twilight, discussing types of gas cookers.

It was now difficult to remember the time when she had not been engaged. Her happiest moment came at the evening's end, when her betrothed abruptly kissed her 'Good night'. He did not linger over these moments and she was relieved to have it so.

But he was happier than he had been for twenty years. He delighted in the discussion and planning of practical details, and hitherto the days had held half an hour here, an hour there, which it was not possible to fill up with arrangements about the chickens or the garden or the eggs and which had too often been haunted by a certain troubling, charming image. But the planning and buying of a home provided endless details to be discussed; they went on for ever; there were—if such a state of affairs could be possible—almost too many of them; far too many to be settled before the date of the wedding.

He had decided to sell the chicken farm, and after the sale accompany Jean to Daleham where she would meet his mother and sisters, and stay with one of his numerous connections while she collected her trousseau. Later on he proposed to enter the firm of J. Hardcastle and Company, Ltd., at first as a learner but later on as manager. He was confident that he had the ability to do this; and Jean wished him to. It would be the dignified, the correct, thing for her husband to have a full-time occupation, and also he would be out of the house all day.

The wedding was fixed for the twenty-eighth of June, and she had done nothing about it except inquire through a friend in the trade about buying thirty yards of white *crêpe-de-Chine* without coupons. She casually confided this to her betrothed, and received such a lecture that she was amazed and sore (though she said hardly one word in her own defence) for days afterwards.

She had never seriously thought about the rights or wrongs of buying through the Black Market. In her world, everyone had done it. In Mr Waite's world, hardly anyone did, and he made her feel ashamed. She had never experienced shame before and she disliked the feeling intensely. She thought how Mr Potter would have received such a piece of news; with a smile and either a 'Good for you' or a 'Naughty, naughty,' according to his fascinating mood of the moment, and, try as she would, she could not help feeling, many times a day, how much more Mr Potter was in accord with her upbringing and outlook and temperament than was Mr Waite.

Ronald had now returned to Germany and Alda had time to turn her attention to her friend's engagement. She observed the couple for a day or two, and decided that they were a pair of old things, though not yet old in years, and that they were inclined to be dim and would grow dimmer as they grew older but at least they were *both* dim, and would suit one another. She congratulated herself upon having introduced them, and forwarded the match in every way that she could, and she thought that if Jean did not appear radiantly happy, that was because she was taking the practical rather than the romantic view.

Alda felt herself particularly fitted to advise upon the practical view because she herself had declined half a dozen men with higher incomes and better prospects than Ronald in order to marry him, on his modest salary, from passionate love.

As for the Dodders, they had soon been disposed of. Jean had called there upon a very hot day. The elder children were out in the meadows, but there were several who could barely walk crawling and tottering about the low, dirty, cluttered kitchen, their velvety faces not much larger than the satiny ones of some peonies in a jam jar. Mrs Dodder, who was still very pretty, received her smilingly; smilingly accepted a large bundle of clothes, and in reply to a timid question, smilingly assured her that all the children was confirmed and went to church and Sunday School regular (Jean tried not to glance at the babies, who were all sitting still and staring at her; their combined ages totalled perhaps five years and it was difficult to believe that they had *all* been confirmed). She said no more. She went away, after a last helpless glance round the room filled with old rags and babies and wilting cottage flowers, and was glad to get its sickeningly sour-sweet odour out of her nose. It was not possible to ask those tiny velvet faces, that sweet vacant smile, if they loved God. Saint Francis of Assisi, who understood non-human languages, would have been the one to deal with them.

When she told Phillip about her visit, he observed that those Dodders were a Disgrace and strongly advised her not to go there again for fear of Catching Something. She was relieved that he took it for granted her visit was charitable rather than evangelical, for once more she could postpone that discussion which she dreaded: her religion.

She had never discussed it with a living soul, and she was eager to keep it entirely to herself until her dying day, but her conscience told her that she ought not to marry a man without first finding out if he were, or were not, a Christian. His occasional references to Christianity were merely patronising. She might find herself like Saint Monica, married for many years to a pagan, and, unlike the saint, fail to convert him in the end. Worse still, she felt no wish to convert him. She only wanted to continue peacefully in her own faith and leave him to flounder about in his. The question embarrassed her, adding to the increasing doubts which she felt about her engagement.

She was sitting in the parlour one Saturday morning, writing to Mrs Waite to announce the date of her forthcoming visit, when a shadow fell across the door, which stood open to admit air and sunlight into the room's dimness, and she glanced up and there, smiling down upon her, stood Mr Potter.

Mr Potter, handsomer, more debonair, than ever; in a loose tweed coat, and bronzed by South African suns, hatless and terribly, alarmingly welcome. At the sight of him she dropped the pen and her heart stood still.

'Hullo, my dear,' said Mr Potter, coming into the room, and as she stood up tremblingly to welcome him, he slipped his arm about her and gave her an easy kiss; alas, a delicious kiss.

At once, while they were exchanging the first sentences of greeting and welcome, she began to play with her engagement ring, according to the nervous habit she had lately fallen into, and in a moment, telling herself that she would break her news to him presently, she slipped it off her finger and into her pocket.

She was still glowing with delight from that casual kiss, and so confused, so overcome with happiness at the sight of him and so alarmed at discovering the strength and nature of her own feelings, that she scarcely heard what he was saying or knew what she said in reply, but presently she realised that he was suggesting they should drive into Brighton for lunch.

She hesitated, for it had been arranged that she and Mr Waite should drive into Horsham that afternoon to place the advertisement for the sale of the chicken farm with the local paper, and do some shopping and take tea at The Myrtle Bough, and she was to meet him at half-past two—but the entrance of Alda and the children gave her a moment's grace.

While introductions were being made, and Alda was welcoming Mr Potter and explaining away the cottage's deficiencies (over which Mr Potter had already cast an incredulous eye) with frank laughter, Jean decided that she would go. She could not resist the temptation. Alda must explain to Mr Waite—and think what she chose. So must he.

'Now, how about it?' Mr Potter demanded agreeably, turning to her. He was seated upon the dreadful little pink chair with its hairy inside coming out, looking very out of place in his light raglan overcoat and elegant grey suit amidst the Victorian fubsinesses of the parlour.

'Oh—yes—thank you, that would be wizard,' Jean answered nervously. 'Alda,' turning to her friend, 'Mr Potter's asked me in to Brighton to lunch, darling.'

Alda's eyes brightened, grew wider, became mischievous.

'What a good idea!' she said, 'but how about your shopping in Horsham this afternoon?'

'Oh—be an angel and explain for me, will you? You can say it's business. I'll just get my coat—shan't be a minute,' and she shook back her hair and hurried out of the room.

Mr Potter sat in easy silence with his legs crossed. He smilingly declined Alda's offer of a cigarette (they were Woodbines, all that Sillingham had been able to offer, and Mr Potter always had his cigarettes made in America with *Oliver Potter* stamped upon each one). The children had quietly taken up their usual

indoor occupations and were stealing glances at him. Presently
Louise asked shyly:

'Did you see any hippopotamuses in South Africa?'

'No, not on this trip,' turning his wide smile and mellow
chuckling voice upon her. He was not accustomed to addressing
children, and therefore spoke to her as if she were grown-up. 'I
was in the Cape. The big game is all up in the National Parks
and Game Reserves.'

'Oh, please, what is a Game Reserve?'

Mr Potter explained, with an attention to detail and a lack
of impatience at her eager questions which caused her afterwards
to declare fervently that he was the nicest man she had ever
met. Jenny also listened with rapt interest but Meg had slipped
outside to harry the ants with her cockleshell. Alda had taken
up her knitting and was studying Mr Potter over the top of it.
Perhaps it would be better if J. married him instead, she thought.
At least he isn't poor, and he isn't dim, either, and she could
soon learn to be his type. He would never have asked her to
lunch if he hadn't been intrigued.

For Alda knew the world from which Mr Potter came, and
had guessed his opinion of the setting in which he had discovered Miss Hardcastle. He had not troubled to conceal completely
what he felt; a look in the eye and a curl of the lip betrayed
him. She was sure that he had never before in his life entered
such a room, and only his good nature prevented his manner
from being downright rude. But what charm in those green
eyes, that big nose, that broad smile! He looked as if he would
be ready at any moment to make a gay plan for everybody's
pleasure, and he was now showing the little girls an especially
ingenious type of propelling pencil; there was something especial
about his wristwatch too, which made it worthy of display, and
after this his lighter and cigarette case must come out and go
through their paces.

Alda, watching, decided that he was what Ronald called a Gadget

Man, with a taste for expensive little dodgems that were always going wrong and taking weeks to be mended; which had to be described and shown to everybody, and which made him uneasy unless he had them all deposited over his person in perfect working order. She thought of Ronald, who carried no gadgets except the fine antique French watch that he wore looped across his slender stomach in time of peace (Mr Potter was inclined to a manly portliness, though he was not yet thirty-five) and the base metal lighter given to him by his batman on the day the latter was killed; and she decided that if Mr Potter did not find her glamorous, she certainly did not find him so. But she could see why Jean did.

Here Jean reappeared, wearing a beautiful dress of blue silk printed with large white flowers under a coat of pale wool, and the finest of stockings. Mr Potter immediately looked relieved, and stood up in readiness for departure. He was afraid I'd pawned all her clothes to buy food for the children, thought Alda, pleasantly accompanying them to the door.

Meg was busily employed with her ants upon the doorstep and (as Jean paused to exchange a word or two with Alda and Mr Potter courteously waited for her) she glanced up at him to secure his attention, then pointed with a fat forefinger at an ant hurrying along by her foot and observed conversationally, 'His name is Gilbert,' but Mr Potter, assuming that his ears had misled him, gave no reply beyond a vague smile.

Alda had not yet thought precisely what explanation she was going to give to Mr Waite about his betrothed's non-appearance, but when Jean lifted her hand to wave good-bye as they went down the path, and Alda saw that she no longer wore her engagement ring, she *did* experience a slight shock; and when she set out after lunch to meet him, she already thought of her friend as lured away and lost, and had got so far as wondering whether Mr Waite would sue her for breach of promise.

'Hullo!' she called cheerfully, waving and smiling as he drove up, and getting in her opening speech before the surprise dawning upon his face could express itself in a question, 'I've got a message from Jean. She's awfully sorry, she can't come this afternoon. An old friend of her father's came down unexpectedly and she's gone into Brighton with him.'

She intended this remark to have a flavour of family-solicitors-and-boring-papers-to-be-signed but, uttered as it was by a pretty woman in a cotton dress with her hair stirred by the wind, it sounded fatally runaway and festive: it chimed with the robust mirth of elderly stockbrokers and the clinking of glasses in secret bars.

'Oh,' he said, after a long, suspicious look, and said no more. He appeared to meditate, staring down at the wheel of the car. He is much better-looking than Mr P. but has no charm at all, thought Mrs Lucie-Browne, who had now made up her mind to get Jean married to Mr Potter. Mr Potter was more Jean's type; Mr Potter had some money and would fit more easily into Lucie-Browne parties; and, after all, the poor pet had always fancied Mr Potter. Well, Mr Potter she should have.

'Why did he come?' asked Mr Waite suddenly, looking at her.

'Oh, just to see her, I think. He knew her people quite well. He's just back from South Africa.'

'I take it that he is well off, then?'

'Nothing out of the ordinary, so far as I know.'

'He must be, if he can take holidays in South Africa,' with a sarcastic little laugh.

'His firm sent him, I think,' said Alda—and of course he pounced on that, saying sharply:

'Oh, he's a young man, then? I thought you said he was old?'

'An old *friend*, I said,' retorted Alda rather crossly. This man would never have fitted in with us, she thought; I'm glad Mr P. turned up in time.

'Did they say where they were going?'

'No. Just to lunch in Brighton. One of the expensive places, I suppose,' she added with a little malice.

'I can't understand why she didn't bring him over to meet me,' he muttered. 'If it's any question of business, I'm the person to be informed now.'

'It wasn't business; he just wanted to see her,' said Alda recklessly, thinking that the sooner he realised how matters stood the better for him and everyone.

'Are you sure they didn't say where they were going? I was thinking—I might run over there and look in at the Ship and one or two places, and join them.'

'They'd have finished lunch by now, it's a quarter to three. And besides, you'd never find them,' Alda said decidedly. 'Look— it's a shame to spoil your afternoon and the children would love to see the sea. Can't you take us to Brighton instead?'

He gazed gloomily at her. She had honeysuckle fastened in her bosom and her hands in the pockets of her old coat as she stood there smiling at him. Since his engagement he had successfully banished a certain troubling image from his thoughts; telling himself that if a man is engaged to one woman he does not dream about another; and the discussion of all those domestic details that Jean found so tedious had helped him to fix his mind upon the future rather than upon the slightly painful present.

Now Jean, upon whom he was unconsciously growing to depend, had failed him. That was how he thought of her behaviour. Heaven knew that he could not depend upon Alda—Mrs Lucie-Browne—to behave sensibly, for one never knew what she would do next, but there she stood; the day was sunny and clear and all over the green country of Sussex people were playing and working in the sunshine, while fifteen miles away, glittering in blue and silver, rolled and murmured the sea. He dropped his hands upon the wheel and exclaimed:

'Go and fetch the kiddies. We'll go.'

The letter to Mrs Waite was still lying upon the table where she had pushed it aside at Mr Potter's entrance when Jean came slowly into the parlour that night. The long summer twilight had not yet left the sky and two moths, a little gold one and a heavy dark creature, were hovering near the lamp. Alda was moving about the room, tidying it.

'Darling! Where have you been?' she exclaimed in a laughing, hushed tone as Jean came wearily in. 'The children are only just in bed. We've had a day out with your fiancé.'

'I know; I saw you,' Jean said, sitting down. 'Is there any tea left? I'm parched.'

'Help yourself. Where were you when you saw us?'

'In the lounge of some hotel.' She pushed her hair back and drank thirstily. 'I saw you coming along the Parade in his car and guessed what had happened. I'm simply dead; we had a lot to drink, too,' she added, half to herself.

Alda stood, looking down at her. She was extremely pale and there were shadows under her eyes.

'Was Phil very cross?' she asked, without looking up, as she poured out another cup.

'He was, rather, but we soothed him down. He didn't say much; it was more his manner. I think he enjoyed being with us; he gave us a very good tea and carried Meg down to the sea to paddle.'

'It was horribly crowded, wasn't it,' Jean murmured.

'Yes, but great fun. The children loved it, bless them. Your Phil isn't such a bad old stick, J. By the way, *is* he still your Phil? I notice you've shed your ring.'

'It's awful of me, I know.' Jean looked up miserably. 'But I just couldn't help it, darling. Oliver really does seem to like me a lot, after all, and I simply hadn't the courage to tell him.'

'Has he asked you to marry him?'

'Not in so many words but—oh, Alda!—he seems to take it for granted that I will. Isn't it frightful! What *shall* I do?'

'Nothing, of course, until you see what they're going to do,' said her friend decidedly. 'Take a firm line with Phil and say

you've a perfect right to go out with an old friend if you want
to——'

'And what about Oliver?' Jean was now leaning forward,
gazing up into the gay, confident face with a slightly less wretched
expression upon her own. Alda would help her; Alda knew
exactly what to do.

'(Is he Oliver? How sweet.) Oh, just string him along. See as
much of him as you can without making Phil furious——'

'He wants me to go back to London. He—he doesn't like
my being down here.'

'Yes, I could see that,' Alda muttered, beginning to fold up
the children's outdoor clothes.

'He says I'm buried here, and we could see so much more
of each other in town. He can't get away except at week-ends,
of course, because of his job. He wants to me to go and live at
an hotel——'

'Well, why don't you?'

Jean stared at her.

'But, Alda, how can I? What would Phil say? I'm supposed
to be going to his mother's next week.'

'Say you've got to get your trousseau or you feel like a change
or something.'

'He wouldn't believe me.' Jean rested her head drearily upon
her hands.

'He'd believe me quick enough; I wish I had the two of them
to manage,' murmured Alda, bending over to raise the lamp wick,
and the brighter glow shone upon her white throat and the
slight smile of reminiscent mischief on her mouth. 'I remember
once when I was going about with Johnny Bradfield——'

'And there's another thing,' burst out Jean unhappily, and her
head sank lower into her hands, '– two other things really—I'm
afraid Oliver may only want me for my money, and——'

'And what?'

'*He* may not be a Christian.'

'Oh really, J., how morbid!' cried Alda crossly; the last quality with which we associate Christianity is elegance, and Mr P.'s clothes, his shoes, his very gadgets were so elegant that it seemed absurd to think of Mr P. and Christianity in the same breath. One of the three writers whose books she loved and knew by heart was Jane Austen, and now, as she suddenly remembered the passage in *Sanditon* where another Mr P. catches sight of the children's bathing-shoes in the shop window and exclaims delightedly, 'Civilisation! Civilisation!' she burst out laughing.

'He's as good a Christian as anyone is nowadays, I expect,' she added, sobering.

'And how good is that?' without looking up.

'Oh—kind and honest, and all that sort of thing.'

'That isn't everything, if—if you really do believe.'

'Oh, J.,' sighing exasperatedly. 'As if you hadn't enough to worry about! What's come over you? You never used to be like this.'

'I know. It's been coming on for years. And until I got engaged I was happier than I'd been for years, too, and now I'm wretched.'

Alda demanded bluntly: 'Are you in love with Oliver?'

'Of *course* I am; I'm crazy about him; that's what's so awful. If I marry him I shall have to lead his sort of life, and perhaps get to hate him because he makes me lead it.'

'What sort of a life, for goodness' sake? (here, have some more tea and don't talk so loud; you'll wake the children).'

Jean was silent. She wanted to speak of her experience in Sedley Church but she could not; the words would not come; she felt that her friend would never understand, and then, suddenly, as she sat there miserably sucking down tepid tea, she felt rebellious.

Why should she have to be worried about Phil and worried about Oliver and bothered about what was right and what was wrong? Some of those hours spent with Oliver had been deliciously happy, filled with the violin-notes that had lately been missing from her personal life. She was suddenly, strongly tempted to do what she wanted to do, and blow the rights and wrongs.

Alda had been watching her downcast face. She now said more gently:

'Lots of husbands and wives don't have the same religious views. You could have your beliefs (whatever they may be) and Mr P. could have his. He could be what Ronald calls a Noble Pagan.* Ronald's one himself, as a matter of fact, but it doesn't worry me. He lets me bring up the children as Christians; he think's Christianity the best of all the religions, actually, only he's too old to believe in it.'

'And what about Phil?' Jean said.

Alda had been so busy arranging the religion of Jean's husband that she had forgotten Jean's fiancé. But she knew just what to do. She said firmly:

'Drop him, J. You've always wanted your Mr Potter and now you've practically got him. Don't give Phil another thought.'

'But, Alda—I've taken his ring—and accepted him——'

'Oh, you can get out of it somehow. Keep out of his way. Go up to town to-morrow; I'll make your excuses. You can write to him from there.'

Jean hesitated, staring down in silence at her hand, now bare of those dim little garnets. How tempting the suggestion was! By to-morrow evening she could be in a cool bedroom in a London hotel, with the muted roar of traffic rising from the streets below; she could be far away from the insistent, silent pressure of these woods and meads that forced her to see too clearly, to feel too deeply; she could be back in the world again, dressing to dine at the Dorchester with Oliver Potter.

She lifted her head and looked at Alda.

'You think I'd better marry Oliver, then?' she said.

* Ronald was quoting Mr Aldous Huxley.

'Of course I do, darling! Haven't I made it clear? I *know* he's just your type.'

'More than Phil?'

'Oh, J.! You are dumb! Of *course*. Why, Phil was only a stop-gap, a last chance, a—a *faute-de-mieux*! If Oliver wants you, for *mercy's* sake snap him up while you've got the *chance*.'

Her face glowed and her eyes were bright in the lamplight, her voice was hushed because of her sleeping children, yet rang with an imperious, compelling note as she leant forward, resting her rounded arms and sturdy hands upon the table. Jean caught her mood; her wretched look vanished; she began to laugh unsteadily, and at last she said, blowing her nose:

'Oh, darling, I really believe you're right! I'll go.'

25

By ten o'clock the next morning she had gone. She awoke early after a night of heavy dreamless sleep, and hurried across to the farmhouse in pyjamas and housecoat to telephone to Oliver. (It now appeared that Oliver had spent the night at Brighton in order to be near his love, and Alda's opinion of him improved.) While Sylvia listened in open curiosity and the Hoadleys got on with their breakfast after civilly assuring her that she was giving them no trouble, Jean arranged for him to meet her on the Froggatt road in an hour and drive her to London, and ran back across the meadows smiling at his warm approval of her decision. The day was already hot and beautiful, the sky a thick dreamy blue. A delightful prospect of action, change, gaiety, opened before her, all smiling in the light of happy love, and as Alda helped her to pack they chattered and laughed and only once sobered their voices to speak rather sharply to Jenny, who asked bluntly *What would poor Mr Waite do?*

It was arranged that Alda should send Jean's heavier luggage after her, and soon she was saying good-bye to them all, kissing them almost impatiently with none of her usual placid kindness, and then, clutching her handbag and suitcase and hastily refusing their offers to accompany her as far as the road, she hurried away.

They watched her out of sight. Louise was mildly interested in the proceedings and Meg was indifferent but Jenny, still slightly sulky from her snubbing, glanced at her mother. She had a fairly clear idea of what was happening and she burned with indignation on Mr Waite's behalf. She did not particularly like him, but

316

yesterday in Brighton he had bought them ices and given them tea, and her strong child's sense of justice was aroused. She described Jean to herself, in spite of the bicycles, as a beast, while even her mother did not escape condemnation.

Alda saw Jean go with lively satisfaction. She was convinced that her advice had been for the best and that Jean had done the sensible thing, which would shortly lead on to the happy thing. She expected that there might be a slightly awkward encounter between Mr Waite and herself, in which she would have to cover Jean's behaviour with some airy remarks until Jean should have written to him, but she hoped that she might avoid meeting him until after Jean's letter had arrived; and for her part she would find it pleasant to have the cottage and the children to herself again, for lately poor Jean and her affairs had definitely been a bore. She made plans for a picnic lunch while they washed up the breakfast crockery, and soon the cottage was ringing with *White Sand and Grey Sand*, sung in a harmonious four-part round.

At a quarter to ten Jean left Pine Cottage on her way to meet Mr Potter. At ten minutes to ten one of the Waite battery chickens, taking advantage of its metal grille slipping aside, escaped from its cell and set off at a smart pace on its way to freedom. At five minutes to ten it was seen and heard by Mr Waite, who was ministering to some other chickens at the far end of the enclosure, and he, setting down his pail with an impatient exclamation, set off after it.

It had a good start. Flapping and squawking, it led him along the grassy paths between the huts and through his own cabbage patch and into his bean row, where it paused long enough to let him nearly seize it and then set off again, half-running and half-flying, across the open fields in the direction of the Froggatt road. He had been hurrying through his morning's tasks in order to walk across to Pine Cottage and hear what Jean had to say for herself about her behaviour of yesterday, and this interruption was therefore doubly annoying. As he came out on to the road he was swearing.

A car was passing at that moment: a large handsome saloon which was travelling at some forty miles an hour, walking pace for such a highly powered engine; the type of car, the very make, that he had always longed to own and which he had lately indulged in hopes of possessing. He caught a glimpse of the occupants: a stoutish, prosperous-looking young man was driving and beside him, with her arm passed through his, gazing into his face, was a girl. Good heavens, it was Jean!

They passed by while he was still gasping. They were already nearly out of sight. But there was no mistake; it was Jean. Hanging on to a man's arm. Staring up into his face. What was she doing with a man in a car at this hour on a Sunday morning? Was this Mr Potter, her father's old friend, the party with whom she had had a business appointment in Brighton? Why, he could not be a day over thirty; he was younger by years than Mr Waite, and what clothes, what a car! He must be wealthy; very wealthy indeed. And amidst the confusion of his feelings he suddenly felt strong indignation with Mrs Lucie-Browne, who had certainly led him to believe, throughout their own excursion to Brighton yesterday, that Mr Potter was middle-aged and of moderate means. He had had his suspicions from the first, and who had deliberately lulled them to sleep? Mrs Lucie-Browne.

He stood there, gazing down the road where the car had disappeared, and a dreary sensation began to creep over him. The chicken, now that he had ceased to pursue her, was wandering towards him talking to herself, and presently, without effort and almost absently, he captured her and began to walk back to his cottage. His anger was increasing. He wanted to have this business out with someone, find out what was going on, blame somebody for Jean's disgraceful behaviour, and he decided to go then and there and have things out with Mrs Lucie-Browne.

He was deeply disappointed in her. They had passed a very pleasant afternoon in Brighton yesterday and he had spent fourteen shillings and sevenpence halfpenny upon herself and her children and (he admitted it) she had seemed attractive; very attractive indeed; all the more attractive because he was not responsible for her opinions and her conduct; she was like a—a lovely and valuable brooch, that you could safely admire because it belonged to someone else and you need not worry about its getting lost or stolen.

Side by side they had sat upon the stony beach on his macintosh, enjoying the warm salt air blowing in from the tumbling waves; they had watched workmen hammering and climbing on the big white hotels as they repaired the ravages of bombing; they had listened to the hoarse cries of men imploring visitors to come out in the *Seagull* or the *Rose Marie*; and had smiled at the long white legs and the short brown legs wandering in and out of the waves. The ice cream, the comings and goings of motor buses, all the gaiety and bustle of Brighton and its glittering sea upon a summer's day, had been shared by himself and Mrs Lucie-Browne, and what had she done to him? Encouraged his fiancée to go off with another man.

He would go and have it out with her at once.

And, pausing only to shove the subdued battery bird into its cell and slam the grille upon it he set off with a grim face for Pine Cottage.

Alda was knitting peacefully in a deck-chair in the front garden when she heard the click of the gate. Mr Waite, looking tall and ominous, was stalking up the path. This is it, Alda thought, and put the knitting down and called gaily:

'Oh, hullo! Good morning!'

It was fortunate that the elder children were indoors preparing the picnic lunch. Meg was playing about the garden but she was fully occupied with her ants.

'Mrs Lucie-Browne, where is Jean?' he demanded sharply,

removing his hat and standing over her. He ignored her greeting.

How good-looking he is, thought Alda, studying him while deciding what to say. He ought always to look angry; it suits him.

'Gone to London,' she answered lightly at last. 'She sent you her love and——'

'I saw her,' he interrupted. 'She passed me on the road only ten minutes ago. She was with a man in a car.' Then he stood perfectly still, hat in hand, looking down at her, and waiting. The muscles round his jaw were white.

'Oh yes. That would be Mr Potter,' said Alda—brightly, this time, and she shook out her knitting. 'He's driving her up. The fact is, she's been feeling run down for some time, and the hot weather and everything, and she thought she'd get some of her things in town——'

'What things?'

'Oh—clothes.' She gazed at him innocently. She had on a large old hat of rusty black straw like a Welshwoman's that she kept for garden wear; under its shade her lovely hazel eyes shone like gold water. Her hair was tucked behind her ears and she was paler than usual but only from the heat; she was not at all afraid of Mr Waite; she had never been afraid of a man in her life and now she was rather enjoying the situation.

He *is* angry, she thought, as he kept silence but continued to fix upon her his brooding, condemnatory eyes. There must be more in him than I imagined. *I* like him better than J.'s Mr P., bore though he is. If he belonged to me I could make something out of him.

She settled the hat further over her eyes.

'She's going to write to you,' she added, giving him a little nod.

'Breaking off our engagement, I presume.'

'Well—yes—I'm afraid—as a matter of fact. The fact is——'

320

His stare, his almost unbroken silence, were beginning to disturb her slightly and she did not like being looked at in that way. There was more in his expression than he himself knew. She had hurt him; hurt him more than Jean had, and as he gazed at her his eyes betrayed the wound.

'It's best to get it over, really,' she went on hurriedly, 'and I do know as much about J.'s affairs as anyone. I may as well tell you. She's always been fond of Oliver Potter and now he's turned up again I'm afraid——'

'It's you I blame,' he interrupted, in a voice so harsh that it startled her. 'You deliberately misled me about this man, didn't you?'

'I did? Nonsense!' and she laughed but colour began to come up under her warm white skin.

'Yes, you did. And that isn't all you've done. You encouraged Jean to get engaged to me when she didn't really want to and you knew it, and now you've encouraged her to go off with someone else who you've known about all along. I think it was a—a dirty trick, and I think you ought to be——'

'And *I* think you're talking rubbish and being extremely rude into the bargain,' she interrupted sharply; she was not going to hear him tell her that she should be ashamed of herself. 'Of course I wanted to see Jean happily married; one always wants that for one's friends if one's happy oneself; but to say that I "encouraged" her to get engaged to you, when I knew she didn't want to, just isn't true. She was very keen to get engaged to you.'

He heard this in silence.

'She likes and respects you,' Alda went on, taking up her knitting, 'and I think if Oliver Potter hadn't come along you and she might have been happy. It's just bad luck that he did. But you can't expect a girl to marry someone she doesn't love when the man she does love asks her to marry *him*.'

'But how could he do such a thing when he knew she was

engaged to me? Or perhaps,' bitterly, 'she didn't trouble to tell him?'

'That's exactly what did happen,' said Alda, thinking that this confession would at least prove how uncontrollably Jean was in love with Mr P. 'She never told him. She even took off her ring.'

At this he swore, and she lowered her eyes, in embarrassment at such depth of feeling, such angry shame, on a man's face. But she had never thought so well of him, and she became more and more convinced that Jean had chosen the lesser man.

Mr Waite was thinking how mean Aunt Janet's ring would look compared with the enormous diamond set in platinum which this Potter fellow would buy for Jean. Suddenly, for the first time, he missed his Jean; gentle, cheerful, submissive Jean, who—dammit! who had been in love with Potter all the time!

At this point he became aware that something was pulling at his jacket. He glanced down and met the insistent gaze of Meg, who had been trying to attract his attention for some minutes. She was holding up a jam jar containing some leaves and four ants.

'His name is Gilbert,' she announced in a loud, threatening voice, pushing the jar at him.

He stared down at her, frowning, hardly hearing.

'His name is *Gilbert*,' she repeated, beginning to swell ominously in voice and countenance.

'What—the ants?' glancing angrily at Alda, who was laughing. 'How can ants possibly be called Gilbert? Run away now and don't be silly, there's a good girl. I'm talking to your mother.'

''Name *is* GILBERT!' roared Meg, bursting into tears, and Louise came flying out of the cottage.

'All right, Megsy. Come with Weez and we'll give Gilbert a lovely picnic, shall we? *Come* along,' and she bore her away, already consoled and clasping the jar of ants to her chest.

'It's her name for her pet ant; of course it's never the same one but she thinks it is,' said Alda. 'We're all going for a picnic on our bicycles presently; it's such a lovely day.'

Then she hoped that he would not suggest coming too; a whole day of him in the woods, lowering at her and accusing her, was more than she could endure.

He now looked slightly bewildered.

'I don't know what to do,' he said abruptly. 'This has upset all my plans. I must write to my mother and sisters, I suppose. It will be a shock to them. I don't know what to say.'

Alda uttered a sympathetic noise. Then she said kindly:

'Won't you wait until you've heard from Jean? Don't write to them at once.'

'Why? Is there a chance of her changing her mind again?' with ferocious sarcasm.

'Absolutely none, I'm afraid. But do give yourself a day or two to get calmed down.'

'Calmed down! It will take me more than a day or two, I assure you, Mrs Lucie-Browne, to do that.'

'Yes, I'm afraid it will,' she murmured. She was relieved to see that his anger with herself seemed to have abated. But he continued to stare at her with his handsome, gloomy, sorrowful eyes. It had been an increasingly pleasant relationship between the two cottages in the meadows, and it might have ended, but for Mr Potter, in a contented marriage. She and Jean had brought the pleasures of feminine society into Mr Waite's dismal and orderly life; and now Jean had gone, and there would be no marriage for Mr Waite, and in a month or so she herself and the children would be gone too, and he would continue to live among his tyrannical chickens, with what Jean called his spooks for company, almost as if the family at Pine Cottage had never been. He has no sense of humour and he is what Ronald calls *a dead bore* but I like him better than I ever did, and he has certainly had a raw deal, Alda thought, folding up her work and preparing to go into the house. Her own part in the raw deal she refused to admit.

She glanced at him. He was standing as if uncertain, frowning at the ground, and turning his hat in his hands. She was struck by his pallor and his drawn appearance. His feelings must be very strong; stronger than perhaps he knew. Then she wondered how much of his sufferings were due to the loss of Jean's fortune.

He looked up, and caught her glance.

'You think I'm only browned-off about the money and the business, don't you?' he said with a sudden North Country bluntness.

'I'm sure you're not,' she replied, with the gentleness that sometimes made her irresistible. 'You wouldn't be human if you didn't regret that part of it but I believe you're miserable about Jean, too.'

'You're right; I am,' he said, and quickly turned away and walked off. He did not look back.

Thank goodness that's over, thought Alda, and she snatched off the Welsh hat and sent it spinning into the air. The very day seemed brighter.

'Has the All Clear gone?' cried Jenny in a conspiratorial voice, peering out of the parlour window with Meg in her arms.

'Yes. Now we can get off. Is the food ready? Come along!'

Twenty minutes later they were riding down a lane under the leafage of June. They passed a delightful day in the woods and the name of Mr Waite was not mentioned between them, but that night it was added to the already lengthy list in Jenny's prayers.

He strode across the meadows in a black rage, full of bitter disgust with the pair of them. He felt that they had made a fool of him and that was the one situation he could not endure. They had more money than he had, they still lived in that world which he had left at the age of twenty-one and to which he had never been able to return, and now, between them, they had robbed him of his chance of returning. And he would never have such a chance again. He would stay on in this cursed hole, and he would get old and die, and that would be the end of it.

He roughly pushed open a gate (remembering with a country-dweller's habit, in spite of his rage, to shut it behind him) and trudged on.

He entered a meadow that was within a month of being cut for hay, and moon daisies and sorrel and slender purple and pewter-coloured grasses dragged about his knees as he walked. It was already very warm and still. He took off his hat and wiped his forehead and paused for a moment. A lark was singing above his head, bird and song rising and falling together in the hazy blue. Then another sound began upon the morning calm; the church bell from the village ringing over the fields. Of course, it's Sunday, he thought, and his thoughts went to Daleham, where Mother and the Girls would now be walking down Swanton Street to Saint James's Church.

At the sound, there descended upon him (like a severe old parson accompanied by a slightly soulful angel) memories of that creed of practical Christian duties and sober church-going in which his mother had brought him up, and thoughts of those Great Teachers who so irresistibly attracted him. Together, in the midst of that field of warm silver grass, they took him in hand. He wiped his forehead once more; he glanced about him and sighed. His rage began to ebb. He was still very angry with Jean and Alda and when he thought of Mr Potter in his luxurious car a vein in his forehead actually throbbed, but he ceased to lash himself towards wilder fury yet, and presently, when he had lit his pipe and was walking slowly on, it began to occur to him that some of all this might be his own fault.

He remembered what it was that he had meant to confess to Jean when he decided to propose to her: that he did not love her. But he had not confessed, though he had had a suspicion at the time that he was, in some way, cheating her. In his home circle a marriage of convenience would not be regarded as shocking. It would belong to the world of Business, from which sentiment was excluded. But at least a pretence of love—romance—whatever you liked to call it—would have been put up; and Buddha—Jesus—all those Great Teachers—what would they have said to a marriage without love? He himself had always, since his first youth, feared love and avoided it, but he knew that they would have condemned a loveless marriage of convenience very severely indeed.

Then he defended himself by recalling that during the last few days, before this chap Potter arrived, he *had* been getting fond of Jean. He had looked forward to seeing her, and had missed her when she was not there, and her hair and the perfume she used and the silly tinkle of those five silver bracelets she wore had been growing less irritating to him. And now, as he pushed open the gate of his garden and sought about for some useful occupation to fill the hours before it was time to begin preparing his solitary dinner, his anger had almost entirely disappeared and he only felt dreary and sore and disappointed; and what he would have liked to do (if only it were not impossible because of her disgraceful behaviour) was to go back to Pine Cottage and talk over the situation with Alda—with Mrs Lucie-Browne.

26

Fabrio's decision to ask Sylvia to be his wife had lightened his spirits. Now he had an object to work for and look forward to. He ceased to buy cigarettes, so that the money might go into Mr Hoadley's care and by the end of June he had saved two pounds, which seemed to him a little fortune.

He did not pay more attention to Sylvia than he had formerly done, for he was afraid that she would suspect his intention, and he did not want her to suspect until he was ready, with money and a gay confident heart, to ask her to share this with him. He dreamed of her by day and by night in a fond, protective, silent way, building an image in his fancy which he would not allow any roughness or crude behaviour of hers to disturb. Sometimes he even believed that she loved him. Her eyes smiled so kindly when they met his own! She praised his voice so warmly! There came a day, an always-to-be-remembered day, when she said, there before them all while they were sitting at tea in the farm-house kitchen, 'Sing, Fabrio. I love to hear you sing; your voice does something to me.'

And so, while he was carrying away the cups to be washed, he sang, and Mrs Hoadley tapped in time with her foot, where she sat languidly by the window open to the summer afternoon.

There had been a noticeable relaxation in the atmosphere of the farmhouse during the last month, for the mistress could no longer dart about all over the farm, crisply shutting doors and whisking objects into cupboards and detecting the livestock in misdemeanours. She kept usually to the cool pleasant kitchen, where she moved slowly about cooking the meals for which the

Italians and Mr Hoadley and Sylvia came in ravenously hungry three times a day, or stayed in her bedroom, where she sat resignedly knitting and turning over an immense mound of pale pink knitted garments threaded with white ribbon. These had poured in from every corner of Great Britain, where seemingly Mrs Hoadley had an old school friend or a cousin or a someone-we-used-to-know, and all her correspondents were so taken by the name Joyanna that gradually she herself began to feel more placid and as time went on she even began to look forward a little to Joyanna's birth.

Privileges crept into the daily routine. One pouring wet afternoon when the Italians could not get on with cutting hay in the Big Meadow, and everyone was hanging about looking serious because if this weather lasted overnight and into tomorrow the hay would be spoilt, Mrs Hoadley invited them into the kitchen to eat hot cakes and drink tea, where Sylvia presently joined them. There was a good deal of laughter, and Mrs Hoadley presided, knitting as usual, and occasionally giving the stifled gasp with her lips pressed together which was her version of a hearty laugh. Mr Hoadley came into a late tea and was not displeased to find all this going on. His wife had been easier to get on with lately (contrary to his anticipations), less finicky, less nervous. Even the arrival of four yards of exceedingly thick and 'felted' flannel, yellow with age and rather whiffy, from old Mrs Hoadley at the Wild Brooks had only provoked a pitying 'Poor old thing—nobody uses those binders nowadays'—and the flannel had been cut up for polishers and ironholders.

Mr Hoadley decided that he would ask the Camp authorities if the Italians might sleep at the farm during the harvest; Naylor's possessed only one large field, a six-acre which was sown in a crop rotation suitable to the soil of this part of Sussex, and this year it was sown with wheat, as was the Small Meadow and both fields must be reaped in August. All the farm work grew heavier as the summer drew on, and he would need all the help that the two men and Sylvia could give him.

As the strength of the sun increased, so did Fabrio's energy and gaiety. His chestnut hair took on a sheen from exposure to the rays, though he was not mad enough, like an Englishman, to expose it all day, wearying himself and giving himself a headache. No; in the granary, high up among the cobwebbed beams, he had spied a big straw hat, the property of some forgotten farm-hand now perhaps an old man. It was ragged at the brim, it had a rat-hole in its tall crown; never mind. Fabrio, who had studied it while lying on his back during the winter, one day climbed leisurely and expertly up the side of the granary, and brought down the hat. It was grey with dust, but he blew that off, and underneath was the sheen of sound straw. Good, thought Fabrio, and put it on his head and went out into the sunlight. Beneath its brim his eyes felt at home; they could move slowly, observantly, within their little cave of cool shadow. He had just such another hat at home in San Angelo. He settled it more jauntily upon his head and went off to show himself to Sylvia.

She thought he looked a guy but did not tell him so. For years her idea of an attractive man had been a huge square creature in squarer American clothes, so naturally a graceful male of middle height wearing a hat that was a comic poem did not attract her; indeed, no one who was not conventionally smart could hope to, but she smiled at him and told him the hat was smashing ('So it is—so it is,' he agreed, putting his finger through the hole, 'all the time it is being se-mashed') and they loitered in the sun for a little while, chatting while she rested her sunburnt arms upon the warm wood of the gate leading out to the Big Meadow. Gusts of soft wind wandered by, lifting her hair and blowing coolly upon his half-uncovered breast: the wheat stood green and high, and overhead in the elm the hidden pigeons cooed.

'It's nice and peaceful here—for five minutes,' she murmured, gazing off towards the Downs veiled in summer haze. 'Fabrio,' turning to him, 'don't you like it better here in the summer?'

'Yes, it is better, Sylvia, much better. But,' his nostrils dilated slightly, while he did not meet her eyes, 'all the time I am think to go home, to my home in San Angelo.'

'Any chance of it?' she asked lazily, swinging on the gate.

He shrugged. 'Perhaps. I do not know. In the autumn, they say in the *campo*. But I do not know.' He did not dare to look at her, for if he did he could not control his words of love; he stared down at his boots.

'What'll you do, when you do get home, Fabrio?'

He shrugged again, and was silent. The pigeon began again on his monotonous love song; roo-coo-coo—then broke off abruptly. Fabrio looked into her eyes and smiled and said confidently:

'I shall work the farm-a. We have a farm: I tell you, Sylvia.' A little anxiousness came into his expression; he wanted to make her believe the farm was large and his family rich, but he could not find the right English words.

Yes, we know all about that, she thought, but her eyes dwelt kindly on him. She was going to ask him teasingly if he had a girl out there, at home, but a slight shyness restrained her, and at that moment the sight of Mr Hoadley in the distance reminded them both that they must get on with their work, and they smiled at one another and moved away.

They often met in this way throughout the lengthening busy days and exchanged gossip and grumbles and occasionally a little teasing, and she came to accept him as a pleasant part of life at the farm, where everything was pleasant now that the summer had come, though the work steadily increased as it mounted towards its climax, the harvest. It was difficult to remember him as the sullen, silent Fabrio of the winter months, for now he sang as he worked and he and Emilio kept up a cross-fire of

insults and jokes in their native tongue which entertained everybody, themselves most of all.

These weeks were enjoyed by everybody except one. The
households at the farm and at Pine Cottage had entered upon
one of those times which are afterwards remembered with an
affectionate glow—'We did have fun, didn't we?—I often think
of those days'—when the daily round of work and pleasure falls
in exactly the proportion to satisfy everyone engaged in it; when
unbroken fine weather makes every task easier and adds the
splendour of sunlight and clear skies to the simplest excursion
or meal.

Mrs Hoadley had, as she put it, taken quite a fancy to Meg
and liked to have her down at the farm almost every day. Alda
always knew where to look for her if she were missing, and this
led to more frequent comings and goings between the cottage
and the farmhouse, Alda often lingering to admire Mrs Hoadley's
knitting or to gossip about the prospects for the harvest and the
arrival of Joyanna, for now that Jean had gone she was sometimes
at a loss for someone to chat and laugh with.

Jean had now been in London nearly a month—'and hasn't
sent me a word, the blighter,' wrote Alda to Ronald, and Mr
Waite had gone back to his former reserved habits, ceremoniously saluting Alda from a distance and occasionally leaving eggs
(only four, now, alas) on the doorstep, but avoiding friendly
intercourse. She brushed all this aside and always ran up to him
to thank him, and sometimes sent one of the children with a
note asking him to tea, but he invariably answered her briefly
or returned some polite excuse and made her understand plainly
that she was in disgrace. Oh poo, let him get on with it, thought
Alda, but all the same she felt a little sorry and a little guilty,
too. The summer hat in which he fed the chickens was an ancient
boater, almost as derelict as Fabrio's but less picturesque, and the
distant view of Mr Waite on a glorious morning suggested a
bankrupt fishmonger. He was the only plainly unhappy person

in the meadows that June, and Alda did feel that it was a pity. Still, there was nothing to be done.

She herself was full of delightful energy; she gardened, she knitted, she took long rides with her daughters and returned with wild flowers which they looked up in *The Wild Flowers of Great Britain and Eire*, she dutifully read a page, or nearly a page, of Mr H. A. L. Fisher's *History of Europe* every evening, or almost every evening, and she made long lists, and worked out plans, and wrote letters to builders and plumbers and decorators living in Ironborough. They were to leave the cottage in October: they would have been there almost a year. The children were beginning to become interested in the prospect of having a home of their own after five years of wandering, and Alda enjoyed describing to Jenny and Louise some of the family possessions which were in store, and discovering if they remembered the Japanese tea canisters or father's Chippendale desk.

In the long, calm, blue days; during the lingering warm evenings when the sky beyond Chanctonbury Ring was pink as the campion growing in the cottage gardens; and the ruts half-concealed in grass and clover gradually became hard beneath the steady downpour of rays from the sun; when the pools in remote meadows thickened and bore sheets of white flowers where the moorhens nested; when the roads were hard underfoot as they are in winter but muffled in dust; when giant white clouds rolled into the west and stayed there at sunset; then Sylvia began to look, as she went about her work, for Fabrio.

She began to listen for his voice as he sang. She missed his singing when he was silent. Then, the farm and its buildings seemed lonely, in spite of the house's curtain of budding roses and the sweet scents and animal odours that hung about it and conveyed a strong sense of life. She no longer wanted to change his appearance and manners, and his hat, which she had at first thought of contemptuously as 'Fabrio's comic lid' now only amused and even touched her. She began to take pleasure in seeing him each day. There's Fabrio, she would think, glancing out under the eaves of her dim, warm, crowded little bedroom into the green and blue open air, where the massive elms lifted their load of leaves into the heat haze above the pond. Then she would sigh; and suddenly, delight in the summer would rush into her heart, and she would thrust her hands into her hair and twist it up high for coolness and wrinkle up her nose at her reflection in the mirror and run downstairs to see what there was for tea.

One day when Alda had called in to fetch Meg on the way home from an excursion to Horsham she said to Mrs Hoadley, laughing:

'Do Fabrio and Sylvia still fight all the time?'

'Oh no,' answered Mrs Hoadley, stirring her tea and shaking her head as if slightly surprised. 'They get on ever so well together these days. They've got over all that nonsense.'

'I wonder he hasn't got keen on her, she's a pretty girl and Italians are very susceptible,' said Mrs Lucie-Browne, who had finished her gardening and knitting and letter-writing and list-making for the day and who preferred a situation under her nose to those described in the *History of Europe*.

This time Mrs Hoadley looked decidedly disapproving. She drank some tea, set down her cup carefully, and compressed her lips, which lately had taken a softer curve. Her eyes (so large as to promise an emotional temperament but in colour a pale and lifeless blue) lifted to meet Alda's.

'I'm sure I hope he won't do that,' she said, 'It would take their minds off their work and might lead to goodness-knows-what.'

'It might lead to his marrying her.'

'She could do better than that, an educated girl like Sylvia.'

Alda did not challenge this statement. If Sylvia were Mrs Hoadley's idea of an educated person, so much the worse for them both.

'Fabrio's quite rough, you know,' the farmer's wife added in a delicate tone.

'Is he? I haven't seen much of him but he struck me as having great natural dignity and refinement,' said Alda bluntly, 'much more than Sylvia has.'

Mrs Hoadley put her head on one side and shook it.

'Oh no. Quite the reverse. He's ever so rough, a mere peasant. Besides, Sylvia's all set for a stage career and I for one don't blame her.'

'I doubt if she'll get it. I think she's rather heavily handicapped.'

Mrs Hoadley replied darkly that you could never tell what would go down nowadays, look at Frank Sinatra, and Alda thought it best to say no more, but she resolved to make an opportunity of speaking to Sylvia.

It was not easy to find one, however, for the girl was always busy about the farm or else Alda encountered her in the company of others, and on her weekly afternoon's holiday she hurried off to be with the girls at the Linga-Longa, while her monthly free Sunday was dutifully passed with her family in London. What Alda wanted was an opportunity to give sound advice, because she was so sure that Fabrio was in love and had honest intentions. She possessed that insight into the workings of a deeper, tenderer nature which sometimes belongs to the happy and virtuous of this world: happiness bestows upon them that kind of intuition which is usually only gained by those who have sinned and suffered, but they do not always use it tenderly. It amused Alda to observe the smile that sometimes passed between the two young people; a silent, friendly, dreamy smile, saying to her experienced eye so much more than either of them realised.

Poor Fabrio! this smile was now his 'happiest thing,' as Maria's letter had once been; and poor Maria, who had detected the first shade of coolness in his letters; poor Maria who, as the coolness became casualness and the letters arrived at longer and longer intervals, was very jealous and unhappy. Maria had been formed by Nature to be a wife and mother rather than a playgirl, and she lacked the titillating arts.

'What is the matter, my friend?' wrote Maria; right out, in so many words, in a manner shocking to those who give advice in the women's papers, 'Are you tired of writing to your friend, or have you found some English girl you like better? Please tell me because I am very miserable.'

Fabrio replied, after a week or so, with a letter describing the work at the farm and the weather in Sussex. He was sorry that Maria felt miserable, but she should not bother him about her feelings when he had enough to do in managing his own, and as the plaintive note in her letters continued, he began to feel irritated with her.

He made up his mind to ask Sylvia to be his wife on the night of the Harvest Supper.

He first heard this festival mentioned in the early weeks of hot weather when the wheat began to shoot up tall and fresh. Mrs Hoadley had said that We Always had a supper for the farmhands after the last sheaves were gathered in, but then (warned by a sudden glint in his eye) she had told him that he must not expect much to eat and drink, because times were not what they used to be. If he had heard any tales from the old folks at the Wild Brooks about veal and ham pies as big as laundry baskets and pigs roasted whole, and all that sort of thing, he had better put them out of his mind right away; because every bit you grew had to go up to some old Board nowadays, and it was as much as you could do to find a couple of chickens and a pint or two of beer, so if he was expecting quarts of cream and bowls of strawberries, she was afraid he was going to be unlucky, and she was only telling him for his own good and didn't mean it unkindly.

Fabrio listened with the deepest interest, for this Supper reminded him of the fun they always had at home at the end of the grape harvest, with dancing and drinking and bowls of steaming macaroni with tomatoes and onions. Mrs Hoadley forgot that she was talking to a peasant of a naturally temperate nation, who had been brought up on fish and dandelion leaves and thought himself lucky if he ate meat once in two months, and she need not have warned him of poor fare. Chicken and beer—the English beer which he had grown to like although it would never taste so good to him as the thick purple wine of his own district—seemed a feast indeed to Fabrio, and when he heard that there would be dancing afterwards, he smiled with delight and asked eagerly if he might sing as well.

'I daresay; if there's time,' said Mrs Hoadley, and then Fabrio and Emilio both said anxiously that they must make sure of getting their late passes for the occasion. But to this Mrs Hoadley answered nothing, because Mr Hoadley was keeping secret his intention of asking permission for both men to sleep at the farm during the week of harvest. He did not want a terrific jawing-set-out beforehand, he said.

To dance! To dance with Sylvia! and afterwards to ask her to be his wife! The Harvest Supper now became Fabrio's continual thought; his fancy played about it, looking forward to it with longing, and when he settled himself to sleep at night, indifferent to his hard bed and thin mattress, he prayed before he composed himself for slumber that nothing would happen, no ruining storm of rain, no caprice upon the part of the mysterious and malign Powers that controlled the camp, to prevent his being present at that triumphant feast.

Sylvia was also looking forward to the Supper. She had listened to a talk on Harvest Suppers on the radio and found it ever so quaint and old-fashioned (though of course the custom was full of superstition, as the lady who broadcast was careful to explain) and she repeated tit-bits from the talk to Fabrio, unaware that her own faith in Reason and Science was already on its way out.

Mrs Hoadley thought that with two chickens and some rabbits and the largest piedish filled with plum fool they could manage a supper for ten people, and she even looked forward, with a kind of resigned pleasure, to the event.

It was delightful to Jean to be back in London, in attendance upon Mr Potter. Every morning she took her breakfast in her bedroom enjoying (for her return to town coincided with the beginning of fine weather) the view over the Thames. In those days, too, guests at an expensive hotel might pay for a daily bath and take one, and Jean did. After that, she smoked and read. Then she telephoned Mr Potter to learn if he were free for lunch. If he were, he taxied down from the City to the Embankment, and they lunched in the room overlooking the river and made plans for the evening. In the afternoon she smoked and read, or had her hair or her face done or went to some large, long, lavish musical Technicolor film until Mr Potter was at liberty to dine with her or take her to the play.

She wore orchids every night, and bought three new dinner dresses through the Black Market because if a girl were not glamorous and groomed Mr Potter became pained; one was black with white sequins, and one was white with silver sequins, and the grey one had a silver net shawl.

A perfect life, many women would think.

Jean's small face within its frame of gilt hair gradually became fuller and more like a doll's She was so smiling and passive and groomed, like a good little idol, that most men would have found her attractive. Mr Potter found her very attractive; so biddable, so good-tempered, so rich. In taxis he seized her and determinedly gnawed her neck and muttered at her and even slightly shook or bit her, the while breathing upon her the fumes of cigar smoke and champagne. This was passionate love; this was what she had always longed for. A few days after she had arrived in town, Mr Potter announced that they were going to be married as soon as she had collected a proper trousseau and one of Mr Potter's many business connections had found them a flat; and Jean said to herself, how very, very, very happy she was; and thought that she must really write the news to Alda.

But the days passed, and she did not write. It was because she was afraid to hear news of Mr Waite; and every day she dreaded to receive a letter from Alda, breaking the silence into which he had disappeared, but as the weeks passed and no letter came, she began to feel easier. She reminded herself that Alda detested writing letters, but surely if *he* were ill with misery or had shot himself, Alda would have let her know. She decided that he was sensibly getting over it, and thought that he must find this the easier because he had never loved her.

Mr Potter, on the other hand, loved her very much. He was always loving her.

He gave her (just as poor Mr Waite had thought he would) an *enormous* diamond mounted in platinum; bulging under her glove like a heat bump or flashing from afar like a lighthouse warning off the poor and the unsuccessful. The ring was slightly too big for her, so that she was afraid of losing it but she was more afraid of asking Mr Potter to get it made smaller.

Her capacious handbag easily contained the little worn New Testament, but it requires more courage than Jean possessed to read the New Testament while waiting for someone in a cocktail bar, and she was afraid (oh yes, she was very weak and cowardly; presently she began to accuse herself of both faults) of Mr Potter's smart female friends noticing it and exclaiming 'How sweet!'

Mr Potter had a number of these female friends, all youngish and smart and groomed, with the very latest gadgets to help them in smoking, drinking and painting themselves. They knew, seemingly by instinct, what it was smartest to wear, and eat, and where it was smartest to go. Their only fear was of seeming innocent or soft or dowdy or serious; they were so smart that they stung.

Mr Potter, of course, never told Jean in so many words that she was on trial before these ladies, but she presently began to feel herself in that position. He liked her to look exactly as they did, helpful gadgets and all, and she willingly spent quite large sums in equipping herself. He also liked her to join in their long, long discussions upon where to obtain this brand of American shoe or that brand of rum (which was at the moment the only shoe and rum to wear and drink) to which he himself listened with the attention and interest the subject demanded.

Her attention occasionally wandered.

The ladies had a sixth sense which warned them when someone was bored, and they became suspicious and hostile towards a woman who might not be as interested as they were in shoes and rum. Presently Jean was referred to among them as 'Oliver's Dim-Out.' This would have surprised her very much if she had known, for she took such pains to look and speak exactly as they did that she was sure she had succeeded.

Mr Potter was a good-natured and easy-going man when nothing occurred to annoy him, and it was quite six weeks before he, too, became a little disturbed about Jean. There was something wrong about her, but he was not quite sure what it was. She wore the right clothes, and said the right things, and did everything he told her to do and yet he did not feel completely at ease about her. He had the same feeling about her that he sometimes had about a golf- or tennis-ball which afterwards turned out to be faulty: it looked all right; it felt all right; and yet——

What could it be?

27

In two days the harvest would begin at Naylor's Farm. Sunlight had poured down for three weeks, uninterrupted by rain or cloud, upon the wheat, and the heads bore that shadowy pencilling on their undersides which appears only when they are ripe; the fields were burnished to pale gold, and blew in the wind with a dry rustle that was yet a luxurious sound, full of promise.

All was going forward cheerfully; with the shed already tidied and swept ready for the Supper, and Mrs Hoadley planning a day's baking on Sunday because there would be no time to bake on Monday when the harvest began; and everybody had sampled the wheat and pronounced that the stalk snapped off sharply when bitten, thus proving its excellence by fulfilling an ancient test. The Land Girl provided by the West Sussex Agricultural Office at Mr Hoadley's request had arrived; she was a merry little thing named Mary Parkes and everybody liked her at sight. And then the B.B.C. broadcast that all over the country there was Risk of Thunder.

At once the farm's pleasant mood of anticipation was turned to anxiety. Sylvia (who was pleased at this threat of drama) frequently stopped her work to scan the cloudless sky, while Emilio (whose mood of late had been divided between fatherly indignation and swelling pride because his eldest *bambino* had been caught robbing an American lorry and promptly adopted by the regiment as a mascot) became sulky. Only Fabrio, bemused with love, hardly noticed what was being said.

However, Mr Hoadley decided to stand by his first plan, for he had a low opinion of the experts upon the Air Ministry roof, preferring to trust to the weather lore which he had followed since his father had taught it to him as a boy, and it was his

340

opinion that there would be no storms.

By tea-time the sky was still tranquil and cloudless and the heat showed no sign of becoming oppressive. Sylvia had the afternoon free, and had spent it quietly for once, resting in the garden at the back of the farmhouse and studying *The Petrified Forest*, in which she fancied herself in the part of Gabby.

Mary Parkes obligingly brought her tea out to her, and Sylvia, having overwhelmed her with loud and surprised thanks, cleared the tray in ten minutes. Then she set it down beside her chair, flung up her arms in a yawn, and decided to go for a walk.

It was too hot to move briskly, and she sauntered along the lanes enjoying the shade of overhanging trees until an open gate attracted her, and she wandered down a path that led through a field of ripe barley into the woods.

Late afternoon sunlight filled the coppices, and now and then a pigeon called among the green shadowy boughs. Her mood was quiet as the hour, and to-day she wanted neither excitement nor noise. She was happy, wandering on with a grass stem between her lips and her eyes fixed dreamingly upon the leafy distances, while there drifted through her mind the image of Fabrio's smiling face. That ever-returning image increased her happiness, and when she remembered that he would be at the farm when she returned, and was to stay there throughout the harvest, she parted her lips and sang softly to herself—in that voice which even his love for her had not been able to praise, but which now, sounding quietly in the stillness, had a lulling charm.

For once she was not thinking of any film hero; she was remembering Fabrio's kiss, and regretting that she had been unkind to him—but here her thoughts shrank in happy confusion—and she pulled a fresh head of grass, while a smile trembled upon her mouth and the woodland light shone down upon her young face.

Then she heard voices. Glancing away down a mossy ride she saw coming towards her Alda and the three children. She called and waved to them and they waved back and hastened to join her.

'Hot enough for you, Mrs Lucie-Browne?' she asked.

'Too hot——' as the party walked on, 'though one shouldn't grumble. It's grand for the harvest.'

'The wireless says there may be storms. It was on the eight o'clock news this morning.'

'I do hope not—it would be such a shame if the wheat were spoiled. We need it so badly.'

'Mr Hoadley doesn't think it'll come to anything. Are you coming to the Harvest Supper, Mrs Lucie-Browne? Mrs Hoadley said she was going to ask you and the kiddies.'

'Of course. We're looking forward to it.'

'Meg too?' glancing down at the small silent figure toiling along by Alda's side, with plump arms and back tanned to gold.

'Oh yes. She can sleep late the next day and it would be a pity for her to miss it—a harvest supper is something to remember.'

Alda was wondering how soon she could introduce the name of Fabrio. She was determined to give Sylvia advice, and here was the perfect occasion.

Usually she did not take much notice of people's appearance, for her practical mind was occupied with the plans and duties of the moment, but now she studied Sylvia and thought that she looked 'attractive' ('beautiful' did not come into Alda's vocabulary unless suggested by a landscape or flowers). Sylvia's white skin had gradually turned to rosy gold beneath the heat of the sun, and her hair, which to-day she wore parted in the centre and spread upon her shoulders in abundant curls, had acquired the glint of copper. Amidst this gold and bronze her blue eyes looked wonderfully cool and clear.

Alda slightly despised her, of course, for her lack of education and her wrong values, but as she looked at her she understood why Fabrio loved her.

'The Italians are staying at the farm for the harvest, aren't they?' she asked.

'Oh yes. Just over the harvest,' Sylvia answered, and that was all. No joke, no mock-rueful 'Worse luck!', none of her usual forthright comments followed, and a note in her voice, the slightest shade of consciousness in her manner, caused Alda to fix her at once with a keen, mischievous gaze.

'How do you get on with Fabrio nowadays?' she began.

'Oh—all right.' Sylvia turned aside to pull off another head of grass; she was suddenly alarmed, for she did not want to talk about Fabrio to anyone, least of all to Mrs Lucie-Browne with that look in her eyes. She wished that she could laugh too, but she could not: she only felt helpless, and her one wish was to keep her thoughts and her feelings about Fabrio to herself.

'Is he still as keen on you as ever?'

'Oh—I don't know—I don't think so. Who said he was——?' Her voice died off in a mutter.

'Nobody. The way he looks at you is enough.'

Sylvia said nothing. A kind of sickening misery was creeping over her. She had been so happy, and now everything was being dragged out and spoilt.

'You look at him as if you liked him, too,' the kind, teasing voice went on. 'You do, don't you?'

'He's all right.' At that moment she felt that she hated him, and Mrs Lucie-Browne as well. She added loudly, with an effort, 'He'll pass in a crowd with a shove,' and laughed.

'Well, you know, Sylvia, I think you might do very much worse than marry him. I'm sure he's going to ask you—he's got that look in his eye,' laughing. '*Has* he asked you yet?' and she inclined her charming face, full of curiosity and laughter, nearer to the girl's.

Sylvia could only shake her head.

'Well, I'm sure he will. And if you take my advice you'll say "Yes." That young man means business.'

Sylvia was trying to think of something to say, but it was useless, and she could only walk along in silence with a foolish smile and burning cheeks.

Alda glanced at her and thought that her sulky expression

was not becoming, then lightly slipped her arm through the other's sunburnt one.

'You're thinking about your stage career, I know. But actors don't make good husbands, Sylvia, and I'm sure that Fabrio would. And then what fun it would be, living in Italy! Sunshine all the year round, and it's such a beautiful place; you can't imagine how beautiful if you've never seen it. (I have; I spent my honeymoon there, in Venice.) You wouldn't be rich, of course, but you'd have a *real* life, with Fabrio's farm to live on——'

'It isn't Fabrio's, it's his eldest brother's.'

'Oh. Well, I expect he'll have a share in it——'

'Not for years, he says. There's a whole tribe of them—dirty, skinny, jabbering Eyeties. No thanks.' And she slipped her arm from Alda's and lifted up Meg, who had suddenly halted and stood gazing at her mother in weary silence.

Sylvia settled the hot little body, scented with sunlight and the sweetness of bruised grass, comfortably into her arms. Her throat ached, but she angrily swallowed, and began at once in her usual tone:

'No, really, Mrs Lucie-Browne, I'm afraid it's a case of no-can-do. I've known girls who've married foreigners and it's never worked. You never know what they're really like until they get you into their own country; they're quite different over here. Besides—hark at me! Better wait till I'm asked!'

'I think you're very silly. There aren't so many good-looking, devoted young men about, you know.'

'I'll chance it,' Sylvia said indifferently, setting Meg down as they reached the beginning of the meadows, and the edge on her voice, the expression on her face, foreshadowed how she would look in twenty years, if nothing befell her to bring the woodland light to dwell in her eyes for ever.

Alda was annoyed but she laughed.

'I'm sure it will be "yes," when he does ask you, all the same,' she said, as she beckoned to her children and moved away.

'I bet you it won't!' Sylvia called ringingly after her, and Alda turned with a mocking wave as she went through the cottage gate.

'What's up? You looked browned-off,' said Mary Parkes, as Sylvia came up the path.

'I'm all right; I've only got a bit of a headache.'

'Oh, I'm so sorry. It's the heat, I expect. Shall I get you an Aspro? You were so full of beans at lunch, weren't you? I've been laughing all over again at some of the things you said.'

Sylvia smiled vaguely and went up to her room.

Fabrio and Emilio had only been informed on the previous day that they were to sleep at the farm, and for the past twenty-four hours they had been alternately in delight, and in agony lest the authorities should at the last minute prevent them from going. Now they were safe; their passes signed and all formalities fulfilled; and here they were, actually spreading two lumpy mattresses upon the floor of a large old chamber, dim with dust and still scented by the apples which it had harboured last autumn, extending over the whole area of the farmhouse, and having one small window through which could be seen the elms, the pond and meadows, the distant woods, and far off the dark hills below a pink sky.

Fabrio's dreamy mood had gone and he was very gay, tossing the mattresses about and peering into all the dark corners of their bedchamber in search of rats or overlooked apples. Somewhere, under the same roof with him, was Sylvia, and the day after tomorrow he would ask her! Emilio dryly inquired why was he so cheerful.

'I am happy to be out of that thrice-cursed place.'

'*This* is not much of a place,' glancing about him. 'They might have given us a proper room with decent beds. For seven years I have not slept upon a proper bed.'

Emilio meant a soft bed, not a clean one.

'They have not enough rooms, as thou knowest well. We shall

be very comfortable here. Look!' and he brought out, from the shadowy corner where he had concealed it earlier in the day, a two-pound pot of redcurrant jelly. 'I will bring bread away from the supper-table and to-night thou and I will have a feast.'

'Ah-ha!' Emilio nodded. 'It is made by the *padrona* and will taste good. She cooks well. And to-morrow thou wilt go to Mass with this upon thy soul?'

Fabrio's expression became confused and sorrowful, and he shook his head.

'To-morrow I shall not go to Mass,' he muttered, and pushed the jar back into its place of concealment. He would go to confession and Mass no more until Sylvia had promised to be his wife, for he feared the keen eyes of Father Francesco upon his happy face, and searching questions as to his state of mind and heart. When once Sylvia was betrothed to him he would go to Mass again, for Father Francis could not command him to renounce a girl, even if she were a *protestante*, and thus break her heart.

As for Sylvia's heresies, he, Fabrio, would deal with them all in good time. She must give them up and become of the Faith, even as her husband was. His joyful expression returned, and he finished the spreading of the beds with a song from *Cavalleria Rusticana*.

He gave a last glance over the expanse of dim leafy country, rejoicing in the absence of hateful barbed wire, and drew in a breath of night air before he felt his way down the black narrow stairs behind Emilio, who was grumbling at the darkness.

He hoped to see Sylvia at supper-time, but Mrs Hoadley had instructed everyone to take bread and cheese and draw a cup of tea from the brown pot standing on the range (which had been lit for the Saturday night baths) without troubling her, and had gone up to bed. The two Italians, Mary Parkes and Mr Hoadley passed an hour or so of gossip with the door open to the twilight, but Sylvia too was tired, and had retired.

And the next day she had left for London before Fabrio was

even awake. Poor chaps, said Mrs Hoadley to her husband, it must be years since they had a lay-in, and he had rather grudgingly conceded that they need not be roused until eight o'clock. In any case, the Italians did not understand fully how to perform any of the tasks connected with the early milking because their own work had always been with the crops and soil, and Mary and Sylvia did the work before the latter left for London.

At home among her family, she threw herself into the loud discussions and chatter and noisy gossip with an interest she had not shown for weeks; vowing that she was sick and tired of the country, and only dying to get back to London and begin looking for work on the stage. Her brothers and sisters applauded, sitting about the kitchen and scattering cigarette ash on their dirty dressing-gowns while they coughed and argued and waved their arms about. The brown houses loured against the pale hot sky, and the ice-cream man's bell rang in the Sunday hush as he pedalled slowly down the drowsing streets. Once or twice the face of Fabrio came before Sylvia's eyes with a sensation of pain, and she laughed the louder and argued more fiercely.

The day passed quietly at the farm and the threatened thunder kept off. Fabrio was disappointed that Sylvia was not there, but the morning passed pleasantly enough for him in gossiping and dozing and roaming about, and in the afternoon he helped Emilio and Mary Parkes to put finishing touches to the long shed where the Harvest Supper was to be held. Two unemployed men from Horsham had been engaged to help with the work, and Mrs Hoadley flatly refused to entertain them in the farmhouse kitchen, fearing that they would stealthily take note of the house's locks and bolts and bars while eating their Harvest Supper, with future burglarious visits in mind. Mr Hoadley thought she was an ass but humoured her.

Mary Parkes was shyly taken by Fabrio's looks, and once or twice tried to draw him into conversation, but he answered politely and without real interest and although he worked

347

industriously his manner was absent, for all his thoughts were with Sylvia who, to-morrow, would be his.

About ten o'clock she came down the path between the snap-dragons and marigolds in the twilight, swinging in one hand a new hat made for her by her mother, and whistling.

'Hullo, all! Poo, is it hot!'

'I hope you've had your supper, Sylvia, for there's only two sandwiches left and Emilio's just finished the last of the lemonade,' warned Mrs Hoadley, peering desolately over plates and into jugs.

'Had some in town, but I could always find room for a bit more; you know me. Poo! I'm nothing but a grease-spot, I had to walk from the station,' and she sat down heavily upon the warm brick doorstep and sighed, pushing back her hair and arranging her dress over her knees. She smiled brilliantly upon the company (which had now started an earnest and most interesting discussion as to why the 9.10 bus from Horsham did not stop at the crossroads, conveniently for late returners to the farm) and offered to the party her cigarettes.

Fabrio was seated in the kitchen beyond the last faint light from the sky, and his eyes were fixed yearningly upon her, waiting for their own happy secret smile, but she did not look at him directly—or perhaps she did, but he could not see clearly in that dim light—and she only spoke to him amidst the general conversation, and when she took her candle and hurried upstairs at the end of the evening she gave him no more than the hasty 'Good night' which she threw over her shoulder at everyone.

That sent him to bed with a slight heartache, and the night was so hot that even he, used to the heat of Mediterranean nights, could not sleep. He and Emilio lay for some time smoking and talking in whispers; then they ate a pound of redcurrant jam and became so ragingly thirsty that Emilio had to make a perilous journey down to the kitchen for water, and tripped over the cat with much uproar and reassuring shouts in Italian to Mr Hoadley.

28

No one had slept well and everyone was irritable and pale as they assembled to begin the day's work. The two unemployed men arrived and their outraged comments upon the earliness of the hour were silenced with a cup of tea, while Sylvia and Mary hurried out to get the cows in and milked, and Emilio and Fabrio were instructed by Mr Hoadley to take the two new men down to the Big Field and lift the ground-sheet off the tractor attached to the harvester which he had borrowed from a large farm nearby.

The wheat stood up shadowy and still in the warm grey light. The sun was not yet risen, and the men's boots, already black with dew from their walk across the meads, soon ran with water as they moved about. There was not a ripple of wind, and the night-scents of wet grasses and the faint strawy breath from the wheat lingered on the air.

'Going to be a storm,' said Spray, one of the unemployed men, pausing to wipe his forehead and look up at the louring sky.

'Do not say so!' retorted Emilio crossly. Fabrio said nothing. He was not very happy but now, for the first time for days, when he saw it spread before him waiting to be reaped, he was not thinking of Sylvia, but only of this harvest, and how to get it in. A harvest was the same everywhere, no matter whether it was olives or grapes or wheat, and a storm threatened it in Liguria exactly as it did in Sussex. He hauled the ground-sheet off the tractor in great folds and packed it into a square, with energy. There was no time to be lost.

'What's your union, mate?' inquired the other elderly man

with mild sarcasm, sitting down on the slip-gate and lighting a cigarette. 'Where's the 'urry?' Fabrio did not answer but his lip curled. This fool was born in a town, he thought.

When the reaper was fixed to the tractor and the machine was ready to start, they went back for breakfast. It was already seven o'clock, and all the others were seated round the table eating hastily and almost in silence. Sylvia's pale face wore a sulky expression and she barely glanced at Fabrio, who ate a thick slice of cold fat bacon and drank off some tea with relish, after darting one loving but absent glance at her. He was eager to be out and at work. Emilio was not, and had to be ticked off for lingering.

At eight the noise of the engine broke the stillness in the waiting field and, with revolving flails, the reaper moved forward. The first swathe fell, pulling down with it one cornflower and a purple vetch, and lay spread. The harvest had begun.

Soon the harvesters were moving in, along the edge of the bronze wheat under the grey sky, stooping and gathering up the heavy sheaves. Down drooped the heads as they were lifted, a sure sign that the ears were full of corn. Fabrio was skilled at the stacking, and deftly, swiftly set each shock in position, and Mary Parkes, who followed him, was almost as expert, but Sylvia, who came after, let the wheat slide apart and topple over. Emilio was instructing the unemployed men, who maintained their air of outraged surprise at everything that happened, and Mr Hoadley drove the tractor.

Presently Alda and the children came down by the hedge, all wearing trousers and slightly too ready to laugh and make a game of the occasion. Mr Hoadley gave them a brief wave, Mary Parkes straightened herself for a moment with hands on hips to smile at Meg, and Alda, sobering her manner to meet the general feeling, crossed over to Fabrio to watch how he set the sheaves, with the stubble pricking through the soles of her soft shoes.

'Hullo, Mrs Lucie-Browne! This is quite like work! You wait!' called Sylvia. 'Come on, Jenny. I'll show you how to do it.'

After a few failures Alda was setting the sheaves almost as neatly as Mary, but soon she began to wish that she had worn long sleeves like the others. The sharp straws pricked her inner arm as she lifted them and soon it showed a scraped expanse of skin. Then her back began to ache, and she was very thirsty, sweat ran down into her eyes, insects settled on her face, and the stubbly furrows were increasingly uneasy to tread. Nevertheless, she was enjoying the work. There was satisfaction in setting each sheaf correctly, in seeing the heavy notched heads loll over into position and settle; in hearing, as if from afar, the stutter of the tractor's engine as it moved across the field, while all about her the pale gold shimmer coming up from the stubble merged into a dreamlike glare which lulled her senses.

Suddenly the glare brightened, and a warmth caressed her bending back.

'The sun!'

'Oh goody!'

'Now there will be no storm!'

'Look, Mudder, the sun!'

Everyone straightened their aching backs for a minute, standing upright and shading their eyes against the splendour rolling out between rapidly dissolving banks of cloud. Overhead the sky was already a dense blue.

By noon the day was brilliant, and two-thirds of the Big Field was reaped, while about half the wheat was in stook. The unskilled workers had kept steadily to their task, the elderly men because they had to in order to earn their wages, and Alda as a point of honour, though she excused the children when they began to complain of weariness and heat. Meg did so after about twenty minutes and went off with Mrs Hoadley. Louise was the next to wander away, leaving a scattered sheaf, and she went down to the little pool at the corner of the field to lie in the long grass and watch the moorhens amidst the bladderwort and water violets, but Jenny kept steadily on, and when the party broke off at noon for lunch Mr Hoadley brought a smile of pleasure to her brown face by calling her a proper little Land Girl.

They were seated in the spreading shade of the Big Meadow's one tree, a majestic oak whose branches stretched out a considerable distance across the waving wheat, while the roots formed little seats for those who despised comfort and ignored insects. The shade was very grateful, for all the land now shimmered in sunny light and the distant hills were black blue in the haze. Everyone was aching, burning with the sun and scratched with the straw.

Mr Hoadley had gone back to the farm to have lunch with his wife, and Emilio, who was not so deft at the stooking as Fabrio, had been sent to bring down the jugs of lemonade and the basket of sandwiches. Now everybody was eating heartily or awaiting their turn with one of the two cups, while the girls had removed their knotted caps to let the damp hair blow loose on their brows. Alda had at one point in the morning's work impatiently grasped her curls, screwed them up, and pinned them on top of her head. Everyone appeared hot and dishevelled except Fabrio, whose face only deepened in golden hue as the sun mounted higher and the heat increased, whose eyes looked blue and quiet under his straw hat's ragged brim. He lay comfortably on his elbow, munching steadily at an enormous sandwich and staring at the far hills. Hours of heavy labour in the heat followed by spells of utter idleness were natural to the Italian, and he was happy. Now, too, that the threatened storm had rolled away and half the harvest was reaped, his attention could turn fully to Sylvia. Slowly turning his head, he looked away from the hills that reminded him of home, and towards his girl.

Sylvia's tongue had been going steadily since eight o'clock in a flow of wisecracks that had kept everybody laughing, even the two unemployed men, who were slightly inclined to disapprove of her exuberance; and her silence at this moment was only due to a mouth full of sandwich. Her eyes, shining with enjoyment, continued to rove about the circle of faces. Only on Fabrio's face those eyes never lingered; their blue flash darted across him swiftly as a kingfisher over a pool, and he could not force her, by his own steady tender gaze, to meet his own.

He was not deeply disturbed. He thought: the little one is shy, and loved her the more. Of all the group gathered there under the oak—the experienced young matron, the poor elderly men with a knowledge of human nature gained in the dreary back streets and humble shops of a small country town, the young woman whose nature brimmed with natural kindness, the Italian experienced in the ways of petty crime—Fabrio alone was fitted to understand Sylvia. All that he believed about her was true. A gentle girl did live within her hoydenish body, and love for him would have set the shy prisoner free. But he made one fatal mistake: he underestimated the power of the tomboy, the rude Audrey, who kept her silent and in chains.

Soon all were at work again except Louise, who had come up from the pool to beg for her lunch and returned to share it with the moorhens. The last strip of wheat, with its population of cowering field mice, had now fallen to the reaper and Ruffler, who had been lying panting in the shade watching the workers, was encouraged by the elderly men and the Italian to go for 'em, boy, sic 'em, fetch 'em out, and so forth. He turned his large eyes upon the hunters as if to inquire, *Do you really think I'm going after mice, as if I were a cat, in this heat?* then shut them with a sigh and put his head down upon his paws.

Mr Hoadley now stopped the tractor and came over to the harvesters to express his satisfaction. Three-quarters of the Big Field was covered with stooks, and so well was the harvesting ahead that he wanted Mary Parkes and Fabrio to attend to various tasks which had been postponed. While they went off (Mary looking willing and Fabrio looking glum) he drove the tractor through the gate and down the road to start on the Small Meadow, and the elderly men were encouraged by the forward state of the work—and perhaps also by his absence—to 'ave a bit of a breather and a fag. Emilio joined them, but Alda and Jenny kept on with their stooking.

Presently Alda became aware through the pleasant daze of fatigue in which she was working that a fourth person had joined the group under the tree, and she glanced up and saw that it was Mr Waite. He happened to be looking in her direction, and ceremoniously lifted the bankrupt fishmonger hat. She replied with a cheerful wave, wondering whether he were telling the men that he Must Help, and in a moment it appeared that he was, for he rolled down his sleeves and came towards her. He looked gloomier, yet handsomer, than she had ever seen him, for he had lost weight and the whiteness of his shirt was becoming to his tanned skin.

Jenny stopped working for a minute to make him warmly welcome, for she continued to think of him as martyred by Jean's unkindness, and then he set to work by Alda's side, and for some time all three laboured in silence. Then Mr Waite remarked abruptly that he couldn't stay long because he had the battery birds to feed, and had only looked in to give a hand so that he could say that he had. ('Like stirring the Christmas pudding,' put in Jenny.)

'Aren't you coming to the Harvest Supper?' asked Alda.

'Oh yes, *do* come!' Jenny hauled up a sheaf almost as large as herself and set it in place. 'Do, Mr Waite.'

He muttered something about being busy or having letters to write and looked gloomier still. But Alda had caught one glance at her that was almost despairing, and felt truly sorry for him, amidst all the pleasant activity and bustle in such glorious weather. Could he be deeply in love with Jean, after all? and longing for some news of her though it might bring him fresh pain? She resolved to break the awful silence which had surrounded her friend's name for the past six weeks.

'Have you heard from Jean?' she inquired cheerfully, bending to set a sheaf in place in order not to look at him. 'She hasn't written to me once, the wretch.'

'No. Er—no, I haven't,' he answered, very stiffly indeed.

At this moment Jean herself was creeping along behind the hedge not twenty yards from where Alda and Mr Waite stood.

There was no need for her to creep, as they certainly could not have heard her uncertain footsteps as she hobbled (she was wearing high heels) along the ridges or jumped awkwardly from one tussock of bleached grass to the next, but her whole manner expressed guilt, secrecy, haste and the desire to conceal herself, and every time she passed a thin place in the screen of thorn and wild roses, she bent herself almost double. If her friend and her former betrothed had glanced towards the hedge they would have seen her white coat gliding by, but they did not, and she was able to gain the safety of the first chicken house and dart behind it.

Then she paused for a rest, feeling the warm wind blowing lazily against her flushed cheeks.

It brought the scent of white clover but was too gentle even to stir the flowers themselves in the grass. There was not a cloud in the deep blue sky, and the only sounds were the voices of the harvesters behind the hedge, the distant throbbing of the tractor engine, and the low remarks of the chickens as they wandered and pecked about her feet. Jean looked all about her. She noticed the sheds that badly needed a fresh coat of creosote, the rusty broken wire enclosing the runs, and, in the grass, that tall yellow flower whose presence means that a field will one day be completely covered by it and the soil ruined. Clearly, Mr Waite's property had declined in value even since her absence; the field and sheds had never looked prosperous, but now they looked far gone towards decay.

Nevertheless, something within her spirit gladly exclaimed 'Oh *yes*!' to this ordinary meadow full of weeds and these shabby sheds under the blue sky. She breathed the scent of the warm clover and felt more at peace than she had felt for weeks. Presently she sat down upon a tuffet of wiry grass with two bellflowers in it, and took off her shoes and smoked a cigarette. She could still hear the voices of Alda and Mr Waite at intervals but she was unable to distinguish their actual words. Later, she heard congratulatory exclamations and gathered that the last sheaf had been stooked, and that the harvesters were about to move on to the Small Meadow. She hastily put on her shoes again and hurried away in the direction of Mr Waite's cottage.

After replying briefly to Alda's question, the latter had said no more for some time, and she simply had not had the courage—so strong was his expression of displeasure—to reopen the subject. She had given him the opportunity to ask questions if he had wanted to, and he had not taken it. If he chooses to make an asinine martyr of himself, thought Alda, he must get on with it, that's all; he's like some hero out of a Victorian novel, suffering in silence and proudly enduring and all the rest of it. Nobody does that nowadays, not even the very young. I give him up.

She had been working steadily since eight o'clock with only half an hour's rest, and now began to feel very tired. She was therefore not surprised—indeed, she was relieved, for the child's deeply flushed face had been troubling her—when Jenny suddenly asked if her mother thought Mr Hoadley would mind if she stopped work now. Alda emphatically assured her of Mr Hoadley's willing consent, and she strolled off to find Louise, but first she so earnestly begged Mr Waite to attend the Harvest Supper that he promised he would. When she had gone, he told Alda that he must get back to the cottage to mix the battery birds' food and then make himself a cup of tea; it was nearly four. 'So late?' said Alda in surprise, and then there came exclamations of satisfaction from Emilio and the hired men: the last sheaf had been set in place.

Alda decided to put some grease on her burning face and re-pin her hair before going on to the Small Meadow, so she returned to Pine Cottage. Tea had been promised about half-past four in the Small Meadow, and to her at least it would be exceedingly welcome, for she was as tired, hot and parched as if she had been rolling in stubble for weeks. She glanced out of the window while at her toilet, and was rewarded by a distant view of Mr Waite, a lonely figure in white shirt and straw hat, walking slowly towards his cottage between the green grass and blue sky.

On arriving at the Small Meadow she found it already reaped and almost half the wheat in stook, for Mary Parkes and Fabrio had joined the others there; six people could make light work of stooking the Small Meadow, which was less than an acre in extent. Sylvia was grumbling loudly about the heat, her tiredness and the flies, but working as hard as at the beginning of the day. Alda noticed that she was at the extreme end of the line from Fabrio, and it now occurred to her that the girl had been in this place all day. Had they quarrelled?

Mr Hoadley now appeared, carrying a pail filled with scalding tea and a garden trug packed with rock cakes baked on the previous day by Mrs Hoadley. Behind him came Mrs Hoadley herself, dressed in a blue smock and leading by the hand Meg, whose scanty hair was curled up at the ends and adorned by an enormous pink satin bow whose ends fell into her eyes. They approached with dignity, Mrs Hoadley looking pityingly at the hot, silent, dusty group sprawling in the stubble under the shadow of a stook, and Meg strutting beside her wearing an expression of insufferable conceit.

'You poor dears, you do look hot,' commented Mrs Hoadley. 'We were the lucky ones, weren't we, Meg, having our dinner in the nice cool kitchen?'

Meg trotted towards Alda, crying:

'Don't I look a lovely girl, Mudder?'

Alda caught her up with a hearty kiss and told her she looked beautiful, while Mrs Hoadley complacently observed that she did like to see the best made of a child's looks. Louise and Jenny came up for their share of rock cakes and tea, and everyone drank thirstily and rested in the shade for nearly an hour, for they were all much wearier than at lunch time, and as the work in the Small Meadow was nearly completed they could afford to take a longer spell.

Fabrio was now disturbed by the behaviour of Sylvia. Not once, all day, had she exchanged with him their smile, not once had she spoken to him apart, or even looked at him. She had kept as far away from him as she could. She would not answer properly when he had asked her what the matter was. She had only laughed and answered, 'Nothing's the matter, what do you mean?' without looking at him. He could not draw attention to himself by leaving his work to speak to her, and he had been able to make only two hurried attempts to find out what was the matter during the rests for lunch and tea. Both had been unsuccessful, and now he lay on the grass, as close to her as he could get (but Jenny and Emilio and Meg were between them) with his gaze fixed imploringly on her as he ate his fifth rock cake. And still she would not look at him! To-day was to be their day of betrothal. What could be the matter?

Mr Hoadley was satisfied with the day's work. Both fields would be harvested by seven o'clock (it was now five) and although it was annoying to have engaged two workers to get the wheat in quickly because of threatened storms that had not come, the extra men had worked well. To-morrow he would go into Brighton and sleep the night there. There was a two-day sale of the contents of a large house in Hove that he wanted to attend in order to buy bedroom furniture, and now he could do so with an easy mind.

The weather continued glorious until the end of that day, and when at last they all gathered round the last sheaf in the

Small Meadow, rubbing their aching arms and vowing to one another to eat and drink enormously at supper, the harvest moon was rising above the field set with rows of sheaves, and the stars promised to be of Southern size and brilliance.

'What's the matter with you and Fabrio? Had a quarrel?'

Alda came into the shed where the trestles were laid, and, seeing Sylvia loitering, went up to her. They were alone. Soft dusk filled the long bare chamber, and on one wall the first moonlight faintly shone. Sylvia had twisted some large pink roses into a clumsy crown for herself and wore the pink and white dress which exposed her throat and bosom. She had been staring moodily at the table but now glanced up.

'Nothing's the matter. I don't know what you mean,' she said irritably.

'My dear child, I've got eyes. You haven't been near him all day.'

'There hasn't been much time to-day for anything but harvesting, Mrs Lucie-Browne. Oh, there's Megsy—doesn't she look sweet—I'm glad you've taken off that awful bow—some people haven't any taste,' and she went off to meet the three children.

If ever a girl longed to say to an older woman, 'Mind your own business,' Sylvia had longed to say it to Alda then. She almost had said it. But her youth, her manners, her pride, had kept the words in check. She had forced them back, and they now worked within her, increasing her anger against Fabrio. If he hadn't behaved like a fool all day, staring at her with sick-monkey eyes, people would not have noticed and made nosey remarks.

At that moment he came into the room, carrying a brilliant lamp whose light shone upon his freshly brushed chestnut head. She turned her back upon him, and unnecessarily rearranged Jenny's dress.

After him came Emilio, also carrying a lamp and with eyes eagerly roving over the supper-table, which at present bore nothing but a white cloth, the farmhouse's muster of second-best cutlery and crockery, and the large Harvest Cake, baked and iced by Mrs Hoadley, and adorned with a miniature sheaf of real wheat tied with blue ribbon, and the words HAPPY HARVEST. (An anthropologist, surveying it, might have marvelled at the distance travelled from the rites of the Spring Queen and the Corn King, but behind Mrs Hoadley's cake the spirit of the latter still dwelt serene.)

Emilio set his lamp down at one end of the table; Fabrio set his down at the other, and they surveyed the scene with smiles (even Fabrio smiled at that moment) of anticipation. Enter the two elderly men, bent beneath the weight of a small barrel of cider, which they arranged upon a bench near the door. They were followed by Mr Hoadley, pushing a wheelbarrow filled with the solid portions of the supper; three cold chickens and a jellied rabbit pie in the largest earthenware dish, a salad of lettuces and tomatoes grown in the farm's kitchen garden, and a vast smoking pot of potatoes. His arrival was welcomed with cries of admiration. Behind him came Mary Parkes bearing a tray with an enormous brown teapot.

'In case the ladies didn't fancy cider,' explained Mrs Hoadley, who brought up the rear, still dressed in her blue smock and now bursting out into little blue bows on either side of her head. 'Now are we all here?' She anxiously counted heads, waving her finger up and down as she recited names under her breath, while Fabrio's heart beat painfully. Oh, would his place be next to Sylvia?

'No!' exclaimed Mrs Hoadley. 'Mr Waite! Mr Waite isn't here. Now I told him supper was at eight o'clock sharp. It's too bad of him.'

'Well, we can't *wait* for Mr *Waite*,' declared Mr Hoadley, and amidst the laughter which followed they all took their places;

the women arranging their scanty flowered skirts and the men climbing awkwardly in between trestle and bench. The soft brilliant light of the lamps shone becomingly upon reddened lips and hair brightened by the sun, upon white teeth and laughing eyes and the jars filled with second bloomings of roses and fresh moon-daisies; it coloured the walls with gold and gave warmth to the lined grey countenances of the hired men and the little face of Meg, already pale with drowsiness, while in the vista seen through the open door, where strengthening moonlight poured down through the still air, it gave deeper blue to the twilight.

Fabrio was in despair. She had turned her back on him—she was going as far away from him as she could—right down to the very end of the table among all those children—she would not look at him——

He started towards her with an imploring gesture; it seemed to him afterwards that he had cried out her name—but it was all useless—she was sitting down between the tallest child and the *bambina*—she had chosen her place for the Harvest Supper, and it was not by his side.

His head drooped and his hands fell hopelessly. He stepped into the place which Mary Parkes was offering him and for some minutes stared dully at the table without speaking. The white cloth shimmered through a rainbow. Presently Fabrio blew his nose upon a far from spotless khaki handkerchief.

'Dear, will you ask a blessing,' Mrs Hoadley was requesting, having put on a special face and voice, and Mr Hoadley stood up, rather embarrassed by the occasion as he had been for the last ten years, and said—while the countenances of those seated about the table became 'recollected,' as if each had received a picture of the sheaves standing in the moonlit fields— 'For what we are about to receive, may God make us truly thankful.'

Everyone except Fabrio muttered *Amen* (God and Our Lady had deserted him; why should he thank them?) and Mrs Hoadley began dishing out pie with a rapid, experienced touch, resignedly loading a single plate with more food than she herself could have eaten at three meals.

When they had been eating for about ten minutes, a step sounded outside in the yard and everyone rightly assumed it to be Mr Waite's; what was unusual was the quick cheerful whistle accompanying it. In he came, his manner brisker than anyone had seen it for weeks, and sat himself down with apologies for his lateness next to Mrs Hoadley. As he did so he glanced at Alda, a good-naturedly derisive glance that said plainly: 'Ah-ha! Guess!' and she spent some minutes wondering what he meant and why he was so spry this evening.

We must now go back some hours, and find out.

29

On finishing his harvesting he had, as we know, walked slowly back to Meadow Cottage, promising himself a cup of tea and a glance over the local paper before starting on his evening duties. He went in by the back way and as he stepped into the kitchen he sniffed. Old Miss Dodder must have brought in a bunch of honeysuckle. But no; that scent never came from real flowers. Someone must be in the house, and, like the Big Bear, Mr Waite knew who it was. He stalked down the passage and opened the parlour door and sure enough there sat Jean.

She stood up at once, smiling and seeming not in the least nervous.

'Hullo, Phil. I'm sorry if you're annoyed with me for coming, but I had something to ask you and I did so want to see you again.' And she held out her hands. When he took them in his (partly because they looked so pretty, with their whiteness and their jingling silver sillinesses, and partly because he was so confused that he did not know quite what to do) she reached up as calmly as possible and kissed him. Then there was a pause.

'I expect you'd like some tea. I'll get it,' he said gruffly.

'I'd love some. I'm parched. I'll come and help you,' she answered.

He wanted to say sarcastically, 'My kitchen isn't fit to receive you, in that coat,' but the words would not come out, because he was pleased to see her.

'And I can talk to you while we're making it,' she continued, following him out to the kitchen, and again he noticed how completely at ease she was. She ought not to be. She had behaved disgracefully. Yet he too felt at ease and he could not be angry with her. He ought to be, but he could not. And what had she got to say to him?

When the kettle had been put on the stove, Jean sat on the table. He silently placed a newspaper beside her and indicated that it would protect her coat and she absently re-seated herself on it. Then she looked at him. With his dark patient face a little lowered, he looked back at her. He was thinner; there were shadows under his eyes; his firm mouth had a new, slight expression of pain. Suddenly her eyes filled and she glanced away. She had hurt him—it did not matter how—in his pride or his ambition or his love—she had hurt him very much.

'Oh Phil!' she burst out, 'I am so sorry I was so beastly to you! I came down here to ask you if you would let me be engaged to you again, only I was going to ask if I might have a holiday by myself in Europe first, and if you would let me try to make you a Christian, but now I've seen you I'm so *very* fond of you, dear, kind—I'm so sorry——' and the tears came, and soon she was sobbing and mopping and incoherently protesting her remorse.

Slowly, but without awkwardness, he put his arm round her. He did not pat her, or say anything. Even when the kettle boiled all over the gas and the kitchen became filled with a most alarming smell, he did not move. He did give one glance at the stove, for this was precisely the kind of disaster which fussed him most, but he did not move, and in a minute Jean said more quietly:

'Put it out, dear, or we shall be blown up.'

He did so, and made the tea and arranged it on a tray with his accustomed neatness, and they returned to the parlour. All this time he had not spoken, but suddenly he said:

'What about—that chap?'

He meant Mr Potter, whose name he knew perfectly well; he merely refused to utter it.

'I don't love him any more. I never did really love him. I just liked kissing him. Phil!' urgently, as his expression changed, 'if we are going to be husband and wife I've *got* to be able to say things like that to you and you must *not* be shocked. You *must* know what I'm really like, and I must know what you're like, too. Haven't you ever enjoyed kissing someone without liking them as a person?'

He made an effort to meet all this as she wanted him to; she could see him trying, and presently he admitted that there had, once, been someone, in Daleham, when he was about twenty, like that.

'Well, then, can't you understand how I felt?'

'In a way, but one doesn't expect a lady——'

'I know, Phil. But I was romantic about him, too. I idealised him——'

Mr Waite thought that she meant 'idolised,' and this error took some time to get straight, but the time was not wasted because she was able to describe the luxurious, boring, wasteful life of Mr Potter and his set so vividly that Mr Waite's hurt pride was soothed. Behind his own materialistic view of life and his longing for money and comfort, there lingered a tradition from hard-working, thrifty provincial ancestors with a serious outlook, and he understood how, though he did not fully understand why, Jean had become satiated with the life of pleasure. He shrank with real horror from extravagance, and to himself he used very blunt words about those lady friends of Mr Potter's who spent a morning in drinking, and an afternoon in hunting down a lipstick.

While she was talking, he studied her. She was sleeker than when he had seen her last, having put on a little weight, and her clothes were even more expensive. But still they were not so smart as to frighten a provincial who was also a quiet man; still they were becoming, and softer than fashion decreed, and as he watched her, tenderness grew in his heart. She had rather queer ideas for a lady, but he would try to understand what she meant. After all, he owed her something. If she had gone off with that chap Potter, *he* had asked her to marry him without really loving her. But now he felt quite different about her. As he sat there, watching her and patiently trying not to be shocked by what she said, warmth and joy and other unfamiliar emotions softly invaded Mr Waite's poor gloomy heart. With any luck, he thought, we shall be happy together for years and years. Happy. I've almost forgotten what that feels like. The last time that he had been truly, carelessly happy had been in Cambridge that week before his father's business had failed. Since that day, his life had been one long suppression of all the softer feelings; one long, dour refusal to laugh or approve or join in.

She was saying:

'I'm a Christian. I believe all of it, with all my heart. You won't mind, will you?'

Habit dies hard, and again Mr Waite was tempted to be shocked.

'*Mind?* Why should I? Of course not. We're all on the Same Road, if it comes to that, and all the Great Teachers——'

'And you won't mind if I go to church?' she interrupted.

'Of course not, Jean. I'm not a heathen. I'll come too, if you want me to.' He got up from his chair and began to put the cups on the tray, for his feelings were so agitating that he automatically tried to calm them by this ordinary task.

'I came down here so pleased with myself,' she confessed, beginning on the cups in her turn. 'I wasn't a bit nervous. I was sure you'd have me back, and I'd got it all planned. Then when I saw you looking so—I felt quite different, Phil. You're sure you really do want me?'

'I do now, Jean. Since you believe in speaking right out,' with an awkward little laugh, 'at first I wanted your money. Oh, I liked you all right,' he added hastily (it did sound shocking, said out loud like that!). 'What I mean is, I thought about the money too.'

'That doesn't matter, so long as we both know it. I—well, I wanted a husband more than I wanted you. But now,' she moved nearer to him and took his hand and looked up into his face, 'we feel all right about each other, don't we?'

Mr Waite pressed the cool hand with its jingling bracelets hard within his own, but he only said severely:

'And how about that other chap? How's *he* feeling this evening?'

'He doesn't know yet,' she confessed. 'I left a note for him at the hotel. I don't think he'll really mind. He'd realised I wasn't his dish, I think, some weeks ago. He'll probably marry one of his hags.'

'Was he after your money, too?'

'Not altogether, Phil. He——'

But she checked herself, and suggested they should take out the cups and wash them. She had been going to say that Mr Potter had truly enjoyed kissing her but she thought it wiser not to tax her new betrothed's sensibilities too heavily. So they washed up the cups in companionable silence; Mr Waite refraining from saying that that chap had been badly treated, and Jean refraining from explanations. She also refrained from mentioning again her proposed holiday in Europe, for now it seemed to her that she had been lonely for a long time, and that master-pieces in paint and stone, viewed in loneliness still, were not what she wanted.

She learned that he had made acceptable excuses for her to his mother and sisters, and that her flighty behaviour had been successfully concealed from them. They were still collecting teaspoons and embroidering table runners in Daleham, and ready to receive her whenever she could come. Everything had been made much easier for her than she deserved, and she felt humbled.

After they had made their plans, they were surprised to find that it was seven o'clock, and Jean said that she must go back to town. She declined without a second's hestitation his suggestion that she should attend the Harvest Supper and he did not press the matter. Alda's part in their affairs had not been mentioned. Mr Waite had mixed feelings about her which he did not care to investigate, and Jean was only aware of one strong wish: not to be exposed to the teasing, autocratic gaze of her friend's lovely eyes. She had taken Alda's advice for fifteen years, and it had led her into the arms of Mr Potter and almost into the unrelaxing clutches of Pleasure. Now she would follow her own reason and her own feelings. Dim and unexciting as their counsel might seem to Alda, they were responsible for the calm contentment of the present hour, and their promises for the future were hopeful. There was a strong satisfaction in managing her own affairs, and she did not want to meet Alda until she was certain that her new confidence in herself would endure.

Mr Waite drove her to the station and remained with her, discussing plans, until the train came in, and then stood waving until he could distinguish no more than a white speck receding swiftly into the distance. Then he hurried out to his car and drove fast towards Naylor's. It was almost eight now, and he did not want to be asked a lot of questions.

He was soberly content as he drove on through the evening light. There were many legal and financial points to be decided and the next weeks would be exceedingly busy, but his attitude towards his betrothed had altered so much that his chief feeling now was joy at having her back again: the practical details were set aside. He hastily assembled the repulsive ingredients of the battery birds' supper and served them before hurrying off to his own, and as he went, he rejoiced maliciously in the defeat of Mrs Lucie-Browne. It would be amusing (Mr Waite relished the word, an unfamiliar one in his vocabulary) to meet her this evening, completely ignorant of what had occurred and thinking of Jean as still engaged to that chap. It would make her look a bit of a fool, thought Mr Waite, and serve her right. She had meddled too much.

As Jean travelled towards London, her mood was as quietly content as his own. She had lately been endeavouring to practise one of the tenets of the Christian Faith, and avoid fussing about the future. She repeated to herself *Sufficient unto the day*—and *Consider the lilies of the field*—and found both sayings increasingly comforting. Her nature had always been placid; she was a spectator, an observer, rather than a doer, and she found herself able to avoid fuss without much effort. She hoped that poor Phil, who was always on the boil, might be encouraged by her example to lower the gas and relax.

Therefore, following her principles, she had broken her engagement to Mr Potter as easily as she snapped a thread of sewing silk. Her note to him was not the result of much careful thought; she had merely written down exactly what she felt, sealed it, and given it to a page boy to deliver.

Dear Oliver,

I don't want to be engaged to you any more as we haven't any interests in common. Thanks awfully for giving me such a good time. I enjoyed it very much. I am sorry if your feelings are hurt. I thought I loved you but I don't. All the best and good luck.

Yours ever,

J.

And poor Mr Potter, who never wrote or said or even thought exactly what he felt, was simply knocked out by it, like the pilot of an enormously complicated aeroplane suddenly blinded by a speck of dust. He just could not believe it. He swelled with mingled fury and suspicion. What was her game? What did she want? He read the note five or six times; he turned it inside out looking for postscripts; he almost smelled it in his passion to read into it some complicated and sinister meaning. The page boy left him sitting in an overstuffed chair with a tiny icy drink before him, reading and re-reading this outrageous little letter, and went away bawling for other, happier gentlemen, and still Mr Potter sat on. Never in all his easy authoritative life had such a thing befallen him.

We hope that some readers are not licking their lips in anticipation of a blazing row between Jean and Mr Potter staged in the Savoy Grill, for we have to disappoint them. We will so far concede to their morbid expectations as to admit that both wore evening dress—rows are so much more satisfying when the antagonists are *en grande tenue*—but they did not meet. Jean had just finished changing her clothes when a telephone call was put through to her room. She removed the receiver, and listened long enough to assure herself that it was his own mellow voice demanding what was the matter with her and appealing for fair play; then she replaced it, caught up her evening coat and rushed out of the Savoy by another entrance. A fleeting notion that it was her duty to stay engaged to Mr Potter in order to save his soul she instantly dismissed as morbid.

She dined somewhere else; and afterwards went on to the last act of a play.

The next day Mr Potter launched the Awful Silence tactic.

Jean allowed it to remain unbroken.

The following day he sent her roses, and she remembered to return his ring, which had been lying forgotten in the drawer where she had thrown it.

The rest is silence—unless the reader cares to hear the verdict of Mr Potter's lady friends upon Jean's behaviour. They all said they had always suspected that she was borderline, and now they knew it.

30

Fabrio cast imploring glances towards Sylvia but in vain; she would not look at him, and giggled and whispered with Jenny and Louise. Emilio, who had an alarmingly weak head, was seated near the cider barrel and stealthily refilled his mug every time Mr Hoadley's attention was distracted from his end of the table; soon he became smiley and knowing and inclined to put his arm round Mary Parkes, who did not like this at all, though she met his efforts with an uneasily good-humoured smile. The low-ceiled shed became very hot in the brilliance and warmth of the lamps, and the motionless air beyond the open door gave no relief. Faces began to shine and flowers to wilt as the generous helpings upon the plates diminished, and conversation became more general and cheerful and was presently interrupted by bursts of laughter. Even Mr Waite made some dry jokes (usually at other people's expense), for his private good news put him in an indulgent mood.

It all seemed most comfortable to Fabrio: the brilliant light and savoury food, and the flow of stinging golden drink from that little barrel; and how he would have enjoyed it all—if only she had been kind! But there was a miserable load where his heart was, and a dreadful anticipation of worse unhappiness to come. He had lived on hope for months and grown used to that intoxicating but unsatisfying diet, and now that it seemed about to be taken away and replaced by starvation or bitter dregs, he could hardly bear it. He had planned such tender words: he knew exactly what he would say to her; night after night as he lay awake in the camp he had whispered those words to himself and imagined the scene—and now, she would not let him speak. His heart was breaking.

Alda observed his pale face and his silence, and pitied him so warmly that she resolved, in spite of the discouraging results of her former attempt, to speak to Sylvia again when supper was over. Every now and then she encountered the ironical gaze of Mr Waite and once he raised his glass to her as if in a toast—a gesture so out of keeping with his usual behaviour that she could only stare, but then she laughed and nodded, showing her pretty teeth and gaily raising her glass in return.

Mr Waite for his part felt triumphant and rather spiteful and years younger. Memories of parties in his youth returned to him, and that love of pleasure which he had ignored for twenty years suddenly, delightfully awoke in him, in spite of the uncouth surroundings and the shabby table appointments. (The poor man did not realise that he was surrounded by the true luxury—beautiful light, flowers, fragrant scents, simple but delicious food—which appeals instantly to the senses and does not rely upon such secondary comforts as stainless steel or draught-proof walls. How far from understanding human beings are those advertisers who promise us electric irons when we crave for fresh grapes!)

Sylvia's anger abated as the supper went on, for she was too devoted to pleasure and too light-hearted to resist the enjoyments spread about her, and she amused herself by twisting flower crowns for the children and piling their plates with food, giggling across the table at Emilio and exchanging jokes with Mr Hoadley and Mary Parkes. So long as she could avoid catching Fabrio's eye she now wished him no harm, but woe betide him—she vowed to herself—if he came up to her and tried getting fresh after supper. Then he *would* have had it.

Mrs Hoadley ate a small meal while keeping an eye upon everybody's plate. She wanted everyone to enjoy the Harvest Supper. No doubt ill-effects would result; those children would have bad dreams from all that meat at night, and it was high time baby Meg was in bed; Emilio must have had a good third of that barrel to himself already, and she noticed that the man

Spray, whose diet at home was mainly sausages and bread, was struggling to conceal hiccups, while cider never did agree with Neil. As for Fabrio, he looked as if he had lost sixpence, and that great camel Sylvia was making enough noise for six. Mrs Hoadley would have preferred a cup of tea and a small slice of the cake alone in the kitchen with Mary Parkes, who seemed a nice refined girl; she used to work in a high-class perfume and cosmetics shop in Brighton, about which Mrs Hoadley would have enjoyed hearing. However, she was glad that everything was going well. Even this old shed did not look too bad, though of course you could not really enjoy yourself in a shed with chipped crockery and bent cutlery and such mixed company.

At this moment Joyanna gave her mother a strong kick, as if telling her not to be such a bore, and Mrs Hoadley's thoughts took another turn.

Mr Hoadley glanced affectionately at his wife's pretty, peaked face. He admired her blue smock and those gallant bows in her hair, which seemed as if they were trying to ignore her clumsy form. Good old Molly, she's the sort that would spread a table-cloth on a desert island, he thought, and for a moment his thoughts left the harvest, with which they had been concerned all the evening, and he hoped that Joyanna (but Mr Hoadley was not sure that it was going to be named Joyanna) would reconcile her mother to life in the country. The country's the place to bring up children, thought Mr Hoadley, and if there's two or three more to come, now Molly's started, there'll be no excuses for moving into town.

At length the last piece of rabbit had been conveyed to the last mouth, and he leant back in the Windsor chair and pushed aside his plate crowded with delicate bones.

'And how about you?' he inquired of Meg, who was seated next to him. 'Ready for plum fool?'

Meg opened her eyes with a start and smiled drunkenly. The thick pale pink cream was already being ladled out, and she did make an attempt on it but so slowly, nodding the while, that Alda hurried her through the last spoonfuls and gathered her up.

'I'll pop her into bed,' she said to Mrs Hoadley. 'It won't take me twenty minutes and she'll never hold up to the end.'

'Mother! You said she could see the cake cut!' cried Jenny sternly.

'It's only once in her lifetime,' pleaded Louise, with enormous eyes peering out under a straggling wreath of willowherb. '*Do* let her.'

'Meg will see the cakie!' at once announced Meg, opening her eyes and lifting her head from Alda's shoulder.

'Meg shall see the cakie,' soothed the cunning Alda, 'look, there it is, in the middle of the table.'

Meg leant forward and peered earnestly, while everybody smilingly watched.

She had on a white dress powdered with blue buds which was long for her because it had belonged to an elder cousin; and her thin silky hair, scarcely confined by a white band, fell about her flushed cheeks. Beneath the frilled hem of the dress hung down her little naked brown feet.

'There! Isn't that a lovely cakie. Now Meg has seen it, she can come to bed.'

'Mother. That isn't fair!' in a disgusted voice from Jenny. 'You said she could see it *cut*.'

But Alda was already half-way to the door.

She had told Mrs Hoadley not to wait for her return to cut the cake, and now everyone caught up a plate and crowded towards the head of the table. Sylvia was going with the rest when Fabrio, taking advantage of the general movement and acting with the recklessness of misery, hurried down the table and slipped into the seat at her side.

'Sylvia! Love!' he muttered, scarcely knowing what he was saying. 'Why are you angry with me? What have I done?' And he tried to take her hand.

Instantly Louise whirled round and stared at him with wide eyes blazing with surprise. He took no notice of her and she stood there, the plate which had been held out so eagerly beginning to droop in her hand as she gazed wonderingly first at him and then at Sylvia, who had also turned quickly round, shaking off his imploring hand.

'Sylvia!' he repeated, and then was silent, staring up at her.

'What on earth's the matter?' she said, laughing angrily, with an embarrassed glance at Louise.

'Will you—will you come away with me a little while? To go for a walk?' he said. 'Please, *Sylvia mia*, come,' and he caught at her arm.

Louise kept her eyes, now grave and wondering, fixed upon his face. She was not yet of an age to understand the scene even dimly, and she vaguely thought that Fabrio must be ill. He looked ill. She felt sorry for him.

'What, in the middle of supper? So likely I'm going off for a walk with you, isn't it?' Sylvia answered roughly.

'But I want to say something—to speak to you, Sylvia——'

The touch of her round golden arm, glowing from the sun's heat, inflamed him. He frowned and turned pale beneath the deep brown of his skin. His lip trembled.

'Sylvia—it is important—you *must* come,' he said loudly.

Here Jenny became aware that something unusual was going on behind her, and turned round. Her brilliant eyes, which no longer looked on the world so innocently since her friendship with June Wilson, took in the situation at once and she exploded into the gushing, uncontrollable, maddening giggles of early girlhood. Louise instantly caught the infection without knowing why and they both bent over the table, letting their plates slide from their hands while they rocked and rippled, their bright eyes stealing sidelong glances first at Fabrio and then at Sylvia and then at one another.

Their laughter irritated Sylvia beyond endurance, the more

because the sight of Fabrio's pale pleading face touched her. She was so embarrassed and confused that for a moment she did not know what to say; then she turned furiously on them, exclaiming, 'Shut up, can't you?' But her tone and expression did not subdue Jenny and Louise, who came of a family which had no experience of violence and regarded bad temper as a joke, and they went on giggling. Fabrio neither saw nor heard them. He only saw his love's face.

'I must ask you something,' he said again, in a quieter tone. 'Please-a, come, Sylvia?'

'I want some cake, that's all I know,' she retorted. 'And so do you, I suppose. Here's a plate,' snatching one and holding it out to him. 'S'sh, now, Mr Hoadley's going to speak.'

Mr Hoadley had assumed a patient attitude as he waited for that chattering and giggling down at the far end to cease. When it did—for Fabrio held the *padrone* in too much respect not to keep silent, though it needed an effort of which he was scarcely capable to keep silent at that moment—Mr Hoadley looked round upon the company, nodded once, and said:

'Well, harvest is over once again and we've had grand weather for it. I should like to thank all those who've helped to get it in, especially the young ones' (here he smiled in the direction of Jenny and Louise and everyone gazed benevolently at them, while Louise felt what she afterwards described as 'awful' at this undeserved tribute to one who had spent most of the day staring at moorhens) 'because it's hard work, as I'm sure some of you have found out by now' (hearty murmurs of assent from the amateurs). 'Well, now let's drink to a good harvest in good weather all over the country. Then Mrs Hoadley'll cut the cake and if the young people don't find the weather too warm for dancing, we'll have a dance.'

He straightened himself and raised his glass, and everyone followed his example, and amidst mutters of 'The harvest—the harvest—' and clinking of mug against glass, the toast was drunk.

Then Mrs Hoadley daintily inserted the tip of the knife into the icing and, having professed herself unable to find strength enough to sever a slice, relinquished the task to Mary Parkes. No one would have credited such a finnick as Mrs Hoadley with being a first-class cook, but she was, and she was also capable of going to any lengths to procure the currants and sultanas, the icing sugar and lemon juice and butter, which must go into a first-class cake. It was loudly praised, and then tea was served and cigarettes handed round. Emilio was arranging the portable wireless (the property of Mr Waite, loaned for the occasion) which stood in a corner, and suddenly there came a burst of gay music, and he sat back on his heels with a satisfied smile, nodding his head in time to the tune.

All this time Fabrio had been sitting in a dejected attitude staring down at the floor, his tea untasted, even his cigarette unsmoked, but at the first notes he started up and hurried across the room to Sylvia, who was chatting with Mary Parkes.

'Sylvia! Dance with me!' he said; so imperiously, so fiercely, that her own anger, which had been subsiding, sprang up again to meet his tone.

'Who do you think you're talking to?' she demanded, crushing out her cigarette with some satisfaction in the stagy action. 'I'm damned if I will,' and she turned her back on him.

He caught her by the waist and swung her round.

'Yes, you will, yes, you will, Sylvia,' and suddenly his sullen young face broke into gaiety; and he made a few gliding steps that were graceful, despite his clumsy boots and rough clothes, and bent towards her in a bow.

'It is a good tune, this one,' he said simply. 'Now come along, *Sylvia mia.*'

Mary Parkes was thinking that if Sylvia were silly enough to refuse she would dance with him herself; but Sylvia too was laughing, and as he swayed eagerly towards her, she held out her hands and he caught them, and they moved away together.

'Mees. You dance-a weeth me,' said a sharp voice at Mary's elbow and there of course stood Emilio, with beady eyes fixed greedily upon her face.

'Oh—I was just wondering if I would—the floor's so rough—and it's so hot——'

'No-a, no-a, the floor is good, Fabrio and me we roll it this-a day weeth a roller, and now the sun is go down it is nice-a cool. Come on, mees,' and poor Mary found herself pinioned by a wiry arm and whirled away.

At first Sylvia was glad to be dancing with Fabrio, because she thought that he was going to be sensible and then everything would be pleasanter, but in a minute she began to feel uneasy. He had stopped laughing and his eyes, their beautiful colour slightly dimmed, gazed sternly, yearningly into her own. She had an impulse to shut her own eyes against that look, but she resisted it, and glanced over her shoulder round the room. Three couples were dancing, for Mr Waite had now stepped out with Jenny, and the rest of the party was seated round the walls, smoking and watching. Clouds of dust were rising from the floor under the dancers' feet and everyone was exclaiming and shaking their heads; it was indeed very disagreeable in the intense heat, and a general feeling seemed to be developing that the dancing had been a mistake.

Suddenly she felt, rather than heard, a low sound from the lips near her own. She quickly turned her head, and met a look of such love that for an instant she did actually shut her eyes, exactly as if they had come too near a naked flame. But she opened them again at once, and then she felt how his arm was trembling against her waist. She looked at him questioningly; she could not think of anything to say; she was becoming terrified and longed to escape from the circle of that hard, trembling arm. She had a confused impression that he had said something in Italian, but she could not even force herself to ask him if he had; for the first time in her life she was silenced by the presence of passionate love.

Yes, he was speaking:

'Will you be my wife? I love you,' he said softly, '*Sylvia mia*, I love you. I love you.' It seemed that he could not say the words often enough; he repeated them as if their sound was a comfort to him. 'Will you marry me?' he said, and then, as if overcome by the dearness of the childish face close to his own, he smiled.

Sylvia's store of memories in later life was the usual human store, quite unillumined by any imaginative glow, but it is true to say that she never completely forgot that smile—which held the tenderness of a father and brother as well as a lover's passion—upon a young man's mouth.

She heard what he said, but her feelings were so confused that she could not answer. She was indignant and frightened, but she was also flattered, and she had a strong hysterical impulse to laugh. In her distress, she glanced away again towards a group close at hand which included Alda. Mrs Lucie-Browne's eyes were at that moment fixed with a mischievous expression upon herself and Fabrio, and as Sylvia met their bright stare, Alda gave her an approving nod.

Sylvia jerked her head away with a furious gesture. Shame overcame all her other feelings. She hated Alda to see Fabrio looking at her like that. What business was it of hers, poking her nose in—giving advice that wasn't wanted, pushing people around? She would show her—and Fabrio too.

He was murmuring in Italian. Her silence had encouraged him, and the clasp of his arm tightened as he gazed eagerly into her face. But she suddenly shook his arm from her waist and flung off his clasping hand. She looked straight at him.

'You've got a hope, haven't you?' she, said, deliberately. 'Catch me marrying a Wop. I'm thirsty, I'm going to get some tea,' and she turned her back on him and walked away.

Alda did not see this, for, immediately after she had encountered Sylvia's eyes and given her that encouraging nod, she had thought that perhaps the young lovers would prefer not to be stared at, and had turned her attention elsewhere. When she next noticed them, the length of the room was between them. Sylvia was drinking tea and laughing noisily with Mrs Hoadley and Mary Parkes, and Fabrio was standing in the doorway looking out at the moonlit yard. Even at that distance she could detect an extraordinary change in him. An exaggerated comparison drifted through Mrs Lucie-Browne's usually sensible mind; it occurred to her that he looked as if he had been kicked.

'Now that's enough, all this dust is making everybody cough, it's enough to choke us,' announced Mrs Hoadley, coughing herself to give point to her words. 'Emilio's got Mr Hoadley's accordion, and he's going to give us all a tune. Gather round, everybody,' clapping her hands to attract attention, 'and we'll have a sing-song.'

This announcement was not received by the company with unmixed pleasure; the children were delighted, and Emilio was all smiles as he bent over the accordion and experimentally squeezed it in and out between his dirty yellow fingers, but Mr Waite was looking sober, and the two elderly men exchanged glances of despair, for they had hoped to get away to their usual haunt, the Wheatsheaf on the outskirts of Horsham, as soon as the supper was over. But Sylvia at once seized Mary Parkes by the arm and drew Louise to her other side to form a circle, and Mr Hoadley looked relieved; he had not liked all that dust and the Italians hopping about with their arms round the girls. Soon there was an animated circle seated about Emilio, who played a few cautious notes, then dashed with immense *brio* into *Teresa*.

In a moment Louise whispered under cover of the singing: 'Mother, what's the matter with Fabrio?'

Alda glanced at the door. He was still standing there, with arms folded and his back to the lighted, crowded, noisy room.

'I don't know, lovey, perhaps he doesn't feel well or he's tired,' she answered.

But she thought impatiently that that idiot of a girl must have upset him again, and badly this time, to give him *that* look. Surely she had not been fool enough to turn him down finally? I certainly will speak to her the minute all this is over, Alda thought.

Louise turned, and studied Fabrio with one long, curious gaze before joining again in the singing. She was not deceived: she knew that he was miserable because Sylvia had been unkind to him. It made her feel uncomfortable. Grown-up people ought not to be miserable; it was frightening. They were there to comfort children, and how could they do that if they too got miserable when people were beastly to them? She suddenly pushed herself closer to her mother and took her hand.

The voices rose and fell in pleasing harmony. They sang rounds; *Great Tom is Cast* and *Joan Glover* and *White Sand and Grey Sand*, but *Three Blind Mice* was the most popular and successful. Emilio proved an expert player, hearing a tune and trying it over only once before mastering it well enough to satisfy an uncritical audience, and they went on from one old favourite to another, each member of the party eagerly making suggestions. Mr Hoadley called for *Roll Out the Barrel* and Mrs Hoadley for *The Temple Bells are Ringing* (this was not among the more successful attempts, and the spectacle of Mr Waite doggedly proclaiming that he lay hidden in the grass was nearly too much for Alda and Jenny). Mr Waite himself, when his turn came to choose, surprised everybody by coming out with *Drink to Me Only with Thine Eyes* in a severe throaty baritone. They had *Lily of Laguna* (bashfully put forward by the man Spray, who had abandoned all hope of reaching the Wheatsheaf and was now enjoying the occasion) and *The More We Are Together* and *John Peel*, a suggestion from Alda, who knew that Jenny and Louise enjoyed making alleged hunting noises in the chorus.

Presently everyone paused for a rest and a drink, and Sylvia took the opportunity to suggest that they should sing some solos. She was not at all nervous, she said with an angry laugh (she was very conscious of the silent figure now seated on the moonlit threshold, still with its back to the room and tactfully ignored by the company) and she would begin with *Night and Day*. She was not trained, she explained to her dismayed audience; hers was a natural voice, more like a crooner's.

So Emilio, with an expression that proved his kinship with the race that bred Juvenal, cocked his eye upon her and kept it there throughout his playing of *Night and Day*, which she duly crooned.

After the polite applause, Mary Parkes was persuaded with some difficulty to sing *I'll Walk beside You*, which she did very prettily, and then Mr Hoadley thundered his way through two verses of *Drake's Drum* in an enormous mellow bass which shook the lamp glasses but ceased abruptly in the first line or the third verse, because he had forgotten the rest. He was unperturbed, and smilingly refused the entreaties of the children to 'sing some more,' but took a very large drink of cider and wiped his forehead, for singing was warm work.

During the last song, Emilio had been glancing from time to time at the figure of his friend in the doorway. He now squeezed a note or two from the accordion, and suddenly called in Italian:

'What's the matter, my brother? Has *La Scimmia* turned you down?'

'Shut up, you, and go to Hell,' answered Fabrio, without turning round.

A musical language does not confine its music to educated voices. The unfamiliar sounds lilted down the room, and everyone felt a little stir of curiosity and pleasure in their ring. What were they saying, these foreigners, one of whom had no self-control? No one knew enough Italian to make a guess, but everyone assumed that Emilio was attempting rough comfort on his friend, and everyone (except Louise, who frankly stared) tactfully busied themselves with their cigarettes and drinks and chatter.

'Ah, you don't want to worry. Cheer up——' and here, Emilio's consolatory words became gaily gross (though he took care not to say anything gross about *La Scimmia* herself).

Fabrio did not answer, and his back continued to look utterly wretched. Everyone was sorry for him except Mr Hoadley, who thought that he was making a fine fool of himself but spared him a reproof because of the occasion, and Sylvia. As he continued silent, Emilio began such a gay tune that everyone looked up in pleased surprise.

'A song-a of *Napoli*. I sing-a it to you,' said Emilio confidently, his narrow eyes twinkling with malice as he glanced from face to face, and he burst into a high-pitched ditty with a catchy chorus that set every foot tapping. No one ventured to ask what it meant; indeed, there was a silent agreement among the elders not to, as, judging by the singer's expression, the words were lively as the tune, but after the last long note had quavered away and the applause broke out, Emilio volunteered the information that it was about a lovely lovely girl who say she will kiss her boy friend much much when her old dad he is gone away out.

Then he squeezed a few more notes out of the accordion, and again called something in Italian.

Again Fabrio answered without turning his head. His tone was low and savage. Mrs Hoadley pursed her lips and shook her head at Emilio.

'Best leave him alone,' she said.

But Emilio called to his friend yet again.

'I ask him sing,' he explained to the company, 'He sing verra nice, you like-a hear him.'

'Not if he doesn't feel like it,' said Mary Parkes in such a quiet voice that hardly anyone heard her. 'P'raps he's tired.'

'No, no, he like-a sing-a,' persisted Emilio, 'you like-a hear him. Oh, come on, don't be a fool, show her you don't give a damn for her,' he went on in their own tongue. 'All the time you sit there like a' (untranslatable) 'she's laughing at you. Come on—show her!'

Suddenly Fabrio got up, and came down the room towards them. He was very pale, his eyes glittered as if with fever, and his nostrils were dilated. He came slowly, swaggeringly, with hands in his pockets, and more than one female quailed as he came. Even Alda, the confident matron, felt that she would not like to be responsible for putting that expression on a man's face, while Mr Hoadley experienced the familiar twitching at the toe of his right boot. Mr Waite thought that the chap was making an exhibition of himself. The two hired men hoped that there was going to be a row. Jenny and Louise were struggling to conceal their overpowering drowsiness; Sylvia stared at her finger-nails.

'All right,' said Fabrio in Italian, standing by his friend. He had not looked at Sylvia.

Emilio glanced grinningly up at him and said something; Fabrio nodded, and immediately he struck up an air twice as impudent as the previous one. It was lively but sneering; in it the sun shone too hotly and there was a breath off the back streets of Genoa. Or perhaps it was not the tune itself that conveyed all this, but the expression on the faces of the two young men, but whatever it was, nobody liked the tune much, and Mr Hoadley was just about to say sharply, 'That's enough, let's have something else,' when Fabrio began to sing.

His audience had been expecting a shock, and it got one. He looked straight at Sylvia; he never took his blazing eyes from her crimson, downcast face while he swiftly sang his gutter-song. It was very short and it was plainly brimming with insult. Emilio was laughing as he pressed the melody in brief sonorous bursts from the accordion and as he finished on a high, quick note like a snarl, Fabrio was laughing too, but now, to the extreme embarrassment, not to say horror, of his audience, his eyes were thickly filled with tears. They spilled over and rolled down his face as he passed, almost without pause, into the song he had sung to Emilio in the winter woods, the song of the fishermen, sailing home at dawn into San Angelo.

The simple air was so beautiful, and his voice now so full of yearning, that outraged feelings were partly soothed, and his audience listened in silent pleasure while visions of assuagement and peace drifted before their minds' eyes. All but Mr Hoadley; he was not fond of music and both toes of his boots were by now almost out of control. Sulking, and singing dirty foreign tunes, and blubbering in public! Where did this Wop think he was, and who? Mr Hoadley was only waiting until the departure of the ladies and children to give Mr Fabrio a piece of his mind which he would never forget.

The song ended on a long note that softly died away. All the females at once broke into hearty applause, except Sylvia.

She sat in a deliberately casual attitude and played with her bracelet as though bored, but she could not look up. She dared not meet his eyes, or even see his face. The first song had filled her with fury and bewildered shame, affronting her modesty although she did not know why, but the fishermen's song had done worse; it had brought a lump to her throat and stinging tears, and now she was hoping passionately that no one, especially not Alda, would stare at her while those two tears were drying upon her burning cheeks. She did not dare to use her handkerchief. She would not let him see his triumph. He would think that she was crying because she was sorry for him, but she was not: she hated him and would never speak to him again; never, never, never. It was only that his voice was so smashing, and music always did something to her. It was such a corny song, too. Round and round went the cheap bracelet on the brown arm, and she stared down at it while the tears slowly, how slowly, dried in the heat of anger.

'Now let's have something a bit more cheerful,' Mr Hoadley was saying, not deigning to cast a glance at the two offenders, who were now sitting silently side by side and giving a distinct impression of Snakes at Bay. 'What about *Under the Spreading Chestnut Tree*?'

'Yes, that's a nice *English* song,' was Mrs Hoadley's helpful contribution; and Emilio, looking bored, picked out the tune and soon everybody was singing as cheerfully as though nothing embarrassing had happened.

When shortly afterwards the evening came to an end with *God Save the King* (only played by Emilio after one enormous shrug of his shoulders to convey his utter indifference to the British Monarchy—a gesture which all the English very properly ignored) and everyone was thanking Mr and Mrs Hoadley, Louise wandered to the door.

The moon was still shining, but a cool wind blew on her upturned face and the western sky was covered in cloud.

'Just in time; there'll be rain to-morrow,' said Mary Parkes, coming behind her and putting both hands on her shoulders.

Mr Waite was deciding that he would not offer to accompany Alda home. It was bright moonlight and she would be there in seven minutes; besides, she might try to find out things on the way. He had no intention of giving her the opportunity. He felt very strongly indeed that he did not want to hear her comments or her congratulations or *anything*; he only wanted to avoid her.

So he bowed slightly and said 'Good night' to her with a slightly less distant manner than of late, but he walked off at once towards Meadow Cottage, and as he strode through the dry warm grass he was whistling.

Mr Hoadley intended to speak to Fabrio immediately the last visitor had gone and was looking sharply about for him among the busy figures folding tablecloths and stacking chairs when his wife came up with a livestock problem that had arisen during the evening and had just been reported by Sylvia, who had slipped outside to cool her hot face. Then the two men had to be paid off and sent home, and arrangements made about his own early start for Brighton the next morning, and when all this was done, the disappearance of the moon behind thick motionless black clouds led to some revision of plans already made, in case the morning should bring heavy rain.

It was not until after eleven that he again remembered Fabrio's outrageous behaviour, and then he was sitting on his bed taking off his boots. He would almost have gone up then and there and pulled Fabrio out of bed to listen to him, had not Mrs Hoadley, who was resignedly wide awake, dissuaded him. He knew just what he was going to say to Fabrio and a few hours made no difference. He fell asleep at once.

Sylvia cried for some time before she went to sleep, although she did not know why. She longed vaguely for some kind and sensible person in whom to confide, yet when Mary Parkes tapped on the wall and asked what was the matter she robustly answered that everything was O.K., she had only had a bad dream. If she had confided in Mary, she could only have said that she was 'upset.' She was miserable, but presently she told herself that it would all come out in the wash, and all be the same a hundred years hence and so forth, and gradually her natural good spirits reasserted themselves. Eros retreated before the philosophy held by the cinema queue, and before Sylvia fell asleep, she had decided that Fabrio, in asking her to share his low peasant existence, had been downright insulting.

At three o'clock the first drops of rain fell in the lowering dawn, and by the time the farmhouse party came down at five to begin the day's work, a wet day had set in.

31

The stooks looked autumnally bronze against the grey sky, for the rain was heavy and continuous and had darkened their colour, but the sight of them cheered the workers as they went about their morning tasks and they exchanged congratulations upon having completed the harvest yesterday. It was difficult to realise that the shorn expanses of dripping stubble were the hot golden fields of twenty-four hours ago, and those sodden white twists in the hedge the bindweed flowers that had waved against the blue sky. After breakfast Alda glanced out of the window and saw a familiar figure making its way across the fields under an umbrella. Where was Mr Waite going to, in his best suit, at this hour in the morning? But she had plenty to do, for the children had all slept late and were tired and cross and dismayed at the rain, and she forgot him at once.

It was eleven o'clock and she was making the beds with Jenny's help when there came a rap at the front door. Jenny ran down, and presently Alda heard her coming up again.

'It's Mary, Mother. I say! gosh, what do you think? Fabrio's run away! Isn't it super? I expect that's because Sylvia was so beastly to him last night.'

Alda ran down to the door.

'I'm awfully sorry to bother you, Mrs Lucie-Browne,' said Mary prettily, standing in the porch with a clean sack arranged over her head in a hood, 'Mrs Hoadley asked me to come over and ask you if you'd seen anything of Fabrio this morning. He isn't at the farm.'

'Are you sure?' asked Alda, staring.

'Quite sure. We didn't notice he was missing until Mr Hoadley had gone off to Brighton in the car just before eight, and we've looked everywhere since and we can't find him.'

'I haven't seen anyone this morning, except Mr Waite in the distance. Perhaps he's gone back to the camp?'

'That's what I said, but Emilio says no. He says they had a permit to stay here for four days, and Fabrio would never go back to camp before his time was up; he hates it.'

Mary looked as neat and sensible as usual, but Alda believed that she detected anxiety.

'You aren't *worried*, are you?' she asked.

'*I'm* not,' with a touch of hauteur, 'but Mrs Hoadley is. She's working herself up into quite a state, and she oughtn't to.'

'She's quite different since that baby started; she used to be so efficient and managing. It is a bore for you all, isn't it? Shall I come over after lunch and cheer her up?'

'Oh, I wish you would, Mrs Lucie-Browne. She's made up her mind he's hung himself.'

'Ass,' said Alda crisply. 'Because of last night, do you mean?'

'Yes. She says Italians are so uncontrolled.'

'They aren't the only ones,' Alda muttered. 'What *did* happen anyway? Did he propose to Sylvia?'

'Yes. She's just told us. She's crying.' Mary's tone was less kind than usual. '*She* thinks he's drowned himself.'

'I expect she's enjoying the excitement,' said Alda, but then a surprised glance made her slightly ashamed of herself. 'And she turned him down?'

Mary nodded. 'She seems to think it was a—a sort of insult.' She paused, then said with feeling—'Asking someone to marry you—well, that is quite something, isn't it? I mean, I know girls—I'm not speaking personally—who would give anything for the chance to get married. I'm older than Sylvia, and you get over all those silly ideas.'

'Age will make no difference to Sylvia, my dear Mary, because what my husband calls "the seeds of growth" aren't in her. I'd get back to the farm now, if I were you,' for Mary looked as if the last remark were rather above her head, 'and tell Mrs H. that he's probably gone off to sulk in the woods. I'll come over after lunch and have a word with her.'

'We were wondering if we ought to contact Mr Hoadley in Brighton.'

'I wouldn't bother him. Fabrio will be back by this evening, I expect, and Mr Hoadley would only be annoyed at a fuss over nothing.'

'It was Sylvia's idea really,' Mary called back, setting out across the dripping grass.

'It would be. Don't let her fuss you; she's a great half-wit.'

The children were so ready to exclaim and enlarge their eyes over the news that after a while Alda refused to discuss it any more, but this did not prevent them from retiring into their bedroom and mulling it over until lunch, and afterwards they returned to it with unslaked interest. Meg took no part in it, for out of sight was out of mind with her, except where her mother was concerned, and she passed the time peacefully in tilting Gilbert's jam jar up and down in order to make him lose his balance.

At the farmhouse there was the atmosphere that might be expected where the occupants are a pregnant woman, an Italian, and a stage-struck adolescent. Mary did help to maintain a more sensible attitude at first, but as the day wore on and the rain poured down, and there was no sign of Fabrio, she too became depressed; and when Alda walked over in top-boots and raincoat early in the afternoon, she found them all seated round the fire, drinking tea and very low. The day's duties were being performed, but in a perfunctory manner, and not one of those odd indoor tasks which Mr Hoadley made it an admirable habit to perform upon wet days had been so much as thought of. Gloomy speculation and fruitless agitation held the field.

Alda smiled at Mrs Hoadley and took up a letter for herself

that had arrived by the morning's post, wondering as she did so when Jean was going to write.

But it was to be eighteen months before she again heard from her friend.

'If only Mr Hoadley was coming back to-night!' said Mrs Hoadley for the seventh time, pushing over her cup for Sylvia to refill, 'I should sleep so much easier if I knew there was a man in the house.'

Emilio looked at her with a bilious eye, but said nothing. He was not quite sure of her meaning, and he was too much under the influence of last night's cider to speak up for the honour of his sex. Let all these women weep, he thought, drinking tea out of his saucer. My brother is no doubt stewing a rabbit somewhere in the woods, glad to get away from *La Scimmia* for a while, and would that I were with him! To-morrow I must go back to that accursed camp; therefore let me make the most of the time still left to me.

'Well, please leave us a *little* sugar, Emilio!' exclaimed Mrs Hoadley with a disagreeable titter. 'That's only *three* spoonfuls you've had for one cup of tea. It's a mercy *all* of us haven't got a sweet tooth!'

'*Scusa?*' said Emilio politely. He was wondering if there were any drink left in that barrel; he had not been able to get near the shed on his last search for Fabrio, and he thought that he would soon go out to look again.

'It's funny; I've got such a strong feeling he is at the camp,' Mary was saying, 'I suppose you wouldn't let me telephone there later on, when we've had another look for him?' to Mrs Hoadley.

Sylvia was sitting by the fire, sulky and red-eyed. She now looked up and said impatiently:

'All right, if you want to get him into the hell of a row. If you telephone, they'll be certain he's done a bolt—gone to London, p'raps.'

'Well, p'raps he has,' said Mrs Hoadley drearily. 'Oh dear, I do

wish Mr Hoadley was coming home to-night. I dread the darkness coming.'

'Well, it won't come until about ten o'clock, thanks to the
Government, and when it does there's a full moon,' said Alda dryly.

'Oh, you don't know—he may be desperate!'

Emilio said nothing, but one yellow eye slid round the corner
of the cup from which he was drinking and regarded Mrs
Hoadley with derision.

'Highly unlikely, I should think,' said Alda.

'Oh, you don't know—men get so worked up—and Italians
are so hysterical—I beg your pardon, Emilio, but you know they
are—and he was in such a state last night. His eyes! Shall I ever
forget them!'

'Oh go on, all of you, say it's my fault, I know you think it
is, and if he's dead that'll be my fault, too!' burst out Sylvia, in
a kind of howl. She stood up and re-knotted her scarf, sobbing
noisily. 'It *isn't* my fault, I never asked him to get crazy about
me, did I?'

Emilio continued to suck up tea. His other eye peered round
the cup, looking equally yellow but this time fixed upon Sylvia.

'Good gracious, Sylvia, don't go on like that. No one's accusing
you, I'm sure I never said a word to her, did I, Mary?'

But Mary, her natural good sense reinforced by the presence
of Alda, was deftly clearing away the dinner, and she glanced at
the clock. It was a quarter past two, a good three-quarters of an
hour later than the farmhouse party usually got up from the
midday meal.

'I must get on, I promised Mr Hoadley I'd get all those flower
seeds into packets for him and then you and I'll have to get onto
the milking,' she said to Sylvia, at whom all the others were now
lackadaisically gazing. 'What are you going to do now?'

'M-m-muck out the bull's shed,' blowing her nose desolately.

'Right. Emilio, I expect you've got plenty to do, haven't you?'
and Mary, having done her best to break up the party, sailed out

into the scullery with a tray of plates. Alda's heart warmed to her, the more because she was sure that Mary liked Fabrio better than Sylvia did, and was inwardly far more grieved for him.

Mrs Hoadley raised her eyebrows. It seemed to her that Mary was taking rather much on herself. She was almost giving orders. Let her have a baby, then she won't feel so brisk, thought Mrs Hoadley crossly. However, Mary's tone had a bracing effect upon her, and she went slowly upstairs to change her morning slippers for neater ones.

Emilio went off, pulling a sack over his head against the rain, and Alda and Sylvia were alone.

'Cheer up, Sylvia, for goodness' sake!' Alda said impatiently, after watching her slowly pulling on her boots, slowly putting on her raincoat, and sniffing the while.

Sylvia said nothing.

'What did you want to turn him down for, silly child?' Alda went on more quietly. 'I told you he was a good match. Now see what you've done!'

Suddenly Sylvia hurled her boot to the far end of the room. It hit a pot of geraniums on the windowsill, which fell to the stone floor with a crash. Earth and bruised flowers and snapped leaves and broken flowerpot were scattered all about. The cat, which had been resting under the table, flew out with a sharp howl and blundered into a chicken which was mincing in from the scullery, where Emilio had left the door open. The chicken rushed out flapping and squawking with the cat after it and the scandalised voice of Mrs Hoadley was heard crying from upstairs:

'What on earth's the matter? Fabrio, is that you?'

Sylvia was blubbering noisily with her fists thrust into her eyes, and Alda could just make out the words: 'All your fault—all your fault!'

'All *my* fault? What do you mean? What rubbish!' she said. She could hear Mrs Hoadley's slow steps coming down the stairs.

'Yes, it is! If you hadn't poked your nose in and told me what

to do—it wasn't your business—nothing to *do* with you——'
and her voice rose hysterically as she remembered Fabrio's smile.
She believed that he had killed himself. Men did do such things,
when they were crazy about women.

'Don't be absurd, Sylvia, you're hysterical. Pull yourself
together,' said Alda very sharply indeed, as Mrs Hoadley entered.

'What's the matter now, Sylvia?' the latter said with an irritable
sigh. 'You'd better go and get on with your work. It'll take your
mind off things.'

More sobs and incoherent sentences in which the words
'shan't!' and 'unkind' were distinguishable.

Alda said nothing. She sat down and picked up the local
newspaper. She had come here intending to chat with Mrs
Hoadley, and Sylvia's tantrums were certainly not going to drive
her away. But she was also slightly embarrassed. Sylvia was an
idiot, of course, making such a fuss and completely misunderstanding well-meant attempts to help her, but Mrs Hoadley might
also misunderstand if Sylvia poured out the story to her. So
much for educating the masses, thought Alda (it was as well that
the passionate individualist, Sylvia's late father, could not hear
her lumping himself and and his family with the masses). Really,
it's getting dull here, I shall be glad to leave at the end of next
month, she thought, quite forgetting how delightful life at the
farm had seemed only yesterday.

Mrs Hoadley glanced from the red agitated countenance to
the calm brown one. It was plain that they had had words, but
she did not want to hear what about. She was too tired after
yesterday's exertions and too worried about Fabrio to want any
more fuss. She said, not unkindly, to Sylvia:

'There, that'll do. Get on with the next job, Sylvia. It's wonderful
what a cure work can be, isn't it, Mrs Lucie-Browne?'

Mrs Lucie-Browne, with her eyes fixed upon the pages of
the *East Sussex Advertiser and Chronicle*, made a non-committal
noise.

Sylvia blundered off. She was raging with bitterness towards Alda. *She* took it all as a joke, did she? *She* thought everything was going to be fine and there was nothing to worry about, did she? Just let her wait a bit, and see! Wait till they dragged the ponds in Saint Leonard's Forest that night, and the hooks caught in Something—and they pulled It up out of the dark waters—and the moon shone on a gleam of chestnut hair! Here the tears spurted again as she went out into the rain. And she had driven him to his doom! By her heartlessness, her coldness. She would never forgive herself. All her life long she would carry the mark of this Horror upon her. The next time she went to see Mr Smedley-Porter at the Canonbury School of Dramatic Art he would tell her that she had gained Something which was of immeasurable benefit to her Art: she had suffered. And however brilliant her career; however large the lights in which her name appeared in the West End, she would never, never forget the Italian prisoner who had gone down into the Dark Places for her.

Here she trod upon a broom which Emilio, another individualist, had cast carelessly from him, and it flew up and bumped her. The sharp undeserved pain shook her out of her orgy, and she realised that the rain was increasing in severity. She drew the sack closer over her head and hoped that Fabrio, if not yet dead, were under shelter. We might have been all right, Fabrio and me, if *she* hadn't interfered, she thought vaguely, with a sudden pang that was not in the least enjoyable, as she cautiously opened the door of the bull's shed.

Alda remained for half an hour with Mrs Hoadley, salting down runner beans into big jars against the winter and listening to every imaginable supposition as to Fabrio's fate; from his having jumped a lorry bound for Brighton and thence made for Dover and the Channel *en route* for home, to his having gone mad and concealed himself in those deserted shacks up in the woods with the object of waylaying Sylvia and murdering her. Later she contrived to steer Mrs Hoadley away from the subject by an account of the new house in Ironborough. This was a happy thought, for Mrs Hoadley delighted to talk about Ironborough; and in listening to a detailed account of the contents of Alda's linen-cupboard, which her mother was storing for her against their return, she forgot Fabrio and his fate for quite twenty minutes.

As Alda went home across the dripping fields, which yet did not look dismal because of the abundance of the surrounding vegetation and because there was still no hint in the air of autumn, she wondered a little for her own part where Fabrio was. She was not surprised that he had gone. How wretched he had looked last night! And he had made no attempt to conceal it! He had behaved like an unhappy child. It would be very tiresome to be married to a man of that type, but of course, no man of one's own class would be of that type. Self-control was the first rule for the gently-bred, and perhaps it was the last remaining characteristic distinguishing them from those who were not.

She still thought that he and Sylvia could have made a match of it, and if he returned in a sobered mood and Sylvia met him in one of joyful relief at his return, they might yet do so. But as Alda cheerfully roused the somnolent children from their books and paint-boxes with the announcement of tea; setting the cups on the table and mixing some cakes which were to be eaten hot and driving her daughters round to find the spoons and the jam, most of her thoughts were turned eagerly towards Ironborough and the new life there, and Fabrio, Sylvia, Mr Waite, the Hoadleys, all seemed on this dim rainy afternoon to belong already to the past. Harvest was over; Jean would soon write to say that she was to marry her Mr Potter at once and that Alda must come to the wedding; and in less than six weeks the Lucie-Brownes would again be living in Ironborough: familiar, smoky city where Alda's family had lived and been respected for sixty years and where her daughters—and now, she hoped, her son—would live in their turn.

'Tea's ready,' she called, coming in with the plate of cakes. 'Come along,' to Meg, who was gazing out of the window. 'Can you see the Big Meadow, lovey, with all the sheaves? The harvest's over, and next month we're going home.'

Of all the party at the farm, Mary passed the pleasantest afternoon, in arranging seeds collected from vegetable and flower garden during the summer in envelopes and labelling them. The large curved seed of the marigold; and the poppy seed small as dust; the flat yellow grain in which dwells the wall-flower; and the large, blue and purple, marbled seed of the runner bean, were sifted out from their litter of withered stem and leaf and neatly classified. Two hours passed so quickly that she was surprised when she heard Sylvia bellowing in the distance that it was milking time (sounding rather like one of those about to be milked, thought Mary, who was getting tired of Sylvia).

. . . Afterwards, no one could remember who first brought Mr Hoadley's rook-rifle into the discussion. Mrs Hoadley always vowed that Emilio had been trying to get his hands on it ever since he first clapped eyes on it, and that he took advantage of the general anxiety about Fabrio to suggest that he should go forth armed upon his search. Mary said that everyone got so moody and upset as evening came on that no one could remember exactly what they did say, and Mr Hoadley (soon to be the father of a perfectly enormous son with lungs like a bullock and a will of iron whom his mother worshipped) blamed everyone impartially. Whoever was to blame, one fact is clear. When Emilio went out at half-past eight to look for Fabrio, he was carrying Mr Hoadley's rifle. He left the women sitting in the kitchen over a final cup of tea as he stepped reluctantly into the twilight.

The rain had ceased, but it had been so persistent throughout the warm, still day that a mist had arisen from woods and meadows as evening advanced, and now lingered among the motionless trees, thick and bluish between their heavy green leaves. Now and again one drop of water fell from the soaked boughs, and the brimming ditches ran fast, with a light covering of petals and dried stems and seeds swirling along their surfaces.

Emilio was so pleased to hold a weapon again that he even made some attempt to carry out a promise to Mrs Hoadley, and search those deserted huts up in the copse. This rite consisted in approaching to within fifty yards of the huts, pointing the rifle at the one which was so ruined as to be practically open to the elements, and shouting in Italian and English: 'Is anyone inside there? Answer or I fire!'

No one did answer, but he thought he had better not fire Mr Hoadley's rifle because of Mr Hoadley, so he went back, almost noiselessly, through the wet, quiet woods; down the hill and across a meadow enclosed by coppices where ran a tiny stream. It was a miniature river gliding between banks a few feet high, which was marked upon a map dated 1530, in the possession of this land's owner. Meadow, coppices and stream covered not more than five acres of land and were only two miles from the main road: but they proved, as they lay there under the grey evening sky in deep solitude, how small England is, and how secret still: in spite of holiday camps, and motor coaches and the horrifying increase in our numbers, how secret still!

Emilio leapt the stream with the rifle gaily pointing at all angles and went through the trees, keeping a look-out for something to shoot. He was enjoying the outing; he had no intention of reporting his friend's whereabouts even if he found him, and now he was on his way to the scene of last night's festivities to try that little barrel for a last drink.

Across the home meadows he went. There were no lights in Mr Waite's cottage, for Mr Waite had not yet returned from London, where he had spent the day with his fiancée (in case anyone should ask, the care of his chickens had been entrusted to Miss Dodder).

Emilio entered the precincts of the farm, and at once began opening doors, with the rifle ready, and demanding in a low tone: 'Art thou there, my comrade?' Soon (having received no reply from the bull's shed or the stable where the little goats were kept) he naturally found himself at the door of the shed he was making for. He opened it, he aimed the rifle; he put his question, but again there was no answer. He shrugged his shoulders and went in, carefully drawing the door to after him. The little barrel was still there, and he went over to it. He turned the tap. Alas, after a few delicious drops which he sucked up with eagerness, there were no more. The barrel was dry. The *padrone*, that monster of injustice, that hard man, had drained it before he left home that morning. Emilio swore, and decided that he had searched enough for one evening. Now he would return, and see if there were anything left to eat.

On the way he passed the granary. He remembered that it had always been a favourite haunt of his friend's, and, almost without thinking, he pushed open the door (which stood slightly ajar), poked the rifle round it, and bawled, 'Art thou there, my brother?'

The rifle barrel was struck violently down. Then it was pulled forward. It was jerked out of his hand. It vanished. The inside of the granary was almost dark. Fabrio's voice said gruffly out of the darkness:

'What art thou doing, threatening with rifles? thou, who couldst not hit a tank at five yards. Do not be a fool, and come inside. I would speak with thee.'

Emilio, who had run some distance, returned slowly. His heart was beating as if to burst his chest. He had always been a little afraid of *Il Signor* even while despising him, and who knew what maggot might not have got into his head since that accursed girl had turned upon him? He might be mad. But he was more afraid to stay outside while Fabrio remained inside with the rifle, and so he walked slowly forward and into the shed.

He could smell cigarette smoke, and a spark glowed in the dusk. He heard a rustle as if Fabrio was making room for him in the straw, and he moved cautiously towards the sound.

'Sit down, sit down,' said Fabrio impatiently, with a heavy sigh, and then Emilio felt himself gripped by an unpleasantly strong hand and pulled down upon the straw. He was next aware of something white extended under his nose.

'Cigarettes,' said his friend, again uttering that labouring sigh. 'Half are for thee—though thou dost not deserve them. Coming after thy comrade with rifles!'

'Didst thou steal them?' inquired Emilio, getting out his lighter. The flame sprang up and illuminated the grey rafters with dusty webs in their corners, the discarded household and farm implements crowded along the walls, the sacks of grain, and the deep pile of straw upon which Fabrio lay. He looked sullen and his hair was very untidy. Otherwise Emilio's avid eyes could detect no such ghastly change as he had expected. He blew out the flame and again they sat almost in darkness save for what light was afforded by the grey summer dusk.

'No. The *padrona* at that place—Amberlei—gave them to me.'

'Thou hast been there? This day? Twelve miles!'

'I waited until the *padrone* had gone away in the car and then I rode in the bus.'

'But why? All day we have been searching for thee. The women—thou canst imagine!' and Emilio drew the smoke down, down, down into his lungs and grinned.

'I wanted a holiday. I hate this place, as thou knowest. And at that place, Amberlei, the *padrona* was glad to see me. She gave me eggs and meat to eat and drink from a little black bottle. It was very good. As for the women, all the women in this place, all the women in this accursed, wet, cold, miserable country, may they all burn in Hell for ever and ever.' And Fabrio spat.

Emilio said nothing for a minute. The smoke burned his throat with its familiar comfort and the scent of grain and damp sacks floating in the dimness was comforting too. Water dripped musically from a nearby gutter. He stretched out luxuriously on the straw. He did not want to move. He wanted to stay here all night and smoke all those cigarettes. But if *he* went off, too, there would be the father and mother of a row, so what was the use of doing what he wanted? He yawned.

'Thou knowest?' said Fabrio suddenly.

'What?'

'What I have done with *La Scimmia*.'

And then and there did Fabrio, in five minutes' talk with Emilio, defile the memory of his love. It seemed to him the only way to heal the wound to his pride. What did it matter if he lied about that creature with brazen hair who had terribly insulted him? He would return her insult with his lies. So long as no one but himself ever knew of that day at Amberley when she had seemed so different; so long as the memory of their secret smile remained his secret alone, what did he care what he said of her, what she thought of him, what anybody said or thought? He spoke as foully as he knew how.

When he had finished, Emilio laughed and congratulated him. He did not believe this yarn, of course; anyone with their eyes put straight in their head could have seen what had happened last night, when his friend's perfectly natural suggestion had been refused by that female monkey. But he felt pity for Fabrio, and also there were times when men must stand together against women. This seemed to Emilio to be one of them. Besides, *La Scimmia* had never shown the slightest kindness towards himself. Let her get the reputation of a loose girl. She deserved it.

So he tapped the side of his long nose in the darkness, and laughed and admired, and presently Fabrio's sore pride began to feel soothed. When Emilio casually suggested a little later that they should return to the farm, he turned sullen again, but made no objection, and later still, having smoked another cigarette, they leisurely set out. Fabrio had no dread of meeting *La Scimmia*, for he would retire again into that reserve with which he had first treated her, never addressing her except when it was unavoidable in the course of the day's work, and soon, very soon, he would ask if he might be transferred to another farm.

Already, as he trudged back beside Emilio through yards dimly lit by the hidden moon, he felt less tender towards the memory of Sylvia. No man could continue to love a woman who had so cruelly insulted him.

Meanwhile, Mr Hoadley's rifle lay forgotten on the damp sacks near the open door where Fabrio had placed it, immediately beneath that musically dripping gutter. It had been raining smartly for quite twenty minutes when Emilio, cursing and swearing, came stumbling into the shed to retrieve it, and during those twenty minutes the rising wind had blown a great deal of water from the gutter over the rifle. On the way back Emilio did shroud it in a sack against the rain, but this did not prevent it from being very rusty indeed the next time Mr Hoadley came to use it. To those readers who were hoping that Fabrio or Emilio would murder someone with it, we tender our unrepentant apologies.

32

Some eighteen months later, a children's party was in progress at the Lucie-Brownes' house on the outskirts of Ironborough on the occasion of Jenny's thirteenth birthday, and Alda had sent out the invitations marked *Please come as a Nursery Rhyme.*

It was a pretty scene. The grey walls in the one room, and the satin-striped white ones in the other, set off the children's brilliantly coloured costumes, ingeniously devised with the help of Eastern scarves and shawls sent home by fathers and brothers still on active service. Alda had economised with coal, in order that with the help of her store of logs she might provide a royal fire, in itself enough to beautify the plainest apartment, in each room. The youngest unmarried aunt was seated at the piano thumping out 'Here we go gathering nuts in May,' and down the long room, through the folding doors flung wide, pranced a row of tall creatures (Jenny's generation is a collection of young maypoles) hand in hand; with plaits flying, skirts whisking, mop caps and turbans flapping, feet thundering on the gleaming floor as they chanted more or less tunefully:

> 'Here we go gathering nuts in May—
>   nuts in May—
>   nuts in May——'

Not all were pretty, but all had the charm of health and youth; their cheeks were like petals, and their brilliant eyes brimmed with laughter.

Meg, who was now nearly six years old but not considered old enough to join in this game, was sitting on a chair by her

mother, surveying the dancers. These were the Big Ones at Miss
Cowdray's school which she now attended; the Big Ones, who
dragged you along in the morning when they were late, and
made you run so fast that your legs almost flew out behind you
and you gasped for breath; who were sarcastically patient if you
should happen to cry; who never stopped talking to one another
about four feet above your head, and squeezed your hand dread-
fully hard as they hauled you across the terrible High Street; the
Big Ones whom, in spite of all this, you greatly admired, for
whose notice and kindness you longed. But you did not often
get it.

And when you turned to humbler circles for comfort, what
did you find? People of nine and ten who only wanted each
other and were always sharply telling you to buzz off and not
be a nuisance, and hiding away from you. And somehow other
people of six were not interesting. Jenny said that six was an
awful age, the worst age of all. She said this poem about it:

> But now I am six I'm as clever as clever,
> So I think I'll be six for ever and ever.

Jenny said that that just showed what people of six were like;
always boasting. It was dreadful to boast: it was the worst thing
you could do, Jenny said. Things might be better, Meg hoped,
when she was seven. Some people of seven were quite kind,
only they always seemed so busy.

But Richard, their new brother, knew Meg now, and when
she came into the room he smiled at her and he stared at her
all the time and turned his head to look at her. Mother said
that he noticed Meg more than the others because she was the
nearest in size to himself. This was very gratifying.

Meg now slipped off her chair and rushed across the room
(right in front of the opposing row of dancers, who shooed her
on with impatient cries in their fresh, thrush-like voices) and

pushed her face into Richard's little soft one, where he sat within Nanny's arm.

'Gently, now,' said Nanny, otherwise Mrs Pakin, in her placid Yorkshire voice. 'We aren't a wild elephant, I hope.'

Meg rubbed her nose against her brother's head, which was covered in down soft as the seed of a dandelion, and of almost the same silvery colour. He was a year old, and already very like his maternal grandfather.

'I'm taking him up now,' said Nanny. 'He's had a look at you all and it's past his bedtime.'

She carried the baby across to Alda, and the aunts admired him and bade him good night, but were not encouraged to give him more than the gentlest of kisses. Then she bore him away.

'How pretty the tree looks, Alda,' said Alda's mother, a comely and active lady in the early sixties who had dropped in on the party, 'but what a business you must have had making all those presents, with everything else you have to do! Who began this fad that *all* the children at a birthday party must have presents? It's something quite new and I call it nonsense. Pampering.'

'I don't know, Mother. It started in the war. One does curse it, but everybody does it, so of course I have to do it too.'

Mrs Norton did not snort but her expression did. Alda said no more, but watched the children with a contented air. It was of no use trying to explain the technique of contemporary living to her mother, who had passed the greater part of her married life, and experienced her motherhood, in the comparative safety of the early twentieth century. Mrs Norton was generous with her own rationed luxuries, her fresh eggs and her bottled fruits, when there was a party at one of her daughters' homes but she always sighed over *my poor grandchildren*, who had to put up with a chocolate biscuit apiece and jellies made from synthetic fruit juice. It was useless to tell her that what the tongue had never tasted the young stomach did not miss, while the Party Spirit crowned all.

Louise was dancing with the others, in a nondescript ruffled garment intended to represent the Queen of Hearts which unbecomingly revealed her lankiness. She had lost her Ice-Maiden look, and was now only thin and fair and rather plain, and retained that habit of gazing with her mouth open which called forth sharp rebukes. She read voraciously, and though she seldom spoke of the convent, and unprotestingly accompanied her mother and sisters to the church which Nortons and Lucie-Brownes had attended for years, Alda knew that she continued to correspond with Sister Alban. She also cherished a rosary. Alda anticipated that these tendencies would come to a head when Louise was about eighteen in a determined attempt to Go Over, which would then be thwarted by packing her off, if she could win a scholarship, to Cambridge, where her father had been. Louise was clever; far cleverer than the gay and vigorous Jenny, who was dancing into her teens with every sign of avoiding completely the awkward age, and was one of a group at Miss Cowdray's known, because of their interests, as The Horsey Dogs.

The Lucie-Brownes have gone up in the world, thinks the Gentle Reader, with their satin-striped wallpaper and their Nanny for the new baby, but in fact these embellishments were less grand than they sound. Nanny Pakin was the mother of one of Doctor Norton's poorer patients; a woman with a large but now grown-up family, who possessed a common and beautiful form of genius; the power to rear very young children. Having declined, several times and with vehemence, suggestions from local employers that she should enter what she roundly called their dirty old factories, Mrs Pakin was happily installed in the large shabby comfortable nursery at the Orchard House for not much more than board wages. As for the satin-striped wallpaper, the old builder who had once decorated Alda's father's house for the homecoming of his new bride had just happened to have that particular piece by him.

Ronald Lucie-Browne now entered the room, and went across to the fire, rubbing his hands and appreciating the warmth after a walk home of several miles through cold, foggy, darkened streets. There was a strike of bus and tram drivers in Ironborough and street lighting had been reduced to save coal. He looked amused and tranquil, and in his head there lingered a line of Alfred de Vigny's which he had quoted that afternoon during a lecture:

Marche à travers les champs une fleur à la main.

It seemed to him that it was still possible to do this, even during a Time of Troubles. He believed that there must have been many families, unrecorded by history, who had contrived to live happy lives even in the darkest periods, until they were finally overwhelmed, and as he gradually reassumed civilian life, he saw more and more plainly that this was what he must lead his own family to do. They were helpless, but they need not be unhappy, for most of the great natural sources of joy were still open to them.

At this point his reflections were interrupted by his mother-in-law, who joined him to congratulate him upon the election of his sister as Labour Member for Ironborough South at a by-election, made necessary by the sudden death of the Conservative Member, and held on the previous day.

'At least,' said Mrs Norton menacingly, '*now* we know who to complain to if we don't get more biscuits into the shops.'

'You take a low view of politics, Jane.'

'And you? What's your view of them these days? I thought there was some talk of *your* standing for Ironborough South as a Liberal, at one time?'

'There was, but Marion has more of the necessary type of energy and brains, and she got there first.'

'She is very clever and has worked exceedingly hard,' said Mrs Norton, in a tone whose scrupulous justice did not in the least conceal the fact that she thought Marion a dead bore.

'Yes. I saw her this afternoon; she has commissioned me to hunt up Jean Hardcastle. She wants her for a secretary.'

'She thinks her money would be useful to the Party,' said Mrs Norton instantly. 'But Jean isn't trained. Besides, Alda told me that she has completely lost touch with her.'

He held up a letter. 'This is from Jean, I believe. It was sent to the college to-day. I suppose she hasn't our new address. Alda will be pleased, I know.'

He crossed the room to where Alda stood by the tree.

'Hullo, lovey,' she said. 'You've just missed Richard; Mrs P. has taken him off. All these women will have gone in half an hour, and then we'll have our supper alone.'

'So I should hope, but look here.' He gave her the letter. 'Isn't that from Jean?'

'The blighter! After eighteen months!' exclaimed Alda, snatching it. 'I'm dying to hear what she's been up to. What's the odds Potter got away?' and she tore open the envelope. Almost at once she began to laugh.

'I say, do listen!' And she read aloud:

'Darling Alda,

'I expect you will be absolutely shattered to hear that I'm *married*. We've got an absolutely *smashing* son aged eight months exactly like Phil (*Phil? What does she mean? Potter's name is Oliver!*) and I'm *terrifically happy*. As you will see by the address we're living in Daleham to be near Phil's family, they're rather dim but awfully kind. *Do* write and tell me you aren't furious with me for not having written for such *ages*. I'm sending this to the College and do hope it finds you. How are the girls, I expect they're *enormous* by now, do kiss them all for me. We must meet *soon*. I'm dying to show you Alex.

'Tons of love,
'from
'J.'

'Then Potter *did* get away!' exclaimed Alda, looking up from the letter at the interested faces of Ronald, her mother, and two younger sisters who had come up to hear what was going on. 'She married Phil Waite after all. No *wonder* she's been keeping out of my way! She is the limit!'

'But I thought you wanted her to marry Waite,' said Ronald.

'So I did, at first, but only because there was no one else. As soon as Potter turned up, I was all in favour of him. Fancy his getting away after all!'

'Perhaps it was Jean who got away,' said Ronald.

'Of course not; she adored Potter,' said Alda absently; she was re-reading the letter. 'Oh well, she does say she's terrifically happy. I'm glad. Good old J., she hasn't done so badly for herself after all. But not a word of thanks to *me*, you notice, and I arranged the whole thing!'

'Never mind,' said Ronald. 'It'll soon be time to start arranging "things" for Jenny and Louise. Have you anyone in mind for Meg?'

Alda laughed, but in fact she did have the youthful sons of various old family friends in mind for all three, and her laugh was a little conscious.

'And then there's Richard,' he went on. 'One can't begin thinking about these affairs too early, can one?'

Alda's expression changed. It became graver, slightly cautious.

'Oh, that won't need thinking about for quite twenty-five years yet,' she said, 'perhaps thirty. With girls it's different, of course, but I really don't approve of boys marrying too young. It leads to all kinds of difficulties. Of course, I shall always welcome any nice girls that he likes to bring to the house and I hope he will bring them whenever he likes, but I should never *encourage* an early marriage where Richard was concerned— what's so funny, Ronald?'

33

It was autumn when Fabrio at last came home.

Across the south of France crawled the dirty, crowded train through the blazing sunlight of the year's decline; stopping at villages still half-ruined, dead and silent in the brilliant light without a sign of human or animal life; then down the tranquil Swiss countryside, where girls came on to the railway platforms offering cherries in baskets lined with the green and golden leaves of the vine and the blue Rhône sprang along, rippling and glittering, beside the train, and far off snow peaks glistened in the haze.

Then, one by one, familiar scents began to be wafted to him, as he sat in the stifling compartment in a daze of discomfort, wedged between ten other Italian repatriates on their way home. Once, near the frontier of France where trees crowded down to the line's edge, there came a breath, between the odours of stale khaki and garlic, from pinewoods warmed by the sun. When he got out of the train at a Swiss station and wandered past the open door of the stationmaster's office, he smelt fresh beeswax from the polished floor. Then, after they had actually entered Italy (but he was asleep, jerking miserably to the movement of the train with his head against his neighbour's shoulder, when that sacred moment passed) he touched and smelled and tasted grapes for the first time in five years.

A *signora* gave them to him, and to every other man in the carriage, together with a drink of fresh water mingled with wine; a real *signora*, with white hair under a decent black hat and wearing many sparkling rings and golden brooches; and as she and her elderly maidservant offered the fruit and water, they made the Sign of the Cross and blessed the returning prisoners. Some of the men blessed them gratefully in return; but others, as soon as she and her maid had left the station to return to the large car and chauffeur which awaited them outside it, hastened to sell the large bunches of fresh yellow grapes to the rich English and Americans on the train.

Fabrio ate his bunch down to the last seed and skin; then he smelled the big fading leaf, mottled with amber, which was still attached to the brown crutch-shaped stem, and bruised it between his fingers to bring out its scent, and lastly he put it away into the worn notebook where he carried the papers that proved he was a human being.

In this wallet he also carried the money that he had saved while working for Mr Hoadley and the farmer with whom he had passed the final six months of his captivity (for his request to be transferred to another farm had been granted, supported as it was by Father Francis and Mr Hoadley himself). This sum amounted to nearly nine pounds in English money. It seemed a fortune to Fabrio, and had done much towards sending him home in a confident, forward-looking frame of mind. *He* was not like the dirty, penniless, feckless creatures with whom he shared the carriage and with whom he had handled the same greasy pack of cards throughout two stifling days and a night. Some, despite their long sojourn in England, could hardly speak a word of English, and others quickly lost in gambling the few lire that they had, while one continually related a disgusting story of cowardice and disease. Some were bad, others were merely fools, but not one of them could read the copy of *Post* that Fabrio (who had always had a weakness for that journal) had brought with him; he was the only one with well-blacked boots and a rag in his pocket with which to dust them, a comb, and in his wallet a fortune in lire! Truly, he was returning home with a higher heart than the one he had set out with as an unhappy boy, nearly eight years ago.

Best of all and thanks to the Blessed Mother of God, I am alive, thought Fabrio, looking out of the window at the Lombard plains going by, covered in the blue leaves of ripe vines and shimmering in the heat. How many, how very many of us, are dead.

Someone paused at the open door of the carriage and glanced in at the sweating, yawning group with black heads bent over the cards. There was the soft thr-p, thr-p as someone shuffled the pack, and exclamations in liquid Italian. Some were asleep, with head flung back against the wooden wall, while others gazed dejectedly out of the window at the dancing haze as if only waiting for the journey to end.

The stranger was a tall portly priest in American army uniform, with grey eyes that looked small and keen behind the lenses of strong glasses. His glance lingered over the men; then smiled and made some pleasant conventional observation on the heat and their destination (which for most of them was Genoa) and passed on.

As the afternoon advanced, the air in the carriage grew so stiflingly hot that it was impossible to do anything but try to sleep. Most of these repatriates had spent four or five years in Northern countries where such summers are unknown, and had lost their native capacity for enduring them; they swore and moved restlessly, crowded out into the corridors to get what air blew in from the burning fields, or made useless visits to the lavatory in search of the drinking water which had not been there for years.

At last, in the hottest hour of the afternoon, the men shouted with excitement and crowded to the windows to stare thirstily at the sea, blue as a sheet of cornflowers, and placidly extending beneath the dazzling sun. Immediately before them lay a large town of which only the slum tenements were at first visible; tall buildings of pale gold plaster with lines of coloured washing looped from house to house, and many a window having an indifferent, dark old face staring out above a pot of growing flowers. The train was entering Genoa.

The men struggled to reach down their suitcases or bundles from the racks, loaded themselves up, and crowded to the door, talking and laughing and staring over each other's shoulders at the station, which was crowded with people struggling to reach the train and welcome their men home. Fabrio sat down in a vacated corner seat and stretched out his legs with a sigh. He lit a cigarette and wondered if Emilio were in that crowd out there.

Emilio had been sent home nearly a year ago. A terrible fate had overtaken his eldest son, the little robber of American lorries. It will not be told here, for we agree with that philosopher of the Ancient World who said that the death of a young child is the only grief which is insupportable, and Ruskin wrote the epitaph of Emilio's son once and for all time when he described the heavy-eyed desperate child gamblers 'clashing their bruised centesimi' in the porches of Saint Mark's. He was a victim of the cities, and of war. Let us try to forget him.

So Fabrio thought a little of his friend, but not much, for already he was beginning to hear the voice of his own home, calling him onwards. With every turn of the wheels bearing him deeper into Italy, the memory of England became fainter. The grey sky, those large dark trees that had dripped cold rain down his neck, the endless mud, those potatoes and that bitter stinging beer, they all faded into the past. Now the sun burned his face and the sky above the sea was turquoise. A girl came past the window selling little fritters fried in fat, and he bought some and put them into his mouth. She was thin, and she looked sad, but she wore a bright pink dress and her dark eyes smiled up at him as she gave him his change. The crisp fritters were not so good as they had been eight years ago, but as he crunched them up all Italy seemed to be in their taste.

As for *La Scimmia*, he scarcely thought of her at all. No man with self-respect would think about a woman who had so shamelessly insulted him. *La Scimmia* was probably still at Naylor's Farm, awaiting the time when the British Government would release her and she could get away to *Londra* to display her shameless person upon the stage, passing the time meanwhile by dressing and washing the *padrona*'s baby. Yes, amidst the potatoes and the mud, under those great trees, *La Scimmia* was shouting and banging still. Let her shout, let her bang. Fabrio cared for her no longer and he was going home.

The train halted for some hours at Genoa, and when it moved on again towards Santa Margherita and the smaller towns of the Ligurian coast, evening was falling. But the air still quivered with heat, and in the carriage where the lights now glared and Fabrio dozed with the three remaining repatriates on their way to the South, it was still stiflingly close. The vine rows in the dry fields were dark in the violet dusk, and he had seen his first firefly. In an hour they would reach Santa Margherita, and there he would leave the train and set out on the twenty-mile walk to San Angelo; or perhaps he would be lucky enough to get a lift part of the way. There would be time enough to think about all that when he got there. He stretched himself out more comfortably and soon fell into his deepest sleep yet, for the carriage was now quieter and he had slept hardly at all on the previous night. The three other men were already snoring.

Distant shouting aroused him some time later; he sat up suddenly, startled and confused, and saw through the window the brilliant lamps and white roof of a station against the night sky. The train had stopped at Santa Margherita. He sprang up, in panic lest he should not have time to get out, and dragged down his bundle of possessions. The carriage was empty save for himself, but he was in such a hurry that he did not think about this, and he dashed down the corridor and out through the door, down the steps, and on to the platform.

Once there, he found that he need not have hurried. The

train made no signs of moving on, but stayed where it was, panting steam into the hot blue night while a few porters and some passengers were occupied with luggage and greeting their friends. He set down his bundle and wiped his forehead and recovered his breath while gazing about him. A white flower with a sweet scent bloomed all down the side of a bank, and his eyes rested absently upon it while he felt, as he did every half-hour or so, in his breast pocket for his wallet.

A sickening sensation gripped his stomach and he gasped. It was not there.

He stared wildly about him. The train still panted steam into the night, showing no sign of departing. He rushed forward towards the carriage which he had just left—the men, of course! the men who shared it with him had robbed him while he slept—but they had gone—they were hiding somewhere on the train and at any minute now it would start—it was hopeless—he had lost his money and he would never get it back. Mother of God, what a fool he had been to sleep!

His hand was on the rail and he had one foot on the step when the train began to move. He sprang down; then set his teeth in rage and sprang on to the step again. The warm air began to move faster and faster past his face, he felt the train's increasing speed beneath his feet. He knew that it was hopeless, even as he rode there: they might have slipped out at the other side of the train and be half a kilometre away by now, and his bundle with all his remaining possessions! he had left his bundle! He looked back and saw it, looking very small in the middle of the empty platform under the brilliant lamps. A man was walking towards it.

The train was rapidly increasing its speed. He swore, and jumped down.

The shock jarred him but he was too wild with fury and despair to notice. He shook his fists at the train, he shrieked curses aloud, he beat his breast in his anguish. Nine English pounds! His fortune—his hope for all the future, which was to show his family and Maria and her family that he had not come home from the war a ruined man! Tears burst from his eyes and, all his hard-won self-control in ruins, he sobbed aloud.

The end of the train was now approaching. Someone tall and portly was standing on the steps of the last carriage, and as he came level with Fabrio, he leant forward and launched something at him. It landed full in his chest with a most comforting thump. It was his wallet.

'There you are, my son, and be a bit more careful with it next time,' roared the American priest in a voice that soared easily above the increasing noise of the train's wheels, 'I caught those boys counting it over and made 'em stand and disgorge. Don't forget to give the Church a thank-offering! Good-bye, my son. God—ble-e-ess you!' (in a vibrating shout) and as the tail of the train passed on into the twilight, Fabrio saw a great hand go up and two fingers held in blessing. He sank upon his knees then and there and vowed a candle, the biggest that Father Mario could supply, to Saint Antony and Our Blessed Lady at San Angelo.

He was just in time to secure his bundle from the porter, who had been about to appropriate it, and this incident turned out fortunately, for he got into a friendly conversation with the man which ended in his spending that night at his home. It was a poor place near the port, but there was food and a bed and the sound of the sea awash on the rocks coming in through the open door and, most comforting of all, there were the voices of Italian women and children in his ears again, and dark eyes smiling at him while he ate and talked and heard all the news.

In the morning he said good-bye to his hosts and left them a little money out of his recovered hoard because they were very poor, and set out on the last stage of his journey.

He left the town of pink and white and yellow houses behind him, and set out along the steep coast road.

The dazzling blue sea lay below, and above there were groves of silver olive that covered the hillside in broad cloudlike shapes, but so hot was the still air that their shade scarcely afforded any coolness. More than once he paused to listen to the cicada, and to wipe his face and neck, and twice he saw the yellow tail of a lizard flick into a creviced stone wall, so quickly that it was barely distinguishable from the shimmer of the heat. He moved slowly on with the dogged rocking pace of a man accustomed to walking in the mountains, and as the road climbed higher the silence deepened, but presently he heard a sound that he had known from boyhood, coming down from the groves of olive and chestnut above him. High up on the little farms half-concealed under blue and golden vines, the coopers were hammering on the casks for the new wine. For the grape harvest had begun.

Wherever there was room, and wherever the sun could get at them, the vines were trained: over trellises, over pergolas, over the walls and roofs of cottages washed with pink or blue or apricot against the fire of the sun; they grew along wires in twisted shapes like rustic godlings of the olive groves and chestnut woods; they drooped from stunted nut or fruit bushes, while the glittering harmless flies and the wasps, wild with the life which heat and grape juice were pouring into their bodies, darted and clung amidst the lavish clusters. He did not pause to look, but kept steadily on. Only his head turned from side to side every few seconds as he took it all in. Home with its sights and sounds and smells was rising about him and closing him in, and he began to feel very happy. During the last months he had almost ceased to sing, but now, warmed by this familiar sunlight and moving through sweet wafts of grape-must while the distant hammering rang in his ears, he sang a line or two, almost under his breath, then more loudly. A bicycle came unsteadily down the road ridden by a young man and a girl. She was seated in front of him, and they only stopped their singing in order to press their lips and their thin young bodies together in ardent kisses. They looked curiously at Fabrio and his song died away as he looked back at them; then all three smiled together and called 'Good morning' in chorus as the bicycle went on down the road. He walked on, and now he was thinking of Maria.

Months ago, while he was still at Naylor's Farm, he had begun again to write regularly to her, and her letters had resumed their cheerfulness. Not a word was said about the future, but each felt the other understood that one day they would marry.

He had written to her (by the Air Mail, for now he was a man of means who could afford such conveniences of the modern world) as soon as he knew the date on which he was to leave England, telling her that if all went well he would arrive at San Angelo upon a certain day, but at what hour he did not know. There had been no time for her reply to reach him before he left, but he knew that she would come out to meet him, if she could leave the harvesting, and accordingly he began to look out for her, gazing along the road that faded off into a distant prospect of hills from which the sun had burned out all colour but the brown of earth and the blue-green of vines.

Soon he began to recognise landmarks that he had known from boyhood. Once he had ridden out in his uncle's cart to search that wood for chestnuts, and had drunk from the fountain at its edge where a statue of Our Lady smiled above the gushing water, now in its summer slenderness. There was the tower of the church at Palazzo, rising between a gap in the hills, and there the fields of white barley and yellow maize that he had countless times seen as he glanced inland and upwards from his hoeing in the field at San Angelo.

He passed familiar farmsteads, where laughter and voices sounded from figures moving with baskets slung on their backs behind the screen of violet grapes and bronze leaves, and more than once some thin young mother or weeping old woman ran down to stop and question him, bringing a faded and tattered letter written—how many months ago!—from Derna or Tripoli, showing it to him that he might see the writer's number and regiment, and perhaps give news of him. Oh yes, a letter had come from an office at Roma or Venezia or Milano saying that he was missing and must be dead, but the war had been in so many places and there had been such miraculous escapes, the dead had returned alive after years, and Our Lady was merciful, She knew what it was to lose a son. Fabrio did his best for them, but their sad anxious eyes and pleading voices wrung his heart and spoiled his own happiness, and as soon as he could he escaped and went on his way.

Women were scrubbing the wine-presses on some of the farms, singing as they worked, and girls stood up above the vine rows in faded ragged cotton dresses to laugh at him and wave thin arms to him as he went by. There were few young men at work, because most of them were still in the army or in prison camps, and the old men at harvest were almost in rags. Fabrio, who had grown accustomed to the decent shabbiness of the English, was shocked by these tatters and naked feet, these dresses clumsily fashioned from parachute cotton, and was glad of his own neat suit and stout boots, though certainly the latter were beginning to feel unusually heavy. He was tempted to remove them and bathe his feet in another trickling summer stream but refrained, because he was anxious to get on.

He was very thirsty, and when a wagon drawn by two large, emaciated white oxen lurched down the road towards him, and the children riding with purple-stained mouths amidst sliding mounds of red fruit tossed him a bunch, he crushed the cluster into his mouth and gratefully swallowed the rough delicious juice. Now and again he put up his hand to feel the wallet hidden in his breast. It was safe; and so, now, was he.

Safety and consolation closed him in and filled his heart more and more strongly as he drew nearer home, even as the familiar hills enclosed him, and already he was beginning to feel that he had never been away. Once San Angelo had been the dream, the unreal place. Now, it was Naylor's Farm.

He took the road that led down again to the sea.

The hills here were lofty, with sometimes a shrine standing on the white grass of the parched summits or at the edge of shrivelled brown woods, but every foot of the lower slopes was crowded with ripe olive, wheat or vine, drinking their last nourishment from the sunlight before yielding their riches to Man; and so he walked downwards between vast, peaceful slopes of yellow and grey and blue-green, under the turquoise sky, towards the glittering sea. It was now noon, for he had started to walk at dawn, and the countryside was at its emptiest and almost silent, under the fierce sun, while the workers in the vineyards and fields ate their midday meal. He had undone his neat collar and put over his head his last remaining khaki handkerchief. As he gazed with half-shut eyes through the glare, he saw, standing motionless at the crossroads where the rough track led down through chestnut and acacia woods to San Angelo, something dark.

It was a small open cart, drawn by a donkey which (he saw as he came nearer) was skeleton-thin and hanging down its head as if asleep. Someone in black was sitting in the cart holding the reins, and all round the donkey's head moved some small objects. He opened his eyes wider to see what they were. Children: yes, they were children. Whose could they be? and who were they waiting for? Him? He fancied he knew that cart and donkey. They were his uncle's; he used them for carrying hay and wood and fish. But surely his old uncle had not come out in this heat to welcome him?

All at once the small figures became agitated, as if they had caught sight of him. He could see them pointing, and jumping about, and then the figure in the cart raised a stick and the donkey lifted its head and plodded forward. Down towards him it came, at a slow walk, and round it danced the children. They were singing. He could hear their weak piping voices through the hot stillness, and now he could see that the woman in the cart wore a black dress with a white collar. His heart began to beat fast. She must be Maria. And the cart drew steadily nearer.

But he felt no desire to run to meet it. Everything was so quiet; the sky, the glittering sea filling the little bay, the blue leaves cascading down below the cloudlike olive groves, all were motionless, and not even the cicada cried. Only the donkey's hoofs rose and fell in the dust and the children's weak voices wavered off into silence as the cart came near. He stood still and let his bundle slide to the ground, and waited.

But this was not Maria! Sick disappointment overcame him. This girl was so thin that she looked quite old, and her great eyes started, and short locks of silky hair stood out stiffly around her head. She had not Maria's dimples, and she was hardly pretty at all. Yet she was looking at him shyly and then she smiled, and he saw that she was Maria. But what had she done to herself? And whose children were these? How they stared!

Suddenly a long ragged boy of twelve or so shouted as if he could keep quiet no longer—'Uncle Fabrio!' and ran forward, but when he was almost near enough to touch Fabrio he stopped, staring doubtfully. 'Uncle Fabrio, is it thou?' he asked, more quietly. 'I am Cesare.'

He saw a sturdy man dressed in brown, with chestnut hair cut close and smoothly combed; he had no hollows in his cheeks, and he wore splendid boots with soles an inch thick. His eyes were very blue and he was very clean. What an uncle to welcome home from the war! Cesare was a little afraid, but he was also proud.

But Maria was only afraid, for she had seen, from her very first glimpse of him, that he was much handsomer and sterner and much more of a man than the boy Fabrio whom she remembered.

Her hair! What would he say about her hair?

Three days ago, an hour after his letter came, she had left her work in the cottage and the field half-done and set out to walk, as fast as she could for the trembling of her legs with excitement and hunger, to Santa Margherita. There she had sold her curling waist-length hair to her former employer, who was an agent for such sales on behalf of a Genoese firm, for the equivalent of five English pounds. (Yes, the girls were getting such prices now for their hair, double the price offered before the war.)

The money would buy her wedding clothes. She had had nothing—no money, no clothes—nothing to offer Fabrio but herself, and she could not bear it. There had always been girls after Fabrio! and most of them had had more clothes and better homes than she. For no other reason would she have parted with her hair, which had been so silky and glittering, lifting itself about her face with its own soft, healthy life like the familiar spirit of her girlhood. Now some smart lady in Genoa or Milan, perhaps even in Rome itself (Maria had seen pictures of such ladies in the fashion papers at the hairdresser's shop) would wear it twisted in a false braid upon her shameless head. *Her* hair, her very own hair that had always been with her since she was little! It made Maria so sad to think of it. And now she was frightened as well. She smoothed her new black dress as if to comfort herself by its touch, but as the cart paused beside Fabrio she was so frightened that she burst out loudly:

'Oh Fabrio, it is thou! After all this long, long time! Dost thou know me? I am—it is Maria! All the others at thy home are busy with the harvest, so I brought the children to meet thee. Art thou hungry? Thou must be hungry, after thy long journey. There is food for thee at thy home and I can stay a little while. That is Cesare, and here is Baldassare and Elena and Giulia—come here, little one——' and now Fabrio saw black eyes looking languidly at him over the top of an old black shawl on the floor of the cart, and a thumb thrust into a small wet mouth—'it is thy uncle, Fabrio!'

Her voice was softer than he remembered. It delighted him. So many years had gone by, such a long bad dream, since he had heard a beloved woman chattering in Italian! He was not at all shy of her; he went up to the cart and put his hands round her waist (how thin she was! That would never do, for she had to bear many *bambini*) and lifted her right out of it with his great strength, and set her feet in their cheap white shoes down in the dust beside him, and surveyed her.

'What hast thou done to thy hair?' he exclaimed loudly, all the reserve and self-control that he had begun to learn from the English melting away under the fire of the black eyes and at the sound of the eager voices around him.

'She sold it!' shrilly cried three or four of the children. 'To buy wedding clothes! Thou shouldst see them! Magnificent!'

Maria hung her head. 'I had nothing. I was in rags,' she said. 'Thou art not angry?' and she looked up at him.

'It will grow again!' cried Fabrio, and swept her (but gently, because she was so thin, poor Maria, and not strong or dimpled any more, and yet he loved her) into his arms. How soft she was, and her hair smelt of some beautiful scent! He eagerly kissed her, and she flung her arms about his neck and smiled up into his face, then turned her head to laugh at the circle of staring children. The black-eyed one in the cart whimpered in a suffering little way without moving, and two of the girls flew to her.

'She is ill,' said Elena shyly to Fabrio. 'There is no milk,' and she shrugged her thin shoulders and rearranged the black shawl.

'I will work for you all, and then there will be money to buy milk on the Black Market,' announced Fabrio, holding Maria more tightly and addressing her as much as the open-mouthed children. Now he was glad that he had been away for six years, and had not starved with the rest at home. He would save them. He had strength and youth and love: he even had money. He had everything. He kissed Maria again and motioned the children onwards. Cesare climbed into the driver's seat and some of the others got into the cart behind him, Elena gathering up little Giulia on to her lap. Cesare whipped the donkey, which awoke with a start.

'Go home and tell them that I am coming,' commanded Fabrio. 'I have *cioccolata*, and later thou shalt have some——'

'*Cioccolata! Cioccolata!*' they cried. The donkey set off at a trot, and Maria cried fearfully after them, 'Elena! Take care of Giulia!'

'I have her safe—do not be afraid, Maria!' and Elena drew closer the stifling folds of the shawl. The boys ran on beside the cart shouting, '*Cioccolata!*' and singing.

Maria was so dizzy with hunger and happiness that she was aware of nothing but the sun's heat striking down upon her skull and the supporting comfort of Fabrio's iron arm about her waist. She allowed herself to be half-led, half-dragged, onwards in silence. Presently she shut her eyes. She had almost lost the sense of where she was, but in a moment something light and cool dropped upon her head and the pain of the sun's rays lessened. He was saying something, but she could not quite hear what. It did not matter: the tone was loving. She opened her eyes and saw that his own head was bare: he had given her his khaki handkerchief. His own handkerchief, brought home from the war! Tears of joy came up into her eyes, and then she heard, soaring out into the warm air, a beautiful, joyful sound. She had not heard it for six anguished years. It was the song of the fishermen, coming home into San Angelo.